Praise for W
and his Father

"William Kienzle is the Harry Kemelman of Catholicism.... Robert Koesler is the Detroit response to Rabbi Small."
—*Los Angeles Times*

"As Kienzle addresses serious modern issues, he stops to digress and tell his wonderful stories ... providing a neat solution with a twist."
—*The Philadelphia Inquirer*

"There are few authors whose books a reader anticipates from the moment he finishes the last effort.... Add William X. Kienzle to that list."
—*Dallas Times Herald*

"As regular as the solstice, the former priest annually provides a new Catholic whodunit from Detroit, inviting readers to shut out the rest of the world and spend a few absorbing hours watching his venerable alter ego, Koesler, peel back the layers of a puzzle to plumb the tortured depths of the human soul and elegantly solve a mystery."
—*Chicago Tribune*

"One of America's foremost mystery writers ... [His] characters bring to mind the early novels of Graham Greene."
—*Knoxville News-Sentinel*

THE GATHERING

WILLIAM X. KIENZLE

FAWCETT BOOKS • NEW YORK

The Gathering is a work of fiction. Names, places, and incidents either are a product of the author's imagination or are used fictitiously.

A Fawcett Book
Published by The Random House Publishing Group
Copyright © 2002 by Gopits, Inc.

www.ballantinebooks.com

ISBN 0-345-45794-3

This edition published by arrangement with Andrews McMeel Publishing, Kansas City.

Manufactured in the United States of America

First Ballantine Books Mass Market Edition: January 2004

OPM 10 9 8 7 6 5 4 3 2 1

for Javan,
my wife and collaborator

Acknowledgments

Gratitude for technical advice to:

George Arsenault, Senior Financial Officer, General Motors Corporation (Retired)
Sister Bernadelle Grimm, R.S.M., Hospital Pastoral Care (Retired)
Dennis Larsson, Tool Engineer
Irma Macy, Religious Education Coordinator, Prince of Peace Parish, West Bloomfield, Michigan (Retired)
Louis Morand, Catholic Financial Development
Werner U. Spitz, M.D., Professor Forensic Pathology, Wayne State University

Any error is the author's.

IN MEMORIAM
Gloria DeGrazia Ankeny—"Joy she gave; joy she has found."

Bob Laurel—He gave us beautiful music and brought Father Koesler to the screen.

Msgr. F. Gerald Martin, Father Anthony Lombardini—
Gaudeamus, igitur, juvenes dum sumus.

1 WHEN STUCK WITH an elephant, it's best to paint it white, Father Robert Koesler concluded.

"Well," said his guide, "what do you think? Recognize the old place?"

Something about the term "old." It was hard to think of himself as old. Just as it was hard to consider this building old. Yet he was seventy-three. And St. John's Center—once St. John's Provincial Seminary—was fifty-four.

He himself was in relatively good health. For which he was grateful. But while his participation in enterprises such as baseball, football, and basketball had been fun . . . no more; he was now merely a spectator. Yet grateful to be able to still care for himself, thanks to a robust immune system.

As for St. John's, upon reflection, his assessment seemed accurate: a veritable white elephant—a rare, expensive possession that had become a financial burden.

Prior to 1949, most Michigan seminarians who graduated from Sacred Heart Seminary college and still aspired to the priesthood headed for their final four years of theology at Mount St. Mary's in Cincinnati. A fate just this side of death.

Events would have continued in that dour manner had it not been for the dynamic, if princely, leadership of Edward Cardinal Mooney.

Mooney was named bishop of Detroit in 1937. Because he was already an archbishop, Detroit, for the first time and forevermore, became ipso facto an archdiocese. Unexpectedly—since membership in the College of Cardinals was at

1

that time strictly limited—in 1946 Mooney was named a Cardinal.

He was gifted with enough foresight to anticipate the coming flood of candidates for the priesthood. So he dragged the other Michigan bishops—some kicking and screaming mightily—into building Michigan's own theologate seminary: St. John's Provincial, serving the Province of Michigan.

Mooney pinched no penny in construction and landscaping, even adding a picturesque nine-hole golf course, which the Cardinal played as much as or more than anyone else, including the students.

There followed unparalleled upheaval in the seminary, the Catholic Church, and the world. These transformations took place in the sixties, a decade of turmoil. The Vietnam War fractured the nation. The Second Vatican Council gave birth to changes that seemed to contradict hitherto changeless verities. Seminaries exploded with hordes of applicants, only to nearly empty when Vatican II either promised too much or delivered too little.

Thought was given to expanding Sacred Heart Seminary. And, indeed, another high school building was erected. Pressure grew to complete St. John's building program.

Then, seemingly overnight, seminarians became an endangered species.

The Province of Michigan—principally the Archdiocese of Detroit—was now running two seminaries, each of which required expensive maintaining. In actuality, either one of them was far more than adequate to house, feed, and educate the ever-shrinking number of priestly candidates.

The eventual decision was to continue Sacred Heart Seminary, eliminating the high school, keeping the college, and adding the theologate. It became Sacred Heart Major Seminary.

And St. John's? It became a white elephant.

Why was Sacred Heart kept operational, with expanded courses, while St. John's was shut down?

The obvious response was the Neighborhood.

Once, early on, Sacred Heart had stood almost alone on the then-outskirts of the city of Detroit. Along the way, the wilderness was replaced by a Jewish community. Its synagogue grew up kitty-corner from the seminary. Eventually, African-Americans replaced the Jewish inhabitants. By 1988, the consensus was that there would be no buyers for all those antiquated buildings.

St. John's, on the other hand, had practically no neighborhood at all.

St. John's went on the block. Sacred Heart circled its wagons ever more closely.

So, back to his guide's question: Did Father Koesler recognize the old place?

"Yes and no," he hedged.

It was an unexpected reply. "It hasn't changed that much," she said, ". . . has it?"

"The shell is here," he said slowly. "The buildings . . . the rooms . . ." He looked about. "But it's so much more beautiful—and larger as well."

"Are you really that surprised? I mean, I know you haven't been back here since it became St. John's Center. But you must've seen pictures . . ."

"Oh yes . . . yes, I have. But the pictures don't do justice to the in-person reality."

"Is there anything else you'd like to see? We've been pretty much through the whole place. But if you want another look . . ."

"No . . . no, thank you. You've been very gracious." He hesitated. "I think I'll just wander around a bit." His smile was flitting. "I don't think I'll get lost. The buildings—at least most of them—are the same. Only the names have been changed. The library reading room still stands . . . though in my day it was the chapel. And so on . . ." he finished somewhat lamely.

Her smile was meant to be encouraging. "Just keep in mind, Father, St. John's is no longer a seminary. Though it is still owned by the Archdiocese of Detroit, it has absolutely nothing to do with educating priests. Now, we hold weddings here . . . even cater the receptions. We provide counseling for troubled parents and children. We have facilities for handling meetings of almost any kind or size, as well as overnight accommodations.

"And there are recreational facilities. There's basketball and handball. And of course, there's golf—"

Koesler nodded, then grinned, recalling countless hours spent by him and his seminary classmates in clearing the fairways of stones. "Up from what it was. Nine holes and lots of space in our day. I haven't been back since the course was modernized and expanded to eighteen holes."

"Now," she said, "it's a pleasuresome twenty-seven."

"But the buildings—at least the ones that were here when we were students . . . they hold memories that will never fade from my life." Half lost in recollection, he looked about, then turned back to her. "Again: Thanks for the tour."

She nodded, turned to leave, then did an about-face. "One thing you ought to be clear on, Father: You are scheduled to meet with your guests at six o'clock in the cafeteria. You do know how to get there?"

"Uh-huh. Another building that wasn't here in the beginning. But you showed it to me in our tour and I remember: It's at the end of the tunnel beneath St. Edward's Hall and just inside the Power House reception area. Don't worry: If any of us get lost, we'll yell for help."

Her eyes crinkled in amusement. "Okay."

Though it was early for the meeting, Koesler was used to being first on every scene. This exceeding promptness had its inception in boyhood, when his mother had shooed him out of the house well before the gathering time for him and his buddies. The habit had taken root. Nor could he rest on his laurels. Even now as an elderly man he grew anxious whenever a deadline or an appointment was imminent.

So, with time on his hands and feeling quite at home in these once familiar surroundings, he decided to let the memories flood in at their own good pleasure.

He was standing in what had been the Prayer Hall, directly beneath the ornate chapel that hadn't even existed during the four years he had been a student here. As he had told his guide, what in those days had been the chapel was now the library reading room. What had been the Prayer Hall was now just a large, nondescript, rectangular space. Years ago, it had been filled with bench seats with snap-up tabletops and kneelers that could be lowered to the floor for prayer. With the tabletops raised and the kneelers down, it was no place for a claustrophobic.

Sometimes the room had been used for classes. At other times, the Prayer Hall had actually been used for prayer. As in morning, noon, and night. Morning prayer was the diciest. That prayer was followed immediately by silent meditation, during which many of the group—those not yet fully awake—fell blissfully asleep. On one occasion a young man was concluding his reading of morning prayer in preparation for somnolent meditation, when he inadvertently turned too many pages. Unmindful of the fact that he was on the last page of evening prayer instead of on the final page of morning prayer, he read aloud, "Let us offer up the sleep we are about to take in union with that which Jesus Himself, took while on earth . . ."

Even the priest in charge had laughed.

Laughter in Prayer Hall was not unique or even rare. There was, for instance, the pre-luncheon examination of conscience. The composure of a couple of hundred students in cassock and clerical collar was sorely tested one day when a mouse came through the doorway, eyeballed the reflecting group, then dove under a nearby lowered kneeler.

There followed a good deal of fidgeting, shifting, and outright jumping as some of the more mischievous boys ran a finger up a neighbor's leg. Their victims were forced either to exercise extreme self-control or hop up on their seats, pulling their floor-length cassocks up around their knees.

All the while, on the podium, the presiding priest, who hadn't seen the mouse, wondered what in hell was going on.

Fortunately, the examination period ended shortly thereafter, and the students, still wary, made their way to the dining room. Sad to say, a few who were fresh from the farm stayed behind to dispatch the mouse, who, with the kneelers now raised, had forfeited any hiding place.

Two floors directly above where Koesler now stood were meeting rooms, which, in his day, had been classrooms. As was true of most of the original buildings, the classrooms were bright and airy with plenty of window space.

Sulpicians had made up the faculty. The Sulpicians were diocesan—or parish—priests on loan from their home diocese and totally dedicated to training young men to become diocesan priests. Thus they were held in high regard by their students.

In addition, the courses at St. John's were at the heart of relevance for the seminarians' future ministry. Core subjects were dogmatic and moral theology, Scripture, Canon Law, Liturgy, and homiletics—the meat and potatoes of the lives these students longed to live.

So intense were some courses that gobs of dogma as well as blocks of Canon Law had to be skipped over in favor of more relevant and immediate material. So dedicated a student had the maturing Robert Koesler become that, almost alone, and on his own, he studied such otherwise neglected matter.

How things had changed over the years! His alma mater had been transformed from a single-minded seminary to a sort of Catholic resort. In Koesler's day, most courses had been taught entirely in Latin: questions, answers, texts, exams—all in Latin. Now, Latin was an elective, with few takers—even though the largest by far of the branches of Catholicism is the Latin Rite, whose primary language remains Latin.

Koesler was engaging in one of his favorite pastimes: remembering the past. Sailing along on this sea of memories, he thought it ironic that he could think of nothing negative . . . nothing of the sort of recollection that causes one to wince.

Actually, of course there had been some less than enjoyable events . . . but they had softened with the passage of time. Even though these students of yore were, by and large, dedicated, they were also young, sometimes bored, and frequently funny.

Koesler continued to slowly make his way toward the meeting place. He paused as he reached what had been the crypt chapels.

Originally, one large space had been divided into five small chambers, each with three walls opening to the central area. Now, it was no more than an oddly shaped room so empty it gave no clue as to its previous use.

Once, each of the five chapel spaces had been equipped with all the necessities for the celebration of Mass. Though "celebration" seemed too grandiose a term for what had taken place there.

Each morning after meditation—slumber—five faculty members went to their assigned cubicles, where the vestments of the day were arranged on the vesting table. Each priest had a student appointed as sacristan. It was the sacristan's responsibility to care for everything. Other students took their turns serving Mass, a week at a time.

Everyone whispered, in a futile attempt to cause no distraction to the others. At least the intention was honorable. With five priests and five seminarians whispering their Latin prayers in a very confined space, there had to be noise. Limited sound, but sound nonetheless.

The most heroic effort at quiet centered around the bell. A very small bell was provided at each altar. It was the server's responsibility to ring the bell—a total of ten times at each Mass—while attempting to keep the sound at a minimum.

One morning, a server tipped his bell ever so carefully and slowly. There was no sound. Eventually, the server was shaking the bell violently. Still no sound. It did not occur to him at the time to look inside the bell where, unbeknownst to him, the clapper had been taped to the bell's interior. The sacristan had been bored.

On another occasion, this same sacristan received a complaint from his priest. The priest claimed that he was being distracted during Mass by a spider that crept and crawled on the cross during each and every Mass. No way would the priest himself contribute to the solution of this problem. That contract was given to the sacristan, who conducted an intense search-and-destroy mission—without success.

Finally, he reached a solution—at least as far as he was concerned.

"My priest," he reported, "gets vested, picks up the chalice, and goes to the altar. He puts the chalice on the altar, takes the corporal [a cloth resembling a handkerchief] out of the burse [a type of purse], props the burse against the wall, spreads the corporal on the altar, puts the spider on the cross, sets the chalice on the corporal . . ."

As far as anyone knew, the spider was never found. Had it been, it would undoubtedly have joined the inquisitive mouse as a sacrificial offering to the peace and quiet of the seminary.

By far, the most intriguing aspect of the crypt chapels—perhaps of the entire seminary—was the once occupied, now empty tomb in the floor.

It had been Cardinal Mooney's wish—and his wishes were law to the faculty—to be buried in this spot where five Masses would be offered simultaneously each and every day during the school year.

And so it came to pass that the only thing missing from this tomb was a body. The roped-off area safeguarded a plaque bearing Mooney's biographical statistics. The major events of the Cardinal's life were noted on the six-foot-long plate—with the exception of his date of death.

Arguably, Mooney may have found the tomb depressing. It surely must have reminded him of his mortality. But undoubtedly he had considered it consoling that he would be laid to rest in so sacred a spot.

In any case, there it was: No guided tour of the seminary had ever skipped a visit to the Cardinal's empty but waiting tomb.

In time, of course, the tomb was occupied. Cardinal Mooney was laid to what was thought to be his final rest on October 31, 1958. At that time no one would have dreamed that anything would ever happen to contravene his order. However, who could have foreseen the drain of seminarians and the change in name and purpose of St. John's Provincial Seminary to St. John's Center?

Eventually, nearly unoccupied, the seminary was officially closed in 1988.

When it became clear that such a drastic change was inevitable, the administration of the archdiocese decided to have the Cardinal's body moved to Holy Sepulcher Cemetery, there to be interred in the section reserved for deceased priests.

A small crew of workers was put to work on the transfer.

They cracked open the seal of the plaque and laboriously raised the heavy casket from the tomb and placed it on a carriage. They rolled it out of the crypt and through the empty Prayer Hall. They maneuvered it up a flight of stairs and pushed it to the front doors of the one-time seminary.

As they crossed the threshold, something eerie and inexplicable occurred. All the power in the buildings failed, and the telephones went dead.

The moving crew was unaware of what had happened. Those few still inside the building of course knew that suddenly the electricity was out and so were the phones. But they didn't know that the outage was in any way connected with the noncompliance with Mooney's order.

Nor, when the stories had been meshed, was the incident made public. Perhaps the powers that be were loath to fan the embers of what could give rise to a cult, a shrine, and/or talk of a "miracle."

Those who knew of the phenomenon ever after shied from the emptied tomb.

As Koesler was recalling these events, he stood motionless at the very foot of the Cardinal's now-vacant crypt. He smiled as *The Twilight Zone* theme sounded in his head.

Koesler resumed his journey in the direction of the Power

House entrance. As he did, his thoughts returned to the present and the upcoming meeting.

At one time, not that long ago, this would have been a gathering of The Six. Over the years, The Six—four men and two women—had formed a special bond that had survived the test of time.

Their relationship had begun some fifty-five years before. It was a bond that could, and did, survive disagreements, misunderstandings, and even enmity. Of course their usual response to one another was just the opposite of such negatives. The point was that the group's comradeship was built on a rock-solid foundation that could withstand all manner of testing.

But what they were experiencing now was a sterner test than any in the past.

They had been six. Now they were five.

Only days ago, one of their number had died. This, in itself, was not extraordinary. Koesler was in his early seventies. The others, all at one time classmates, had been one year behind Koesler. Now they too were in their early seventies, a year or two younger than he, depending on their month of birth.

It was the cause of this demise that was ambiguous. Rather than dying of a sharply defined illness or from so-called natural causes, the death could be attributed to either an accident, or suicide, or murder. Whatever the true cause of death, it seemed possible—albeit unthinkable—that one of the surviving classmates might have been responsible for the death, had assisted in the death, or was an accessory.

Koesler had reason to believe he knew the answer.

2 IT WAS 1942 and young Bob Koesler wanted to be a priest. Never had he planned on being anything else.

In three months he would enter high school. The ninth grade was the earliest he could start on the process of becoming a priest. All he needed at that point was a seminary.

Until about the middle of the eighth grade, he had taken it more or less for granted that he would attend the Redemptorist seminary in Missouri. The Koesler family belonged to Holy Redeemer parish on Detroit's southwest side. Redemptorist priests—lots of them—staffed the parish.

The Redemptorists were founded by St. Alphonsus Ligouri. They were supposed to be preachers and teachers, but most of them had, for all intents and purposes, become parish priests. So, young Robert put two and two together: He wanted to be a priest; the only priests he knew were Redemptorists—ergo, he was preparing to leave for Missouri.

Then a friend of the family, a Maryknoll priest, opened young Robert's eyes to a seminary virtually right under his nose. He wouldn't have to leave home; there was a seminary in Detroit that was only two streetcar rides away.

On this warm and bright day in May, Robert was following the directions mapped out by his anxious mother. The directions brought him to the massive institution called Sacred Heart Seminary. He arrived to find the gigantic playing field filled with boys competing in various track and field events.

Annually, at Sacred Heart, one Saturday in early May was set aside as Field Day. This meant races, jumps, and similar fun events. The object was to get nearly all the students out

11

of the buildings so the incoming candidates could be processed.

As far as Robert Koesler could tell, three different categories of young men filled the Gothic corridors: There were seminarians excused from participating in the Field Day in order to organize the applicants. There were small groups of applicants from various home parishes. Each group hung close together, seeking comfort in numbers. Finally, there were unaffiliated boys who were here for the first time. These unattached individuals seemed lost; most of them were overwhelmed and scared.

Robert Koesler knew no one. He stood stockstill in a virtual vortex in the middle of a corridor while young male bodies circled him in roughly a clockwise motion. So bewildered was he that he was sorely tempted to retrace his steps and retreat to the security of home.

But he couldn't do that. What sort of priest would he make if he turned and ran every time he was even slightly daunted?

Just then a boy about his size and age stopped in front of him. "You new?"

"Yeah," Robert replied. "I really am!"

"You gonna be a freshman?"

"If I can find out how to do it." Robert extended his hand. "Bob Koesler."

The other boy shook his hands energetically and identified himself. "McNiff—Pat McNiff."

"You know where you're going?" To Robert, his new acquaintance didn't seem nearly old enough to be one of the seminarian guides.

McNiff grinned "I was here last year."

"So . . . ?"

"I wasn't accepted."

The possibility of being rejected had never occurred to Koesler. Till now he'd thought that all one had to do was register and then begin school. "Is . . . is there some test we're supposed to take?"

"Didn't you get your application form in the mail?"

Panic began to again grip at Koesler's nervous system. "I didn't even know there was an application form."

"You're kidding!"

"Wish I was. What'll I do?"

"The best you can, I guess. Look, I'll take you to the study hall where the freshies are supposed to meet. Take it from there. Maybe it'll work . . . you never know."

Koesler followed McNiff through the crowd until they reached an impressively large room filled with desks and chairs, a bunch of boys, and a balding older man in a cassock. Probably a priest, Koesler concluded.

"This is it," McNiff said. "Good luck."

"What about you?" Koesler was reluctant to lose the only friend he had made.

"I'm gonna apply for the tenth grade. Last year I had a lot of trouble with the English test. So I really burned the books this year. I've got all the English they can throw at me—at least for the tenth grade. Maybe I'll see you later."

"I hope so." It was almost a prayer.

Actually, the two would see much of each other.

Pat McNiff failed to realize that while he was working on English grammar in his ninth-grade curriculum, those in the seminary were inundated with Latin grammar. McNiff was eminently qualified for the tenth grade as far as English was concerned. But with no Latin, he would be slated for the seminary's ninth grade. Though McNiff was a year older than Bob Koesler, the two would be classmates.

But first Koesler would have to gain entrance.

He approached the elderly priest and tried, haltingly, to explain that all he had to submit to the seminary was himself.

"You haven't got your application?" The query was delivered far more loudly than necessary, thought Koesler.

"No, Father."

"Here . . ." The priest plucked a form from a stack of papers on a nearby desk and handed it to Koesler. "You've got about fifteen minutes before we hand out the test papers. Fill out as much as you can now and finish it after the test.

"And get a move on! I don't want to spend our first nice spring day waiting for you to get your act together."

At this point Koesler almost could pray that the earth would open and swallow him. But he had to ask; there was no other way. "Father . . ." He spoke just loudly enough to be heard by the priest over the subdued noise in the room.

"Well?" the priest growled.

"I wonder . . . I don't have a pencil." Koesler realized he must sound like Oliver Twist begging for "more gruel, please." But his options were few.

"My God, man!" the priest thundered. "Here's a guy shows up without bringing anything with him! Anybody got a pencil you can lend this poor soul?"

Several pencils were thrust immediately at the blushing candidate. He accepted the first pencil he saw. Fortunately, it didn't need sharpening. If it had, he would have had to ask the location of the sharpener.

He was so confused he had some trouble remembering how to spell his family name.

He filled out the application form as best he could. And just in time to commence the test with everyone else. Before beginning, however, he delivered the completed application to the priest, who seemed slightly mollified by the dispatch of the accomplishment.

Upon reflection, Koesler was grateful that he hadn't known he would have to take this academic test. He would have crammed ceaselessly without knowing what exactly the test would be about.

As it turned out, it was a potpourri of subjects blessedly familiar to him. He would do best in English and worst in math, with everything else on the high side with English.

Some applicants finished early but were advised that they must wait the full hour and a half before proceeding to the next step, an interview with one of the priest faculty members.

Koesler's head was in a whirl. So many things had been thrown on his plate with such little preparation on his part!

He felt like a zombie. He was beginning to wonder why any-one in this seminary would want him as a student.

And now there would be another hurdle to clear. An in-terview. Once again, this was news to him.

Well, he thought, take them as they come. He finished the test with a few minutes to spare. He ran through it one more time and changed only a couple of his answers. He thought he'd done well. Pretty good, at least.

A huge electronic bell mounted on one wall let loose a blast.

Bob Koesler was to learn—without even knowing he was being taught—that this was a wondrous system. For people in authority at least. Merely by ringing a bell one could get hundreds of young men and boys to do whatever it was time for them to do.

The bell woke them in the morning. It summoned them to chapel to pray and to attend Mass. It called them to eat—not much, but enough to survive. It ordered them to exercise, to study, to attend classes. In short, a bell programmed their lives.

In the swirl of students, Koesler searched in vain for his one and only contact, the McNiff boy. It would have been a deus ex machina had Koesler found McNiff. And God was not being a machine this day.

By observing other applicants who were scanning signs posted on various pillars, he discovered which office he was supposed to be at. He did not want to cap this day's adven-ture by getting in the wrong line and wasting what easily could be hours. So he not only searched out and ascertained his destination from the bulletin board, he asked directions of anyone and everyone who appeared knowledgeable.

When his time came, he entered a small office. Awaiting him was the antithesis of the gruff, elderly cleric of the study hall. Later, Koesler would learn that his interviewer was the chief executive officer of this enterprise—the rector of the seminary.

In short order, the rector discovered that Koesler had virtually come in off the street. He was asked for—and did not have with him—his certificates of baptism and confirmation, his parents' Catholic wedding certificate, and a transcript of his grammar school grades.

Once more the less than intrepid boy panicked. He volunteered to go directly home, get all the required documentation, and return with them this very day.

Father Donnelly almost smiled. He assured the boy that, while these documents were absolutely required before his admission could be considered, it would be sufficient to mail them in within the week.

Donnelly and Koesler also chatted about the boy's reasons for wanting to be a priest. From this discussion, it was apparent that young Koesler wanted the priesthood as much as or more than any other lad making application this day.

On concluding his interview with Father Donnelly, Koesler checked diligently to be sure there was no other procedure required of him. Finally, satisfied that he was done for the day, and intent on getting the required documentation in the mail, he headed to the designated corner and waited for the streetcar.

He could see clearly the games going on all over the outsize field. Happy kids, he concluded: all this fun and activity and studying for the priesthood to boot.

It would be a headache trying to round up all those records. But his family, most especially his mother, would willingly endure the discommodity to come up with the required documents.

The easiest certificate to obtain would be his scholastic grades from his parochial school. The others—baptism, confirmation, and marriage record—were spread around the Detroit metropolitan area. Young Robert's family had relocated from time to time based on the senior Koesler's employment. Thus, each vital statistic had its own separate parish.

But the entire family was indeed most supportive in Bob's quest for ordination. Gladly would they travel all over creation to locate the requisite parishes.

This was the initial test of how far Bob and his family would be willing to go for his vocation.

In a few days, the mission was accomplished. The records were tucked into an envelope and dispatched to the seminary. Robert was able to breathe a tad more easily.

And then the waiting game began. Allowing two days—three at the most—for delivery by the postal service, each and every morning the family expected mail from the seminary. What could be taking so long?

Robert's adrenaline rush had long since subsided. Initially, the path had seemed to lead toward Missouri and the Redemptorists. A priest at Holy Redeemer had started making arrangements.

Robert had never been long away from home and family. His mother feared that homesickness could end his aspirations. Then they had learned about the Detroit seminary, and suddenly things were upside down. Mrs. Koesler was relieved. Her son could be a day student and live at home.

The Redemptorist who had been counseling Robert took the change in plans in stride. The priest was aware that should Robert for any reason leave the diocesan seminary, he could still try Missouri. But it was not vice versa. If Robert were to attend, then leave the Redemptorist seminary, he would not be accepted at Sacred Heart.

Though the Koeslers didn't know it, they were on the safest path. Sufficient to tap into this alternative plan was the Redemptorist's thinking—*if* it became necessary.

Robert, however, was getting worried. So far, he was committed to the diocesan seminary. But the deadline to apply to the Redemptorist seminary was fast approaching. What if the deadline for Missouri passed and he was then rejected by Sacred Heart Seminary?

In such a case, he would be attending Holy Redeemer High School. And his dream of the priesthood? At best, put off till next year, when he would be applying for the tenth grade, as had the McNiff kid.

The worst scenario? He would not be accepted by either school. And his dream of the priesthood would be shattered.

He didn't want to think of that eventuality. But he couldn't suppress the worry.

Then it came. He had been accepted for the ninth grade at Sacred Heart Seminary.

Catholics were no strangers to the belief in miracles and Divine intervention. Young Robert interpreted his acceptance into the seminary as a portent that he would persevere over the twelve hurdles ahead.

None of the other applicants had anywhere near that degree of confidence.

Whatever, considering the size of the school, its history, the number of students, the caliber of the faculty, its service to the Archdiocese of Detroit, Robert Koesler would soon be a very small fish in a very large pond.

3 HOLY REDEEMER ELEMENTARY grades and high school
took up a heap of land on Detroit's southwest side.

From day one, boys were separated from girls. The IHM
Sisters, Servants of the Immaculate Heart of Mary, taught
both boys' and girls' elementary classes through the sixth
grade. From the seventh grade through high school, the Brothers of Mary taught the boys, while the nuns taught the girls. In
those final six years, not only were the two sexes segregated by
classrooms, they were in separate school buildings.

As if anticipating the Age of the Automobile, Holy Redeemer church spawned an extravagant asphalted parking
lot. In the early forties and before, the entire city had easy
access to mass transportation in the form of streetcars. The
time had not yet come when the auto giants would contribute
to the demise of the streetcar system. Redeemer parish made
ready for a parking crisis. If there was a car in every garage,
there would be room for churchgoers to park those vehicles
while attending Mass.

But on any hot summer's weekday afternoon, the parking
lot was virtually unoccupied. The sun beat down and baked
the smooth surface.

Two boys were engaged in a nameless game of bouncing
a tennis ball so it would ricochet off the ground, hit the
church wall, and be fielded by the alternating player.

The *da-dum, plop, da-dum, plop* reverberated against the
surrounding school buildings.

As they played, the two boys chattered.

19

"Man, this vacation is goin' way too fast," Manny Tocco observed.

"Yeah." Mike Smith couldn't argue the point.

Da-dum, plop. Da-dum, plop.

"Man, I wish there was a swimming hole around here."

Smith grinned. "The Detroit River's just a few blocks south . . ."

"And the ocean's just a few states east."

"Yeah. Then there's Ozanam." Mike smiled at the memory of his two weeks at that summer camp.

"You just got back, dintcha?"

"Uh-huh."

"That's on a lake, isn't it?"

"Yeah . . . Huron."

"That musta been great."

"It woulda been if the stupid water wasn't so cold."

Da-dum, plop.

"This late in the summer?"

"Yeah, well, one of the counselors said it gets swimmable in late August. It looks great . . . especially when you first get there. The weather's hot as hell and all you can see is blue water sort of forever. Canada's across the lake, but you can't see it. Just water. And then they let you go in . . ." Mike would never forget the shock of that water that turned one's skin blue.

"Besides havin' a lake you can't swim in, how was it?"

Mike tossed the tennis ball from one hand to the other. "Too many rules"—he tossed the ball back—"and just too many campers."

Manny's brow knitted. "How does that figure?"

"Well, they had more'n two hundred kids—and less'n twenty counselors. In each season there's five groups of kids. Each group has a two-week stay. So the groups keep changing. But the same counselors stay for the whole summer." He looked thoughtful. "Maybe that's why they had so many rules . . ."

"It sure doesn't sound like my kinda place . . . 'specially not for a vacation. Man, we got enough rules in this Catholic school without gettin' an extra bunch shoved down your throat."

"Oh"—it came out as sort of a sigh—"it wasn't as bad as it sounds. Besides"—Mike grinned—"the counselors were kind of neat." He wound up and fired the ball toward the wall.

Da-dum, plop.

"They're all seminarians. Older guys . . . not long to go before they get ordained." He pursed his lips and nodded. "One thing I got from my stay there: Those guys—the seminarians—they're human. I mean they lost their temper about the same as any other guy." He grinned again. "Even used bad language once in a while."

"So what's so different about that?"

Mike shook his head. "Just that they're almost priests. They get ordained, they don't suddenly become plaster saints. They're *human.*"

Manny pondered that. "These guys—these seminarians—they go to school the same place we're headed?"

"Yup . . . Sacred Heart."

"Is that smart?" Manny turned to Mike. "I mean, we were all set to go to the Redemptorist place in Missouri. Are we makin' a mistake? I mean, you convinced me it was a good idea to go in for high school . . ."

"Instead of waiting for college? Yeah. I'm convinced we better make our move early—and make it here. Matter of fact, I was talkin' to Bob Koesler. He just got the word that he's been accepted at Sacred Heart. He's goin' in next month. He's on cloud nine!

"But he told me about a guy he met who got rejected on the entrance test. He said it'd be a good idea to really crack the books in the eighth grade. Especially English."

Da-dum, plop.

"Well," Manny admitted, "it does make a helluva lot of sense to stay here . . . I mean, I wasn't nuts about goin' all the way to Missouri."

"Yeah, I feel the same way." Mike tilted his head in thought. "Funny how this worked out. We would all be going to Missouri if it hadn't been for that missionary priest who clued Bob into Sacred Heart."

"I know. Now the joke is on the other two guys in Bob's class: They're packin' to go to Missouri."

"Bob was barely able to get into Sacred Heart himself. He didn't even have time to tell those other guys. He's lucky he made it." He turned up one side of his mouth. "I guess he's on his own now."

"Until we get there next year."

"That's not a lead-pipe cinch, you know: We gotta get accepted first."

Da-dum, plop.

"Hey, don't worry, we'll make it. We're not dummies. And we've got lots more time to prepare than Bob had . . ."

Manny was tiring; it was just too hot to expend even this small amount of energy. He put an extra measure of smoke on his next throw.

Da-dum . . . dum . . . dum . . . dum . . . da . . . da . . . Mike missed the rebound. The two watched as the ball bounced away. It rolled about twenty yards, where it reached a level drain in the pavement, rocked a bit, then lay still.

"That's eleven," Manny said. "I win."

They walked over to the inert ball.

"Wanna play another one?" Manny was definitely running out of steam. Still, he wished Mike would be willing to bet a nickel or so on another game. He sighed; he could have relieved his buddy of pocketsful of loose change in almost any athletic competition, but it was an an exercise in futility even to imagine that Mike might gamble.

They had talked about what Manny liked to call "putting your money where your mouth is." They had talked about the morality of gambling. As students at a parochial school, they had discussed the morality of a lot of situations. On the question of gambling, Mike and Manny disagreed. Manny could see no problem whatsoever in gambling any amount as long as you could cover your bets. Mike was convinced that no one should risk the cataclysm that could well occur.

Last year Mike had asked the priest who visited their

classroom periodically what the position of the Catholic Church was on gambling. It seemed to the young student that the priest waffled. Most of the time gambling was bad; however sometimes it could be a harmless, innocent recreation.

To Mike, in his youth and with his rigid upbringing, everything was black or white; nothing was gray. His Church was the only guaranteed source of truth in life. It was one, holy, Catholic, and apostolic. He lost a bit of respect for any visiting priest who was willing to compromise.

In a more capsulated way, Manny was confident that he could beat anyone at anything. Mike had no comparable self-confidence. Mostly, he just couldn't bear to lose. Thus he was reluctant to wager. Even in situations where he might be reasonably confident of winning, it went against his conscience to take money from the loser. What with one thing and another, Mike couldn't stomach gambling.

It didn't surprise Manny that Mike didn't want to continue the game. It *was* too hot. Only a wager could have motivated him to any further outdoor physical activity today.

They retrieved the tennis ball and walked back toward the slight shadow cast by the huge buildings. En route, Manny continued to bounce the ball as if he were dribbling a basketball.

"You gotta play with that thing?" Mike said.

Manny snickered. "Sore loser."

The two were in the same phase of development. Each was about five feet five. Each was thin. They would both grow to be adults, but not in the near future. Judging from their parents, Manny would be heavy-set; hirsute, with dark black hair; and ruggedly handsome. Mike, should he favor his father, would grow only a few inches taller than he was already. Possibly five feet nine or ten. He would remain slender; his hair would stay reddish brown until it turned gray or white. Eventually he would lose much of it to male-pattern baldness.

But for now both had a great deal of growing up to do.

"Maybe," Mike said, "I'd be sore if we'd had any money on it. But we didn't have a bet."

"Yeah, that's a snowball's chance in hell. Or maybe a warm water's day in Lake Huron."

They laughed.

"Don't get me wrong," Manny explained. "I don't mind playing any game for fun. I just can't feel the killer instinct unless something's riding on it. I don't know . . . it's just the way I am.

"Take you, for instance," he continued. "You're not bad at all. You can stay even with me pretty well. But you don't do as well as you could. There isn't any time that you ever go for the jugular. I've seen you sometimes when we're playing: You get an opponent on the ropes—and then you back off."

"Winning isn't everything."

"It's something."

Mike shook his head. "You know, it's a good thing you're gonna be a priest."

Manny stopped bouncing the ball and stood still. "What in hell has anything we just talked about have to do with becoming a priest?"

"Well, if you weren't going to the seminary, you'd probably get involved with varsity sports. Certainly the major stuff: football, basketball, baseball. You'd be playing for Redeemer. And Redeemer's in the top league."

"Yeah? So?"

"You said it yourself: There's no betting on games in high school or college. That'd take you out of serious contention. You'd want to play pro ball. But you'd never get there because the amateur leagues wouldn't pay you. So you'd never make it to the majors."

"How long has it taken you to figure out my future?"

"Actually, just now. But it's been in the back of my mind for a while. It fell into place when you were just talking about how you've got to have something riding on the game before you go for the jugular."

Manny studied his friend. "You may have something

there. But I don't think so." He shrugged. "The question will answer itself if and when I become a priest."

"One step at a time," Mike cautioned.

"One step at a time, eh, guy? Well, what's first on the hit parade?"

Mike's brow knitted. "Well . . . we start to gather the documents. You know, it's not as easy as it sounded when Bob told me about it. He didn't bring anything with him the first time he went to the seminary . . . things got pretty involved."

"Wait a minute! Wait a minute! What documents?"

"You don't know? Didn't you talk to Bob?"

"A little. But he didn't mention any documents. It never even came up. Of course," he said, after a moment's reflection, "mostly I was just asking him questions." He shook his head. "Nope; it just didn't come up.

"So"—he looked at Mike intently—"what's it all about?"

"According to Bob, in addition to a pencil, and a transcript of your grammar school grades, they want three documents. Three certificates, really: your baptismal and confirmation records and your parents' marriage certificate."

"I haven't got any of these." Down deep, Manny felt the beginning of panic.

"I don't have them either."

"Then what—"

"You've got to go get them."

"Where?"

"The parish where you were baptized and confirmed. And the parish where your parents were married. You just go there and ask for them. Bob said they have to have the parish seal on them. But Bob said the priest or his secretary would probably know that."

Manny could see his dream vocation crashing before it got in the air. "I think maybe I got a problem."

"What?"

The two sat on the cement stair in the blessed shade.

"My dad. He's not a Catholic. Will he be able to get a marriage certificate?"

"Were your folks married in a Catholic church?"

"Yeah. My mom told me all about the wedding a long time ago. Actually, they were married at a side altar. Because my dad wasn't a Catholic."

"So what's that got to do with getting the damn certificate?"

Mike thought about that briefly. "I don't think it has anything to do with it. Remember in our Religion class when we were studying the seven sacraments? If one party is Catholic and the other isn't, they call that a mixed marriage."

"Yeah." Manny brightened. "A mixed religion marriage."

"Well, if your folks got married in a Catholic church like you said, then it's a valid marriage."

"Even if they did it at a side altar?"

"Why not?"

"Yeah, why not?" Manny hesitated. "But there's more to it than that, isn't there? I mean, don't they have to get something?"

"Get something? What something?"

"Something about . . . uh . . . permission . . . no? Permission to get married even though both of them weren't Catholic?"

Mike's eyes widened. "You mean a dispensation?"

"That's it: a dispensation."

Mike's memory faltered. "From what?"

"I don't know. I just remember the word."

"Wait a minute," Mike said thoughtfully. "It's simple. They can't get married 'cause one of them is not a Catholic. It's prohibited. So," he said triumphantly, "they get a dispensation from the prohibition. Then they can get married in a Catholic church . . . even though it's at a side altar."

"Man," Manny exclaimed, "you got some memory!"

Mike smiled. "Not for everything. I figure we ought to know all we can about the Catholic Church . . . after all, it's gonna be our entire life."

Manny was uneasy about the Church being his "entire life." He wasn't sure he wanted to make that total a commitment. "Is that all there is to it?" He sensed there was more than merely getting a paper that said his parents were dispensed so they could get married in the Catholic Church.

Mike thought. The Brother who taught their Religion class was pretty thorough about Church stuff, especially about the sacraments. Brothers were more demanding than nuns. At least it seemed so; they hit harder. "Seems to me there's something people have to do before they get their dispensation." He looked up as if the answer were somewhere in the sky. "Something they have to promise. Promise . . . oh, I know: They have to promise to raise their kids as Catholics."

He turned to Manny. "Your folks certainly lived up to that. Heck, I see your dad at Mass practically every Sunday."

"Yeah. I never thought much about it, but Dad does go to church every Sunday . . . and so does my mom. But"—he sighed as he tilted his head and pursed his lips—"she *has* to go or she'll go to hell." He thought for a moment. "I don't think my dad *has* to go. He says we ought to go together— like the family we are. Even though he can't take Communion.

"I never thought about all he had to go through to marry my mom." Manny thought about it now, then, eyebrows raised in recognition, he nodded. "That was pretty neat."

"Do you think your ma would have married him if he hadn't made the promise or just refused to do anything to get the dispensation?"

"Man, I don't know."

"If your dad didn't get the dispensation, they wouldn't have been able to be married in church. Would she have married him anyway? I mean, then she would've been excommunicated."

"Man, I don't know what she would have done," Manny repeated.

"It's just that I think that if that had been the case, then you would have a real hard time getting in the seminary."

"Because she'd've been excommunicated?"

"I think so. I heard my folks talking about it a long time ago. One of my cousins married a lady who was divorced.

Then they had a son who wanted to be a priest. But the seminary wouldn't accept him . . . just because of his parents."

"Man, that's miserable. Why pick on the kid? I mean, just for something the parents did—or didn't do?"

"That's the law. And you're right: Now that we're talking about it, it *doesn't* seem fair."

"No, it don't!" Manny said in emphasis.

"But . . ." Mike shrugged. ". . . it's the law of our Church. It must be right."

They continued to sit still. It was cooler in the shade. It would have been more tolerable if there had been a breeze. Not only was there no wind, but it was humid. Languidly, they bounced the tennis ball back and forth to each other.

Across the parking lot, a couple of boys appeared in the car entrance.

They walked with purposeful direction. There could be no doubt they were headed toward Manny and Mike. They didn't appear to be in a mood to play games. Their demeanor was downright menacing.

Each set of boys focused on the other.

4 To MIKE IT was creepy.

The two strangers were advancing toward him and Manny with deliberation. They were now near enough to be identifiable.

"Do you know them?" Manny asked, out of the side of his mouth.

"No," Mike said in a faint voice, "I don't think I've ever seen them before."

Manny grunted.

The newcomers had halted and now stood some ten to twelve feet away. Each was considerably larger than either Mike or Manny. "What's your names?" the taller one demanded.

Mike's impulse was to tell them. What harm could come from answering a simple question? But before he could respond, Manny spoke. "What's yours?"

The newcomers looked surprised. They had obviously expected to instill fear, whereas they were being defied.

"I'm Switch," said the taller one. "And my friend here is the Blade." The two laughed humorlessly.

"Cute," Manny said.

Switch, though the taller, was by no means well developed. The Blade was slightly better built.

They looked to be in their mid- to late teens. Their clothing was soiled and ragged. They could have profited from a shower—possibly even a delousing.

"Well," Switch said, "*your* names?" Though it was a

question, it was issued in the tone of a command. Mike felt an even stronger impulse to provide the information.

But again, before Mike could say a word, Manny spoke. "We don't think you'll have much use for them." He began to bounce the tennis ball against the pavement.

Switch and the Blade were taken a bit aback; they had definitely not expected anything like this show of resistance.

"That a new tennis ball?" The Blade tried an oblique approach.

"You see a gift wrap anywhere?" Manny's reply was rhetorical. "If it ain't wrapped up like a present," he said, "it probably ain't new."

Switch and the Blade traded glances. The two made a habit of doing exactly what they were trying to do now: intimidating smaller, younger boys. Bullies, ordinarily they picked their targets at random. As long as the prey was vulnerable, the two were confident of taking booty, like pirates.

Mike wanted out of here as badly as he had ever wanted anything. But, for starters, he doubted that Switch and the Blade would give him safe passage. More important, he would never abandon his buddy in such a threatening situation.

But, oh, how he wished Manny would get rid of the chip that had unexpectedly appeared on his shoulder.

"Wanna play a game?" Switch was definitely the spokesman for the twosome; outside of his oblique question, the Blade had done nothing more than nod when his cohort spoke—and try to look menacing.

"We just got done," Manny said.

"Yeah, but I know a real good game." Switch's grin was malevolent.

"What's it called?"

"Keep Away."

"Same as Monkey in the Middle?"

"Sometimes." Switch's smile was smug.

"Or Let's Steal the Ball from the Squirts?"

Switch's chin thrust forward. "You accusin' us of being thieves?"

Manny's lips curled down in an ironic smile. "And I would guess not very good ones." The two hoodlums were furious. Manny had verbally cut them down to size. Their bluff had been called.

They all knew where this was going.

Manny tossed the ball behind him. His gesture was clear: If you want the ball you'll have to go through me.

Mike's eyes bulged with fright.

Switch, though livid, was the talker. The Blade was action. He dove at Manny.

Switch and Mike had little choice but to follow suit; they began to scuffle. But although each ripped the other's shirt, their hearts weren't in it; after less than a minute they called it quits. They stood, irresolute, staring at the action between Manny and the Blade, both of whom, though exerting maximum effort, seemed strangely immobile. Like Ursus and the bull in *"Quo Vadis?"* Or like two powerful arm wrestlers straining toward a draw.

For the moment, all four combatants seemed frozen in time.

Then, as Manny and the Blade continued to push against each other, the Blade's anchor foot began to slide to the rear. His knee buckled, and he fell backward, taking Manny down on top of him. Manny immediately pulled upright. Then, seated on the Blade's chest, he rained punches on his now powerless opponent—rights and lefts from one side of the Blade's face to the other.

The Blade was now thoroughly defeated. It mattered not to Manny; it appeared he would continue his pummeling until the Blade was seriously battered and/or beaten senseless . . . or even possibly dead.

The entire episode had reversed from its initial premise.

The Blade, who had single-handedly raised the ante from a verbal confrontation to a fistfight, was now helpless. His head, like a barely attached punching bag, reeled from side to side under Manny's blows. Still, Manny, a seeming automaton, gave no indication of letting up.

Mike and Switch, now almost totally oblivious of each

other, both tried to pull Manny off. For only the briefest moment, Switch considered taking Manny on.

That would not have been advisable. Switch could not hold a candle to the Blade when it came to street fighting or hand-to-hand combat—and Manny had totally disabled the Blade.

Switch knew his arithmetic.

Together, he and Mike were finally able to pull Manny off his unresisting adversary. Manny's parting kick to the Blade's ribs put the final punctuation to that story.

Adrenalized, Manny, still in fighting mode, turned full attention to Switch. Mike was shouting, urging, pleading with Manny to cease and desist. Switch, fists clenched, glared at Manny, took half a step forward, thought better of it, and turned to his prostrate buddy.

Amazingly, in spite of the drubbing, the Blade, with assistance, was able to stand. The red on Manny's shirt belonged mostly, if not exclusively, to the Blade, who was bleeding copiously from nose and mouth.

Leaning on Switch for support, the Blade staggered from the parking lot. But not before shooting a mixed look of wrathful defeat and sworn revenge at Manny.

Manny collapsed on the steps. He reached behind him and picked up the tennis ball. Mike watched him carefully. Manny's hands trembled as if with Parkinson's. Slowly the adrenaline subsided.

Mike was in a state of near shock. When this altercation had begun, he'd thought the worst: that they would suffer anything from the humiliation of having to surrender their ball to getting a beating.

Then, completely unexpectedly, Manny had taken the field and saved the day. At the same time, he had revealed something about himself: Manny had a temper that could be explosive.

"All this blood," Manny mused. "How am I gonna explain it? Ma'll kill me. If she doesn't, Pa will."

At this point Mike couldn't think of anyone who would or could kill Manny. "Why don't you just tell the truth? We were just playing when a couple of jerks tried to take the ball away from us. You wouldn't give it up. From that time on, it was self-defense."

Manny brightened. "Yeah. I guess that would work. And it *is* the truth."

The picture was getting clearer in Manny's mind. His mother would bawl him out for fighting. She would tell him that he could get hurt. "Look at all that blood! Was it worth all this mess? Better you should let them have the silly ball. We can always get you another toy. You sure you weren't hurt? Lemme look you over. Okay. Take off those dirty clothes and take a bath. Look! Your pants are ripped in the knee! I'll try to fix them. Now clean up before your father gets home and sees this!"

But that ultimate threat wouldn't come to pass the way his ma threatened. Rather, when Manny's dad arrived home from the factory, Manny would tell him what had happened. And, as Mike suggested, he would tell the truth. Dad would let him finish, then he'd ask, "The kids were bigger than you and Mike?"

"Yes, Dad."

"And you didn't start it?"

"No. Like I said, they wanted our ball. They just came up and said so."

Mr. Tocco would shake his head. "Hooligans! Pickin' on little kids. Did you get hurt?"

"No, Dad. I just got kinda dirty—well, bloody. But it was the other guy's blood."

Manny's dad would feel a surge of pride. He would try to hide any indication of this. But it would be there.

No, on second thought, the prospect of going home bloody and torn didn't seem nearly as foreboding. As long as it worked out the way he projected.

Mike's voice returned Manny to reality. "Why did you do that anyway, Manny? I was all for giving them the stupid ball."

Manny began again to bounce the ball. Mike noted that

his friend's hands still trembled, but not as pronouncedly as they had.

"I don't know, Mike. I've never felt like that before. It was like these guys just had to be stopped or they would be pushing littler kids around forever."

"Weren't you afraid?"

Manny thought about that. "No. I wasn't afraid. I didn't even think about being scared.

"Anyway," he said after a moment, "I didn't start it. *They* did. That guy Blade did. I think Switch would've just talked away if the Blade hadn't been there."

"You did toss our ball behind you."

"Yeah, I almost forgot. I don't know why I did that."

Mike hesitated. "Well, you couldn't have thought that was going to bring peace."

Manny contemplated the ball he now held. "Mike, honest, I wasn't thinking of anything. I just wasn't thinking. What they were doing was wrong. I couldn't let them get away with it—especially so easily."

"You never ran into anything like this before, did you?"

Manny shook his head. "No . . . not like this. This was so . . . so black and white. They were goons. If we had given them the ball, they probably would've just thrown it away."

"Well, you sure were impressive."

"Maybe then. But I don't think now."

"Whaddya mean not now?"

"Now that I think it over. Now that I *can* think it over, it scares me. I think I actually could've killed the guy. That's scary."

Mike's mouth formed an *O* of disbelief. "You wouldn't have gone that far? . . ."

"Yeah. I think you know better. You were pretty strong yourself . . . or you couldn't have pulled me off him."

"I refuse to believe it. You would have stopped. You were counting on us—better make that on *me;* Switch wasn't working that hard—you were counting on me to pull you off."

"No. I just wanted to make sure he didn't have any fight left in him."

They were silent for a few minutes.

"Whaddya say, maybe we ought to go home," Mike said finally. "Let's get the explanations out of the way. My ripped-up shirt, and all that blood on you."

"And the tear in my jeans."

"Yeah . . . oh, and one more thing," Mike added. "When the Blade's buddy was helping him get out of here, did you see the look Blade gave you?"

"I saw."

"He sure looked like he was thinking about revenge. Shouldn't we be doing something about that?"

Manny thought a moment. "I can't live that way. If he comes, he comes. But"—he shook his head—"I don't think he will. He got beat up pretty bad."

Mike turned to leave, then stopped. "I don't care how cold Lake Huron is, I sure could use a little corner of that Great Lake right now." He grinned. "See you tomorrow."

"Yeah."

5 ROSE SMITH WAS brushing her hair. One hundred strokes. It was a nuisance to observe this beauty tip religiously each night. But it seemed to be paying off: Her blond hair was lustrous and silken.

Alice McMann was another case; she considered such self-pampering a futile extravagance.

The Smiths and McManns were neighbors and close friends. Whenever Rose's or Alice's parents were called away or had a night out, the one girl would spend that time at the other's house.

Tonight, the two girls, each in bathrobe and pajamas, were in Rose's bedroom. Alice's parents were off to a wedding in Philadelphia.

Alice was paging through a movie magazine. Had she her druthers, she'd be downstairs listening to Frank Sinatra records. But she thought it better to wait for Rose.

The Smiths had not yet retired for the night. They were listening to the *Jack Benny Show*. Mrs. Smith was knitting. Mr. Smith was leaning back in his upholstered chair, smoking his pipe and living the word-pictures the Benny ensemble was painting.

Mike, Rose's twin brother, was doing homework. Since learning of the importance the seminary placed on English courses, he had taken a renewed interest in grammar, especially the diagramming of sentences.

The family group was a contributing factor in Alice's decision to wait for Rose to complete her nightly ritual rather than going downstairs without her.

36

If she had joined the others downstairs, she would've been a fifth wheel. The adults could be counted on to silently communicate with each other. While Mike, oblivious of the radio comedy, would pore over his studies. If she were there, she would be intruding on the adults, who would feel impelled to make conversation for her benefit. As for Michael, he would effectively freeze her out.

So Alice held to the routine that had developed between the Smiths, and Mike and Rose. Except that Alice found the magazine boring. She allowed it to slip from her fingers and fall to the floor. The soft noise caught Rose's attention. She turned, while continuing to brush her hair. "I don't blame you, Al," she said. "Those movie and entertainment mags aren't worth the trees that have to be cut down to make the paper they're printed on.

"Well"—she stopped brushing for a moment—"that was an awkward sentence. But you know what I mean."

Alice nodded, as Rose turned back to the mirror. The brushing continued.

Alice sprawled on the bed. "Why does Mike hit the books so hard? He hardly needs to. He's a genius—just like you."

Rose giggled. "We're not geniuses. Oh, we may be kind of smart—but we both have to work to live up to our potential. Right now, Mike's working harder than I am. It's for the seminary. He doesn't want to repeat the fiasco that Bob Koesler went through. Of course, Bob hadn't brought the documents they wanted because he didn't know they were required. Mike wants to be completely prepared."

Alice absently twisted a strand of hair around her index finger. "How about that fight Mike and Manny were in last week? That's getting to be a popular topic around school . . . around our class anyway."

"Nothing to it, really," Rose said.

"I heard there was blood . . . lots of blood."

"You don't want to believe everything you hear."

"No blood?" Alice sounded disappointed.

"The other guy's. But Mike's shirt was torn up pretty

bad." Rose hoped the shredded shirt would satisfy Alice's seeming fascination with senseless violence.

"How about Manny?" Alice pursued. "Was that just scuttlebutt too? About how he took the big bully to the cleaners? And got him pretty well beat up too?"

Rose grinned. Alice couldn't see the expression. "No. That seems to be the God's honest truth. And my information is firsthand—from my brother. After all, he *was* there—and God knows he tells the truth."

Silence, as Rose reached fifty-three strokes and Alice busied herself in trying to untangle the knot she'd made in her own hair.

"And all that over a tennis ball!" Alice exclaimed. "Boys!"

"I think it was kind of brave of them," Rose said thoughtfully. "It's like they say about the war . . . you know: We're making the world safe for democracy. Well, Mike and Manny are making the playground safe for other kids.

"Besides . . . it's already done some good. The Brothers have set up patrols of seniors and juniors to keep a watch when school's out and on weekends."

Alice thought about the ramifications of what Manny and Mike had done. Manny more than Mike. But Mike had made a contribution. "I guess," she said, "the guys were pretty brave."

"Especially Manny. He's the one who came up with a re-action 'above and beyond,' as they say."

"Yeah," Alice agreed, "but what kind of priest is he gonna make? I mean, priests aren't supposed to get physical, are they? I never heard of one who did, anyway. Look at Father Flannigan of Boys' Town. He doesn't go around boxing guys' ears."

Rose laughed. "Al, Manny hasn't turned into some kind of goon or thug. Remember: Manny didn't start this whole thing. He just responded to the bad guy's challenge. Like the war: We didn't start it. We didn't even want to get into it. Then came Pearl Harbor."

"Yeah . . ." Alice pondered that incontrovertible fact.

"Mike and Manny . . ." Alice reflected.

"Mike and Manny . . ." Alice repeated. "Do you realize, Rose, that Mike and Manny are the only two guys in our class that I know? And I know them only because I know you. You're Mike's twin. That's how I know Mike. And Mike's best friend is Manny, and that's how I know Manny.

"Doesn't that seem odd?"

"Um-hmm."

"Think about it," Alice persisted. "Public school kids seem to know everybody . . . I mean everybody in their own class anyway. And you and I know a sum total of two boys!"

"And all our girl classmates," Rose reminded.

"It just doesn't seem right. We go through seven years; we're in the same building—at least through sixth grade, then all of a sudden we're not only not in separate class-rooms, we're not even in the same building."

"And," Rose added, "the boys aren't taught by the nuns. Their teachers are the Brothers of Mary."

"That's right. Why do you suppose the boys have to wait until seventh grade to get the Brothers? I mean, they're al-ready in separate classrooms. How come they don't get the Brothers right off the bat? In first grade."

Rose paused in mid-stroke. "I suppose it's simply supply and demand."

"Huh?"

"Maybe there aren't enough Brothers to go around. It comes down to numbers."

"Really?"

"Mike and I have talked about it."

"And?"

"Well, take the girls . . . our classmates . . . ourselves. The plan—at least in Redeemer—is for all the girls to be taught by nuns, with maybe an occasional laywoman. When the girls graduate, most of them get a job. A few go to col-lege. But, in any case, practically every one of them is look-ing for a husband. After all, being a housewife is the ultimate goal . . . right?"

"Hmmm. Yeah . . . I guess so. But what about girls like us . . . who want to go to the convent?"

"Then . . ." Rose was having trouble keeping track of the strokes. ". . . we go to the convent. Ordinarily, girls like us naturally go to Monroe—to the Sisters, Servants of the Immaculate Heart of Mary. You know, that's the religious order that trained and taught us.

"But even if we don't go to Monroe . . . if we become, say, Dominicans from Adrian . . . we'd still be the same essentially. We'd be nuns. Just members of different orders, that's all."

"Sure. But what's that got to do with the Brothers? That there aren't enough to staff all twelve grades of boys?"

"That's where Mike comes in."

Alice shook her head. "I don't get it."

"How many boys from Redeemer intend to become priests?"

"I dunno. A couple . . . maybe three or four . . ."

"From the whole high school?"

"No. I meant by class. I'd say"—Alice ran the figures through her mind—"a couple—as many as four or five . . . from each class."

"Okay. Why do you think these kids go to the seminary?"

Alice shrugged. "Because they want to be priests."

"Yes. But *why* do they want to be priests?"

"Well, going to a parochial school doesn't hurt. Having Catholic parents. Like that."

Rose nodded. "And Mike tells me it's not only those things. It's also because they think being a priest is exciting. They want to get in on the action."

"I couldn't argue with that."

"It's right from the horse's mouth. Mike said that. And he also said that not many of the kids understand what the Brothers are up to. And that's why the Brothers don't inspire many kids to join up."

Alice looked surprised. "Gee, I don't have a problem with that. The Brothers of Mary we've got here are classy guys. Real men and real teachers."

"But they're not teaching *us*. So we don't experience them the way the boys do. Anyway, how many boys in Redeemer High School, do you think, sign up to join the Brothers?"

"I . . . I don't know. Not as many as want to be priests."

"Would you believe one or two in the whole high school? Mike says the kids appreciate being taught by men for the first time in all the years in school. He says he just doesn't see the Brothers as a vocation. One of Mike's teachers asked him if he wanted to become a Brother."

"What did Mike say?"

"He said he'd never thought of being a Brother. He said the Brother looked kind of hurt. Like he'd been personally turned down. But Mike had said it and he couldn't take it back.

"Mike told me he couldn't understand the vocation. Brothers aren't dumb. Lots of times they're smarter than priests. So why go half way?"

Alice could hear the radio being turned off downstairs. She couldn't make out which program was going off. But the sound had stopped; the Smiths were getting ready to retire.

Alice, on the other hand, was ready for some Sinatra. Her desire would cause no problem; it was shared by Rose.

"How are you getting along?" Alice asked.

"What do you mean?"

"The brushing. How many strokes?"

Rose brushed. "That would be ninety-three," she said without breaking stride.

"How can you do that?"

"Do what?"

Alice sat upright. "We've been having a conversation. You had to be involved in what we were talking about . . . at least part of the time. How can you talk and still keep count of your strokes?"

"It's not hard; it's just a matter of thinking of two things at the same time."

"That's easy for you to say."

"You find it difficult?"

"Me and most of the rest of the world."

"There." Rose put the brush down and shook her shoulders, which were somewhat stiff after this monotonous exercise. "All done." She turned to Alice. "Some music?"

"You bet!"

By the time the two girls reached the main floor, the Smiths had retired to their bedroom. Michael, also in pajamas and robe, was stretched out on the living room floor.

None of them felt awkward. They were friends and no more than that.

Rose went directly to the phonograph. In no time the pleasantly nasal voice of Vaughn Monroe was crooning "Blue Moon."

The two girls sat together on the floor roughly halfway between the record player and Michael, who, pencil in hand, continued to work on English drills.

Alice, lost in Monroe's distinctive voice, seemed mesmerized by the lamentation.

"Blue Moon, you saw me standing alone, Without a dream in my heart, Without a love of my own . . ."

Without a love of my own. How depressing! Was that the lonely life she was slated to enter?

Alice had no real knowledge of convent life. No one who had not lived that life could comprehend it. In her naïveté, she was quite sure that what she saw she certainly would get.

She would wear the time-honored uniform, popularly known as a religious habit. It stood for something. She would be set apart in a most secular world. She would dedicate herself, body and soul, to the Roman Catholic Church.

If she joined almost any other religious order than the IHMs, she would be invited to express her preference for one of two paths: teaching or nursing. The fact that she would not necessarily be allowed to pursue the one she had chosen merely spoke to the dedication that religious life would demand of her.

But there was something to be said for either occupation.

If she were to teach, she would be instilling in young minds the ancient and ever-present truths of Catholicism. Her students would remember—some for the rest of their lives—what "Sister said." The aphorism "Once a Catholic, always a Catholic" would, in many cases, be the legacy of her vocation.

That—even the demands on her freedom—was all on the positive side. There would be pride in what she had accomplished and a reverence for what her life signified.

If she were directed to the nursing field, it held similar possibilities. She would have to be qualified as a nurse. She would work in a Catholic hospital where uniforms abounded and nurses' caps identified the wearer's school of training. But among all those uniforms of various shades, hers—the religious habit turned white—would be the most distinctive.

She would be warmly welcomed by patients stricken with nearly every sort of illness. Her prayers would be solicited and promised. Patients would go forward with renewed confidence: What better insurance could there be than a nun's prayer?

She would be with those who would not survive. Being encouraged and given good hope as they passed from this life to the next. She would be with the bereaved, offering consoling words, a reassuring presence, and the promise of more prayer.

All these were positive and motivating arguments for the life she proposed to pursue.

She could not imagine what it would be like to live in a community of women who would compose one's "Sisters." She hoped that that would be worth the price of admission. Still, there were doubts.

What if she were to find herself locked away with no companions other than women who were more strangers than Sisters?

What if she were housed with one or more women with whom she was flat-out incompatible? Alice guessed there would be no remedy for that. Obedience—blind obedience—would be the required response. The Community saw fit to send her to this school, this hospital, and/or this convent. That mission then would be God's will—no matter how unpleasant the atmosphere might be.

Monroe's voice reinvaded her consciousness. That about which he was singing was the real sacrifice she would have to face. She felt that it would be the most difficult gift of all—a veritable oblation.

Loneliness.

And not just under a Blue Moon.

She would see it everywhere.

And it would be worse as a nursing Sister. Teachers deal with students, kids more than likely. More times than not it would be on an adversarial basis. She recalled a cartoon of a nun at a blackboard lecturing other nuns. On the blackboard was the stick figure of a little boy in open-neck shirt and jeans, with a slingshot sticking out of his back pocket. The cartoon caption: "THE ENEMY."

Teaching nuns had little to do with adults, unless the parents' little darlings were in deep scholastic or disciplinary trouble.

The nursing nun dealt with everyone from infants to the elderly. Not only did these nuns care for the ill and infirm, they also interacted with the next of kin: husbands, wives, children, friends, relatives, lovers. Sometimes the love among these people was all but palpable. They would hold hands, be near, kiss.

None of that for her.

Could she do it?

Right now, Mr. and Mrs. Smith were in bed together. Whether or not they were making love, at least they were together—touching, caring, sharing, being in love.

Not in her life. Her life would have its pluses—and its minuses. Could she carry it off? No telling till she gave it her best shot.

No one had said a word during Monroe's song. Alice and

Rose each had her own thoughts and daydreams. Mike was deep into lines connecting adjectives to nouns, adverbs to verbs.

Monroe had finished. Time to put on another record.

Time to share a little conversation.

⑥ MIKE PACKED AWAY his books, rolled over onto his back, and stretched. "No wonder they call Monroe the Iron Lung; he sings practically every song his band plays."

"Stop picking on him." Rose was lighthearted. "At least he's good at it."

"He sounds like someone pinched his nose with a clothespin," Mike replied.

What has been said of twins' closeness was true of Mike and Rose. Even as infants they had paid more attention to each other than to the toys their parents lavished on them.

Although Mr. and Mrs. Smith had planned a large family, Rose and Mike were the only offspring they had and the only ones they would ever have.

The Smiths had not expected twins, although they certainly welcomed the two, who would, they thought, provide a great start toward the desired large Catholic family.

The bad news was the discovery of a cancerous growth on the mother's uterus. The growth was excised, of course. But to do so, the entire uterus had to be removed. There followed an extended period of watching and praying that the surgery had removed any possibility of recurrence.

The parents' initial reaction was to lavish the twins with toys and games. Eventually, they saw the light and settled down to provide their children the only things they really needed—tender, loving care.

"It's not that I was looking for a specific singer," Alice said. "It's the song I wanted to hear."

46

"How come?" Mike asked.

"Oh, I dunno. I guess I was feeling kind of alone."

"You should've told me," Rose said with genuine concern. "We had plenty of time to talk about it upstairs. It certainly wasn't going to do you any good to listen to such a sad song. Besides"—she was trying to be encouraging—"toward the end, it says, 'Now I'm no longer alone . . .' "

"I guess the melody is what I was looking for," Alice said. "It's sort of sad and melancholy." She smiled. "But now that I've heard the song and listened to you guys, it's better."

"Remember," Mike said, "you only get to feel like this"—he paused for emphasis—"once in a blue moon. That's what it means: once in a very long time."

"You would make this cerebral," Rose scolded. "Al just was feeling down. I'm sure that it happens to everybody now and then." She turned back to her friend. "Is something bothering you, Al? Don't be put off by Mr. Meat-and-Potatoes there. Believe it or not, he does have feelings."

"I know he does." Alice smiled at the now blushing Mike. "I was thinking . . . I got to thinking about what we're planning on doing."

"Which is what?" Mike asked.

"Going into the convent," Alice replied.

"Is *that* it?" Rose's tone was dismissive. "Good gravy, that's not for another five years. First we have to go through grade school *and* high school. That's a long way to go. We've got plenty of time to decide for sure. Heck, Mike here has only one year to make up his mind. Once he finishes the eighth grade, it's off to the seminary—if they'll have him," she said with a mocking grin.

"I'd appreciate it if you didn't joke about that," Mike said. "If Bob Koesler had a rough time, I'm not expecting a smooth slide."

"Sorry," Rose said. "But you shouldn't be so touchy. You know you're gonna be accepted."

"Okay. But so do you two."

"It's different with us," Rose protested.

"Oh?"

"We—the three of us," Rose said, "along about this time next year will graduate from the eighth grade. Then Al and I will start high school at Redeemer. Nothing much will change for us. But you," she addressed her twin, "will be going to a very special school where you'll start a long process to figure out whether or not you want to be a priest.

"When the three of us graduate from high school, you'll continue to be a student. Nothing much different will happen in your life. But our lives—Al's and mine—will change terrifically. We'll be in a convent. We'll be postulants. We'll be wearing a religious habit. We'll be well on our way to becoming nuns."

Silence for a few moments.

"I see what you mean," Mike admitted finally. "Once we get out of grade school, my life will change—a lot. I'll be a seminarian. But you and Alice; well, nothing much will happen to you two next year. Then, when we graduate four years later, I'll still just be a seminarian . . . whereas you two will be beginning religious life in Monroe."

"I'm not sure . . ." Alice hesitated. ". . . about Monroe."

"What?" Mike was puzzled. "You gotta go there. That's where they make IHM nuns."

The girls ignored Mike's flippant phrase. "I'm just not so sure I want to be an IHM," Alice said.

"What?" It was Rose's turn to be surprised.

"The IHMs are teachers," Alice said. "That's what they do. Oh, here and there one might be an infirmarian, so she'd likely have to be a nurse. But there's no real choice when you enter Monroe: If you stick it out, you're going to be a teaching nun."

"Maybe that's why you were playing the Monroe record," Mike teased. "You were thinking of being lonely in Monroe." He chuckled.

"We can do without your feeble puns." Rose turned to Alice. "I'm really surprised, Al. I thought you and I had the same plans. I mean, we know the IHMs. I didn't think there was any question."

"I haven't mentioned it," Alice admitted, "but I have been giving it some thought."

"What is it?" Rose probed. "You getting cold feet about the convent?"

"That's not it . . . at least I don't think that's it. I think it's the question of having a choice."

"I don't understand," Rose said.

"There are lots of different orders," Alice explained. "There are teachers and nurses and . . . and missionaries! We haven't even discussed missionaries!"

"Do you think you might prefer one of those alternatives? 'Cause if you do, I wouldn't want to stand in your way. I mean, it's too big a choice for you to depend on somebody else to make."

Silence. Even though the girls were clearly aware of his presence, Mike felt as if he were eavesdropping.

"I want to be with you," Alice said finally. "That's part of it. But I also want a bigger choice on what I'll do with my life in a religious order." Her brow wrinkled. "I'm confused."

"Well . . ." Rose shook her head. Her freshly brushed hair danced about. "We can't plan that we'll be together. We have to give up a lot of personal freedom when we become nuns. Far as I know, we'll have precious few choices. Even our new names in the Order won't be up to us. We can request, but others will decide them. And if we don't even get to choose our own names, it's not likely we'll have much say in where we'll serve or with whom."

Mike might as well have been invisible.

"I'm confused," Alice acknowledged. "I want to be a nun. I want to be a 'Bride of Christ.' I want to wear the habit and I want to live up to what the habit stands for. I want to willingly—gladly—accept any sacrifice that I'm called to make.

"That's today. Yesterday I didn't want to be a nun. Tomorrow I may want to get married and have kids. I don't want to keep changing my mind, going backward and forward. It's driving me nuts." A tear slid down her cheek. More tears filled her eyes, waiting to fall. She wiped them away.

Rose moved closer and put an arm around her friend's

shoulder. "I had no idea," she admitted. "I just had no idea. Isn't there anyone you've talked to about your decision? Isn't there anyone you could discuss it with? One of our teachers? Your folks?"

"Oh, Rose, I've got more confidence in you than in anybody else. I know . . . I really know that you're the one to help me make up my mind once and for all."

"I don't know what to say, Al. I want to help you. But I've got to be objective. I'm just a kid. Like you. I don't have any experience with something as important as this."

"Prayer." Mike spoke the word with no particular emphasis.

"Huh?" Alice wasn't sure what he'd said.

"Prayer?" Rose echoed.

"I don't mean to horn in on your discussion. But"—he shrugged—"I really couldn't help it."

"I don't mind," Alice said. "In fact, I was kind of hoping you'd throw your two cents in."

Rose was smiling. "You hit the nail right on the head, brother. The one thing we should've thought of right away. Here we are, talking about a religious vocation, and we've done a great job of missing the point. We plan on spending our lives in prayer . . . and we forgot all about it when it most counted."

"You two," Mike said, "have been carrying on as if we were going to ship you off to the convent tomorrow. Migosh, you've got five years! Plenty of time, if you use it well."

"You're right, pal," Rose said. "And who knows what'll happen during these next years?" She turned back to Alice. "You might even find a nun you have confidence in—somebody you can really open up to. But more than anything else we simply have to pray about it. And that means all of us: praying for ourselves and for each other."

From upstairs, Mr. Smith's voice cut through their thoughts. "Hey, it's almost eleven o'clock! Aren't you kids ever going to bed?"

"We'll be up in a few minutes, Dad," Mike called.

"Don't forget the lights!"

"We won't."

7

THE TOCCOS REACTED about as their son Manny expected.

He arrived home from his bout with Blade bloody but unbowed. Maria Tocco made a great fuss over his torn, dirtied, blood-spattered clothes. After she checked to make sure that the blood had not flowed from holes in her baby, her main concern was the condition of his hand, especially the thumb and index fingers. She was unfamiliar with the term canonical digits. All she knew—and that mostly from observation—was that those were the fingers the priest used to hold the communion wafer. Lacking one or more of those fingers . . . well, God knows; she assumed he would not be allowed to become a priest.

As a child in parochial school, she had listened wide-eyed, as the nuns related the martyrology. Now, she remembered all too vividly the tales of the tortures suffered by the early Jesuit priests and missionaries at the hands of their Native American captors.

Father Jean de Brebeuf—they cut out his heart and ate it while he watched. (A little hyperbole there, but what did the innocent pupils know?) Father Isaac Jogues—they chewed off his fingers and ate them. Brebeuf, of course, died. Jogues escaped and applied to Rome for—and received—permission to offer Mass sans fingers.

Maria took from these accounts two puzzles: How does one go about offering Mass without fingers? And why, though mutilated, would a living martyr need to apply for the Vatican's permission to offer Mass?

After hearing this nausea-inducing tale, one of Maria's classmates—the class comedian—had added his own contribution to the Litany of the Saints: "From the nuns who teach us precisely what the Indians did to the Jesuit missionaries, Good Lord deliver us."

Manny had come through his violent altercation in one piece. The blood had to have come from the bully. And all fingers were present and accounted for.

His mother breathed a sigh of relief, then imposed penance: Manny must confess his misdeed to his father. And so, when 'Fredo arrived home from work he was met by a still-steaming wife and a browbeaten son.

Typically, Tocco wanted to know whether either Manny or his friend Michael had been injured. Then, having ascertained that neither Manny nor Mike had started the fight, the big question was had his son triumphed over the bully, or had he come out second best?

And, finally, the damage. A shirt beyond repair, pants torn but mendable. 'Fredo mentally shrugged; the clothes were Maria's bailiwick. She would mend what was repairable; what was not would be replaced.

There followed a halfhearted lecture on the necessity of trying just about everything else before fighting might become inevitable.

'Fredo's pride in his son was only thinly disguised. Manny had fought the good fight. There was laid up for him an extra dessert.

That was then. This was now.

Manny had gotten some drastic news from the horse's mouth: Brother Vincent—or, as the boys invariably referred to him, Bro. V. Brother Vincent was principal of Holy Redeemer High, boys' division.

The Brothers were—in the parlance of war—bugging out.

It was all but a done deal. The battle had been waged over several years. Essentially, the school office argued that the peculiarly segregated situation at Redeemer was no way to run a parochial educational facility. After all, why have a coed school when there's complete separation of boys and girls? Either you have boys and girls sharing classes and rooms or you have a school for just boys and a school for just girls.

The Brothers, hitherto happy with the status quo, were now willing to fight to preserve their educational philosophy. And so they did. However, as one archdiocesan office after another climbed aboard the bandwagon, the Brothers' ship of state began to sink. The result was, in a word, inevitable.

Their decision to leave only weeks before school was scheduled to open bordered on the vindictive. It was a bombshell.

Nevertheless, the Sisters, Servants of the Immaculate Heart of Mary, and the archdiocesan school office rose to the challenge. The Brothers got their marching orders and began to break camp.

The final decision was supposed to be kept tightly under wraps. Here and there some leaks occurred, but by and large the secret was kept.

Bro. V told Manny Tocco because the two had grown close in the past year. Vincent knew that the Tocco family would face challenging decisions as to Manny's scholastic future.

Privately, Vincent did not think that Emanuel Tocco was up to the intellectual demands of the seminary. Not Sacred Heart Seminary. It was questionable as to whether he could pass the entrance test. But even if he did, he might well be overwhelmed by the exigencies of an intensive liberal arts program with a strong emphasis on English and Latin.

Moreover, considering Manny's already significant muscle power, if his physical growth continued as could be expected, he might well enjoy an impressive athletic career elsewhere.

Redeemer was a Class A school. Regularly its football team played other large parochial school teams. Not infrequently

Redeemer played in the post-season Soup Bowl, competing against the top public high school team for the city championship.

The point was it was possible—probable—that Manny Tocco could be a big fish in a fairly large pond.

Yes, one could realistically project a career in sports for Manny. Who knew; he could even enter the pro ranks.

But not from the seminary.

The seminary did have some excellent athletes. But sports in the seminary were intramural. There were no headlines, no media coverage, no visits from scouts.

Originally, Bro. V. had had plans for his protégé. In Manny's last year before high school, Brother Vincent would make sure that Manny understood what he was passing up by not attending Redeemer High. The choice, of course, would be Manny's. But Vincent would exercise his considerable influence to try to convince Manny to stay where he was—on the Redeemer path, where fate had directed him.

In this endeavor, Vincent enlisted Alfredo Tocco's cooperation. 'Fredo quickly became firmly convinced that Bro. V. was right. All Mr. Tocco and Bro. V. had to do, besides convincing Manny to see the wisdom of their position—which would not be all that difficult—was to make sure Maria Tocco knew nothing about this.

The two men were convinced theirs was the perfect path for Manny. Both gave full credence to the strong possibility that this was God's Will.

But now some of the building blocks were coming loose. Bro. V. was not to have his final year before Manny's enrollment in the seminary. As much as he desired his dream for the boy, Vincent could not delay the termination of the Brothers' tenure at Redeemer. The prospects of one lad could not be important enough to derail the collective course. Besides, the decision to leave now had been reached by the governing body of the Brothers.

The best Vincent could do at this stage was to clue Manny in. He told the boy this had to remain a secret until it was officially made public.

Manny had two questions: First, could he tell his father?

Of course; Vincent wanted the father informed. The Order's rules of secrecy on the matter mandated that the parents were not to be advised in advance. Brother Vincent was following that mandate; he had not told 'Fredo. But there was no rule that said that Manny couldn't tell his father.

Manny's second question: Could he tell his best friend, Michael Smith?

Considering the closeness between the two boys, it would be cruel to demand silence on the matter. Besides, the story could break at any time. Yes, Manny could tell Mike.

Manny engaged his dad in a game of catch in the back alley. It was early evening. They had just eaten—meatballs and spaghetti again. Maria good-naturedly shooed them out of the house so she could wash the dishes and clean up in the kitchen.

'Fredo sported an almost-new catcher's mitt. He needed the protection for his hand, he admitted—pridefully; his son, though still young, had a stinging fast ball.

Even with the mitt, after some thirty minutes, Mr. Tocco cried uncle.

Father and son sat on the front porch glider, absorbing the peace and tranquillity of a late summer evening. 'Fredo fingered the baseball, then dropped it in what Manny called his glove box. 'Fredo reached into the box and took out what looked like a large marble bag. Out of the bag 'Fredo took another ball, a ball that held fond memories.

It was a major league ball. They'd gotten it some two years back at Briggs Stadium. They couldn't afford to go to many Tiger games. So when they did go, 'Fredo made sure they had excellent seats.

For this game, their seats were along the third base line just behind the Tiger dugout. In a late inning, Hank Greenberg hit a towering foul ball that just reached the seats. Many fans wanted that ball, but 'Fredo had to get it—for his son. So, although he was not very tall, he had more intense desire working for him. He leaped as high as he could and speared it. He brought it down, clasped it close, plopped into his seat, turned, and carefully handed it to his son.

To Manny, his dad might as well have been Greenberg, Gehringer, Higgins, and all the rest of those superb professional athletes rolled into one. Manny and his dad: two people in a crowded ballpark who took pride in and loved each other.

Words unspoken, Manny knew the next move was his. At game's end Manny scrambled across the dugout roof and stretched out prone at the spot where Greenberg would pass on his way to the locker room. As Greenberg neared the dugout, in a hurry to shower and leave, Manny waved the ball at him.

There was something in the boy's eyes. Greenberg couldn't resist. He stopped, took the ball, and reached for the pen Manny held out to him. The boy always brought a pen to the park—just in case. The lines around Greenberg's eyes, begrimed with sweat, crinkled. He signed the ball, handed back the pen, then reached out, dropped the ball in the boy's outstretched hand, and in the same movement, tousled the boy's hair.

Manny vowed he would never again wash his hair. It was a vow no one in his family would let him keep. But from that day on, anyone who bad-mouthed Hank Greenberg had to answer to an aggressively faithful Manny Tocco.

As for 'Fredo, he would never forget the look on his son's face, and he would be forever grateful to Hammerin' Hank.

'Fredo twirled the ball, stopping at the sacred signature. "Remember this?"

"How could I forget?"

"Maybe, someday . . . well, you never know . . . I keep thinking that someday you'll be out on the mound for the Tigers. Or the Yankees or the Red Sox. Some kid will ask for your autograph, and you'll remember Hank and what he did for you."

There was a long pause. The glider rocked back and forth.

"Ain't many priests playin' in the majors," Manny said at length.

"It's an even longer road getting to be a priest than it is getting to play ball in the majors," 'Fredo commented.

"Nothing personal, Pop, but extra-large is not a measurement that runs in our family. Most of my uncles and my cousins are kinda small. Even you, Pop—no offense intended."

"That's okay. But you don't have to be seven feet to play ball. You're strong. Just look at how you handled that bully the other day. Ask him if you're a contender or what."

Silence.

"And on account of you I had to spring for a new catcher's mitt. You got some arm, kiddo. And, what are you—thirteen years? Why, you're just into your teens. You get eighteen or nineteen and as long as you're serious about building yourself, you're gonna be somethin'. Ya know that?"

Another pause. Maria had turned on a popular music program. The caressing voice of Bing Crosby could be heard. Smoothly, not noisily.

"Pop . . ." Manny said softly, "there's something I gotta tell you."

'Fredo had heard this song before. It almost always meant bad news was coming around the corner. He didn't reply.

"I just heard about it today," Manny said. "The Brothers are pulling out of Redeemer."

"What!?"

Maria heard her husband over the radio's volume. She stirred, but didn't rise. She'd learn what it was about in due time. For the moment, she'd let father and son work it out. The two were as close as any parent and child she knew of.

"The Brothers are leaving, Pop," Manny repeated.

"How do you know?"

"Bro. V. He told me today."

"That can't be! School starts in just a few weeks! Your mother and I haven't heard a word. I can't believe it!"

Actually, he could—and did—believe it. He had to

believe it. His son would not lie. If Manny said that Brother Vincent had told him the Brothers were leaving, then the Brother had, indeed, told him so. And the entire group—all those excellent teachers—all of them were leaving without so much as a reasonable notice.

But while 'Fredo, in his inner being, had to believe his son was telling the truth, the father was having trouble absorbing the ramifications of this news. "So, what's supposed to happen?"

"I guess this has been going on for a long time. The Church officials downtown didn't think a school should be segregated like Redeemer is. It just came to a boil over this past summer."

"But . . . but . . . who's gonna teach you in the eighth grade? Who's gonna teach you if the Brothers are gone?"

"The Sisters."

"The Sisters—! The Sisters who're teaching the girls now?"

Manny nodded. "The Sisters. Plus any lay people they need to get the job done."

"On such short notice . . ."

"I guess."

"Some business! They tell us it's a sin not to send your kids to a Catholic school. And then they pull the rug out from under you."

For the moment, 'Fredo said no more. Nor did his son.

"I don't want my kid to be taught by women," 'Fredo said finally, but without vigor.

"They're not women. They're nuns."

'Fredo looked sharply at his son. They had been over the "birds and the bees" routine. It wasn't that Manny didn't realize that nuns were women; he just didn't look at them in that light.

'Fredo cared that the Brothers were leaving, of course. But much more than that was involved. A conspiracy had been entered into. Together, Brother Vincent and 'Fredo had planned to steer Manny into attending Redeemer throughout his high school years.

From there on the plans were obvious. A starring athletic career, maybe a crack at the big leagues. But now Brother Vincent was leaving—all the Brothers were leaving. And with them would go the plans for Manny's future.

That was the burning, sinking ship 'Fredo saw in his mind's eye. "Wait a minute . . . the seminary has an athletic program, doesn't it?"

Manny nodded. "A darn good one. I asked Bob Koesler and he asked around.

"They got all the majors: football, basketball, baseball, handball—just about everything. But outside of basketball, everything is in-house. Intramural, they call it. So there isn't any press coverage. No national attention."

'Fredo knew, by its absence from every sports page in town, that the seminary was in no competitive league. The outside basketball teams they played probably counted their meetings as practice games! But 'Fredo was not that concerned about basketball; Manny would never be tall enough to make a mark in that sport. No, baseball was the focus.

"So," 'Fredo said, "do me a favor: Soon as you can, find out whether the seminary lets the kids play in summer leagues."

"Sure, Pop. First thing."

Summer leagues in the Detroit area were extremely popular. There wasn't much going on otherwise. Not infrequently these leagues were covered by the press, and one could find sports reporters and even scouts in attendance.

This might not be a lost cause after all. As he himself had remarked earlier tonight: "It's an even longer road getting to be a priest than it is getting to play ball in the majors."

8

TWO DAYS LATER and the news was out. Now everyone knew.

The archdiocesan education department had tried to keep the decision under wraps as long as possible. The purpose was to buy time. Every day the transition looked better to them.

There were interminable meetings involving administration people from the archdiocese as well as from Redeemer.

Sister Mary Gracia, IHM, was now principal not only of the segregated boys and girls in the first six grades, as well as the girls from grades seven through high school, but of the boys too. The whole shebang. Grades would be divided not by sex, but in good old alphabetical order.

Sister Mary agreed that the entire school should be integrated. If only she had more time and help to get the job done before school opened in September!

With the announcement of the change picked up by the Detroit press—*News, Times,* and *Free Press,* and the neighborhood papers—it was the talk of the town. The corner of Vernor and Junction, the entire southwest side of the city, was buzzing. Seemingly everyone had an opinion.

There was no poll taken. But if there had been, the citizenry would have been split roughly fifty-fifty. Most of the argumentation was philosophical. Segregation (long before it became a racial consideration) or integration: Which was the better means of education?

The principals in this movement had little time for debate. For them, it was full speed ahead.

Now that they had had their way in making the announcement, the Brothers could take their own sweet time moving. Those in the archdiocesan administration who had no luxury time and were not frantically involved in the logistics of nitty-gritty busied themselves in trying to light a fire under the Brothers. Their presence had become awkward. They, as far as Redeemer and Detroit were concerned, were the past. The IHM nuns were the present and the future.

By and large, the transformation was going as smoothly as possible.

There was little mutiny. After all, the school was not circling its wagons. It would be the same size. The classrooms would be as large as ever. And filled. There just would be no Brothers of the religious persuasion. There would, in fact, be no male teachers at all. Not at first, anyway.

Mr. and Mrs. Smith were stunned. They'd had no inkling such a massive change was in the offing. They were aware—everyone was—that the debate over sexual segregation and integration was alive if not particularly well.

They puzzled too that their twins had known of the change before the decision was made public. Odd, particularly, that the twins should have heard it from Emanuel Tocco.

The Smiths were not all that fond of Manny. But as he and Michael had hit it off so well and had become pals, the Smiths had decided to go with the flow. All the while, they would keep a weather eye on the relationship.

The recent fight that was rapidly achieving legend status was a case in point. The Smiths made it clear to Michael that they were not pleased. They were grudgingly grateful that Manny had saved the day. But they impressed upon Michael that they would have much preferred that he had just given the ruffians the stupid ball, thus making even the slightest altercation unnecessary.

As for the teaching change, the Smiths actually were more pleased than not. They had affection for the nuns—more so than for the Brothers.

Michael's parents had learned, through their son, of the

closeness of Brother Vincent and Manny. They were certain that the Brother had approved of Manny's defense of his rights.

The Smiths were somewhat concerned over the influence integration would have on Rose and Michael. In particular they wondered what, if any, effect such integration would have on plans for the twins' vocations.

The Sisters had taught Michael for his first six school years. Then, in the seventh grade, the Brothers had taken over. Now Michael would have but one additional year with the Sisters.

Then he'd be off to the seminary, to be taught again by men. But this time by priests—the cream of the crop.

The Smiths, Henry and Lucy, wanted an undemanding life. Didn't everyone?

Their own lives were in apple-pie order. They belonged to the one, holy, Catholic, and apostolic Church. Their Church had laws, lots of them. But if you kept those laws, heaven was assured you. Don't kill, unless it is justifiable. Don't covet: wives or goods. These laws also inveighed against immoral thoughts, which, as long as they remained thoughts, were venial, not mortal. Or, as the joke had it: A priest asks a confessing parishioner whether the man had entertained impure thoughts. "No," the sinner replied, "they entertained me."

As for coveting goods: It was all right to want a car like one's neighbor had—but not okay to want one's neighbor's car.

And so on they went, through Ten Commandments, 2,414 laws, and more. Priests were expected to at least be familiar with almost all of them. As for lay Catholics, they knew that they must attend Mass on Sunday and financially support the local parish.

The point was that as long as one did not seriously violate any of the significant laws, all was relatively well.

As for what was expected of lay Catholics, the Church took it as a given that their personal lives would be properly ordered. Most would marry before a priest and in the presence of two witnesses. They would have marital relations, every act of which must be open to the creation of new life; no artificial birth control. They would have children, likely more than they would have planned—or could really afford.

If a Catholic family had the supreme good fortune to have one or more of its children enter religious life—priest, Sister, or Brother—parental responsibility would stop at the door of the rectory or the convent or the religious domicile.

The Smiths were batting one thousand on all counts. They did not want the cart toppled. Thus their concern over their twins' gender separation in school.

Michael would have his one and only scholastic experience with girls in class this coming year. What could happen with sharing a classroom with eighth grade girls?

Plenty. Henry Smith well remembered the onslaught of teen puberty. It was awful—having those urges and no place to put them. For the coming year Henry would keep his son on a short tether.

Then there was Rose. For a young lady she had her act pretty much together. But Lucy remembered her own early teen years. Girls that age discovered that they could be both desirable and desired. They, too, could have raging hormones.

And Rose was not going to go through just one year of mingling, as was Michael. She would have five years to keep herself virginal and chaste. School—even a Catholic school—could do only so much to safeguard the adolescent girl. Both Henry and Lucy would keep a special eye on their exemplary daughter.

They would shepherd their twins along the path toward religious life. If this enterprise was successful, their children would be delivered to the Lord intact. After that, it was His problem. Henry and Lucy would have heaven locked up.

It was left to the McManns to see to their daughter on their own. This was not a familiar position for Nat and June McMann. In a way, they played follow the leader. And their leaders, in almost every endeavor, were the Smiths. It was an effort to keep up with the Smiths.

If, for example, the McManns hosted the Smiths at dinner, the menu was sure to reflect the Smiths' taste and preference. It could be said that the McManns lived in the Smiths' back pocket.

And as proof of the axiom "The apple does not fall far from the tree," Alice McMann shadowed Rose Smith like a faithful puppy.

It was almost a given that Alice's desire for the religious life sprang from Rose's. Had Rose opted for marriage and family, to the best of her ability Alice would have found someone who was a friend of Rose's intended. Someone who was apt to want to live near his good friend. In which case, Alice would then be living near her best friend. And the cozy relationship of the parents would be mirrored in the lives of the children.

Alice's greatest fear was that something would interfere with her relationship with Rose.

Undoubtedly, Alice's own choice for a vehicle through life would not have been the religious life. In her deepest heart she would have wanted a good, dependable husband who would love her and be unashamedly romantic long after the pronouncement of the vows. And, as a good Catholic couple, she and her husband would welcome all the children God would send.

Should Rose change her mind sometime before taking her final vows as a nun, Alice would be more than ready to follow suit. She would think it a heavenly gift.

But Rose seemed to have no doubts about the life she would choose. Rose seldom changed her mind; metaphorically, her decisions were carved in stone.

So Alice didn't let herself dwell on what lay ahead. She would simply be living in Rose's shadow. And there be as happy as a pig in sunshine. For now, Alice had five more years to enjoy adolescence with Rose.

Actually, Alice's only hesitation concerned exclusivity. Rose was not only Alice's best friend; she was, for all practical purposes, Alice's only friend. All the others were classmates, or at best, acquaintances. Rose, on the other hand, was a popular girl. She had lots of friends. Admittedly, Alice was her best friend—but not her exclusive buddy.

Alice, when forced to dwell on this disappointment, was saddened. For the moment, she tried to brush her sorrow aside and enjoy her special friendship with Rose.

In this little circle, though not bound as closely, were Manny Tocco and his parents.

The Toccos scarcely knew the Smiths and McManns. The three couples had little in common. As for their kids, it was a mixed if predictable relationship. Manny and Michael were close friends, spending hours together. As for the girls, there were times when Manny had to ponder to remember their names. And the girls knew Manny only as one of Mike's friends.

At this time in Manny's life, girls were not a prominent fixture. Some of that feeling could be attributed to the gender separation in school. Some of it lay at the door of the confusion of puberty.

In any case, Manny's parents were the first to learn the startling news of the Brothers' imminent departure. No chance the news could have been garbled or false: Manny had gotten it straight from Bro. V.'s mouth.

For the first time in his young life, Manny would be in a classroom with girls. His parents now bombarded him with advice. He didn't think he needed all this counseling. But he did. And he was not alone.

The Brothers' imminent departure and the ensuing mixture of boys and girls from first grade through high school seemed all that anyone could discuss. Whether or not each parishioner was directly or personally affected by this drastic change seemed irrelevant; everyone had an opinion. And each felt free—nay, compelled—to voice his or her concern.

Compared with some of the other parishioners, the Toccos were rather laid-back. They'd had a headstart in being exposed to the news. In addition, if 'Fredo's and Maria's plans stayed in place, this state of affairs would exist for only one scholastic year. What could possibly happen in one scholastic year?

Plenty.

Boys and girls realized their opposite grades existed. But

they were unsure what the differences were or what those differences might signify. And now was the time to learn.

At this period in their lives, girls became aware that they could drive boys wild. Something as basic as hairstyles could be provocative. Clothes that hinted at what made girls different from boys were chosen and worn for effect. Aided by her perception of Hollywood's version of femininity, a girl's deportment might range from super-sweet to super-suggestive, her gait from undulation to flounce.

Boys, most of them, affected an air that decades later would be termed macho. They too were influenced by Hollywood. Emulating filmdom's depiction of U.S. servicemen, the more daring sported a cigarette pack in the rolled-up T-shirt sleeve. They considered themselves dashing in dungarees (with cuffs also rolled up) and penny loafers. They carried themselves like their favorite sports heroes—all in hopes of proving themselves desirable to girls. In actuality, at this phase of puberty, the girls were more interested in the boys than the boys were in the girls. Mostly, the boys were interested in sports; girls served mainly as something to discuss with one's fellows in so-called bull sessions. At such times the more advanced boys pretended to have "gone all the way" or at very least to "know the score." Which was rarely the case.

'Fredo Tocco was supremely confident that his son would survive it all. Manny knew where babies came from. For faithful Catholics, there was only but one means of preventing an event that could seriously compromise their future: Abstinence. 'Fredo would have put his last dollar on Manny's self-control.

'Fredo didn't express his positive feeling about his son's one—at least—year in mixed company. Actually, 'Fredo would not be at all upset should this year lead to four more in coed classrooms. In such an event, he would, of course, do his best to comfort his stricken wife. But, if truth be known, he wouldn't be at all disappointed.

No way could the Tocco family afford one of those fancy

all-boy schools—even for one year. Maria knew that. She didn't even mention the subject.

She herself had been a student in a parochial school. Of course it had been coed. She well remembered the fun of teasing the boys. And as for 'Fredo, in the concluding days of their courtship, Maria had driven him near mad with desire. Now things would come full circle.

Girls would roll up the waists of their skirts as soon as the nuns were out of sight if not out of mind. They would push the proper behavioral boundaries. They would experiment with ways to enflame Maria's little boy.

That Manny would come through untainted and unscathed, and persevere in his vocation to the priesthood became the number-one intention of Maria's daily Mass attendance.

9 OUR LADY OF Guadalupe Parish encompassed a neighborhood of near valueless homes close to the heart of downtown Detroit.

One of the area's few boasts was the Olympia, a gigantic indoor sports arena. Primarily, the Olympia was home ice for the Red Wings, Detroit's professional hockey team.

Originally, the National Hockey League comprised only six professional teams. Though most of the players were born and bred in icebound Canada, four of the six teams represented U.S. cities.

It seemed a happy compromise; Canadian youth learned to ice skate before learning to walk. But the money to support the teams and their league was found in New York, Chicago, Boston, and Detroit. Toronto and Montreal completed the roster.

Even areas that had no hockey teams were familiar with the names Howe, Abel, and Lindsay. These three were dubbed the Production Line—as in what Detroit made: automobiles built on production lines.

Hockey nights at the Olympia created an anomaly: The neighborhood made money providing parking for fans who otherwise would never have darkened the neigborhood's streets.

The Olympia also hosted events such as wrestling, boxing, and basketball, all of which featured fighting, sometimes in the arena, sometimes in the stands.

Our Lady of Guadalupe boasted few parishioners. So only one priest was assigned to that church . . . popularly, if incorrectly, pronounced Guadaloop. Although Archbishop Mooney kept harping on the paucity of priestly vocations for Detroit, most parishes had at least two priests, and many had even more.

Measured by this scale, Guadalupe could hope for no more than one lone pastor. And that's what it got, along with the veiled threat that it might well be closed entirely.

The present pastor, Father Ed Simpson, knew—if by no other sign than that he was assigned to hold the fort here— that he was low in the archdiocesan pecking order. Thus, he was forever looking for ways to improve his image and thereby climb at least a few rungs.

He was the butt of many a put-down by his clerical colleagues. He tried to remove some of the sting by joining in the lighthearted camaraderie. On such occasions, he was wont to fall back on the phrase used by earlier pastors assigned to less-than-optimum parishes: "a little wrinkled, but a plum."

Try as he might, Father Simpson was unable to scare up more than one or two new families per year. Actually, he was more apt to lose one or two.

Man did not live by Olympia events alone. Whenever a breadwinner could earn a little more bread, the moving van—or, more likely a friend with a pickup—would empty the house, and the erstwhile resident would never look back.

Unsuccessful at drumming up added parishioners and equally ineffective at increasing weekly contributions, Father Simpson grubbed for some means to improve his profile.

The only possibility of attracting a favorable chancery eye would be to come up with a candidate for the seminary or the convent.

The likelihood of sending some girl to the convent was ever so much more realizable than coming up with a seminarian. But he would just be providing another woman who would not be under archdiocesan control. The various religious orders of women serving in Detroit were managed and directed by superiors of their own order.

However, sending a boy to Sacred Heart Seminary would

be furnishing a greatly desirable commodity: Diocesan priests belonged to the local bishop and, as such, were definitely prized.

Granted, some much larger and more viable Detroit parishes had not fostered even a single seminarian in a good many years. But these other parishes achieved such other commendable deeds as adding new members to the parish lists, thus delivering in a timely fashion their quota of diocesan taxes and generally evidencing life and growth.

It seemed that parishes staffed by charismatic priests contributed the majority of the seminarians. But charismatic priests seemed to skip over "the parish next to the Olympia." Concisely, nobody wanted to be like Father Ed Simpson. Bing Crosby's Father O'Malley, yes; Ed Simpson, no.

But now old Ed had an idea—an idea that, if it worked, might bail him out of this moribund parish.

Even registered parishioners of Guadaloop rarely attended Mass regularly. It was next to impossible to come up with lads to serve as altar boys at Mass.

With one exception.

Little Stanley Benson was fidelity personified. No matter what the occasion—Mass, Benediction, Rosary, Novenas—even periodic celebrations: Forty Hours, Parish Missions, Confirmations—there was Stanley Benson, scrubbed clean, resplendent in laundered and pressed cassock and surplice. Often his cheek or neck was blotched with red—the lipstick smudge of a mother's fond kiss.

Little Stanley, Father Simpson reasoned, was in church so often . . . why not? Maybe he could become a priest. Maybe he could be Father Simpson's ticket out of Guadaloop and onto the upward ladder.

One morning Father Simpson broke one of his own nonnegotiable rules: He invited someone to the rectory for no more than a social event. At least it seemed to Stanley and his mother that there were no strings attached.

What they did not know was that Father Simpson subscribed to the axiom "There's no such thing as a free lunch." Or, in this case, breakfast. So, at the appointed hour, Stanley, freshly cleaned and pressed, showed up at Father Simpson's doorstep.

Father Simpson invited him in the front door, ushered him into the kitchen, and sat him down at the kitchen table. The priest then proceeded to whip up some eggs and fry some bacon. He had no fulltime housekeeper; the tortured budget held no money for such a post. And, for most prospective housekeepers, there wasn't enough gold in Fort Knox to woo them into working at Guadaloop.

Stanley was particularly well turned out for this morning's rare invitation. His mother had run down the articles of polite behavior so that Stanley would not shame the Bensons.

"So, Stanley," Father Simpson opened, "what grade are you going into this year?"

"Eighth, Father." Stanley's hands were folded and placed on the edge of the table.

"Eighth!" Simpson enthused. "Why, it's just about time for you to make up your mind about what you're going to do when you grow up."

Silence. Stanley could see no question to be fielded.

"So," Simpson solicited, "have you made up your mind? Got any ideas?"

"I don't know, Father. I'd like to be a secretary, I think."

"A secretary!" Father Simpson exploded. He did that well.

"Or not," said Stanley agreeably.

"Girls become secretaries. Men *have* secretaries."

Stanley wondered where was the secretary for Father Simpson. But he didn't ask.

After piling three quarters of the bacon and eggs on his own plate, Simpson slid the rest onto Stanley's plate. "You know you're the best altar boy we've got," the priest observed.

"Yes, Father." There was no doubt in Stanley's mind; he had been sole server too often to wonder if all those absentees were in the running for fidelity.

"You know, Stanley, we old bucks start looking for someone to take our place when we begin to run out of steam."

"Yes, Father." Actually, the lad had given no thought to the matter of succession. Now that his attention had been called to it, he wondered what this had to do with anything.

The toast popped up. Simpson took a piece, hesitated, and looked at Stanley's plate. The boy had consumed only a meager amount of food. The priest took both slices of toast for himself.

"What gets me wondering, Stanley, is why I never hear you talk about becoming a priest."

"A priest!" It was as if Stanley had never before heard the word.

"Yes, my boy. You must've pictured yourself saying Mass someday. Don't tell me the thought has never crossed your mind."

"Sure, Father. But I can't be."

"Can't be a priest! Whatever gave you that idea?"

"My father isn't Catholic."

"That probably explains why I never see him in church. But what's that got to do with your becoming a priest?"

" 'Cause my folks weren't married in church."

"They weren't?"

"A justice of the peace."

"Well, well."

"My mother and I talked this over before. She told me she was proud of me—serving Mass and all—and did I ever think of being a priest. I told her no. I like serving Mass, but I don't want to say Mass."

"You don't!"

"No, Father. Then she told me that was good because Church law said I couldn't qualify for the vocation."

"She did?"

"She told me about my cousin in Ohio . . ." Stanley nodded vigorously. "My cousin wanted to be a priest but he was turned down by his pastor."

"Because his parents weren't married in church?"

Stanley nodded again. "My mother told me about all this

because she said she didn't want me to be disappointed. And I told her not to worry because I would offer it up."

"What if we got your folks married by a priest? By me?"

"I haven't told you the whole story, Father. My dad was married before. The pastor—the one who was here before you?—well, he told them they couldn't get their marriage blessed because my dad was married before. That's what made it impossible for my cousin. The difference is that my cousin wanted to be a priest. I don't." Stanley went on eating slowly.

Father Simpson was no expert on Church law. Few of his contemporary peers were. But the situation Stanley had described rang a bell. Things that might scandalize the Faithful—like a physical deformity, or being an ecclesiastical bastard—such circumstances formed an impediment to Holy Orders.

What to do about this?

Simpson was skidding emotionally from an ecstatic high to a depressing low. He had thought he'd stumbled across a ticket out of Guadaloop. Now it seemed the ticket had already been punched.

Things were so serious he put down his knife and fork. Then a light began to appear at the end of this tunnel. "Stanley, my boy, how would you like it if we could get your folks married?"

"You could do that?"

"I think so. There's been a lot of movement lately in granting annulments. That would clear the path for your father to be freed from his previous marriage. Then he could marry your mother in the Church."

Actually, the Church movement toward easier annulments was occurring only in Simpson's imagination and desire.

Father Simpson was heading down an extremely risky road. Should he continue in this direction, he could find himself in a lot of trouble. But as protection, he was counting on location. After all, Guadaloop was not a Grosse

Pointe address. Who cared what went on in this depressed neighborhood?

Was it worth a try? That depended on how badly one wanted to escape the slow quicksand of Guadaloop. This one, Father Simpson, wanted out enough to lie, simulate a sacrament, and engage in fraud.

Simpson's only qualm was whether the mere fact that he had produced an honest-to-God seminarian from this parish might not be sufficient for the chancery to see him in a new light.

Would they delay recognition—make him wait for Stanley's actual ordination? The boy was just entering the eighth grade. Plus twelve years in the seminary would make thirteen years all told.

Could Simpson hold on—could he abide for that length of time? Yes! Even thirteen years down the road was worth the investment. He would still have a few good years left, God willing. Years in which he could enjoy his just reward.

"You could do that?" Stanley's face radiated happiness.

"I think we've got a good chance."

"Would my father have to become a Catholic?" The boy's brow knitted. "I don't think he would go that far."

"No, he wouldn't have to convert," Simpson assured him. "He would be happy to do this for your mother, wouldn't he . . . don't you think?"

"Oh yes! Sure! He would do anything for my mother." Stanley hesitated. "He might even become a Catholic if he had to. He went that far before when they first got married. But the other priest said he couldn't help even if Dad did want to . . . become Catholic, I mean."

"Fine! Dandy!" Simpson enthused. "I'll set up an appointment to meet with your parents. Then you can get busy with the eighth grade so you'll be ready for the seminary's entrance test."

"Entrance test? I don't understand, Father . . ."

"Don't worry about it. You're a smart lad. It'll be a breeze . . . you'll see."

"But I don't want to be a priest, Father. I told you." Stanley felt close to tears.

"What can be so bad about a seminary? You'll get a first-rate education. Besides, just entering a seminary doesn't guarantee that you're going to be ordained. It's a time when you decide—*gradually*—if you really want to. And all the while the faculty has to decide whether you're qualified."

"But I don't need to go there! I already know I don't want to be a priest!"

Simpson took a deep breath, then exhaled slowly. "Son," he said gravely, "do you have any idea how much your mother wants you to be a priest? Do you know how happy you'd make her by becoming a priest? You must see that!"

Stanley's tears overflowed.

"I've got a hunch," Simpson, heedless, continued, "that you are going to be surprised at how much you'll like the seminary. You'll make friendships there that will last a lifetime."

"But . . . but . . . my mother never said anything about my being able to be a priest—"

"That's because before this it was an impossibility. But think: Now it's going to be a possibility . . . a distinct possibility. Think how much it will hurt her when she knows that you refuse to go to the seminary even though you are free to do so. And suppose you make it all the way through and you're ordained: Can you imagine how happy and pleased and enraptured she'll be when you give her your first priestly blessing?

"That's what it comes down to, Stanley. It comes down to: How much do you love your mother? Are you going to break her heart or are you going to make her one of the happiest women in the world?"

Silence.

"May I go now, Father?" Stanley's words were a near gurgle through the sobs in his throat.

"Certainly. But don't say anything to your parents until after I meet with them. Let me break the news and explain everything to them."

Young Stanley nodded, then left, his shoulders sagging.

Simpson rubbed his hands together. Not a bad ploy if he did say so himself. He had always thought Church law was crazy when it came to marriage. It wouldn't bother him in the least to smash a couple or three of those laws.

Now he would have to enlist the willing cooperation of the boy's parents . . . to get Stanley into the seminary—and keep him there.

No problem anticipated in that direction. Mr. Benson will see the advantage of having his son's education taken care of. And Mrs. Benson—well, Mrs. Benson will be on cloud nine!

And I, he exulted, I'll be on a fast train out of Guadaloopville!

He smiled—totally self-satisfied.

10

HOLY REDEEMER'S SCHOOLS opened on schedule. The IHM nuns taught grade school in the same building and the same classrooms they had been using over the years. Except that now there was no segregation by sex. The elementary pupils were given slips of paper informing them which classrooms were theirs. The pupils were assigned alphabetically.

High school was another story. Not only were the boys and girls integrated—again alphabetically—but the Sisters had replaced the Brothers.

The new system would require time and patience to get used to. Initially, the high schoolers missed the Brothers' rough-and-tumble manner. Of course the students had had nuns as teachers from grade one through grade six. But the Brothers had taught the boys from grades seven through twelve.

Everyone from the archdiocesan education office downtown to the teachers in the classrooms were prepared for disciplinary problems and even some defections.

The reality was heartening. The high school boys seemed to consider their female teachers as ladies who should be treated as such. They were deferential. The nuns were quietly grateful.

Here and there were empty seats of students expected to be aboard but who were not. The seats were quickly filled from a sizable waiting list.

Among those who would be sorely missed were Rose

Smith and Alice McMann. Although they were not leaving the Sisters, Servants of the Immaculate Heart of Mary, they were kissing the integrated halls and classrooms of Redeemer High good-bye.

They were excellent students—though Rose was by far superior. The two would have raised the bell curve of academic achievement markedly.

But the faculty was certain that Redeemer would somehow survive without them.

Henry and Lucy Smith had exploded on learning of the planned integration of Redeemer's schools.

There were vague threats to remove their children from that school. Cooler heads prevailed, though there was precious little time.

The first decision was to leave Michael in Redeemer's eighth grade. He would have girls his own age as classmates, but only for one year. If he couldn't withstand temptation for one scholastic year, he didn't deserve to be a priest.

Besides, in his buddy, Manny Tocco, he would have a strong personality to steady him.

Until now, Mr. and Mrs. Smith had not been all that happy over the boys' friendship. Manny could be too rough on occasion. There was that famous—or infamous—fight that everyone seemed to be talking about. Both Manny and Michael had learned valuable if unexpected lessons from the singular episode.

Ordinarily, honest-to-God upperclassmen, particularly those who had just entered high school, would lord it over eighth graders, who seemed neither fish nor fowl.

Not that many schools housed all the full twelve grades. In the schools that comprised the primary grades, the eighth graders became king of the castle. But they would be at the bottom of the heap when they moved into the ninth, the first year of high school.

However, at schools such as Redeemer, eighth graders

would, in effect, go nowhere when they eventually passed into high school.

There was something decidedly out of the ordinary in the way in which upperclassmen—high schoolers—treated Manny and Michael.

It seems that Switch and Blade were familiar to many Redeemerites. The duo's MO was identical in repeated forays, especially in the parking lots of the church and school. Switch would play provocateur; Blade would take the lead. They would never attack more than two at a time. And that only if the prey were small and not likely to put up much of a fight.

That's what made their encounter with Manny and Mike so pivotal.

Undoubtedly the villains had reconnoitered Mike and Manny as the boys played their innocent game of catch. Since neither of the boys was particularly large, they appeared to be easy pickings.

The tale of how Manny took Blade was repeated and embellished as school got under way. Everyone seemed to defer to Manny and, by extension, Michael.

To top off the straight story, neither Switch nor Blade had been seen anywhere in the vicinity of that celebrated parking lot since.

Manny did not anticipate further fights. For one thing, Mrs. Tocco would not overlook another torn and bloody outfit. For another, Manny had fought that day only in self-defense. That would be the only reason he might fight again. And with his reputation as it was, that seemed a remote possibility.

Though he had played a minor, almost negligible role, Michael had indeed been part of that war of liberation. Besides, he was Manny's sidekick and, as such, shared in the respect newly accorded his friend.

All the while, Mike was learning that it definitely paid to be aggressive on occasion. If one never asserted oneself, one stood a good chance of being bullied. Later, much later, this principle would play a defining part in Mike's life. For now, Manny's reputation protected both him and Mike.

This benefit was not a one-way street. Mike tutored Manny, who did well in his studies. But he could have done better.

Both boys took to heart Bob Koesler's warning that the seminary was serious about study and accomplishment. At his suggestion, they concentrated on their English studies and even anticipated the beginning of a long career in Latin. After all, they *were* members of the Latin Rite of the Roman Catholic Church. And one day, please God, they would conduct almost all the Liturgy in that ancient language.

It was, however, not all study and no play. Manny and Michael made Redeemer's eighth grade intramural football and basketball teams. Together they starred in an unbeaten season. Their simple formula was for Michael to get the ball to Manny and watch his teammate score.

From the stands, the Toccos and Smiths cheered on their sons.

All seemed well.

But unbeknownst to anyone, seeds had been planted that would ripen in ways no one could have anticipated.

Sacred Heart Seminary, was, unlike all Gaul, divided into only two entities: Day Dogs and House Rats. It depended on whether the student was a boarder or one who lived at home and commuted.

Both Bob Koesler and Pat McNiff lived close enough to commute to school. Based solely on their chance encounter on registration day, each became the first friend the other made. There would be many other circles of friendship.

Most of the boys came from parochial schools. Nothing odd about that. The priesthood enjoyed a preferential place in Catholic schools. Almost everyone who became a seminarian had been encouraged in his choice by nuns, who were always on the lookout for candidates for the religious life.

Bob Koesler alone had come directly from parochial

grades staffed by the Brothers of Mary. Even so, it was a bit of a cultural shock now to be taught by priests.

Perhaps Bob's biggest surprise was his fellow seminarians. These were young men pursuing the most sublime calling in all of Catholicism; he had half expected to find them wearing subtle halos.

Surprise: They were typical boys, pulling practical jokes, breaking nonessential seminary rules, competing fiercely in everything from physical games to academic achievement.

In no time, he fell into the rhythm of the place. In no time, he and his classmates might just as well have been together for years instead of mere weeks.

Bob did not need to be reminded that his goal was twelve long years off. But it seemed they were going to be good years.

He had no way of knowing that he might have profited from an academic minor in the police procedures of murder investigations.

The upcoming drastic change in the staffing of Redeemer's schools outraged the Smiths, who felt betrayed. Their feelings were mirrored by those of the McManns.

Henry Smith "chaired" a meeting of the four parents. The young people were not invited.

All agreed that they could do nothing to challenge the move. Legal action was out of the question; the school obviously was within its rights in making this policy change.

So, what to do?

"Let's begin," Smith said, "with Michael."

"You can't do that without considering Mike's buddy Manny," his wife suggested. "They're practically inseparable."

"I've already talked to Mike about that. The Toccos have decided to let Manny continue at Redeemer for the eighth grade. Then, when his class gets to high school, he'll be going to the seminary."

"The alternative," Lucy Smith said, "is to send Michael

to an all-boys Catholic school for the eighth grade. Then he and Manny would join up again for high school in the seminary."

"Of course," Nat McMann interjected, "there's the question of a significant raise in tuition . . . and transportation."

Nat and June McMann might as well have been disinterested bystanders when it came to the boys, neither of whom belonged to them. But there existed the possibility that their daughter Alice might be swept up in the Smiths' plans for Rose.

"That's true," Smith agreed. "What we've got to decide is whether that kind of move is necessary."

Lucy Smith toyed with her wedding ring, sliding it up and down her finger. "I think," she said, "that we're making a mountain out of a molehill. After all, it's only one year of integrated classes. And it *is* our parochial school. Remember, Henry, one of the main reasons we chose to live here was the high reputation of Redeemer's schools—"

"With gender segregation," Henry interrupted.

"Gender segregation or integration," Lucy said, "it's not as if our school has turned into Martin Luther Reformation Academy."

"I think," June McMann spoke out, "we've forgotten something: The nuns are all qualified teachers. And I don't think there's another parish school in the archdiocese that doesn't have nuns as teachers."

"Lucy's right," Nat McMann said. "It was nice having the Brothers . . . but not essential. As for segregated classes, well, what can you say? It was a noble experiment.

"Sure it seemed to work for us. But what do we know? The priests who run our parish—and even more so the guys downtown who are in charge of education for this archdiocese—they're the ones who made the decision. And I think it was rightfully their call."

Nat and June had discussed all this prior to this meeting and had agreed that they would try to swing the scales in favor of having Mike—following Manny—stay in Redeemer for that problematic eighth grade.

They felt sure that as Mike went, so would Rose go.

The McManns knew they themselves could not afford the tuition for any given private Catholic school. No matter how insistent their Alice was certain to be, the money just wasn't there.

They knew that the Smiths would be similarly strapped if both Mike and Rose were to be enrolled in a private—as opposed to a parochial or a parish—school.

"Nat's right," Lucy said brightly. "With or without the Brothers—even with or without the segregated classes—it's still a good school. And the tuition is reasonable. I say we enroll Mike in the eighth grade at Redeemer. And, frosting on the cake, he stays with his buddy."

"It's *your* daughter," June observed. "I don't think Nat and I need vote on it. But since our Alice will insist on accompanying Rose, I think you ought to know that I"—she stole a glance at her husband—"and I'm sure Nat goes along—*we* think Mike should stay at Redeemer."

Henry looked from one to another. Each face had an "affirmative" expression.

"That does it, then," Henry said.

"Now," Lucy said, "we come to the much more tangled situation of the girls. For them, it's not a matter of a single year. Rose and Alice face attending high school for all those years . . . wanting to become religious, but having to cope with all those distractions . . ."

"You mean boys?" June almost giggled as she identified *the* "distraction."

"Well . . . yes." Lucy's tone made it clear that she didn't think it was all that funny.

"If you don't mind," June said soberly, "Alice and I have been talking about this. We considered the various possibilities. Now, I don't want you to think that we anticipated what all of us as parents would decide. But high on the list . . . well, we thought you might agree that Mike should be at Redeemer with his friend for this scholastic year. And now we all seem to have reached that consensus . . ."

"Did you and Alice," Nat said with some affront, "come

up with a solution for her and Rose too?" This was the first he had heard of the tête-à-tête between wife and daughter; he was piqued that he had not been consulted.

"We think we did. But only if it was decided that Mike attend Redeemer this year. Which"—she looked at the Smiths—"is what you have decided.

"Incidentally, dear," she addressed her husband, "Alice and I didn't mean to leave you out. It just started as girl talk and eventually got more serious—"

"Well," Henry interjected, "let us in on what you and Alice concluded. We sure could use another consensus right about now."

"Immaculata," June said.

"Isn't that the girls' school out near Marygrove?" Lucy asked.

"Never heard of it!" Nat was still in a minor pout.

"Well, I have," Henry Smith said firmly. "I just can't think of why it slipped my mind."

"Is it or isn't it near Marygrove?" Lucy pressed.

"It's on the campus." June warmed to what she sensed would be quick approval. "Right on the Marygrove campus."

"It's Catholic?" With a name like Immaculata what else could it be? But Nat didn't give in easily.

"Owned, operated, and run by none other than the IHMs." June's response was aimed at her husband.

"Tell us about it," Lucy said.

"Well, as I said, it's on the Marygrove campus. Now you know Marygrove is an all-girl liberal arts college . . . very Catholic, modest tuition. Immaculata is sort of Marygrove's younger sister."

"Okay, okay," Nat said. "I know about Marygrove. But what's with the other place?"

"Immaculata?"

"Uh-huh."

"In effect, it's a prep school. It prepares Catholic girls for Marygrove. And when you get to Marygrove," June added, "you're in Monroe's backyard."

"You mean the girls could graduate from Immaculata and then—more or less—begin their religious life?" Lucy asked.

"Exactly."

"What about transportation?" Nat was determined to play devil's advocate since he'd been left out of the planning that had occurred in his own house.

"We examined that carefully," June said. "It's not far out of the way for both you, honey, and Henry. You could take turns driving the girls. And, in a pinch, they can get there by streetcar."

"Let me get one thing straight," Henry said. "Rose and Alice would go to Redeemer this final year, then start high school at Immaculata."

"Right."

"Then they graduate from Immaculata and go on to Marygrove? Do all the girls from Immaculata go on to Monroe to become nuns?"

"No, silly."

"I didn't think so."

"As I said, it's a prep school," June explained. "It prepares the girls for Marygrove but not necessarily for the religious life. The group that Alice and Rose will belong to will go on to Monroe and study and live there. But their academic records will all be kept at Marygrove.

"Now," June concluded, "I think we've touched all the bases—"

"Wait a minute," Nat objected. "What about Rose? Does she get a say in all this?"

"We just completed our study a couple of days ago," June said. "We haven't had the opportunity to get Rose's input. But"—she looked questioningly at Lucy—"both Alice and I are sure Rose will welcome this solution."

Lucy nodded.

"In that case, it's settled," Henry said. He looked at the others in turn. "Mike attends eighth grade at Redeemer. He'll be taught by the nuns instead of the Brothers. Then it's off to the seminary.

"Alice and Rose will do the same, except they'll go on to attend a high school that is more appropriate than Redeemer for preparing them to be nuns."

"Then it's full speed ahead," Lucy said. "Let's get the kids together and talk it all over with them."

"Shall we include Manny Tocco?" June asked.

"If he wants to join our group, tell him to come aboard," Henry replied.

11 ROMAN CATHOLIC DOGMA was a strange animal, Father Simpson thought, as he tried to puzzle out the canons, the Church's laws affecting marriage.

This was about as academic as he got.

Ordinarily, Simpson's reading did not go beyond the sports and comics pages of the daily papers. Actually, this was the first time he'd cracked the *Codex Iuris Canonici* (the Code of Canon Law) since his final year of Theology. But he had a stake in the present case, so it was worth his while to try to work it out.

The Bensons, along with their son, Stanley, had accepted Father Simpson's invitation. The priest had been the soul of cordiality, ushering the threesome into the rectory dining room. He offered the parents coffee, which they accepted. Stanley had a Coke.

Father Simpson understood that the couple had consulted his predecessor about their marital state and how—or whether—if necessary, it could be regularized.

Father assured them that he was not impugning his predecessor's expertise in Church law. But laws change. Perhaps that might reflect on their marital status. It couldn't hurt to take another look.

In reality, Church law changed about as often as the bishop of Detroit paid a visit to old Guadaloop. No one could remember such an occasion.

But Father had to set the scene . . . give them hope. Because one way or another they were going to have their marriage validated. Then the stage would be ready for Stanley's entrance to the seminary.

That, of course, was why Stanley's presence was required. As a rule, some of the topics to be discussed tonight would not be considered appropriate for one of Stanley's tender years.

Questions and answers regarding failed marriages as well as intimate details could be dicey. But Father Simpson was certain that he could end the evening on a high note of hope. He wanted very much to have Stanley see how much this would mean to his mother. His mother's happiness was the big stick that Father Simpson was betting all his marbles on—the impelling force that would see Stanley into the seminary . . . and the priesthood.

That was enough for Simpson. Once he had produced an honest-to-God priest from this godforsaken parish, the chancery would be bound to recognize the magnitude of the feat.

So, they had their meeting. Stanley fidgeted throughout the evening. Nonetheless, he endured. By God, Simpson thought, there might be some backbone there after all.

Father Simpson asked obvious questions. The Bensons bared their thoughts, emotions, and deeds. Then, everyone exhausted, the threesome went home.

The very next day found Father Simpson buried in textbooks. The problem, as his predecessor had concluded, was Mr. Benson's previous marriage: There was nothing canonically wrong with it.

Mr. Benson—George—had been Lutheran. He had married another Lutheran. That marriage, childless, had failed.

People tend to think the Catholic Church does not recognize marriages between non-Catholics. Not so; the Church presumes any attempted marriage valid unless proven invalid.

Aside from the fact that the couple had been incompatible, nothing in that marriage could be attacked canonically. Both had been baptized (in the Lutheran Church, but that was recognized by the Roman Catholic Church). No one had forced either of them to marry. Neither had been married before. Neither was under age.

There being no impediment to the validity of the marriage as far as the Roman Catholic Church was concerned, George Benson's first marriage was therefore declared valid. And that was why—even though the marriage had been a Lutheran ceremony, and even though the couple subsequently divorced—George could not, again as far as the Roman Catholic Church was concerned, marry Lily. In the eyes of the Roman Catholic Church, he was already married, and he could not marry canonically again unless and until his first wife died.

Father Simpson really did not expect to find any loophole. His predecessor had known much more about Church law than he himself could ever hope to. But he owed it to himself to reexamine the marriage. After all, if he was able to validate George and Lily's union to the satisfaction of the Church, he would have no fear whatsoever of a sanction aimed at him.

Of course he had little fear in convalidating an impossible situation. The comparative anonymity of Guadaloop should protect him. But should both belt and suspenders be available, Simpson was ready to use them.

Having found no solution in the domain of reality, he was now in the realm of fiction.

He couldn't send a signed form to the Tribunal. He didn't have a case.

Some would have found such a situation discouraging. Not Father Ed Simpson. No, Father Simpson knew enough about Catholic dogma and law to open his own emporium of dispensations and decrees of nullity.

Once the Church had insisted that baptism was needed for salvation. All well and good, but what about babies who died without being baptized? Were we going to send these otherwise innocent souls to eternal hell just because the parents were negligent and postponed the ceremony until it was too late? Or because it was a stillbirth?

Even the most adamant Canon lawyer could not look at

that package of innocence and envision its soul burning forever in hell. Well, some few could, but they would be the exception.

In any event, clearly, something had to be done. *Voilà!*— the invention of Limbo.

Limbo came to be described as a place of natural happiness. A place containing all one needed to be perfectly happy, lacking only the vision and presence of God. Sort of a Garden of Eden without apples.

Limbo would be the eternal destiny of all who were unbaptized through no fault of their own, and were guilty of no actual voluntary serious sin.

In more recent times, the concept of Limbo was becoming less logical. And when a dogma such as this lost its logic, it began to fade like the Wicked Witch of the West. Most now would concede such innocents as welcomed into heaven.

Father Simpson needed an explanation for the dispensation he was about to grant. But he wasn't going to find it in Canon Law.

It just needed a good excuse, a good reason for solving a problem that had not been foreseen. Like Limbo. Or like purgatory.

There is no mention of purgatory in the Bible. But purgatory answers the question: What happens to someone who is not bad enough for hell, nor good enough—yet—for heaven? Everyone seems to know such people.

On its face, that arrangement seems fair enough. Merciful, even. But dogma was loath to be *too* merciful. So the punishments of purgatory and hell were described as similar, if not exactly alike. The unending, nonconsuming fire awaited all who were either condemned to hell or sentenced to purgatory. Except that hell was eternal and purgatory was circumscribed. Purgatory continued until . . . until purgation took place.

That span could be as brief as the twinkling of an eye or could last hundreds of thousands of years; no one knew. Indulgences helped. But the duration of purgatory and what suffering it comprised were no more than opinions.

Recently, Father Simpson had heard a fellow priest deliver his concept of purgatory. He compared it to a ticket for an extremely attractive amusement park. You couldn't get in until your ticket number was called. It was very frustrating to be on the outside looking in. It was, indeed, a mild form of torture not to be able to get in and enjoy the park.

The crux was that you were *going* to get in. Meanwhile, you learned lessons of patience and other virtues you had not attained on earth.

Frankly, as far as Father Simpson was concerned, that was way too merciful. People need a dose of hellfire and brimstone—for hell as well as purgatory.

Yes, thought Simpson, I need a tag, a name for my new law. Something descriptive—like Limbo or purgatory.

He rose from the table with its books invitingly open but leading nowhere. He headed for the kitchen, opened the refrigerator, and found a stalk of celery. He was embarked on a quasi-diet.

Somebody sometime in antiquity must have come up with the concept of Limbo to explain how the nonbaptized avoid hell.

Somebody sometime in antiquity must have come up with the concept of purgatory to provide a place in the next life for people who were neither good enough for heaven nor bad enough for hell.

Father Simpson had not met anyone in his volumes of law, dogma, or morals who had invented a means of making it possible for George Benson to marry Lily when he had already been canonically married.

Things looked dark. The thought of working Guadaloop until he dropped made things look even bleaker.

As he walked back to the dining room, he passed a statue of the patroness of his parish: Our Lady of Guadalupe. Composed of plaster of paris and painted garishly, the statue depicted a young Latina woman framed by a robe brimming with roses. A rosary—not part of the original sculpture—

was draped over the fingers of her right hand. The rosary undoubtedly had been placed there by one of the previous pastors of this parish.

Father Simpson had never paid much attention to either the statue or the addended rosary.

Now something made him stop and think.

The rosary.

Something about the rosary. Any rosary.

But what?

Way back when he had been ordained . . .

As a brand-new priest, still wet behind the ears with the oil of ordination, what was it that had bugged him most?

Blessing rosaries!

It seemed that each and every Catholic owned at least one rosary, which, in time, was lost or broken, though probably not stolen. And all those rosaries—each and every one—had to be blessed by a priest.

Maybe it was just his imagination, but the young, newly minted Father Simpson felt that he was spending an ungodly amount of time on such an enterprise. The blessing, in Latin, took a solid five pages of the Ritual. Multiply those pages by the hundreds of rosaries awaiting his ministration and one had a blueprint for madness.

Then what should he find in his mail one day but a gimmee letter from a missionary organization. He had come close to throwing the packet in the circular file, when something—he no longer could remember what—caught his eye. Possibly it was an attractive layout. Whatever the reason, and whatever the missionary order—its name had long since escaped his memory—he had read the letter.

One could join their missionary efforts in some distant, exotic land by sending a fixed stipend—he no longer recalled the amount. His face contorted in an effort to remember these long forgotten minutiae. No matter; the point was that this missionary organization had received from Rome a fringe blessing: permission for contributing priests—those who donated to this worthy cause—to bless rosaries with merely a simple sign of the cross.

And it was a one-time-only donation. Send them one hundred bucks (or whatever amount was required) and in perpetuity the donor could simply trace a sign of the cross over the beads and they would be blessed. As blessed as anything requiring five Latin pages.

There were additional benefits to the rosary owners—like a reduction in one's time in purgatory—just for using these specially blessed beads. One could enter the amusement park sooner than one might have otherwise expected.

Father Simpson couldn't have cared less about the other fringes. He had sent his financial gift, received the authorization, and never again flinched at the outstretched hand bearing an unblessed rosary.

And now, once again a missionary organization would come to his aid. But this time the missionaries would be of his own invention.

The plan was so simple it required no time to put it in operation. But for the sake of credibility, he waited a week before calling George, Lily, and Stanley Benson in for the good news.

Meanwhile, Father did not let slip any hint that he had or had not been successful in his quest for the Bensons' salvation.

When he finally opened the door to the family, the look of struggling hope on their faces was all too evident.

He ushered them into the living room. No one cared for coffee or any other beverage. They sat on the edge of their chairs, waiting . . . waiting for their destiny to be revealed.

He told them bluntly that relief for them was nowhere in Canon Law—Church law. Their case, as his predecessor had found, was canonically hopeless.

Their attitude bottomed out.

However, he went on—after a pro forma pause—he had recalled, in a providential moment, a missionary society that had contacted him years before. Said society had offered a special privilege to priests who would, for a small stipend, spiritually participate in their missionary effort at catechizing the natives of a country in Africa.

As a reward for contributing to their effort, the order was empowered to grant a share in a dispensation they had gained from the Vatican.

Father Simpson had the Bensons' rapt attention.

One of the biggest problems facing missionaries, Simpson explained, was the status of marriage among the natives. It was extremely common for men, especially tribal chieftains, to have many wives—many, many wives.

The missionaries could catechize to their hearts' content, but, in the end, as much as they had convinced their catechumens of the necessity of becoming Catholics, still and always there were those impossible marital situations.

The missionaries could bring these people to the very threshold of Christianity, where, in the vast majority of cases, they would slam into the unrelenting door of multiple marriages.

Did the Bensons follow so far?

Yes, they nodded. The condition made sense, though the Bensons had never really reflected on it.

"Well," Father Simpson continued, "it was a stalemate, a Mexican standoff, as it were."

What these missionaries did, Father Simpson explained, was to take the problem to the Vatican authorities. The missionaries convinced Rome that there was no way in hell—Father Simpson asked pardon for his French—that they could ever walk these well-meaning people through the intricacies of canonical procedures.

So, in a one-time-only exception to Canon Law, a compromise was reached. The Vatican Congregation would allow each man of these tribes to pick one of his wives to be his one and only wife. In other words, once each man had made his choice, that was it! No more multiple marriages. One choice, one time.

Even with such a generous offer, the dispensation didn't solve all the problems, but it helped.

"Now," Father Simpson semiconcluded, "you may wonder what all this has to do with you."

Yes, they nodded, they did wonder.

The missionaries, Father Simpson explained, couldn't accomplish all that might be accomplishable without help—both spiritual and material.

Which is why the Vatican granted the Order permission to solicit priests around the world to contribute both money and prayers for the work of these African missionaries. And, in keeping with the one-time-only rule, this would be a one-time-only solicitation.

Father Simpson paused. He was approaching the nub of his fabricated story. It was crucial that the Bensons believe what would follow, else the priest would be up a creek, paddleless.

George and Lily looked as if they were ready to believe anything. Besides, Simpson's story was not that incredible—especially if one had only a superficial grasp of Church machinations. Simpson picked up his narrative.

In return for their generosity, the contributing priests were allowed to share in the boon bestowed on the missionaries. Each native man would be permitted to select a member of his harem to be his one and only wife. Therefore, the power to grant a declaration of nullity without consulting any Tribunal or submitting any documentation would apply not only to the members of the missionary Order but also to those priests, worldwide, who contributed to this missionary program. They would each be empowered to grant one similar dispensation to a couple whose canonically impossible union could not otherwise be dissolved by law.

Everything about this unique relaxation of law, known as the Missionaries' Privilege, was on a one-time-only basis. (There it was: that one-time-only rule. Obviously, the powers that be were concerned about not setting precedents.)

Each male tribal member who had God-knows-how-many concubines would, upon this application, have just one wife. Aside from the death of that spouse, he could henceforth have no other wife. It was a one-time decision, which did not completely solve the problem—some refused the choice—but it did help in many cases.

What was relevant to tonight's gathering was that Father Simpson had contributed to the missionaries' fund. He, therefore, had received permission to utilize this power once and only once in his lifetime.

He had never used it, he told them. But now he had decided that the Bensons deserved the benefits of this remarkable privilege. Lily Benson had been more than faithful to her Church lo these many years. Not to mention that this dispensation and convalidation would clear the path for Stanley to enter the seminary.

George had a reservation. "Do I have to join the Catholic Church? I mean, I got no objection. It's great for Lily, so I'm all for it. And I don't really know why Stan wants to go to the seminary. Hell, that's up to him.

"But not if I have to join the Church!"

What George Benson did with his immortal soul was beyond Simpson's immediate interest. "No, George, you don't have to become Catholic. Actually, you don't have to do much of anything. We just make a date to meet in the church. Both you and Lily can look on this as a renewal of your vows. Stan can be the witness.

"Well," he summed up, "what do you think?"

George shrugged. "It's okay by me . . . as long as I don't gotta join."

"I can't believe it." Tears streamed from Lily's eyes. "How good of you, Father . . . to let us benefit from your Missionaries' Privilege." She shook her head in wonderment. "It's as if God was saving this wonderful gift in your care. I can hardly believe it. But"—she smiled through her tears—"I do. I'm just so grateful."

She turned to gaze adoringly at her son. "And you, Stanley: You may one day be my very own priest!"

Stanley could scarcely breathe. He had let others, primarily his father, think he wanted to go to the seminary because he had been so certain all along that Church law would block him.

Now, as far as he could know, Father Simpson really had this Missionaries' Privilege, which could be used only once. And that once was now!

This was one of the worst days of his young life.

Father Simpson leaned back in his chair, quite self-satisfied. He had pulled it off.

Still there were some loose ends. "I must caution you: This—what I've told you—must be our secret. You may tell no one . . . no one. For one thing, if this got out, people would be knocking my door down. They would never understand that I lost this privilege when I used it for you. I was given this power to use only once. And that will be used for you. Once we go through with this convalidation ceremony, the power I have to do this will be gone.

"It's like a genie's three wishes," he said, driving his point home. "Once the last wish is used up, that's all there is; there isn't any more. And that's the way it is with this: Once we do it, that's all there is; I can't do it again . . . for anyone . . . any time.

"On top of that, how many other priests were given this power I don't know. This Vatican decision took place only once, and it happened many, many years ago. I have no idea who the other priests were. And it was so long ago that I'm sure that most, if not all, are either dead or have used the privilege long ago. We're just lucky that I saved my power till now.

"So," he pronounced, "for the sake of my sanity, it's our secret."

They nodded, wide-eyed and solemn.

"One more thing, Lily: Once we go through this ceremony, just begin living your faith again. What I mean is, don't confess what we've done. There's no reason you should confess it. It's not a sin. Just begin receiving Communion again. If any parishioners ask you about it, just tell them—without going into detail—that we were able to fix things.

"Do you all understand?"

All nodded, again wide-eyed and solemn. They understood.

Lily was ecstatic. George was happy for her. Stanley was numb.

He loved his mother. In his young life, he loved no one as much as he loved her. He had never seen her as happy as she was now. What would happen if he were to tell her his true feelings about going to the seminary?

It wasn't that he didn't love the Church. It wasn't that he didn't respect the priesthood. He just didn't want to be a priest.

That should be easy enough to understand. Not everybody who becomes an altar boy pines for the priesthood.

He wanted to be a secretary, an office clerk. He would be good at that. He loved detail work. He enjoyed picking up loose ends for others. He was not the type who dreamed gigantic dreams. He was the indispensable one who dotted i's and crossed t's.

A priest doesn't do that, he thought. A priest isn't a detail man. A priest is that heroic figure who runs huge parishes, who builds churches and schools and rectories and convents.

A priest finds jobs for the unemployed. He counsels people. He instructs people. He leads and guides.

He wears a special uniform that everyone recognizes. When he enters a room, conversational language becomes instantly self-cleansing.

He presides at weddings and wakes and funerals. And when somebody dies he knows just what to say to comfort the mourners.

Stanley did not want to do any of that. More fundamentally, he didn't think himself capable of those enormous responsibilities.

On the other hand, he loved the Mass. For him, it had proven to be the perfect prayer. He could well see himself at the altar wearing all those majestic vestments, whispering the sacred words that change bread and wine into the living presence of Jesus Christ.

But that was it.

Mass usually took from thirty minutes to an hour. The question that frightened him was, What to do with the remaining twenty-three hours of each day?

He couldn't do it. But he had to do it.

It was the perfect example of a dilemma.

Was there an alternative?

He could wait until this Missionaries' Privilege was used, then find some excuse for not going to the seminary.

But what sort of story would deliver him? Health problems? Granted, he wasn't the most robust kid in captivity; he was skinny and caught colds frequently, along with an annual case of the flu. But just about everyone suffered those same winter woes.

Was he too dull to qualify academically? Hardly. On the contrary, he was a better than average student.

And not to be disregarded was his history as a pious and faithful altar boy.

Prima facie, he had to admit he was a pretty fair candidate for the seminary, if not the priesthood.

Stanley was desolate.

As he and his parents prepared to leave, Stanley was further shaken when Father Simpson asked him to stop by the rectory tomorrow after Mass.

What could Father want to see him about now?

Father Simpson had everything he wanted.

He had bugged Stanley unmercifully. And now things were looking up for everyone involved.

Except Stanley.

The next morning, faithful as usual, Stan served the Mass. He then accompanied the priest to the rectory.

As they ate breakfast, the priest turned from small talk to more serious subjects.

"Son," said Father Simpson, who would never be a father

in the conventional sense, "I know you'll be going to the seminary mostly for your mother's sake . . ." He paused, hoping he had set the proper mood.

"By now," he picked up, "I'm sure you're going to apply for the seminary next spring. I mean, that's settled . . . right?"

"Yes, Father." The words were barely audible.

"Speak up, son. I can hardly hear you."

"Yes, Father!"

"This thing that we're doing for your folks is pretty complicated. Do you understand it?"

"N . . . no, not really."

"That's all right." In fact, as far as Simpson was concerned, completely missing the point was perfect. The less anyone knew of this concoction of Simpson's the better. "Even the Vatican knows little about this favor granted to the missionaries and through them to me. So we don't want to mess this up . . . do we?"

"No, Father."

"Okay. Good. Now, this is what we're going to do: Next May when you apply for the sem, your folks will give you your certification of baptism and confirmation. I will give you their marriage certificate. It will be predated to the day when their civil marriage took place—that's so we don't have to go through all that paper chase and explanation of how you were born out of Church wedlock and only much later were your folks married in the Church. It's water under the bridge.

"So, son, this is how we're going to do it—" He stopped, noting the boy's abstracted expression. "Believe me, Stanley, it's done all the time," he assured. "Just goes to show you: If you want to mess things up and create problems for everybody, you can do it. But why is what I say! Why?" His gaze fixed on Stanley. "You clear on that, son? Any questions?"

There were indeed questions, but Stanley trusted his priest and was used to doing as he was told. "No, Father."

"Good. Now, there's only one more thing—but it's a biggie."

Stanley's attention was riveted.

"From now on," Simpson declared, "you've gotta hide your light under a bushel. Now I know you're a smart cookie," he said, before Stanley could remonstrate. "But you gotta rein yourself in. No raising your hand every time you know the answer. Answer if you're asked—but no volunteering. You can shine on written exams. That way you and your profs will know that you're not slow. You can pass everything without your classmates and pals knowing just how smart you really are.

"Got all that?"

Stanley frowned. "I think so, Father. But . . . if you don't mind: What's all this for?"

"A decent question, son. What we want you to become is an average—maybe a little better than average—student. You see, we don't want you to be singled out. Better to be a statistic rather than a star.

"Suppose you are outstanding in something—anything to do with the priesthood. Supposing one of the chancellors discovers that you're outstanding. Maybe he wants you to be named a monsignor, or, heaven help us, a bishop.

"Then they start digging into your past. They want to make sure you can do the job they have in mind. Certainly they want a biographical sketch for the newspapers.

"Suppose they discover that your folks were married in civil law but there's no record of their being married in the Church . . . no notice of it in the marriage register, and nothing in the baptismal book.

"You see, son, that's something even I can't do. I can't push the lines apart enough to enter a marriage record.

"But I don't want you to worry. It's all on the up and up. It's just that it'll work out better if you don't stir up any sand in the water. I mean, I don't know whether Rome could even find the record of the Missionaries' Privilege in the archives by this time.

"I think that what we—you and I—have got to keep in mind always is that beautiful smile your mother wore when she understood we could fix up her marriage. And the even more beautiful smile when she called you 'my priest.'

"Now, what I want you to do, Stan, is make a big success of your eighth grade, and get ready for next May, the application, and the test.

"After that, just aim to be no more than ordinary, just average. You're not to stand out in anything. Got that?"

"Yes, Father."

"That's the boy! Now, if you have any doubts or questions, bring them to me . . . nobody else. Got it?"

"Yes, Father!"

"O . . . kay! Now, let's see a smile on you that is as perfect as your mother's."

As he left the rectory, Stanley tried to hold the smile. It felt so artificial. He would have to work at it.

He would have to work at many things. But he would work on those things. He would do it motivated only by his love for his mother.

Damn Father Simpson!

No, that was not too strong a curse. For some unfathomable reason, this priest wanted Stan in the seminary and ultimately in the priesthood.

Was there such a thing as the Missionaries' Privilege? Maybe. There were lots of things Stan didn't know or understand about his Church.

But all those things were of no account. He was going to make his mother happy.

12

THANKSGIVING DAY, 1942.

The dinner was scheduled to be celebrated at the Smith home. It would be a sizable gathering. The Smith twins of course. The Toccos had given permission for Emanuel to dine with his friends. Alice McMann was grateful to be with her friend Rose.

And for good measure, Dick Trent, who worked with Henry Smith, would attend, together with his wife, Peg, and their two children, Judy and Jerry—the latter known familiarly as Jiggs.

Quite a crowd. Fortunately, the Smith home was large enough to accommodate the guests. Two card tables were set up as an adjunct to the dining table. A tight fit, but no problem as long as everyone caught the joy of the holiday.

While the adults would be preparing dinner and conversing, the six young people were shipped off to a matinee presentation of *Yankee Doodle Dandy,* starring Jimmy Cagney as George M. Cohan.

Odd ones out were Jiggs and Judy Trent; they had previously met none of the other teenagers. But Jiggs already had his eye on Alice McMann.

It had been a toss-up. He could just as easily have gone after Rose. But she had a twin in tow. Jiggs figured he could intimidate Michael if necessary, but sufficient unto the day was the complication thereof.

By the time they arrived at the movie house it was jammed, mainly with young people. No way would the six be able to sit together; they'd be lucky to find any adjoining seats. Manny found three and held up three fingers. He entered the row, followed by Alice and Jiggs, and all settled in for the show.

The noise made by hundreds of children—some of whom had attended the J. L. Hudson parade earlier—was deafening. Not only were they communicating with each other at peak volume, they were also trying to get warm.

Finally, the lights dimmed, the noise diminished, and comparative silence reigned. That it was an excellent movie could be ascertained by the attention the kids paid it.

Jiggs waited patiently until the movie was well under way. Then he slowly, unobtrusively, moved his right arm across the top of the seatback.

No reaction from Alice.

He let his arm fall slowly until it was touching her shoulders.

It was a first for Alice; she was unsure what was happening. She had heard some of her schoolmates talking, although she was unclear what they were talking about. There had been a lot of giggling and snickering, but it was all Greek to her.

Could this be what the girls had been giggling about? Maybe what's-his-name . . . Jerry? Or . . . what did they call him? Jiggs. Yes, that was it. Well, maybe Jiggs was just stretching his arm because he was cramped or uncomfortable.

But having stretched, he made no effort to remove his arm. Now she was really puzzled. Her puzzlement was somewhat amplified when she heard a couple of girls in the row behind whispering and giggling. Alice realized she was the subject of their hilarity.

It—whatever the girls had been talking about—*was happening to her!*

She leaned forward, hoping Jiggs would take his arm away.

He didn't. Instead, his arm lowered until his hand was touching the small of her back. He began to massage the spot. Alice let out a small squeal.

From the bright light of the screen it was obvious that Jiggs was grinning from ear to ear.

A muffled whisper came from Alice's right. "Change places with me."

She wasn't sure she had heard correctly. "What?"

"Change places with me," Manny repeated.

Wordlessly, Alice stood and changed seats with Manny. The maneuver happened so smoothly and unexpectedly that Jiggs's hand was almost pinned by Manny's weight. "What the hell are you doing, buddy?" Jiggs said in a low growl.

Manny grabbed Jiggs's hand, grasped the thumb, and gave it a violent tug backward.

Jiggs let out a shriek of pain.

Shushes came from all around.

"If you don't shut up," Manny whispered, "I'm going to snap your thumb off and feed it to you."

Jiggs gasped; his hand went limp. Manny let go and whispered, "Enjoy the show."

For the first time in her life Alice could appreciate the concept of a Knight in Shining Armor.

Not another word was said. It was hard to know whether the other members of their group were unaware of the contretemps. But Rose thought she had heard Alice gasp.

The movie was coming to a close.

An aging George M. Cohan was marching down a Washington street alongside uniformed soldiers. The soldiers presumably were headed overseas to fight World War II. Cagney/Cohan joined the troops in singing *his* song "Over There."

Jiggs was oblivious of the screen action until the very end. He had spent almost the entire time planning revenge. He couldn't even recall the kid's name . . . Manny, or Danny, or some such. But the little snot wasn't going to get away with it! He, Jiggs, would see to that.

The stirring patriotic finale distracted Jiggs. He was caught up in the soldiers' enthusiasm in getting a chance to prove their manhood. He wanted to join them, to fight and maybe even die for his country.

The group reunited in the midst of the exiting crowd and headed back to the Smith home. Jiggs caught up with Manny and pulled him a few steps behind the others. "Listen, buster—"

"If you want to finish this," Manny broke in, "when we get to the Smith house, let the others go in. You peel off to the right. I'll meet you there—at the driveway."

Jiggs stopped in his tracks as the others moved ahead.

There was something in Manny's voice . . . and when the two boys turned toward each other briefly, something in Manny's eyes promised a fight to the finish.

Actually, Jiggs hadn't been all that serious about a fight. He was somewhat larger than Manny; he had expected to scare the other boy and win the day by default.

Jiggs's bluff had been called. He did not respond to Manny's challenge. When they reached the Smith home the others entered the house, shed their outer clothing, and began to give the adults a blow-by-blow description of *Yankee Doodle Dandy*.

Manny planted himself squarely in the middle of the driveway. He looked up to the porch, where Jiggs hesitated in indecision. Manny's eyes were fixed unwaveringly on Jiggs. Finally, Jiggs turned and entered the house.

Manny shrugged. He was just as glad there would be no fight. If there had been, Manny had no doubt he would have won. But he would probably have ruined his good clothes and have been shipped off to a less than cordial reception at home.

But it was Jiggs's call, and that young man had decided that a fight would not be a smart move. Beneath his brash exterior, Jiggs didn't like what he'd seen in Manny's eyes.

Now that the young people had returned, the dinner party could begin. It was the traditional Thanksgiving feast with all the trimmings.

Alice blushed almost all through dinner. Most of the others, if they paid any attention at all, ascribed her rosy cheeks to the weather. Manny and Jiggs said nothing; the two hardly looked up from their food. But Rose was concerned; she could read her friend like an open book.

The party ended early, and the guests departed shortly thereafter, expressing heartfelt gratitude for the meal and the company.

As they left, Manny and Jiggs exchanged one last long look. Jiggs tried to communicate silently that this was not the end. The next time they met, if there was no one to intercede, the fight would commence, and it would not end until Manny was dead—or close to it.

Manny's expression said he couldn't care less.

Alice and Rose had volunteered to clear the tables and do the dishes. The offer was quickly accepted; preparing the dinner and the energy expended in high spirits had exhausted Lucy. As for Henry, he was too full to do more than sink into an overfed near stupor on the couch.

Having finished the cleanup, the two girls went up to Rose's room and closed the door. Rose took out her hairbrush and the routine began. "What happened today at the Stratford?" she asked without preamble.

"What do you mean?" Alice's voice was a whit unsteady.

"I heard you give a little gasp—or was it a shriek?"

Alice's face reddened. "You could hear?"

"I know you. So . . . what happened?"

"Jiggs tried to get fresh."

"What do you mean, 'get fresh'?"

"Well . . ." And Alice proceeded to tell about Jiggs putting his arm across her shoulder and how she'd thought he just might've been cramped and maybe just wanted to stretch, but then, when she'd leaned forward how he'd started to rub her back . . . "and that's when Manny got involved."

"Oh?"

"He told me to switch places with him. So we did. Then Manny did something—I don't know what—to Jiggs. Whatever it was, Jiggs made a noise like he was in pain."

"Sounds as if Manny hurt him."

"I guess. Anyway, Jiggs didn't try anything after that. He said something right after we switched places. But I couldn't tell what it was. Jiggs said something. Then Manny said something, and that was it. Neither one of them said anything at all after that."

"Mmmm. I did notice neither of them said much of anything during dinner . . . and even after when we were sitting around and the rest of us were talking."

"Yes. I'm sure you're right . . . something was going on between them." Alice laughed for the first time since before the movie. "Heck, even if they had tried to say something, they would've had a tough time getting a word in edgewise what with little Judy . . . she's a regular magpie."

"How do you feel now?" Rose asked, without stopping her brushing.

"About what Jiggs did?"

"Uh-huh."

"I really feel I want to talk this out . . . but only to you."

"Shoot." Amazingly, Rose put down her hairbrush and turned to communicate face-to-face.

"I feel horrible . . . violated."

"Al! All he did was touch you. Through all those clothes you had on, he couldn't have gotten much of a feel."

"But I didn't do anything to stop him. I didn't even tell him to cut it out."

"You hardly had a chance. From what you say, it all happened so quickly. So he made a pass at you. But you hardly had a chance to get control of the situation before Manny stepped in. God bless Manny."

"Amen!"

"So why should you feel 'violated'? Nothing happened."

"But what if Manny hadn't been there?"

"You would've put a stop to Jiggs's getting fresh."

"That's the part that gets me, Rose: I don't know."

"What do you mean, you don't know?"

"I . . . I kind of . . . well, I kind of liked it."

"What!"

Alice reddened again.

"What do you mean you liked it? Jiggs would've been all over you if nobody had stopped him. You liked that?"

"It's the first time anybody—boy or girl—ever did anything like that to me. Of course I felt sinful." Her face contorted in unhappy thought. "I probably even committed a sin."

"You didn't do anything!"

"A thought can be a sin. You know that. And I was having all kinds of thoughts."

"For the love of Pete, you didn't have time!"

Alice shook her head. "It doesn't take long . . . I found out." She looked imploringly at Rose. "I couldn't tell this to anyone but you."

"Not even a priest? Now that you think you're some kind of sinner?" Rose spoke in a pooh-poohing tone.

"No. Well . . . not in detail anyway. But I've got to tell someone . . . you, if you'll let me."

Rose sighed. "Go ahead, Al; get it off your chest."

"I felt all warm and moist. It was like my blood was racing through my body. It was the most insane feeling of delight and guilt all at the same time. I've never felt like that before."

Silence.

"Okay, Al," Rose said finally, "you had feelings I don't think I've ever had. It sounds like maybe they're what sex is all about. I don't think you were responsible for them. For sure it wasn't your fault. But, okay, if you want to confess those feelings, this parish has enough priests you can go to."

"Yes, I know. And that's what I'm going to do."

"So?"

"What I'm really concerned about is entering the convent."

"Why ever would you be concerned about that? What's one got to do with the other? Look, they don't cut out your feelings, your emotions, when you enter. We—none of us—can help what we feel . . . especially when we're tempted.

"Al, when you were telling me how you felt when Jiggs

was grabbing at you, all I could think was that if I had been in your place, I probably would've felt the same way you did." She neglected to add that it would've taken someone far more romantic than the bumbling Jiggs to reach her.

"You really think so?"

"I really do. And remember, Al: In a few years we'll enter the convent and take gradual steps toward becoming nuns. We'll see if we're ready. And they'll see if we're ready. But, please God, we'll never stop being human."

"Thanks, Rose."

Silence.

"Can you remember how many strokes you had when I interrupted you?"

Rose picked up the brush and began stroking. "Thirty-three, thirty-four, thirty-five . . ."

"Amazing!"

It was Thanksgiving evening and the Benson family was relaxing. George and Lily sat on the tattered couch listening to the radio and holding hands. Stan was in his room updating the pins he had pushed into his wall map—his way of following the progress of the war.

Today had been a restrained celebration for the Bensons. Still, they were thankful for their modest meal.

Everything about the Bensons was modest to threadbare. If their financial situation had been significantly better they would not be living in Olympiaville.

Outside of following the course of the battles, and praying for a successful conclusion, Stanley rarely thought about the war. Of course, there was always the possibility that divinity students would lose their 4-D status. But that was not likely.

In any event, for now, Stanley would just have to play the hand he'd been dealt.

He had decided to warm up for the sort of changed student he'd have to become once he was admitted to the seminary. The challenge was to convince his teachers that he had somehow changed from an excellent and aggressive learner into a disinterested, mediocre lump. So, where he had once pulled down straight A's, Stan had let himself sink to B's, C's, and even an occasional D.

His homeroom teacher, Mrs. Brown, took him aside a few days before the Thanksgiving holiday.

"Stan, what's happened to you? I've seen you go from the first to the eighth grade and each year you've gotten better. Until now. These past three months I've seen a different Stanley Benson. You almost never volunteer an answer. Before, I had to deliberately bypass you to call on kids whom you have beaten to the draw—just so that somebody besides you could contribute to the class."

Stanley offered no reply, just hung his head.

"You're passing, of course. I don't think you could do less than that. But I am concerned. And so are your other teachers." She paused. "Stanley, is there something wrong? Is something troubling you?"

"I . . . I don't know. It's probably just some kind of slump."

"Do you think your folks should take you to see a doctor?"

"Oh, no, Mrs. Brown. I'll be okay. I think this Thanksgiving break will be a big help."

Mrs. Brown's deeply furrowed brow indicated she was not convinced that whatever was wrong with this promising student would be cured by a few days off. "I want you to feel free to come see me anytime you want or need help. I am—all your teachers are—here for you."

Stanley nodded and stood. "Thank you, Mrs. Brown. I hope you have a Hap—a Blessed Thanksgiving."

She smiled. "And you too, Stanley. And please give my regards to your parents."

"Yes, Mrs. Brown; I will."

Stanley had had a lot to think about as he'd walked home that day. And during the days that followed.

Even now he was lost in thought. He pushed his chair back and gazed at the map. But he didn't see the soldiers and sailors and airmen whom he normally pictured in his mind's eye. The imaginary warriors who would parade through the streets of Europe and Asia, receiving the joyous cheers of the deliriously happy inhabitants of liberated countries.

Somehow the war had been brought home to Stanley. Now his imagination showed him GIs, cold, dirty, unshaved; combat boots rotting off their feet; wolfing rations whenever they got the chance. The reality confirmed an earlier critique: War is hell.

There was no doubt in Stan's mind that he wanted no part of this war. He did not relish pain, injury, death . . . neither suffering it nor inflicting it.

Still, he would have preferred the misfortunes of war to this steady, ineluctable treadmill tramp toward the priesthood.

Other young men could march off to war to, among other considerations, Make the World Safe for Democracy. While Stanley would remain protected from war by a benevolent deferment. And Stanley would clutch that deferment to his bosom for the sake of his mother's happiness and continued mental health.

The person who dominated his life at this point was Father Ed Simpson. He it was who had singlehandedly turned Lily Benson's life from consuming guilt to confident joy. Stan could be grateful for that . . . extremely grateful.

But in doing this, Father had made Stan's life a meaningless mess.

Stan switched off the light. He could hear the soft sounds of music from the radio. He would try to say his night prayers. Prayer did not come to him as readily as it had in the past.

He would not pray for Father Simpson.

Thanksgiving vacation was over, and the students had returned to school.

From various sources, Rose learned that her bosom buddy, Alice, had just barely escaped being saddled with the reputation of a teenage slut.

Rose and Alice went on a fact-finding mission.

It seemed that Rose, Alice, Mike, and Manny were by no means the only students of Holy Redeemer who had been at the Stratford that fatal day. Neither Alice nor Rose had adverted to the fact that they were virtually surrounded by Redeemerites. Constantly changing images appeared on the screen; at times the lighting was bright, at other times shadowy.

Once the film had begun, the moviegoers became entranced by the story. However, unrelated movements such as those of Jiggs and Manny naturally distracted those seated behind and alongside them.

But the exchange had begun so suddenly and was over so quickly that the various onlookers interpreted what happened in different ways.

Some said Alice was the instigator . . . that she attempted to seduce this—as far as they knew—perfect stranger. In this interpretation, Manny had broken up this blatant temptation before anything totally sinful had occurred.

Other theater patrons with a better perspective had recognized what was really going on. They saw clearly the kid with the stereotypical maneuver. One arm circles the girl's shoulder. If allowed to rest there ever so briefly, the hand begins exploring.

This group of patrons realized what had actually transpired. They even overheard some of the revelatory dialogue between Manny and Jiggs.

Fortunately, at bottom, the latter interpretation won out. Thus Alice's reputation emerged comparatively unsullied. And her advance toward the convent continued.

For the most part, Rose and Alice seemed to overlook the protective role played by Manny; instead they focused on the boorish Jiggs. And a newly used expletive entered the girls' speech pattern: *"Men!"*

* * *

Holy Redeemer students were not the only ones who had been treated to the off-screen entertainment provided by Jiggs, Alice, and Manny. Jiggs's younger sister, Judy, had been sitting two rows directly behind the busy threesome. She would gladly have testified for the plaintiff had the case gone to trial.

In addition to the play-by-play progression of that scene being apparent to Judy, she knew the perpetrator. She knew his MO. She had often heard him boast of his conquests. But this was the first time she had seen him in action.

Jiggsy wasn't very effective, in Judy's judgment. However, his scattershot approach seemed more successful than she'd expected.

She knew what her brother would do. Returning to his field of play, he would regale his buddies with what would have happened had Manny not intervened. Reality would go out the window, and Jiggs's imagination would describe the dream sequence that followed the arm-fling opening.

Judy was a small girl. Thus, it was easy for her to remain unnoticed. She heard the challenge and she saw her brother back down.

Later, she took her brother to one side. She told him what she had seen and heard.

He raised his arm to punch hers. But he hesitated when Judy held up a warning hand. "There won't be any more pounding on little sister," she said, in calm, measured tones. "From now on, my arm is off-limits to your fist. Or all your buddies will know what a chicken you are and how your boasting and bragging are so much hogwash. Pound me, and your little game is over."

The Allies should have had such a deterrent.

13 CHRISTMASTIME 1942.

Bob Koesler was full of wonder after his first several months in the seminary. Being taught exclusively by priests—diocesan priests at that—was a new and somewhat daunting experience.

Holy Redeemer's Liturgy—Mass and Devotions—was excellent. But Bob found the seminary's version even more inspiring.

His courses were in the Liberal Arts field, with a clear emphasis on English and Latin. It was not difficult to understand why. English was all but the official language of the United States. It was the language in which the seminarians would preach, should they be ordained. Ordained into the Latin Rite. Their most sacred function would be to offer the holy sacrifice of the Mass, which would be recited in Latin and sung in Latin.

At this time, it was taken for granted that none of the Liturgy would ever change. That fact was beyond question.

Bob Koesler and Patrick McNiff had become fast friends. And, led mostly by the gregarious McNiff, Bob had made many other friends.

But there was no question that Bob and the other freshmen were at the bottom of the totem pole. The sophomores wouldn't let the lower classmen forget. The sophs had taken it on the chin last year. This year was theirs.

Bob had a lot to be thankful for. Not the least was his family, which wholeheartedly encouraged and supported him in his pursuit of the priesthood.

In addition, he was grateful to the Maryknoll priest who had selflessly introduced the Koesler family to the diocesan seminary. Bob, as well as his family, relished his being able to commute to school.

Rose Smith and Alice McMann were getting used to having male classmates.

". . . seventy-four . . . seventy-five . . . seventy-six . . ."

"I thought you usually did that at night," Alice commented.

"You mean"—Rose paused to consider—"brush my hair?"

"One hundred times?"

"Yes. And you're right: evening or nighttime. But we're going to a Christmas party tonight."

"And you're now at—?"

"Seventy-nine . . . eighty . . ."

"Incredible."

"It must be something like the ability to play the piano by ear. If you've got it, you can't understand why just about everyone can't do it."

"And you can't play by ear," Alice said.

"You know I can't. I can play . . ."

"Beautifully."

"Thanks. But not by ear. It's my mom who has the real musical talent."

Almost on cue, Alice began to hum a show tune. She peeked over Rose's shoulder and studied herself in the mirror. She wished she could get her dark hair to lie flat. But try as she might, it always popped up in curly waves.

The rest of her was developing slowly but nicely. She was particularly proud of her newly perky breasts. Puberty promised her good things to come.

But to what purpose? She was going to be a nun. Whatever curves she had would be covered under yards of religious habit.

More's to pity Rose and her pampered, stroked hair.

Both girls were well aware that their crowning glories would be sheared and their scalps shaved. Secretly, Alice sometimes fantasized her friend stroking her bald head one hundred times nightly. How could anyone break such a habit?

"Like what you see?" Rose was smiling at her in the mirror.

Alice blushed. "I was just . . . looking."

"But you are developing beautifully. I'm happy for you."

"You should talk! I'll never be the natural knockout you are."

"It's enough that we both have good looks."

Now thoroughly self-conscious, Alice sat back on the bed and toyed with a Teddy bear that had long been a favorite of Rose. "I've been thinking . . . about where we'll be and what we'll be doing next year at this time."

"You mean at Immaculata?"

Alice nodded. "How about you? Do you ever wonder?"

"Ninety-nine . . . a hundred. There!" Rose laid the brush on the nightstand. "I don't think about it so much. We'll be in another school starting the ninth grade."

"And there won't be any boys." Alice sounded disappointed.

"Have you actually seen much difference than before?"

"Not as much as I thought." It was up for grabs how much Alice had changed consciously and subconsciously because of boys. She felt that this was a time in life when boys her age became aware of breasts. Probably because this was the first visible sexual change that was distinctly feminine.

If the boys were going to look, Alice would enhance. Depending on what she was wearing, occasionally she would tuck some tissues in her bra.

"I think I'll miss them," Alice said wistfully.

"I think I will too," Rose admitted. "At least a bit. I mean, we've been without boys in our classes for seven years. And then they're here for a year and we're gone again.

"But," Rose brightened up, "I hear that Immaculata is nice. It's in a beautiful setting . . . you know, on Marygrove's campus with all those huge trees. It must be especially impressive this time of year."

"And that," Alice said, "will be our high school. A lot of choice we had in picking the place." She sounded resentful.

"Alice, you shouldn't be bitter."

"Why not? It's our life, and we weren't even consulted. We were just told where we'd be going."

"There really wasn't much choice," Rose reasoned. "We're headed for the convent and our folks are trying to help us reach our goal. So they wanted to find a good Catholic school that's all-girl. And Immaculata fits that bill.

"Tick off the positives," Rose urged. "We'll be with girls whose parents care enough to send their daughters to a good Catholic school. It's really a prep school . . . preparing girls for college. We'll be with other girls who want the convent. We'll just sort of graduate to Monroe and start our road to the convent.

"Think of it: We'll start our college and our religious life in Monroe! Our grades and marks will be kept at Marygrove. We'll be surrounded by the IHMs just as we've been from first grade. And on top of all that, we'll be able to have our dads take turns ferrying us to and from school. And when we finish high school we'll be in residence in Monroe. See?" Rose clearly was comfortable with her analysis.

"Sounds nice," Alice agreed. "But there's still a problem."

"I think I know what you mean."

Alice nodded. "I know you know."

"It's nursing, isn't it?"

"Uh-huh. The IHMs are a teaching order. That's all they do, aside from the occasional infirmarian who takes temperatures and sees to sprains, bruises, and tummy aches."

"Exactly." Rose nodded.

"So, Alice, if we want to get into an all-girl Catholic school where we don't have to commute, where we don't have to pay room and board, Immaculata is pretty much the least common denominator."

"But, Rose, I don't know if I can make it as a teacher . . .

especially in a system where you have nothing to say about who you're going to teach, or when and where."

"Be realistic, Alice. That's about what we'd get no matter which religious order we enter. If we joined the Religious Sisters of Mercy or the St. Joseph Order in Kalamazoo, or any of the other Orders that offer both teaching and nursing, we still wouldn't get to pick our spot, or, for that matter, anything else about our lives. We give ourselves to Jesus and serve Him in children and sick people."

"But, Rose, don't you see? You said it yourself: Once we're in the convent, we give up all decisions to our superiors. This—the Order we select—is about the last decision we're going to make. I wanted to make that one."

Rose pulled her slip over her head. There wasn't much time before the Smith family would be leaving for their dinner party. Rose turned and studied her friend—her best friend. "Al, you're overlooking the obvious."

"What might that be?" Alice was a bit defensive.

"You can make the decision as to which direction you'll go in. As a matter of fact, you've got to."

"I'm going to Immaculata and then I'm going to Marygrove. I'm going to be with you."

"Al, I know how you feel. My life would be pretty empty without you too. But this decision is bigger even than our friendship. This is about our vocation. If you're uneasy about Monroe, if you prefer the RSMs, then that's the path you ought to take."

"And live apart from you all our lives?" Alice's eyes filled with tears.

"Al,"—Rose placed her hand on her friend's arm—"there's something I've got to tell you about—something I never told you."

"G'wan!" Alice smiled through her tears. "I can't believe you've held anything back from me. I've never held anything back from you."

"Well, this is something my family keeps as a solemn secret."

"Wha—I don't understand . . ."

"I have an aunt who was a nun."

"An aunt!"

"She's my dad's sister. Years ago, she joined the Religious Sisters of Mercy. She wanted to be a nursing Sister. The RSMs teach or nurse. She entered with the understanding that she would be a nurse."

Rose sat on the bed next to Alice. "The time came for my aunt to get her first assignment. She was assigned to teach."

Alice shook her head. "But she had an understanding . . ."

"I know. But her Mother Superior explained that although at that time the RSMs had an oversupply of nurses, what they needed were teachers."

Rose ignored Alice's "No!" "She was told that she would begin training as a teacher."

"So what did she do?"

"She became a teacher. She was sure that she would eventually be switched to nursing. But time passed and there was no sign that her administration had any intention of moving her into the field she wanted.

"Then"—Rose paused—"then she learned that a few of the new postulants had been channeled into the nursing field.

"She went to see the Mother Superior. My aunt was certain there'd been a mistake . . . that she had been inadvertently left out.

"But she hadn't been. Mother Superior explained she had done so well as a teacher that the Order would leave her in that field.

"It was a while afterward that she did what I guess she thought was the honorable thing: She petitioned to leave religious life. It was a long and brutal ordeal. But, eventually, she was 'returned to the world.' "

"Where," Alice asked in a small voice, "is she now?"

Rose shook her head. "We don't know."

Silence.

Finally, Rose spoke again. "Do you personally know any former nuns?"

Alice didn't need to think very long. "No. I guess I just thought once you're a nun, that's it."

"No. I gather it's a disgrace to leave. Especially after taking permanent vows.

"So our family—Mom and Dad, and their relatives, particularly my dad's relatives—what there are of them—well, they all act as if there never was a Sister Margaret Mary, RSM . . . that she never existed. And even more, that there never was a Bernice Smith."

Alice looked shaken. "How cruel!"

"Nobody seems to think of its being cruel. Aunt Bernice moved away without any family contact at all. It wasn't cruelty; it just was how things were done."

"Do you remember her?"

Rose sighed. "This all happened before Mike and I were born. My folks have never mentioned it. Another aunt told us about Aunt Bernice. And whenever we tried to bring the subject up with my parents, we got shot down.

"Alice, I'm telling you this partly because I know you'll keep it a secret . . . and also because it's important for you to know what can happen."

"That wouldn't happen to me."

"It happened to my aunt. If it happened to her it can happen to anyone."

There was a long pause while Alice mulled over what Rose had told her. Rose finished dressing.

"It is depressing," Alice admitted.

"It's one of those things," Rose said. "It all depends on how you look at it. You can't always be in command of things that happen." She smiled. "It's like a poster I saw in school: 'If you want to make God laugh, tell Him your plans.'

"Think about it," Rose urged. "It could easily happen that you don't get what you want in life. Say you want to be a doctor—but you finish your testing just out of qualification. Or you want to be in stocks and bonds but they happen to be cutting back. Or you join the Religious Sisters of Mercy, like my aunt did, wanting to be a nurse. But instead they don't have a need there. So you become a teacher.

"There's one gigantic advantage. We can be crushed by being turned down or discarded by a secular enterprise. That's because we can be desiring something we want. But when we go to the convent, we go to do God's will . . . or so I'm told.

"I feel sorry for my aunt. I wish I had known her . . . either as Bernice Smith or as Sister Margaret Mary. But I think she maybe wasn't meant for religious life.

"It's not that I could've done anything about it—after all, I wasn't even around at the time. No . . . it's just . . . well, I just would've loved to have known her."

Rose finished putting herself together. It was almost time to leave for the party. "Are we on the same wave length, Al?"

"I think so. I've been trying to figure this out for myself. And 'for myself' is what's important. I could join an Order that offers both teaching and nursing. If I picked nursing and didn't get it, I'd wind up a bitter old woman . . . or leave my congregation just like your aunt.

"As it is," she concluded, "I want to be a nun and I want to be near you. The world won't stop because I'm not a nurse. I've got to see this as God's will . . . which it is.

"But"—she smiled—"it's time for your party. Talk to you tomorrow?"

"Sure. And I'll tell you all about the party."

Alice knew her way around the Smith residence as well as her own. Nor was she a stranger to the family. No Smith would take it amiss to find Alice roaming through their house. She made her way downstairs and let herself out.

Did I give her the right information, Rose wondered. Should I encourage her to try an Order that offers nursing? Will our friendship provide strength sufficient for her to weather the demands of religious life?

She's a good girl, Rose thought. I'm lucky to have a friend like her. But then, she's lucky to have a friend like me.

Rose slipped into her coat and waited by the front door for her family.

Enough serious thought. It's Christmas. Enjoy!

14 CHRISTMAS DAY.

Mass had been attended, presents had been opened, good wishes had been extended all around. And something new was about to be tried.

Henry and Lucy Smith had little extended family. A few cousins now scattered about the country and a few overseas; an aunt who had disappeared after an attempt at religious life. So as a twist on the traditional Christmas dinner, the Smiths suggested a party of sorts for five young members of Redeemer parish who planned to enter religious life.

All five were connected by various ties. First and oldest was Bob Koesler, who had been prepped to flow easily into an out-of-state seminary, there to begin studies to become a Redemptorist priest. Several of his Redeemer classmates had gone off to Wisconsin. One of the three had returned home. His reabsorption into his parochial freshman class was proceeding, though he was viewed through jaundiced eyes.

Most parochial students were conditioned to expect some of their number to enter seminaries or convents. After all, parochial schools were geared to be incubators for religious vocations. Such decisions were applauded.

But when a young man embarked on such a course only to return several months later, understanding flew out the window.

The likely cause of such retrogression was homesickness. Classmates in parochial school tended to look upon the returned one as a quitter.

That same fate could have befallen young Koesler but for the fact that he had become a day student in a local diocesan seminary. In any case, he had stayed the course so far.

But Bobby wouldn't have gone this route if not for the intervention of a Maryknoll priest who had steered him toward Sacred Heart Seminary.

Koesler, in turn, influenced the life choices of Michael Smith and Emanuel Tocco. With Manny taking after Michael, they too had been headed for the Redemptorist Seminary.

Bob Koesler introduced them to the perfect alternative. The information he passed on had to do with favorable odds. Should a boy attend Sacred Heart Seminary and—for whatever reason—drop out, he could still be considered for the Redemptorist Order.

However, should he try the Redemptorists and leave—as had Bob's unfortunate classmate—he would be barred from any attempt to enter Sacred Heart.

Michael and Manny liked the odds. They also appreciated the idea of living at home.

All three had lots to learn about the priesthood in general and what it would be like to be assigned to parish work. One striking point of difference was that—try as they might—religious orders did not produce parish priests. No order could overlook the fact that their group, or their religious community, had been founded for a specific purpose. They might have been dedicated to preaching—or even more specifically, preaching against heretical groups. Or they might have been established to ransom captives, or committed to pursue, combat, or deal with any number of issues that seemed impelling at the time.

Many founders of religious orders had subsequently been proclaimed saints. Most—or at least many—of the erstwhile impelling issues were no longer very impelling.

And so, in going down the list—Dominicans, Franciscans, Oblates, Carmelites, Jesuits, Redemptorists—few of the orders were still engaged in the work that their founders—

Dominic, Francis, Ignatius, Alphonsus, etc.—had established them to accomplish.

Of the more than three hundred parishes in Detroit, only one was staffed by Redemptorists. They functioned as simple parish priests, not as the vanguard of preachers against heresies. The overriding difference between Redeemer and most other Detroit parishes was quantity. This parish comprised many more priests than any of the other parishes.

Thus, Catholics who moved from Redeemer to just about any other diocesan parish might complain that there were only two or three confessors ready to absolve of a given Saturday. Whereas Redeemerites had a choice of some sixteen.

But the method of operation of parish life would be exposed to Sacred Heart students. It was a step toward the mutual testing that was geared to help the student accept or reject the seminary, while at the same time the seminary measured whether to accept or reject the student.

Somewhat like Australian tag team wrestling, the Maryknoller touched and changed Bob Koesler's life. Then Bobby would touch and change the lives of Michael and Emanuel.

Michael could not have begun his overture to religious life without the influence of his twin, Rose. Then, through Michael, Rose was distantly connected with Manny.

And because Rose and Alice were best of friends, the group expanded accordingly.

Some in this group knew each other intimately or well, others only passingly.

Whatever their backgrounds, it was the intention of Mr. and Mrs. Smith to bring them all together. Hopefully, they would bond over the years and each would be a source of strength for the others.

All the parents—the Smiths, McManns, Koeslers, Toccos—agreed: They would arrange a Christmas dinner party, then step aside and leave the young people to mingle.

The adults made arrangements to go to downtown Detroit, where several soup kitchens needed volunteers.

This was a banner day for the homeless, who had nothing, or nearly nothing. It was a grand, if infrequently available, festive meal. And the parents who wanted to serve Christ actually served Him this Christmas Day in the person of the poor and needy.

Michael and Rose acted as hosts, since the dinner was at their home.

Initially, conversation was a bit stilted. Under ordinary circumstances, the young people would've been there to share food and small talk. Perhaps this present formality was due to the fact that each was increasingly conscious that he or she was heading toward a celibate life.

But the awkwardness soon thawed. And by the end of the main course everyone helped clear the dishes. Mike and Rose served dessert, and a sense of camaraderie permeated the atmosphere.

"You know, it really was nice of our folks to throw this party for us," Bob Koesler said. The others nodded agreement. "I guess it's kind of clear what they're trying to accomplish," he added.

"They hope we'll find lots to pull us together," Mike said, "and that we'll become friends."

"Some of us are already," Alice said.

"True," said Bob. "Now that I think of it, I'm practically odd man out. I haven't really been that close to any of you here. But I'd like to be." He looked around the table. "I think our folks want us to realize that we all share much of what we want to become as adults. Three of us want to be priests . . ."

"Of the diocesan variety," Manny said.

The others laughed.

"That's right," Bob agreed. "It's not that there's any shortage of priest candidates from this parish. Probably more men get ordained from Redeemer than from any other single parish in the diocese."

"And all of us who do get ordained," Mike said, "whether

as Redemptorist or as diocesan priests, share in the same priesthood. Still," he said, after a moment's thought, "there will be differences."

Bob nodded. "For one thing, our friends who become Redemptorists can be sent anywhere in this province—anywhere in the world, for that matter."

"And," Mike added, "wherever they may be, they'll be together in a uniquely special way. These guys at Redeemer stick together. I mean *really* stick together. They take days off together, vacation together, recreation together. As far as togetherness is concerned, they'll have it way over us."

"I guess that's the way it ought to be," Manny said. "They eat together and pray together. Face it: They're tighter than we'll ever be as secular priests."

"I can vouch for that," Bob said. "First, the Brothers of Mary invited me to join them. But I never intended to become a Brother. When they became convinced of that, I never heard about it again. Then the Redemptorists tried to enlist me. But when I entered the diocesan seminary, the Redemptorists lost interest."

"They did?" Rose, though she had hitherto said little, had been following the conversation closely.

Bob nodded again, this time vigorously. "Granted, I haven't been a seminarian very long . . . just a few months. But early on, the rector at Sacred Heart advised all of us to report regularly to our own pastors. He assured us our pastors wanted to get to know us.

"So, when Christmas vacation started, I went over to the rectory and asked to see the pastor. He came out, looked me over, and wondered why I was there. So I told him what the seminary rector had said. He nodded, though he seemed kind of puzzled. Told me to have a nice vacation and make sure to attend Mass every day. Then he walked off, leaving me standing in the vestibule."

They all thought that amusing.

"The point is," Bob continued, "we really ought to stick together, just like our folks obviously intended."

"Yeah," Mike agreed. "We've got to be there for each

other. It's a cinch the Redemptorists aren't going to take us under their wing. Heck, I doubt they even know us by sight now, so just think: If we go off to the seminary, they'll spend a lifetime trying to figure out who we are. If we hadn't already guessed that, Bob's experience pretty much illustrates the situation."

"But hang in there, Bob," Manny said. "Just hang in there. And after this school year—the good Lord willin', we'll be with you in the flesh."

They all laughed again.

"That sort of takes care of us," Mike said. "We'll all be at SHS. We shouldn't have much trouble sticking together."

"Of course," Manny said, "we'd be closer if we were boarding. Then we really would be cemented. But we don't want to board unless we have to. And I guess that's around the middle of college . . . right, Bob?"

"That's what they tell me," Koesler replied.

"This thing we've left out," Mike said, "is the girls. They're going to the convent, not the seminary. How do they get to function in this club?" He knew his twin could take care of herself. Right now, he was thinking more of Alice than of Rose.

"I wondered when you were going to get around to us," Rose said. "When you"—she looked at Bob—"said we really ought to stick together, all I could think was: How we are going to do that when we—Alice and I—are going off in different directions from the rest of you?"

There was silence as the others all looked as if they were trying to figure out this weighty problem.

Rose smiled. "Look at it this way," she said, as she answered her own question. "We're united in our goals. We"—her gesture included all—"want to dedicate ourselves to service to the Lord. We can be cooperative and supportive to each other."

"Rose is right," her twin affirmed. "Heck, someday we might be assigned to the same parish. Not all of us at the same time . . ." He smiled. ". . . but someday Manny and Alice, for instance, could be assigned to staff a parish where

Alice is teaching in the school and Manny is assistant pastor . . . maybe even pastor. But even if a situation like that never happens, we'll always be there for each other."

Mike's commentary lost Manny. At first mention of a joint assignment, Manny fell into a daydream.

The reverie, as in Mike's scenario, revolved around him and Alice.

Manny's contact with Alice had been very limited. Typically, get-togethers involved him and Mike—usually stopping off at the Smith home going to or coming from some athletic event.

They would occasionally bump into Rose and her sidekick pal, Alice. For some reason—perhaps because Rose was Mike's twin—Manny never considered Rose in any sexual way. If he'd given it any thought he wouldn't have been able to explain this reservation; it was as if any sort of sexual activity between him and Rose would be . . . incestuous.

No similar reservation blocked his awareness of Alice's allure. As in the attraction of any couple, there were no rational reasons; it just happened.

However, there was no indication that his feelings were reciprocated.

Manny reasoned that it was better that way. An infatuation was not a sound basis for a chaste and celibate life.

The conversation continued as the participants searched for ways that this—what? club, group, association?—could be of service to or provide help for the two girls who now stood out, as a second-rate punster might have said, like sore nuns.

The group searched for some way of providing an even playing field.

The boys were on one level. Particularly in a parochial school, boys who leaned toward the priesthood were number-one class entities. Teaching nuns nurtured them, priests became companions to the present and future seminarians.

Next—and definitely ranking second—were the girls headed for the convent. So it had been and so it was now.

How would two girls headed for the convent be able to "be there" for three boys destined for the altar?

On this score, religious life did not differ all that much from secular life. Women had their place. In the convent, in the classroom, in the pews, in the hospital, in the cloister. All subservient to the priest. In secular life, the kitchen, the laundry, and, of course, the bedroom. Subservient to their husbands.

Manny's distraction notwithstanding, the group pledged to convene as often as seemed useful. Little did they know then how much support each would one day require.

15 CHRISTMAS DAY.

The Benson family had attended Midnight Mass on Christmas Eve. Stan was one of the altar boys for this ceremony. Three other boys also served. There was never a problem getting kids to serve at Christmas and Easter. Like their parents, they could be counted on to be in church for one or both of these reverent feasts.

This was a most solemn occasion for Lily Benson. Now that Father Simpson had "legitimized" her marital state, this was the first Midnight Mass since her earlier necessarily civil marriage to George Benson that she had felt worthy enough to receive Communion.

Most of the other people at Mass today would attend services sporadically throughout the year. For them, Mass attendance was little more than a superstition.

Not so with Lily.

Though not able sacramentally to participate due to her canonically invalid marriage, still she had attended Mass almost daily.

But all that had been fixed. That miracle-working pastor, Father Edward Simpson, had seen to that.

Now Lily was the life of the party. Not that she had embalmed and buried previous parties. But now there was a contagious lilt to her laughter and a special sparkle in her eyes.

The annual Christmas celebration was an occasion for joy and singing well-remembered songs. It was a time that provided a universal greeting for friend or stranger.

Merry Christmas.

Lily Benson was a special case. And those closest to her sensed that.

She bounced about the dining room, making sure all the decorations were firmly mounted. She had visiting privileges to the turkey. Periodically, she swept through the kitchen to baste the bird.

On one of these excursions, her sister Peg invited herself along. "Need any help, Lil?"

"If you want, sure." Lily was surprised. So lost was she in her private happiness that the offer caught her off guard. Ordinarily she wanted no assistance in her kitchen, where she reigned supreme.

Lily checked the pie, while Peg mashed the rutabaga.

Peg had guessed that her sister's extra spark had some connection with her spiritual life. All Lil's relatives were lately aware of and wondered at her taking Communion. Only Peg had the special entrée to question her sister. "Lil, what's with you and Communion?"

Lily spun around to face Peg. "I'm okay with the Church."

"That's great, Lil. But after so many years of your being away, it's natural for us to wonder . . ."

"Don't wonder. All you've got to know is that my wonderful parish priest fixed it all up."

Peg paused in her mashing. "How did he do that? I remember all these years ago, just before you married George, how we tried to get you married in the Church. I was even a witness for you. I mean, I know the problem was with George's previous marriage. But I testified that you were the kind of person who would not lie under oath no matter how you might be hurt by the truth."

"Don't remind me of that. It was the darkest time of my life."

"But," Peg said, unheeding, "the verdict went against you and in favor of George's first marriage."

Lily shuddered at the memory.

"And so the two of you were married by a judge. And I was your matron of honor."

"I remember all too well," Lily said. "You got into trouble because of being in my wedding party."

"It was worth it . . . for you, hon. Besides, all I had to do was go to confession and get the living hell bawled out of me—followed by a whopping penance . . ." Now it was Peg who shuddered. "Fifteen rosaries, as I recall."

They both laughed.

"So," Peg asked, "what happened? How come all of a sudden you can take Communion? C'mon, sis: After fifteen rosaries, you owe me!"

They laughed again.

Lily gently touched her sister's arm. "If I could tell anyone, I would tell you. All I can say is that Father Simpson has this wonderful dispensation that he had been saving for what he called a very special case. I'm not sure how George and I qualified for this great gift . . . but I'm not about to look it in the mouth.

"Just be happy for me, Peg. Just be happy."

"I am. You know that, Lil. And I promise: No more questions."

Lily brushed aside a tear. "Thanks, Peg."

"And I will personally shoot down anybody who bugs you about this."

"Thanks."

"Now," Peg said, "I hear that Stan is planning on going to the seminary . . . true?"

Lily glowed. "I've never seen him so happy. Of course, he's trying to keep it hidden. But I know my boy." She looked thoughtful, then continued. "I'm not sure that he really understands the whole situation. But he knows that George and I are ecstatic. And now he can go off to study to be a priest. It's what he's always wanted to be. I've had the hardest time trying to explain to him why he never could be a priest.

"He knew that I was very unhappy because he was blocked. But I tried never to let him know how guilty I felt.

It was my marriage that was blocking him. My choice of loving and wanting George stood in the way of what my son wanted for himself.

"All I can tell you, Peg, is that George and Stan and I were basically unhappy people. And now we're filled with joy."

Peg was grinning from ear to ear. "And I'm happy for you all. But, one thing, sister mine . . ."

"What's that?"

"You still owe me fifteen rosaries."

A modest-sized Christmas tree with all its lights and baubles stood in the small living room. In the Benson home everything was small: kitchen, dining room, bathroom, etc. The presence of the tree simply made the area seem more cluttered.

But this was Christmas Day. The feast only enhanced the miraculous events that had recently transformed the Benson family's life.

Dick Trent, Peg's husband, sat alongside George Benson, absently listening to some athletic event on the radio.

In the dining room, three young people played gin at a card table that would do double duty as a dining table.

Judy, twelve, and Jiggs, fourteen, belonged to Dick and Peg. The third was Stan Benson, close to Jiggs in age.

Though it was quite cold outside, still the thermostat was set higher than needed. Thanks mostly to the heat, Dick and George were fast losing whatever interest they'd had in the radio program.

"I hear," Dick addressed George, "that your boy is thinking of going into the seminary."

George, who had nearly fallen asleep, came to with a start. "That's the way it looks."

Silence. From the excitement in the announcer's voice, it seemed that one of the teams had done something noteworthy.

"How do you feel about that, George?"

"It puts me in a pickle."

"How's that?"

"I used to say that no man should have a boss who expects him to come to work in a dress."

Dick thought about that for a moment, then chuckled. "Yes, I remember. But what's the problem? I thought it was kind of cute."

"Clever, maybe. But not too smart," George replied.

"Not smart?"

"I said that when the kid couldn't go to the seminary . . . couldn't be a priest. I was trying to make it easier on him."

"Easier?"

"Yeah, you know—less disappointing. I mean, the whole thing . . . well, it was mostly my fault. You know how it was when Lily and I got married—"

"I should. Peg and I stood up for you and Lily at your wedding."

"Yeah, well that was that. We tried to get married in the Church. But the Church wasn't having any part of me and my first marriage.

"At first, I tried to bow out." Noting the surprise on his friend's face, he hastened to explain. "Oh, it wasn't that I didn't love Lil. Heck"—he smiled and shook his head in memory—"I loved the hell out of her. But"—the smile disappeared—"I was taking her away from her Church."

"That must've been rotten."

"It was! It wouldn't even have helped if I had become Catholic. Which I was willing to do. But it wouldn't have done any good: The Church wouldn't let me out of that first marriage. Or, rather, they wouldn't recognize that I was out of it . . . even though it was a disaster from day one. The best thing my first wife and I could do was bury our relationship . . ." He snorted. "Hell, it was long since dead anyway."

Silence. The small radio droned on.

"Boy," Dick said "do I remember that wedding of yours!" He shook his head. "I know the bride gets to shed a few tears. But part of the time Lil was acting as if it was the happiest day of her life—and the rest of the time it was like she was being taken to the electric chair."

"That's 'cause she was kissing her Church good-bye."

"So, what happened? We go to Mass with you and all of a sudden you've got more Christmas spirit than any ten guys I know." Dick turned slightly to face George. "And I've never seen Lil so happy . . . so really happy!

"C'mon now, what happened?"

"I can't tell you."

Silence. Dick frowned. "What do you mean you can't tell me? Am I your friend or not? Especially if it's good news—and from what I can see, this is plenty of good news."

George looked pained. "Dick, we—Lil and I—well, we're sworn to secrecy.

"But I can tell you this much: This pastor we've got over at Guadaloop—he's a miracle worker . . . a real miracle worker."

"You mean all it took was one guy to straighten this out?"

"Yup. He fixed everything. But, listen, Dick: If it gets out that he did this for us, it would—what was the word he used?—it would *compromise* him."

" 'Compromise him'? What in hell does that mean?"

"I don't know what the hell that means. All I know is Lil is back in her Church, our kid can go be a priest if he wants, and—you're not gonna believe this—I'm going to be a Catholic."

"No!"

"Yes! It's the least I could do for what Father Simpson did for us. Lil can be a complete Catholic. My boy can at least try to get to be a priest. And that makes him happier than a pig in sunshine. And that makes the old man"—George patted his paunch—"very happy too."

George peered around the corner. He could see about a third of the kitchen. But no activity. "And not only does it make the old man happy," George said, "it also makes him hungry. I wonder when they're gonna put some food on the table."

"Go easy on the girls," Dick said. "They're having fun."

The two men tried to interest themselves in the radio broadcast. The game being over, the program consisted of Christmas carols.

"Nice music," George said, "but by this time I'm a little tired of it."

"Want me to turn it off?"

George considered. "Nah; leave it on. It adds to the spirit of the day."

The three young people were now quietly playing Monopoly. They knew enough to keep the noise down. Otherwise their elders would shush them.

Judy and Jiggs Trent were aware that their aunt Lily was unusually joyful, much more so than even the season might have engendered. But they didn't know why. Stanley, of course, did know.

Judy shook the dice, counted the spaces, and moved her piece along the board. Try as she might, she just couldn't concentrate. "Are you excited?" she asked, beaming at her cousin.

"You mean about going to the seminary?" Stan had expected that next year's schooling would be a popular topic of conversation today. "Sure," he replied with as much enthusiasm as he could muster. "But it's still a long way off. First I've got to get through the eighth grade, and then pass the entrance exam. And I don't even know how important the interview is.

"So, as I said, it's a long way off."

"You'll do just great!" As far as interpersonal relations went, Judy knew two truths: She greatly admired her cousin, and she abhorred her brother.

"Yeah, you'll do great all right," Jiggs said. "You'll stay at home while us guys protect you."

"Jiggs"—Judy's voice cut the otherwise quiet atmosphere—"don't be such a jerk."

Stan blushed. He had come to realize that almost no one was without a strong opinion about ordination to the priesthood and the seminary training that preceded it.

As for Jiggs, there was no possible doubt about his allusion: The war and enlistment.

Stan felt a strong urge to reach across the table and belt his cousin. The more restrained response had much more going for it. It kept things relatively quiet. It was the Christlike thing to do. And it saved Stan from a bloody nose. Say what you will about Jiggs, he was built for combat.

"It's okay," Stan reassured Judy.

He turned back to his cousin. "That was not nice of you, Jiggs. The government sets up the rules; we just follow them. I know that if I'm accepted into the seminary, I'll be classified 4-D. But I didn't have anything to say about it."

Jiggs snorted. "Four-D! One rank above the guys who are deaf, blind, and crippled."

"I said," Stan repeated, "I didn't have anything to do with getting that classification."

"Why don't you leave him alone, Jiggsy?" Judy knew her brother hated being addressed as "Jiggsy." "It's your turn anyway."

Smirking, Jiggs threw the dice. He landed in Jail. "That's okay, little cousin. I'll keep the place warm for you. That's in case you don't get into your sissy school and you have to become a draft dodger."

Stan did not respond.

"Oh—!" Judy was at a loss for words.

The game continued virtually without speech.

The United States had not been officially involved until Japan bombed Pearl Harbor. So the war effort had now been underway for barely more than a year.

In the months immediately following Pearl Harbor, Stan had not given much thought to his being drafted. After all, he was only in the seventh grade. But if the war continued for another few years—and it looked as if it might—the possibility of his being drafted was a lurking reality.

It became clear that Jiggs was going to worry this topic as a dog would worry a bone.

Several turns went by. Without any particular effort, Stan was winning big.

Jiggs was not amused. "You know what I'm going to do?"

"Drop dead, I hope," Judy said through clenched teeth.

"Shut up, twerp, or I'll poke you in the arm!"

There were times when Judy had thought she might end up with a paralyzed arm from one of Jiggs's jabs. After that episode at the Stratford when she had threatened to reveal what a coward he was, Jiggs had backed off. But lately, he'd shown signs of reverting to his former abusive self. However, as long as he didn't follow through physically, she would keep quiet . . . at least for now.

It was Christmas Day.

The game continued.

In the blissful silence of concentration on avenues, railroads, utilities, and Jail, Stan relaxed a bit. He rested his chin in the palms of his hands and reflected on recent events.

Since school had started in September, this had been the most difficult period of his young life. The eighth grade became a testing zone for what he understood would be his seminary routine.

In all humility, Stan knew he was intelligent, and that he had an ear for languages. Memorizing the Latin responses for Mass had been a snap; in fact, his Latin was better than Father Simpson's. Stan's responses were clear and crisp, Simpson's mumbled and elided.

As a result of Stan's efforts not to stand out, his grades had plummeted. Oh, he was passing all his subjects—but in lackluster fashion.

He was doomed, he knew it. He would spend the rest of his academic life suppressing his ability, stifling his talent, and camouflaging himself in a cloak of mediocrity. And all because this crazy pastor for some unfathomable reason was set on Stan's becoming a priest. And Stan was trapped, with no way out without subjecting his mother to heartbreak.

Every way he turned, there was his proud and happy mother beaming at him. He knew he could sail through the seminary entrance exam. All he'd have to do was blow a sufficient number of answers in order to be rejected by professors who wanted intelligent students.

He could outright flunk the test. But there was Mother brought low again.

He could fake an illness. He could bumble the interview. He could do any number of things to make himself unacceptable.

He could even tell the truth: That he had never wanted to be a priest, did not now want to be a priest, and would not ever want to be a priest. More emphatically, he would be willing to do anything as an adult except be a priest.

In a way, he was hoist on his own petard. Hitherto, he had stood no chance of being accepted into the seminary—and thus not into the priesthood either. Secure in that knowledge, he had let his mother believe that he would have aspired to the priesthood had that door been open to him. It seemed to give her some comfort that he had an ambition that was sacred to her.

Before Father Simpson's heavy foot had entered the picture, Stan could luxuriate in two worlds: He could make it clear that he felt called to the priesthood and was saddened that he was not permitted to respond to that call. Meanwhile, he could be at ease in the knowledge that Church law barred him from pursuing the calling.

In a sense, he had dug his own grave.

Simpson had come up with the panacea. He had convalidated the Bensons' marriage by means of some sort of Missionaries' Privilege. Thus taking down the "Keep Out" sign that had happily barred Stan's entrance upon the path to the priesthood.

Stan was despondent. His emotions, his insides were in turmoil. And yet he was condemned to create the impression—and keep up the pretense—that he couldn't have been more satisfied, more fulfilled, more happy.

Meanwhile, he would be forced to carry on that mediocre existence. He had never even conceived of anyone purposely pursuing far less than he could easily achieve.

What a mess!

The doorbell rang. Only George and Lily knew who was

there: Father Simpson—their miracle worker—had been invited to join them for Christmas dinner.

Simpson had gladly accepted the invitation. While he did not check on Stanley's every activity, neither would he neglect an opportunity to follow up on his project—his investment.

Simpson stamped the snow off his boots, entered the vestibule, and accepted George's and Lily's effusive greetings.

The other guests exchanged wondering glances. Who could this be?

Simpson entered the living room every inch the hail-fellow-well-met. All eyes focused on his clerical collar.

"Who is it?" Jiggs whispered to Stan.

"That's our pastor."

"What's he doing here?"

"I don't really know," Stanley admitted.

George made the introductions. Following which, Lily announced that dinner was ready and, aided by her sister, brought the food to the table.

The diners gathered. Lily invited Father Simpson to "say the blessing." He leaned on the traditional, "Bless us, O Lord, and these Thy gifts, which we are about to receive from Thy bounty. Through Christ Our Lord. Amen." His articulation, as usual, left much to be desired.

He even messes that up, thought Stan. Simpson had, indeed, mumbled his way through the grace.

Young Judy Trent, eyes popping, was obviously deeply impressed. She had never related to a priest in such a relaxed setting. Her previous contacts had been quite formal. The pastor who ruled over Judy's parish church and parochial school was far more remote than this priest. She saw her pastor when he handed out report cards, moving from classroom to classroom, obviously taking only superficial interest in the young students.

Then there were Devotions, Mass, thundering sermons, and the like.

Judy was fascinated that a priest could be so . . . human.

And prove his humanness Father Simpson did. He led the opening table talk down the path of athletics—primarily football. Along the way he tossed off a compliment in Judy's direction.

He had won her heart forever. Or at least for as long as a young lady's infatuation would endure.

Father Simpson remarked on how grateful he was for an altar boy like Stanley. Always in attendance whether assigned or not. Always faithful.

It was all Jiggs could do to stifle a sneer; the priest might as well have been talking about a loyal pet beagle!

Unaware, Father Simpson turned his attention to Jiggs. "What a fine, strapping young man you are," the priest enthused. "What do you plan to do as an adult?"

Jiggs brightened. "I'm going to be a football player."

Simpson smiled knowingly. "Good idea, lad. You're built for it. But what about after that? The body can't take that kind of violence forever."

Jiggs's brow furrowed. "I don't know, Father. I'd have to think about that. But," he brightened again, "I know, before all that, I'm going into the Army. First chance I get. I wanta get me a Kraut or a Jap before they're all gone!"

His mother and his aunt gasped—but quietly, so unobtrusively that no one noticed.

The men, particularly the priest, smiled at Jiggs.

"Dear Lord," Simpson half prayed, "it does a person's heart good to hear such patriotism. So you want to get the enemy and win the war?"

Jiggs's father and his uncle grinned approval.

"More power to you, son," Simpson said. He turned to Judy. "And what about you, little lady—what are you going to do when school's over?"

"Oh, I'm going to work in one of the factories—you know, a war plant. I'm going to put planes and tanks together and help bring the boys home."

Simpson chuckled. "Until young Jerry here wins the war."

Everyone but Judy and Stanley laughed. Judy did not want her brother brought home dead or buried in some distant land. On the other hand, she was not about to line up along Woodward Avenue to welcome him back.

For one thing, how could she throw up her arms in celebration if Jiggs started hitting her again? She'd be totally paralyzed.

Stan once again sat lost in thought, only vaguely aware of the table conversation. He apprehended enough to appreciate the billing he and his cousin were getting. There was measured praise for Stanley's fidelity in Churchy things . . . mostly for his various services at the altar. And that was pretty much that.

Jiggs—Jerry—on the other hand, was a patriot whose lust for battle and killing was in the best tradition of Ethan Allen, General Grant, Admiral Perry, and the rest.

If Father Simpson was so gung-ho about the priesthood—ready and willing to ruin Stan's life—how come there was no push to recruit young Jerry Trent to the seminary and the priesthood?

Stan was tormented by one question for which he had no answer: Why me?

It was as if this priest had diligently made plans that left Stan with no relief, loophole, or escape hatch. If this was a deliberate ploy, it was devilishly clever.

Father Simpson was basking in the glow that virtually every Catholic home would on occasion provide: Nothing is too good for Father.

Merry Christmas.

George and Lily Benson looked on the priest as if he were another Padre Pio, with the power and willingness to work miracles on behalf of an otherwise uncaring Church. George and Lily were blissfully at ease in their newly achieved state of grace.

Merry Christmas.

Dick and Peg Trent were happy for their friends. They were grateful to Father Simpson not only for what he had done to bring the Bensons to Communion in the Church, but also for the attention the priest paid to Jiggs and Judy.

Jiggs seemed particularly taken with Father Simpson. That was all to the good; the boy was not as strong in the faith as his parents prayed he would be.

Merry Christmas.

Jiggs had been dreading this dinner. He was certain he would be cast as Peck's Bad Boy. After pussyfooting around for years, his cousin Stanley had apparently made up his mind to become a priest. How could Jiggs compete with that? In another setting, Jiggs's willingness—eagerness—to march off to war would have taken precedence. Here the spotlight would be on Stan. And so it had been until this enlightened priest had praised Jiggs's courage and patriotism.

Merry Christmas.

Judy had never expected to actually converse with a priest. Priests were so far above other people. In school, priests were known as "other Christs." One does not share small talk with a Christ. But here was a priest who was emptying himself, lowering himself to give full attention to a mere young girl. He had even applauded her vow to help win the war.

Judy was concerned. Had she given the wrong response? Most priests would have reminded a young girl of her calling in life. The pinnacle a Catholic woman could reach would be as a good and faithful wife and a generous, caring mother. Judy had answered bravely if not cautiously when she had declared that she would be active in the war effort. A sort of Judy the Riveter.

Merry Christmas.

Finally, there was Stan. A lad whose life had been turned upside down. He was trapped into becoming a priest. There wasn't even any doubt about his ability to achieve that goal.

Some seminarians had great difficulty meeting the academic standards of the seminary. Stan not only would not know that fate, he would have to compromise his own intelligence in order not to stand out. Even more would be required of him. He would have to adopt mediocrity as his way of life. All this so as not to risk arousing interest in his family history. His would be a lifelong concern, to hide from everyone his birth as an ecclesiastical bastard.

And once a bastard, always a bastard. The mere fact that, at this late date, his parents' marriage had been legitimized did not change the fact that he had been conceived and born out of Church wedlock.

The documents that he would present to the seminary in about five months would indicate that:

(a) He had been baptized. (That was correct even unto the date.)
(b) He had been confirmed. (Which he had been on the date in question.)
(c) His parents had been married in the Church. (In ample time before Stanley's birth.)

The marriage certificate would be a fraud, perpetrated by Father Simpson. And Stanley, unbeknownst to all but a few, would nonetheless be a bastard unworthy of and thus barred from the priesthood.

He was willing to accept Father Simpson's pronouncement that the laws and rules governing marriage in the Church were silly. But they *were* the rules.

He would be carried forward by his mother's happiness. That left Stanley in a dilemma too profound for one so young. It would take its toll on him.

Until now, Stanley had never hated anyone. He disliked his cousin Jiggs . . . but he did not hate him. Father Simpson stood alone as the object of Stanley's hatred.

Merry Christmas.

16 NINETEEN FORTY-FIVE WAS a monumental year. World War II ended with the unconditional surrender of both Germany and Japan. It was a time and a cause for great celebration.

On a much smaller scale, our seminarians were progressing in their advancement to the priesthood.

In September, just after the close of the war, Bob Koesler entered his senior year of high school. In almost any other scholastic setting he would be king of the hill. But Sacred Heart Seminary was not the usual academic scene. After four years of high school, the students simply passed into the first year of college. No ceremony, not even a certificate of graduation. And, of course, no prom.

Bob Koesler and Patrick McNiff had been the earliest in their class to bond. All due to that mixup when they'd first come to enroll. However, the bonding had expanded into a sort of subculture at three Catholic summer camps staffed by students of Sacred Heart Seminary.

These young men were together from September to June, studying, praying, engaging in athletics—all in intensely close quarters. Finishing their school year, the young men— now camp counselors—supervised, watched over, taught, and entertained campers from June through early August. Aside from special vacations such as Christmas and Easter, for these counselors late August was the only time to be with one's family.

Koesler was brought by McNiff onto the staff of one of

146

the three Catholic boys' camps, Camp Ozanam. It was funded by the St. Vincent de Paul Society.

Meanwhile, Koesler brought his fellow Redeemerites into this tight-knit group. The three, Koesler, Mike Smith, and Manny Tocco, became newly appreciated in their home parish. One cause of their acceptance was a new pastor, who saw the priesthood in its universal oneness. Another reason for this open-door policy was the dearth of Redemptorist seminarians.

This situation made Koesler ever more grateful for the Maryknoll missionary priest who had steered the young man to Sacred Heart Seminary.

A singular event took place halfway through the season of Lent. Starting on Laetare Sunday, Sacred Heart High School seniors were given permission to smoke at specific times and in restricted areas. It got to be a rite of passage.

On that Sunday, students who had started smoking earlier had their habit ratified. Those who had waited for Laetare— meaning Rejoice—began their coughing introduction to adulthood. A few—Bob Koesler was not one of them—declined the honor, but almost no one wondered if the habit might prove dangerously unhealthy.

Early on, when Koesler was a sophomore and his Redeemer schoolmates were freshmen, their relationship was more precisely defined. Koesler, McNiff, and their buddies would teach underclassmen the importance of being even one year ahead. In the spirit of kindness that should characterize the priesthood, the upperclassmen would make themselves available to the younger seminarians.

Naturally, Koesler offered his services to Smith and Tocco. The offer was pro forma. Smith was a gifted student, with a history of tutoring Tocco.

It was just as well Koesler remained unencumbered. Another student needed him.

Stanley Benson, classmate of Smith and Tocco, was on the scene, having passed the entrance exam and interview. Thereafter, he became virtually invisible.

At this age, Benson was the epitome of the ordinary.

Physically, he resembled a young Trotsky, while possessing none of the firebrand leadership of the Marxist martyr. His dark stringy hair looked as if he had combed it with an eggbeater after having survived a tornado.

Benson knew what was in his inmost mind. But he kept that a secret from everyone, including even his priest-confessor.

From his earliest days as a seminarian, Benson took stock of the dramatis personae.

The young man named Michael Smith would have been happy to add Benson to the list of those being tutored. But Benson knew the last thing he needed was help with his studies.

He had been careful to pass the entrance exam comfortably. Actually, he could have come close to perfection. But that would have attracted attention.

And that's how it had continued to this day in the autumn of 1945.

The whirlpool hair and indifferent grooming were part of his plan. No one considered Stanley Benson prime material for the priesthood. Because he . . . well, he just didn't look like a priest.

He had no need of academic help in any case. So he graciously turned aside Smith's offer. Benson needed to soft-pedal his talents. If he needed anything, it was to present a mediocre personality . . . and he would have to form that himself.

There was a student, however, who appealed to Benson: Bob Koesler.

Left to himself, Benson would have died on the vine. He seemed to have no athletic skills whatever. And seminarians—particularly those at Sacred Heart—were expected to develop athletically.

Stan would have been happy to be covered with spiderwebs. But that would have seemed counterproductive to what the seminary wanted to produce as priests.

The consensus appeared to favor exercise. *Mens sana in corpore sano*. A healthy mind in a healthy body. Besides, the object all sublime was to build asexual macho men. Sports aided in the creation of that matrix.

From Benson's observation, Koesler was a moderate to successful athlete, and he seemed genuinely eager to help.

Koesler, of course, was aware of Benson's presence on campus. But if he had been even two years rather than one year behind Koesler's class, Benson might well have disappeared in the mist. It came down to Koesler's knowing Benson's name and virtually nothing more.

But that was not Benson's aim. Underexposure was as bad as overexposure when one intended to stay lost in the middle—the goal of mediocrity. And so Benson approached Koesler, wondering if the senior might act as a quasi-coach.

A cloud passed before Koesler's eyes as he tried to place this scrawny kid coming toward him across the gymnasium floor. The face was familiar, but Koesler couldn't come up with a name.

Benson could see—he had expected it—that Koesler was drawing a blank. "Stan Benson," he identified.

"Oh, yeah, sure." Koesler extended his hand and gripped a weak fish.

There was a time-out on the floor and Koesler was toweling off perspiration. "Anything I can do for you, Stan?" If there was anything, Koesler couldn't imagine what it might be.

Benson explained his plight. He knew, and basically agreed, that exercise was good. But for one reason or another—not health; his health was fine—he just couldn't compete enough to participate in any of the demanding games that seemed so popular at Sacred Heart.

As Benson spoke, Koesler looked him over. He tried to imagine this lightweight in a football game. In time, a player might well wonder whether he should center the ball or Stanley.

Benson concluded with a plea. "Can you help me, Bob?"

Koesler looked him over once more. This was a case for Vince Lombardi. Except that Lombardi wouldn't have taken on the challenge. To think of Benson as having a killer instinct was to think that lambs are ferocious. "I dunno . . ."

"Please."

"Well, okay. We've got a half day tomorrow. Why don't we meet here in the gym after lunch and we'll see what we can do."

The next day, promptly at 1 P.M., Stanley, attired in brand-new basketball togs, showed up in the gym. His father had gotten the uniform for him. Delighted that his son was finally interested in sports, George dreamed of the day Stan would make a varsity team, even if only to sit on the bench. George Benson was a jock. Stan Benson was whatever the opposite of a jock might be.

Koesler strolled onto the court dribbling a basketball. He almost doubled over at the sight of Stan, but managed to contain himself in a Christian manner.

"Is this okay?" Stan's question referred to his uniform.

"I . . . basically, I guess so," Koesler said. "I don't know what 'team' you're playing for. But there's one important thing."

"What's that?" Benson was eager.

"That elastic thing you're wearing on top of . . . uh, on the outside of your shorts . . ."

Benson looked down at it. "Yes—?"

"It's called a jockstrap, and it's supposed to be worn under . . . uh, inside your shorts."

"Oh . . ." Stan was embarrassed and confused. He did want to be au courant, but he realized that to get the strap on correctly he would have to take off his shorts as well as the strap. This would have made him temporarily naked from the waist down. He hesitated, indecisive.

"Don't bother with it now," Koesler said. "Let's just get warmed up."

"Okay." Stan was determined to at least master enough of athletics to get lost in the crowd.

"Here . . ." Koesler called. "Catch this." He lobbed the ball at Stan, who awaited it with open arms.

The pass hit him in the chest and knocked him backward.

Koesler trotted over to make sure he was all right. He was.

Koesler led his protégé to one of the baskets. He started to explain the game.

"I know the object." Stan didn't mean the remark sarcastically; he just wanted to hurry things along. "No offense!"

"None taken." Koesler handed the ball to Stan. He didn't want to try another pass just yet.

Time after time, Stan threw the ball upward toward the basket. Stan was, thought Koesler, setting world's records. In perhaps fifty tries, not once did his shot reach the basket's rim.

Koesler considered mentioning this, but assumed Stan would realize that if there are going to be points scored, the ball would have to at least go over the rim.

Conclusion, after nearly an hour and a half: Stan Benson had no coordination. None at all. About the only thing accomplished was the providing of entertainment for boys who were entertained by seeing an athletic supporter worn in so imaginative a fashion.

Even a dogged Koesler had to admit that Stan would never score a single basket. Too bad; Koesler liked to see progress even on a modest scale.

Next, the teacher took his student to the basement handball courts.

There were six four-walled courts. As the twosome approached, the familiar thunk-thunk-thunk of the balls against the walls could be heard as in an echo chamber.

One court was open. Fortunately, it was the singles court. Stan wouldn't have to run as far. They descended into the pit.

Stan had never seen this game before. A few words of explanation were in order.

It didn't matter. Stan could neither serve nor return the ball. The shots that came anywhere close to being kill shots were the ones that hit Stan. And the only marks he got were the contusions that pock-marked his skin.

As they rested, though only Stan was perspiring, Koesler took stock. He had never encountered anyone so completely uncoordinated. In motion, Stan was a danger only to himself. Any opponent, in whatever sport, could damage Stan at will.

As the two sat on the floor, backs against the wall, a word came to Koesler.

Walk.

Walking must've been among the earliest exercises known to mankind. *Homo erectus,* wasn't it? The great primates who stood up on their hind feet.

When we first stood erect, there were no planes, cars, scooters, roller skates, bicycles, or anything else to ride. We walked.

"Stan, do you ever walk?"

Benson looked at Koesler as if he were an alien. "Well, yes. Of course."

"I don't mean 'walk' as in how you got to these handball courts. I mean serious walking . . . with some attention to speed and distance."

"Hmmm. If you put it that way, no. Not really."

Koesler told Stan to change into casual clothing—without jock strap, either inside or outside—and meet him at the seminary's elongated back porch.

Surrounding an area large enough to contain three football fields or five baseball diamonds, depending on the season, was a red-brick walk that did not lead to Oz. It didn't lead anywhere. If one stayed on the walk without surcease, one would travel in circles endlessly.

So, the two began to walk. It didn't take long for Stan to tire and experience breathing difficulties. At that point, Stan was willing—eager—to quit for the day.

But Koesler divined that should he let Stan off the hook, the boy would misread the purpose of this walking. Reminding Stan of the goal he had set for himself, Koesler permitted them the indulgence of resting on one of the benches along the pathway.

When Stan regained his breath, off they went again.

Fearful of his own weakness in backsliding, Stan asked if Koesler would continue walking with him. Koesler did not hesitate. Anytime there was a recreation break too brief for an organized game, there they'd be: Koesler and his protégé, walking around and around on the red-brick footpath.

As they walked, they talked . . . that is, once Stan was able to coordinate walking and talking.

As a tribute to Koesler's endurance and patience, before graduating from Sacred Heart Seminary, it was possible for Stanley Benson to participate on the basketball court.

Without the slightest possibility of helping his team in any fashion whatever, at least he could catch the ball. He could neither throw, dribble, nor score with it. But Koesler took inordinate pride in getting Stan out on the court without threat to his—or anyone else's—life.

They continued to walk together. To walk and talk together. Over the years they learned much from and about each other.

17 MEANWHILE, BACK AT Holy Redeemer Parish, the integrated high school students had long since gotten used to each other.

At first, there had been feelings of awkwardness and self-consciousness. Boys felt uncomfortable that, in general, girls knew answers much more frequently and speedily.

In time, competition gave way to an acknowledgment that it wasn't so much a case of gender as it was that some—be they girls or boys—were better students, were naturally gifted, and/or worked harder.

Mixing boys and girls in classes throughout the school still triggered differences of opinion. Some thought it was a healthy sort of phenomenon that would, in time, lead more gradually into the marital state. Which would be the destiny of almost all these young men and women.

Others agreed with one educator who warned that this physical proximity would lead to "the premature and un-healthy pursuit of girls."

Even though Rose—and Alice—no longer attended Redeemer, both girls continued to attend school programs, parties, and other social events.

According to those who dabbled in such ratings, Rose was among the prettiest girls in both Immaculata and Redeemer. She was also among the most aloof.

Making out with Rose would have been a dream come true for those who competed in that sort of thing. As yet, no one had even tried to bluff such achievement, although Rose was the object of many a pubescent male fantasy.

Eric Jorgenson, captain of the varsity basketball team, decided to give it a try. He was not averse to having Rose's scalp on his trophy wall. This in the face of dire warnings, from priests, and especially nuns, that premarital sex was sinful, harmful, and not all that much fun. It did not escape the attention of some students that these admonitions came from chaste celibates who really never should have had such knowledge.

Almost every school—in some instances, almost every classroom—had a boy who bore the distinction of being a filth fiend. This was true not only in public schools but even—gasp—in parochial schools.

In the parochial setting, the role of filth fiend was outstanding mostly because few could qualify. The opposition—those priests and nuns, not to mention Monsignor Fulton J. Sheen, and of course the Pope—had all the howitzers.

It helped that Eric was a jock. Not only was he captain of the basketball varsity; he was outstanding in football and baseball. The advantage of being, arguably, the top jock in school was that he was awfully good at physical activity. And his approach to romance was nothing less than physical.

Eric the Vike (for Viking) Jorgenson did not fish for perch. Girls with round heels were not worth his time and trouble, not to mention his reputation. So, one fine day, when the boys were feeling jocular in the locker room, the gauntlet was thrown. Would Eric the Vike accept the challenge?

Of course.

Eric was not a moron. Nor was he, like *Streetcar*'s Stanley Kowalski, more brutish than human. Although the term "delayed gratification" had not yet raised its sociological head, Eric was, all unknowingly, a proponent in that he was not unable to contain himself if the eventual reward was worth the wait. And in Eric's book, Rose Smith was close to priceless.

As added incentive, it was common knowledge that Rose was headed for the convent. That sort of feather had not yet found a home in the Vike's cap. Since Rose went to Immaculata and Eric went to Redeemer, his chances were few and far between.

But Eric had a plan. One constant in Rose's life was her attendance at Redeemer's cheerleading practice. Not because Rose was a cheerleader, or was even interested in becoming one. It was because Alice was a cheerleader ... rather she had been a cheerleader. And as such, when the Redeemer girls asked her to coach them in cheerleading, she said yes. And since Alice went, Rose went along with her.

Often, the cheerleaders practiced at the same time as the boys' varsity team. The bleachers in the gym were moved back against the wall, creating room for the cheering group to go through their paces. Rose would sit on a folding chair and alternate between studying and watching her pal coach Redeemer's up-and-coming cheerleaders in their routines.

On this Wednesday, Alice was busy at her cheerleading chores. Rose kept her eyes on Alice, but her mind was on Herman Melville's *Moby-Dick*. She had been assigned to make a report on the classic next week.

Rose's nose told her that someone had approached. The odor of perspiration—musky perspiration—was not unpleasant, just something that could take some getting used to.

She glanced to her left. It was Eric the Vike. His long brush cut stuck together like spikes. Sweat coursed from his hairline and ran off his nose and chin. He had plunked himself down next to her on a folding chair. "Rosie," he said, in as deep a voice as he could muster, "how's it going?"

"Rose," she corrected him pointedly.

He shrugged. "*Rose*. What's in a name? Somebody wrote that. Whatever. A rose by any other name . . ."

It didn't matter to him how important a name might be to a girl, as long as she had all the right equipment. And, judging from the curves stretching her sweater, Rose was endowed.

Basketball practice continued. Eric had decided he'd had enough limbering up. So where better to sit it out for a while than next to Rose? There was little that the coach or Eric's teammates could do about his dropping out. Their task with regard to Eric was to humor him. More than likely he would win the game for them with or without having participated in practice.

Rose shifted in her chair and moved slightly away from Eric.

He didn't crowd her; he stayed in his place. "I've been wondering," he said, "how come you show up at practice but you're nowhere in sight when we play a league game?"

She turned to look at him. "How in the world could you know that with all those people? . . ."

"It just goes to show you, how pretty I think you are." He smiled.

She was thoughtful. The gym could hold two to three hundred screaming fans. When it was Standing Room Only, three to four hundred. In such a crowd, how could anyone tell there was one missing girl?

And the reason? Because he thinks she is so pretty that she is outstanding in a field of hundreds!

Outrageous! Juvenile! Provocative! Inordinate! Preposterous!

But, somehow, sweet and touching.

Why would she fall for a line like that? Did God really make women that gullible? Even a young lady with both feet solidly on the ground? Even a young lady headed for the convent? Was this one of God's plans for procreation?

Whatever, it had softened Rose. She felt herself blushing.

Not far away, Alice stood motionless as the cheerleaders continued their practice. She shot Rose a disapproving glance that was close to a glare.

Well, who does Alice think she is!

Little Alice, who was almost groped in a darkened movie house. It was all well and good for Alice to feel warm and wanted and . . . female. At least she'd experienced the feelings that probably were part of foreplay. Alice could go off to the convent never to feel this warmth again, but at least she had the memory. While Rose would enter the convent totally virginal in every sense and wondering for the rest of her life what it might be like.

When Rose did not respond, Eric shrugged. "Well," he said, "who cares why you're never there for a game?"

He wasn't angry, was he? That set Rose to wondering. Eric was the jock supreme. He must have cared that she didn't attend the games. After all, it was his starring moment. He was the center of attention. Except that he didn't have her attention. Maybe there was something to this Viking after all. Maybe he wasn't all horns.

A basketball went whizzing through the air, a seemingly errant pass headed straight at Rose.

"Watch i—" An aborted warning from the player who'd thrown the pass. That warning was all there was time for. Peripherally, Rose saw the ball headed directly at her. In that split second, she was aware only that she was going to be badly hurt.

A split second later, Eric raised his hand and caught the ball. Not just knocked it away; he caught it. One of his ham-like hands shot up and caught the ball turned projectile. He grinned as he tossed it back onto the court. "Watch where you're throwing the damn thing! There are pretty girls here."

Rose blushed again.

She would have to rethink her opinion of jocks. Suppose she'd been sitting here with her brother . . . or with Bob Koesler. She would have been knocked senseless before either of them could have raised a hand to deflect, let alone actually catch the ball.

She had to leave Manny Tocco out of this scenario; Manny was undoubtedly able to perform athletically almost as well as Eric the Vike.

The boys on the court laughed. They had reason. This was number 12-B in Eric's playbook to set up girls for dates. And all it took was the collaboration of one of his teammates.

However, the feat of catching a screaming pass one-handed was all Eric's. He grinned at her. "I guess you owe me your life."

Rose bristled. "I doubt it would've killed me. But thanks anyway."

" 'Thanks'! That's it?"

"Well, what?"

"Tell you 'what.' We play St. Theresa Saturday afternoon. Come to the game. Wait for me afterward and we'll take in a movie. Then, maybe a burger and a shake. How 'bout it?"

It sounded innocent enough . . . perhaps too innocent. But she did not in any way intend anything more than an innocent acquiescence. "Sounds good."

"Terrific! The game, a show, and a snack."

"Okay."

Eric returned to the court and immediately sank four sensationally tricky shots. He was showing off for Rose and everybody knew it. The cheerleaders, impressed by the athleticism of Eric the Vike, looked at Rose with envy.

But not Alice. And she would have her say before the day was over.

18

THEY MET AT Alice's house. Rose arrived first; Alice had stayed behind to shower after her stint as cheerleading instructor.

By almost every breath they took, the McManns revealed that they lived in the shadow of the Smiths. The McMann house was a tad smaller, more "lived in" and older. The appliances that were new, or close to it, in the Smith home were on their last legs at the McManns'.

And of course Nat McMann worked for Henry Smith.

Alice arrived about half an hour after Rose. She went directly to her bedroom, where Rose sat with her nose buried in *Moby Dick*.

"Sorry I don't have a suitable brush," Alice said.

"What? Oh, it doesn't matter; I'll brush at home."

Alice did have a hairbrush, but it was a bit uneven. Her verbal swipe rolled unnoticed off Rose's back.

The point Alice strove to make was that she was poor—or thought herself such. And Rose was rich—or relatively so. "So did you enjoy yourself at the gym today?" Alice asked.

"About the same as always, I guess. Why?"

"Oh, nothing. It's just that you seemed to really be having a good time—at least that's what it looked like."

"Is there something I'm missing here? What are you getting at?"

"I'm talking about the Vike—"

"What about him?"

"You didn't exactly move away when he came over and sat next to you."

"Al!"

"You didn't move an inch all the time he was with you."

"Al, you make it sound as if I was seducing him."

"That's not the point."

"Then what *is* the point?"

"You were letting him seduce *you*."

"Oh, Al, that's ridiculous. For one thing, I did move away—right after he first sat down. And anyway"—she tossed her head—"all I was doing was talking to him. Just talking, that's all."

Alice plunked herself down on the bed. Her countenance was knowing. "Did he have something to say about how you never go to a game?"

Rose felt butterflies. Had she been taken in? She didn't want to believe that. "He said," she protested, "that he knew I never went to a game. But he certainly didn't seem terribly put out about it."

"And then you asked him how he knew that. And he said you were so beautiful that he would have picked you out of the crowd . . . even if there were hundreds in the stands."

"Some . . . something like that."

"And you believed him?"

"Why shouldn't I?"

Alice shook her head. "I never thought you'd fall for that kind of line."

Rose, the butterflies turning into worms, grew belligerent. "Okay, smart guy, if it was empty flattery, how come he knew that I never attended a game?"

"It's part of his routine. Two of the cheerleaders are in his harem. They're always talking about Eric. 'Eric this,' 'Eric that'—his pickup lines, his swagger, what a neat dancer he is, how they melt when he grins . . . blah, blah, blah."

Rose looked dubious, but inside the worms were turning to blocks of ice.

"Think, Rose: Has anybody—either a boy or a girl—asked you recently if you ever attend basketball games?"

She thought back. And the ice turned to an icicle. She didn't know why she remembered it, but it was suddenly quite clear in her mind. One of the cheerleaders had asked her that exact question. And Rose had replied that no, she never went to the games.

Wordlessly, she nodded. Then: "Why didn't you tell me?" It was almost a moan.

"How did I know you'd been questioned? And that bit about saving you from the ball? That's part of the routine too. It all fits. And don't tell me; let me guess: He's invited you to go out after the next game, hasn't he?"

Rose, now zombielike, nodded. "This Saturday," she said in a small voice. "The game. A movie. And a snack afterward."

"Watch the snack. That's when it happens."

"What?"

"The seduction. He'll probably take you to a little restaurant on Clark. It's a dark, backstreet place. There's a booth in the rear that, for all practical purposes, is his . . ."

"I'm an idiot."

"Don't be too hard on yourself. You are definitely not the first . . . just the most beautiful and intelligent."

The two fell silent. Now that Eric's little game had been revealed, Rose was thoroughly embarrassed and ashamed.

How *could* he have known she didn't attend the games? It was one thing to spot someone in the stands, quite another to know that in all those packed hundreds one person was not there.

And Eric's reaction to the seemingly wayward pass? Well, when you thought about it, it *was* somewhat incredible. Given the fact he could catch one like that, he'd almost have to know it was coming.

She had been a fool.

"How 'bout it, Rose? Want me to call it off for you?"

Rose pondered. Then: "No. Let me think about it for a while."

"You're not going to—"

"Let me think about it," Rose repeated firmly.

"Okay. You should be able to take care of yourself. You're nearly out of high school and almost into the convent. And I know you: If you say you'll think it over, that's what you'll do. So, we won't discuss it any more. You're a big girl now; you can take care of yourself."

Saturday afternoon. The gym was like church on Christmas or Easter: packed to the doors. Not even any standing room available.

Rose smiled as she stood, back to the wall, shifting from one foot to the other. Sure, in a crowd like this Eric easily could have been aware of the absence of one girl. Yeah, and if you want to buy the Ambassador Bridge, I'll give you change.

St. Theresa's team was out on the floor warming up. Then came the purple-and-gold-clad Redeemer Lions, led by Eric the Vike, dribbling the ball and leaving the ground gracefully for an effortless dunk shot. The crowd went wild. The outcry deafened Rose. She pressed her hands over her ears.

The din continued unabated, as Redeemer proceeded to first avalanche, then bury its archenemy.

Actually, the contest was between the entire St. Theresa's team and Eric the Vike. In the middle of the fourth quarter, Eric was benched. By that time the game was on ice. Redeemer's coach would save his superstar for future contests. Why take the chance that Eric could be injured and out for the season?

As the Vike left the court, the fans leaped to their feet in raucous ovation.

Eric sat on the bench, a towel draped over his head and shoulders. He seemed to be looking for someone in the stands. But he gave no indication that he had located the object of his search.

Sure, sure, thought Rose. He could tell that I either was or was not at those games. Ha!

The crowd filed out of the stands. The Redeemerites were ecstatic.

Rose took one of the now empty seats. She wondered why she hadn't delegated Alice to break the date. Oddly enough, Rose was keeping this date in reaction to Alice's last remark on the subject: Rose was a big girl who could take care of herself.

In time—in his good old time—Eric appeared. A mixed group of adults, high school and grade school kids ringed around, asking for his autograph. He was the soul of graciousness, signing each and every surface presented, including one young woman's arm. She vowed she would never again wash that arm. "I'll count on that," the Vike cooed.

Finally, aside from the janitor, who had begun cleaning-up operations, Eric and Rose were alone.

Eric, completely relaxed, walked over to Rose and extended his hand. Wondering where this was going to go from an innocent handshake, she shook his hand.

"How 'bout the Stratford?" The theater was only a couple of blocks away.

Rose beamed. "That'd be great. They're showing *National Velvet*. I'd really like to see that."

"Perfect! We'll get there just about showtime."

There was a fair crowd for a Saturday early show.

Rose was captivated by terrific performances by twelve-year-old Elizabeth Taylor, and Mickey Rooney in a strong supporting role.

Meanwhile, Rose waited, wondering when the assault would begin. She would tolerate a certain amount of hanky-panky . . . just until she had experienced what it was like . . . just until she felt what Alice had felt.

Truth be told, Rose was jealous. Alice shouldn't be allowed to experience one of life's more intimate relationships unless Rose could do the same.

But no furtive arm encircled Rose's shoulders. No roaming hand squeezed or caressed any part of her anatomy.

Perhaps he was saving the intimate stuff for the restaurant. If so, he seemed to be missing a good opportunity. Outside of the screen, the theater was pitch dark, and no one was seated anywhere near them. It seemed that the other patrons were completely absorbed in Mickey and Elizabeth and that magnificent horse.

The film ended. The lights went on. The patrons began to file out.

"Hungry?" Eric asked.

"Starved."

"I've got just the place. A little restaurant just a few blocks from here. Dave's Grill. Ever heard of it?"

"Yes, I've heard about it. It doesn't have a very good reputation."

Eric shrugged. "One of those things. The grub is first-rate. Neighborhood's not so hot. But"—he smiled down at her—"you don't have to worry about the neighborhood while you're with me."

What an ego! she thought. He can do anything—or thinks he can. Nobody would dare cross him; the consequences would be disastrous. Well, he *was* a good-sized, well-built young man. And any sports devotee in the area would recognize him.

Here it was: Dave's Grill. The neighborhood lived up to its reputation graphically. And the Grill followed suit. The food must be terrific, thought Alice; it certainly had nothing else to recommend it.

The interior of the Grill was paneled in dark wood and the lighting was at best muted. The owner—Dave?—smiled and nodded when they entered. At least Rose thought he smiled and nodded; her eyes hadn't yet adjusted to the dimness.

Eric ushered her to the rear booth. It was empty, as were most of the other booths.

Rose sat down with her back to the front door and next to the aisle . . . at least for the few seconds it took Eric to slide her over to the wall by edging into the booth alongside her.

Dave, still smiling, appeared. Now she could see that his smile was aimed at Eric.

"Hamburger okay?" Eric asked her.

"Sure."

"Two burgers, Dave. Mine well done." He turned back to Rose. "And yours?"

"Medium rare."

Eric nodded, then added, "And two Strohs."

Dave winked, and headed for the grill. He hadn't written down the order.

"Eric!" Rose said loudly, "we can't have beer. We're under age."

Eric smiled. "You're never under age when you're famous."

Dave returned with two beers. The aroma of the sizzling hamburger cut through the odor of stale tobacco and alcohol. Rose wondered whether she would be carrying this peculiar stench home with her. If so, how would she explain it to her brother—not to mention her parents?

Eric chugalugged almost the entire bottle. That she could understand. He must be terribly dehydrated and thirsty after all that sweating during the game.

She tasted her Strohs, and shuddered.

Eric laughed. "You've got to get used to it. I felt just like that when I had my first brew. Stick with it. You'll see: Before we leave, you'll be a changed girl."

She didn't think so. She didn't want to be a "changed girl."

Dave brought the burgers and two more beers.

Again Eric almost drained the bottle in one uninterrupted gulp. He urged Rose to drink up. Knowing she would never catch up, she forced herself to drink, but in a ladylike fashion—or so she hoped.

This was her first taste of an intoxicating beverage. Her head was beginning to spin. It felt a foot away from her shoulders. She shook her head as if to clear it. Eric urged her to eat; that, he promised, would cut the alcoholic effect.

She finished her burger and found another bottle of beer at her elbow.

"No more, please, Eric! This is my first time . . ."

"I wonder . . ." Eric was grinning. "I wonder what else may be your first time. Let's just see."

He cupped his index finger beneath her chin and raised her lips to his. Her resistance was only pro forma, not vigorous. She let her lips stay joined to his. It was pleasant.

Then she felt his tongue. He was pressing her lips to open. Her mouth loosened, and his tongue was inside, moving, exploring, probing.

She'd heard of French kissing, but this was the first time she'd experienced it. She felt the warmth build inside her. This had to be it; this had to be what Alice had experienced, if briefly. This was all Rose needed.

But Eric's breathing had turned to panting. Now he was all over her. His hand found her breast and began pumping it. Then his other hand was pushing up her skirt and forcing his fingers between her thighs. She tried to fight him off, but she was no match for him.

Finally, she was able to push him far enough away to be able to speak. And speak she did. At first, she demanded. When that had no effect, she pleaded, while continuing to fight him with all the strength she had.

Ruefully, she remembered Alice's final word in the matter: You're a big girl; you can take care of herself. And Rose had agreed: She was a big girl now; she could take care of herself. Sure! Then why was she struggling as if her life was at stake?

There was movement in the adjoining booth. Eric was oblivious. Singlemindedly, he was pursuing his goal. But he couldn't ignore it when two other bodies slid into his booth.

To say that Eric was not happy was a rank understatement. He had been *that* close to orgasm. Right on the brink. And these two voyeurs had cramped his act.

Eric relaxed his hold on Rose. She wriggled out of his embrace. She had never been more embarrassed. That two strangers had seen her like this! She looked over at them and gasped.

Her brother Mike and their friend Manny sat across from Eric and Rose.

No one said anything for several seconds.

As Eric glared at the visitors, a light began to dawn. "I know you jackasses, don't I?"

Mike nodded. Manny simply stared at Eric, face impassive.

"We played you somewhere this year." Eric snapped his fingers. "It was a practice game. We only played one of those this year. You're the guys from the seminary." Eric snorted. It was all coming back to him now. So what in hell are you doing in this bar? And why in hell are you horning in on my date?"

"It seems as if she was your victim rather than your date," Mike said.

"Wait a minute . . ." Eric looked at Mike more closely. "You look enough alike to be her—"

"Twin," Mike supplied.

"Twin! I'll be damned! A twin! So, your sister is a big girl. She can take care of herself. Why don't you two be nice seminarian girlies and blow! Before I really get angry."

Rose didn't like what she was hearing. Once her brother and Manny arrived on the scene, she was relieved, thinking her ordeal was over. Now, it was obvious that Eric intended to take up where he'd left off. Her heart sank. It was decent of Mike and Manny to come to her aid. But what could even the two of them do against this—properly termed—Viking?

"My sister is leaving now!" Mike could not have been more assertive.

Eric glanced at Mike, weighing the effort that would be necessary to lay this insignificant girl. Replacing Rose was simple enough. But what about his reputation? What would happen if it got around that he'd backed down before two draft dodgers?

As the seconds ticked by, details of that practice game reimpressed themselves on Eric's mind.

Father Karl Hubble, seminary faculty member, and coach of the varsity, was a friend of Dev Sheedy, Redeemer's coach. The two had arranged the preseason game. As the game progressed, either coach could whistle a halt and make necessary changes. No score was kept, but, as usual, Eric Jorgenson scored almost at will.

Thinking back, Eric remembered Mike only vaguely. After the game, Eric never thought of him again—until now. If it came to a scuffle, Eric was sure he could take Mike with no sweat—literally.

Now Manny was something else. This fellow Eric did remember. Manny was tough. He couldn't hold a candle to the Vike, of course. But he could absorb punishment.

After a couple of hours—practice games had no time limit—Eric had actually gotten tired of using every dirty trick he knew. His elbows had jabbed just about every bone and muscle in Manny's body. Yet the young seminarian had asked no quarter.

Yes, Eric remembered Manny. Now Eric was trying to figure out the next development in what was becoming a Mexican standoff.

Manny, still impassive, met Eric's gaze unflinchingly. "Maybe," Manny spoke softly but decisively, "I can help you."

"Oh?" Eric leaned forward. Secretly, he wished he could have Manny on his team. The two, working together, could strike terror into any opponents.

Impossible. But a thought.

"We are going to leave here with Rose," said Manny. "You can step aside and let this happen. Or, you can try to stop us.

"If you try to stop us, there'll be a pretty fair fight. I don't know if you remember the game we played. If you do, you'll remember that you played dirty and I played clean."

"Wait a minute—"

"No, *you* wait a minute. Just listen. Then you can decide what you want to do."

Eric leaned back with a sardonic grin. *Okay,* he seemed to say, *have your piece. Then I'll beat the shit out of you.*

"Now," Manny said, "I wouldn't have been as bloodied in that game if I had sunk to your level of playing dirty. So I ask you to keep that in mind. And, keeping that in mind," he repeated, "if you want a fight, by God, you're going to get one.

"Now, any way you want it, Mike, and Rose, and I are going to walk out of here together. If we have to walk over you, we will." He paused. "Or, we can leave peacefully."

All this time, Rose, now squeezed as far into her corner of the booth as she could get, sat wishing the floor would swallow her up. There was no way she could free herself. Eric blocked every path of escape. She could not drop to her knees and slither under the table—there was not enough room between the seat and the table's edge. And even had there been room, Eric's muscular legs barred the way. Rose had no choice but to sit and watch and listen—like a scared rabbit cornered by two boa constrictors. How could it have come to this?

"I suppose you've forgotten Dave," Eric countered, referring to the eatery's owner. "Not that I can't take out the both of you by myself," he blustered.

Manny didn't even glance at Dave, who was hovering within earshot, but out of arm's reach. "I doubt Dave wants a fight in here, whether he's in on it or not. The first thing that would happen would be that his establishment would be smashed to pieces."

"Before that happens, Dave calls the cops," Eric shot back.

"After serving alcohol to minors?" Manny shook his head. "I don't think so. One whiff of your breath—or Rose's . . ." Only now did Manny look up at Dave, who was sidling out of harm's way. Clearly, Dave did not want a fight. He certainly would not take part in it. And he desperately hoped that Eric would take his horns and get the hell out of what the proprietor hoped would continue to be Dave's Grill.

Eric watched contemptuously as Dave executed a strategic withdrawal, then turned back to Manny. "Look, little man"—Eric did not attempt to hide the derision in his voice—"what it comes down to when all your big talk is done, it's you and me." He flexed his fists. "If you aren't a whipped yellow dog, you'll step outside and we'll settle this."

"Eric, lad . . ." Manny was smiling like a bridge player who held the game-winning ace of trump. "Eric, lad," he repeated, "you've seen too many B movies. I'll go out with you anywhere you want. Anytime you want. You may beat me pretty good. But as you may recall, I can take all you can dish out, and come back for more.

"And just so you know I'm not volunteering to be your punching bag, remember that I can give as good as I get. And think about this: You sat out the fourth quarter of today's game. Coach Sheedy didn't need to rest you . . . and he wasn't trying to hold down the score. No," Manny enunciated slowly and emphatically, *"he . . . didn't . . . want . . . you . . . to . . . get . . . hurt!*

"Think about it, Eric, my lad: If we fight, I can hurt you. That I can promise. And I *will* hurt you. And that is not a threat; that is a fact.

"Your coach is *not* going to be happy. And if I hurt you enough, there go your scholarship offers. There goes your pro career."

Manny leaned back and awaited Eric's decision. Though he had spoken calmly, his fists were white. He'd been clenching them so tightly the blood had a challenge getting through.

Eric was angry. Probably more angry than he had ever been. Angry to the point of blood-boiling fury. But he couldn't dismiss the threat Manny posed. Even in his rage, he couldn't ignore the logic of Manny's reasoning.

Still, everything in Eric wanted to fight. It was all his combative spirit could do not to throw logic to the winds and take on this wop. But . . .

Eric stood up, took a step into the aisle, and, with a broad, sweeping gesture, he wordlessly invited them all to leave. The gesture was a graceful one, but his lips and his eyes were slits.

The trio had taken only a few steps toward the exit when

Eric called after Manny in a barely controlled tone, "You know this isn't over. I'm going to get you. You know that."

There was no response. The trio walked out of the restaurant without looking back. Mike and Manny were on either side of Rose, supporting her. She needed it.

After the stench of the bar, her first breath of fresh air hit Rose hard. "I need to get to the alley," she pleaded. "I think I'm going to be sick." And she was.

Mike supported his sister as she bent almost double and her system divested itself of the noisome elements.

Manny backed away. Suddenly he felt like an intruder. He knew Rose was terribly embarrassed. Having her twin by her side . . . well, that was what families were all about. But right now, he himself was an outsider, an eyewitness to Rose's humiliation. His usefulness, he felt, was over now that they'd gotten past Eric and out of the Grill. "Maybe it'd be better if I just left you two. You'll be okay now."

Mike was about to accept Manny's offer, when Rose lifted her head. "No. Don't go. I don't think I can be any more ashamed than I already am. Please: Won't you stay with us . . . at least until I get my equilibrium again?"

Reluctantly, Manny agreed. "Okay. I'll stay till we get you home."

"Home!" Rose's face contorted. She was reminded of the inevitable: She'd have to go home. "How can I face Mom and Dad? How can I go home?"

Mike stifled a laugh. "Where do you think you're going to stay before you head for the convent?"

"The convent!" Home was one thing . . . but the convent—! Her eyes closed momentarily in emotional pain. "That's never-never land now. After what I did today, how can I even *think* of becoming a nun?"

"Rose," Mike said, "you didn't do anything."

"Mike's right," Manny affirmed. "You didn't do anything. You were a victim. One more trophy the Viking wanted on his wall. You were an innocent victim."

"Then why do I feel so . . . *unclean*?"

"I guess because Jorgenson came so close to having his way," Mike said.

The memory of it flooded her consciousness. His tongue in her mouth. His hand on her breast. And worst of all, his fingers prying between her thighs. At least her breast was covered by clothing; under her skirt was bare flesh. She shuddered, and waves of nausea washed over her. She had begged him to stop. How could anyone be so cruel as to take advantage of a helpless being?

For his pleasure alone. That's how Eric operated. She could envision him torturing a dog, a cat . . . any sentient being. If Manny and her brother hadn't shown up—! Wait a minute: How did they know? Granted they were life-savers . . . but how did they know? The only person she'd told about her prospective date was Alice. It had to be Alice!

Now Rose felt anger. Her shame had caused her to be angry with herself. Now she could dissipate this self-directed anger by projecting it against Alice. How dare she!? How dare she violate a trust!

Rose put her suspicion into words launched like a weapon. "How did you know?"

Mike knew his sister; he anticipated her anger. "Now, don't get angry . . ."

"It was Alice, wasn't it?" she spat.

"Mike's right," Manny said. "You shouldn't be angry, Rose. Alice tried to talk you out of this, didn't she?"

Rose, head hung, nodded.

"When you wouldn't take her advice, she was scared for you," Mike said. "And she was right to be scared. You told her you'd be going to the game and then to the movies, and then for a snack. She didn't know which show you were going to see. And she wasn't sure which restaurant you'd be going to—although, based on Eric's reputation, she had a pretty good idea.

"But the only thing we could be certain of was the game."

"We had the devil's own time finding you in the gym," Mike said.

"But we figured you'd be in the background . . . and there you were—right against the wall."

Another county heard from, thought Rose; there was no way anyone could be sure that somebody *wasn't* at a game.

"It gets a bit sticky here," Mike admitted. "We followed the two of you from the gym to the Stratford. It wasn't easy, but once we realized you were headed down Vernor we guessed you'd be going to the Stratford."

"You didn't notice us, did you?" Manny asked.

"No, I didn't. And Eric didn't know either of you well enough to recognize you even if he had seen you."

"We sat several rows behind you," Mike said. "There was hardly anyone sitting around where you were."

"We thought," Manny added, "that he'd make his move when the two of you were alone in the dark. We were ready to move in. But nothing happened."

"Tell you the truth," Mike said, "when nothing happened there, I began to think nothing *would* happen."

"I didn't share Mike's opinion," Manny said. "Jorgenson is such a louse, I figured he would never pass up a chance like that."

"Anyway," Mike said, "we followed you, hanging back as far as possible so you wouldn't become aware of us right behind you. When we walked into the Grill we didn't see you at first. But Alice had told us about the rear booth. So we took the next booth. We didn't want to butt in unless it was absolutely necessary—but when we heard you pleading with him to no effect—well, we knew it was time to step in."

Her escorts were aware that Rose now seemed to be walking quite normally. "I think you can operate on your own now," Manny said. "How about it?"

Rose tried a few steps. She had her sea legs again. She turned to Manny. "I'll never forget what you did for me today. Never. Without the two of you I would feel that I didn't have anything to live for."

"Whatever *might* have happened would not have been your fault," Manny said. "Can't you understand that? *He* was the rat. You were his victim. Remember that, and don't ever forget it." He smiled at her. "I'll split now." He looked at Mike, then back to Rose. "We were supposed to call and let Alice know you're okay. Would you rather do that? I think you might want to talk to her yourself."

Rose nodded. "I'll do it. And again"—she grasped both his hands—"thank you, thank you, thank you!"

"Come on, sis," Mike said. "And whatever you do when we get home, don't let Mom and Dad get a whiff of your breath. You smell like a brewery."

"Still?"

"Still!"

Manny felt like punching something . . . smashing something. His adrenaline was high. He half wished that Jorgenson had gotten physical. They both probably would've been bloody by this time. But it would have been a relieving flow.

His habitual instinct to throw himself into a fight hell bent for leather had been muted. He attributed that mostly to the seminary.

Early on, the rector had made it crystal clear to the new seminarians in the ninth grade that fighting would not be tolerated. And that fighting was not only forbidden but could lead to expulsion.

Manny did not want to be expelled. As a result, he tried as diligently as possible to suppress this combative propensity of his and to settle disagreements reasonably and without escalation.

He sincerely thought today's altercation might have been an exception to the rule. Still, he was glad he wouldn't have to excuse himself for having come to blows.

Manny decided to walk a bit before going home. He needed to cool off, dissipate the adrenaline so that by the time he got home he could act as if nothing had happened. Concealing his feelings would be easier now than it would be if he had to greet his parents with torn clothing and a bloodied face.

Peace! There was a lot to be said for it. Getting through

today's confrontation without throwing a single blow seemed to him very definite progress in self-control.

What would he do if Jorgenson followed through on that threat of getting even?

I'll cross that bridge when I come to it.

19

LITTLE BY LITTLE, Stanley Benson was accepted into the fivesome of Bob Koesler, Mike and Rose Smith, Alice McMann, and Emanuel Tocco.

There was no perceptible reason for his admittance to this coterie. Granted, Stanley was the classmate of Mike and Manny. But an onlooker wouldn't have known it. Stanley just didn't seem to fit in anywhere.

With the exception of this small circle no one took him seriously. He occupied a seat in class. He participated in compulsory school activities.

Occasionally, he attended varsity basketball games. Bob, now in college, played on the college varsity, while Manny starred for the high school team. Also on the high school team was Mike Smith, mainly in a benchwarming role.

And then there was that walk around and around the huge playing fields. Now, albeit rarely, Bob and Stan might be joined by Manny or Mike, or both. But their addition to the core duo was generally the result of being in the company of Bob. And because, for short recreation periods, the walk was the exercise of choice.

Bob was aware that when he and Stan were by themselves, the younger boy chattered on about many things. Those who knew him no more than peripherally—that would include most of the others—just drew a blank when it came to his evaluation.

In class he was what might be termed mediocre—neither bright nor ignorant. He passed his tests with room to spare. Still, he remained little more than a body filling a space.

Before Stan entered the seminary he knew practically no one in his age group. Aside from his parents, he was close to no one, not even schoolmates. As for those who were assigned to serve Mass, when they condescended to show up, Stan would have a few words of greeting. He was never abrasive or mean-spirited, but never offered more than a casual hello. He was grateful for their company; it saved him from having to relate to the once distant, now overly familiar Father Simpson.

Because Bob Koesler willed it so, Stanley had his first peer friend. Stan had initiated the bonding. And, much as he would a poor waif, Bob had accepted Stan. In so doing, he had, in effect, invited the boy to come close and to open up.

Each year, the seminary rector delivered a lecture on what he liked to call "particular friendship." Since this sermonette was preached once at the beginning of each school year, any student who survived both high school and college heard the talk eight times.

And such a student would eventually find the theologate rector lecturing on the same subject. So those who endured all the way through high school, college, and theology would have been exposed to the subject twelve times.

During these repetitions, it might dawn on the student that the rector was referring to homosexual dalliance. Little time was spent treating heterosexual relationships. Thus, over the years, the seminarians learned, almost by osmosis, that females were the Enemy. Of course, as long as there were no females in the seminarians' lives, there couldn't be any problem relating to heterosexuality.

As mentioned, the seminary's objective was to form the asexual macho male. Not a simple task, but in a strange way it made sense. Quite simply, there was no expression of sex either in the seminary or the priesthood. Sexual activity was appropriate only within the state of matrimony. And then, only when the expression was open to procreation.

Everything else was forbidden. And most everything else was "intrinsically evil," a mortal sin. That included everything from masturbation to orgies.

Stanley Benson learned all this in an incoherent way. The elementary school he attended tiptoed around the subject. In the seminary the teaching was confusing and embarrassing, particularly to the priest-teacher whose lot it was to explain the subject.

Nor did he receive any enlightenment at home. His mother thought his father should be the author of one or more man-to-man talks. His father thought someone in Stan's school would surely inform him about the birds and the bees. In fact, Stan's dad was not even certain just how it worked for the birds and the bees.

The bottom line was that Stanley knew little outside of the obvious fact that boys and girls, men and women, were different from each other—and that, somehow, women had babies.

It was while he was in mid high school that Stanley had his first nocturnal emission, or wet dream.

Bewildered, he didn't know what to make of it. He couldn't recall ever having wet the bed. If he had, he'd been too young to remember it. He was most reluctant to ask any of his priest-professors. Not one gave any indication that he wanted to be of help with this type of problem.

So, in one of those walks around the playing field with Bob Koesler, Stan brought up the subject.

Fortunately, Bob's experience with wet dreams was a year earlier than Stan's. And that seemed natural, since Bob was a year older than Stan. Bob knew, from his own experience, that what bothered Stan most was the accompanying sense of guilt. That Stan had brought his problem to Bob was a rare blessing for the younger boy.

"Stan," Bob said, as they rounded the turn, "I did some checking around and I asked some questions. What I can tell you is that it's a natural occurrence. It happens to everybody. It's natural. There's nothing wrong. It is not a sin."

"Girls too?"

"Girls too, what?"

"Girls have wet dreams?"

Koesler stopped walking. So, also, did Stan.

"I don't know," Bob confessed. "I honestly don't know."

"If you find out, you'll tell me, won't you?"

"Sure. Of course."

He did find out. And he did tell Stan.

Even in the face of opposition from every side—home, school, Commandments, rules—nonetheless sex was a force with which to contend.

One could suppress it, confine it under the surface—but, like a cork, it tended to resurface. And it continued to be mysterious and confusing.

Stan had what might be described as a natural curiosity about the feminine sex. He had few resources to satisfy that obsession. For studies of human anatomy, there was the *National Geographic*—particularly when the magazine featured an article such as a study of equatorial tribes. For inhabitants of such areas there was little covering of breasts or buttocks. There was not all that much, if any, complete nudity in those pages. But the *Geographic* came closer to displaying the unclothed body than any other general magazine of that time. And the seminary library did carry the *National Geographic*.

As copies of this magazine piled up, those issues that featured exploring the North or South Pole remained in pristine condition, while those that showed the state of undress in places too hot for clothing were dog-eared nearly to shreds.

Sex was a subject that fascinated adolescent boys. And they reacted adolescently.

However, it puzzled Stanley more than it aroused him. He seemed more interested in the near-nude males than the near-naked females.

He wondered if something was wrong here. He might not have known that his reaction would be termed "unnatural," "gravely sinful," "barbaric." All he knew was that he was more physically aroused by males than by females. He didn't know why. Nor did there seem to be anything he could do about it.

What was natural to him was unnatural to most others. Not knowing what was happening—or what had happened—to him was frightening. One thing he did know was that he had to fight this concern alone. This was not a case of lack of coordination, or awkwardness in athletics, or walking around that stupid circle.

The question of whether he was homosexual was vital not only to his presence in the seminary but to his entire lifestyle. Stan had been presented with a dilemma that defied a facile solution.

Granted that he would become a priest and that he would keep all the rules, he would never know exactly what his sexual orientation was.

He would never know what sexual preference was his since he would never lie with either male or female. The prospect of "never" was so final. The thought caused him to question again whether he belonged in the seminary much less in the priesthood.

Resolving the ultimate question, as it always did, as well as every correspondingly similar question, was the awareness of his mother, her joy in his vocation—and her bitter disappointment should her dream of his priesthood go down the drain.

So, the only practical question was the public stance he would assume with regard to what he felt. Should he sympathize with the plight of the homosexual? Should he glory in the religiously correct stance of the heterosexual?

But each time he pondered this, he came to the same conclusion: He must, he knew, straddle the fence, as he ended up doing in each and every case. He would take neither side.

Stan was getting so tired of exhibiting a slithering backbone. But he had to face the fact that this would be his life, courtesy of his loving mother and his meddlesome, officious priest, Father Simpson.

20

IT WAS 1947. Bob Koesler was entering the second year of college. Mike Smith, Manny Tocco, and Stanley Benson were entering their first year of college.

What was happening to them could not hold a candle to the changes experienced by Rose Smith and Alice McMann.

They had been accepted as postulants, probationary candidates for membership in the religious order of the Sisters, Servants of the Immaculate Heart of Mary. They were seeking acceptance by the same order of nuns who had taught them from grade school through high school.

The postulants quickly learned that it would not be an easy life.

Symbolic of their "death" to the secular world, they dressed entirely in black, in the first of the habits they would wear on their progress toward final vows.

They would begin their academic study as college students, taking subjects such as English, history, and math. They would be affiliated with Marygrove College, while living full time at the Monroe Motherhouse. Academic success was of prime importance: They were seeking membership in a teaching order.

Alice, of course, knew this going in. She was not strong in the three R's. That was why her first inclination had been to join an order with the option of nursing rather than teaching. In the end, though, she went along with Rose to Monroe and the teaching nuns.

In the early years in the convent, the postulant, and later the novice, would be testing this new life to learn whether

182

this might be God's will for a lifelong vocation. But much, much more than that, the IHM order would be testing these young women.

The administrators looked for strengths and weaknesses. They looked for fidelity and humility. The spirit of poverty, chastity, and obedience—the three vows that would bind the professed to God in a special way.

Having stood the test of all this scrutiny, entrants prepared to test their vocation as postulants—probationary candidates. If successful, the next two years they would be novices. The first of those years was termed a canonical year, during which they took no secular courses. Instead, they studied such Church-related subjects as theology, Scripture, and chant. After their second novitiate year they took the three vows of poverty, chastity, and obedience, for a three-year period. This period was followed by temporary vows for another two years. Then came final vows—ostensibly forever.

It was a program tested over centuries that gradually led to a total gift of self to God. After being received into the order, on the ring finger of the right—not left—hand the professed wore a wedding ring. This signified that they were "brides of Christ."

Where the priest on ordination became an *"alter Christus"*—another Christ—the professed nuns became brides of Christ.

Other Christs and brides of Christ; two groups who in theory might be presumed to be made for each other, yet who in actuality could not be further isolated as far as marriage was concerned.

Little by little, the IHM postulant was introduced to a swamp of rules and regulations.

In the beginning, for instance, postulants could entertain visitors. However, the nuns themselves, after final vows, were not allowed to attend the funeral of both parents, only one. Rules such as these could test one's wholehearted submission to obedience.

Alice, Rose, and all the other young women, most of

them fresh out of high school, walked through the doors of the motherhouse to study, to learn, to test, and to be studied and tested.

Once inside the motherhouse, the postulants saw—most of them for the first time—the marble staircase that everyone was forbidden to use.

Welcome to a mysterious life.

This was the final academic year that Bob Koesler would be commuting between home and school as a day student. This would also be the final academic year that he would wear exclusively lay clothing.

Beginning with their third year of college, seminarians would wear a cassock and clerical collar. As long as the young man was within the seminary property—and not engaging in athletic events—he would be expected to wear this uniform during all waking hours.

On vacation, at home, or for a special occasion, regular clothing could be worn—preferably a black suit, black shoes, black hat, white shirt, and a black tie. Ordinarily, there was no problem with this ensemble. But occasionally . . .

Some forty seminarians were going to a University of Michigan football game. They—all of them—wore the prescribed black suit and white shirt.

The problem began when their bus driver lost his way. The contingent arrived at the stadium approximately twenty minutes late. A block of tickets awaited them. In the otherwise packed stadium, a vacant section of forty seats stood out like a sore thumb. Then the black-and-white-attired group arrived and one by one filed into their seats.

The sight of all those solemn-faced black-suited young men processing in made the crowd gasp, then laugh. Soon, members of the Michigan journalism class were joined by the opposing team's journalists—both factions attempting to interview the young men. Each team figured the other had hired these young men to pose as morticians, there to bury the opponent's team.

The seminarians were thrilled—ecstatic—to be permitted

to wear the cassock and collar, a distinctly priestly garb. For each seminarian, to one degree or another, desperately wanted to become a priest.

Next year, this distinction would be Koesler's. The following year it would include Smith, Tocco, and Benson. But for now, they dressed in civvies.

It was just as well. On their commutes, they rode streetcars that were usually crowded. Had they been wearing clericals, things would have been awkward, to say the least. In civvies they were just students boning up for class. Which—after all, was exactly who they were and what they were doing.

Koesler, Smith, and Tocco had long since perfected their scheduling. They almost always met simultaneously at the corner of Vernor and Junction to catch the streetcar and ride together to school. Frequently, depending on what extracurricular activities might delay one or another of them, they would meet for the homeward trip.

Stanley Benson figured in none of this. The Redeemerites lived in southwest Detroit. Benson lived in west-central Detroit. Their commuting paths were separate.

This late September morning was brisk. The conductor, stationed midway in the car, where he called out street names and collected fares, had turned on the heat. Though it was not hot inside, the passengers' conglomerate body heat made heavy coats uncomfortable.

Manny Tocco's stocky yet solid body warmed easily. He shed his coat. His two schoolmates retained theirs. All three pored over their homework.

"Did you find a mnemonic for all the words you had difficulty with?" Manny asked Mike.

"There weren't that many I didn't know," Mike replied.

"You'd better be serious about these mnemonics," Bob warned. "Father Merrill is serious about them."

Since he was a year ahead, Bob Koesler was able to tell his comrades what they would be expected to learn and how much emphasis the various priest-teachers would put on each subject. Expectations didn't change that much from year to year.

The students were given a series of frequently misspelled words. They were to report on the morrow, when they would either spell the words correctly from memory or have made up a mnemonic to help them get the words right.

Each time a student misspelled, he invariably leaned on the lame excuse that "I was sure I knew how to spell that word." Some performed in Barrymore fashion; some were rotten actors. Koesler well recalled Father Merrill's nearly going berserk when some of Koesler's classmates, searching for an excuse for having misspelled a word because they had not come up with a mnemonic, pleaded they had thought they knew the correct spelling. Father Merrill had hit the floor and the ceiling simultaneously.

Koesler was trying to prepare his schoolmates for an assignment they should not take lightly.

"Okay," Manny said, "here's one that's got me stumped: 'principal.' Now, I know it can be spelled two ways. Both are pronounced the same, but each spelling means something different. One spelling means the head of something like a school. The other means a rule or code of conduct. My problem is: How do you tell them apart?"

"I gotta say," Koesler offered, "that's one of the easier mnemonics around. You think of the head of your school as a 'pal' and that gives you the last letters of the word. So, by the process of elimination, you know that principle, ending in p-l-e, is the other one—the rule or code of conduct."

"I've got one," Mike said. "S-t-a-t-i-o-n-a-r-y and s-t-a-t-i-o-n-e-r-y: One means standing still, and the other is something you write on. But which is which?"

Bob by now was gaining the reputation among his protégés as one of the world's greatest authorities on mnemonics. "That was always a tough one for me until I stumbled on this," he said. "The one ending in 'ery' is the writing paper—station*ery* and pap*er*—they both have 'er' at the end. And again, by the process of elimination, that means the other one—the one ending in 'ary'—means something that's standing still."

"Hey," Manny exclaimed, "I think I'm catching on!"

Bob laughed. "Okay, I'll give you a free one. It hasn't come up yet, but it will . . . especially if you stay around here."

Both Mike and Manny smiled. This was fun!

"Okay," Bob challenged. "How many Great Lakes are there?"

Silence, as the two tried to recall.

"Three," Manny said finally.

"No," Michael corrected, "four."

Koesler shook his head. "Five. Now, can you name 'em?"

Manny took a stab. "Huron, Michigan, and Superior. But that's only three and you said there are five."

"And I said four," Mike said. "So, I can add Erie. But we're still one short . . ."

"Right," Koesler affirmed. "The missing one is Ontario. And now we come to the mnemonic: Homes."

"Homes?" Manny looked puzzled. Then his face lit up. "I've got it: Huron, Ontario, Michigan, Erie, and Superior." He grinned. "Hey, that's easy. I don't think I'll ever blow that one again."

The three returned to their studies.

It was standing room only in the streetcar. But the few who were left standing were men dressed for manual labor. Had there been one or more women standees, one or all of the seminarians surely would have stood and offered his seat. The trio's privately shared slogan was: Chivalry is not dead; it's just ailing.

Many of the passengers near the threesome were smiling. Some realized that had they themselves studied so diligently when they were in school, they might now be headed for a job at somewhere other than an automotive assembly line.

Bob Koesler shook his head in silent wonderment. He was preparing for what his teacher called a "pepper-upper" test. The subject was Latin/Religion. All it involved was translating the faithful old *Baltimore Catechism* into Latin.

To Bob, the project seemed useless—as if the Department of Studies had run out of honest-to-goodness subjects and, in desperation, had turned to the Catechism as a fill-in.

But he had to admit that at least it was an exercise in becoming more familiar with Latin.

For parochial students, the Catechism's questions and answers were as old hat as the familiar prayers the kids had memorized long ago.

"Who made me?"

"God made me."

"Why did God make me?"

"God made me to know Him, to love Him and to serve Him in this life and be happy with Him forever in the next."

It went on, seemingly interminably, through questions and answers about the Creed, the Sacraments, Church law, and the Commandments. By the time Koesler started this course, the *Baltimore Catechism* was like a tired old friend.

But the language of his Church rite was Latin. In only a few more years, when he and his classmates reached the theologate, Latin would be the language of textbooks, prayer, tests—and sometimes even conversations.

Getting more familiar with the language now made sense considering how frequently it would be used by major seminarians and priests. Every morning of every day, Bob would celebrate Mass at least once, speaking and chanting in Latin.

On second thought, he concluded, turning the venerable Q and A of the *Baltimore Catechism* into Latin was not such a bad idea.

He tried to write on his pad. It was challenging. Detroit streetcars ran on ancient tracks. There was a fair amount of swaying and bouncing. It was difficult not only to write but also to read.

The repeated jerking and swaying, and the heat pouring from the registers induced a subtle temptation to nap.

The car squeaked to a stop to let some passengers leave and others board. Suddenly everyone was aware of a new element. Raucous voices could be heard coming from the front of the car.

What was causing the problem? Only those toward the front could know.

The driver's voice could clearly be heard. He was telling the latest boarders that they would not be permitted to bring something into the car—something that from the sound of it they very much wanted to keep with them. The driver could be understood. The other voices were unintelligible.

Koesler thought he might as well go back to the *Catechism* and its Latin challenge as try to translate the loud gibberish emanating from the front.

Michael Smith glanced at his two companions. They both shrugged. Mike rose from his seat and stretched in an attempt to see what was going on. He wasn't quite tall enough. He too shrugged, then resumed his seat and his study.

The dispute up front intensified. The streetcar was not going to move until whoever or whatever the driver wanted removed was gone.

Something akin to an undercurrent of anger made itself evident. The passengers were not taking a streetcar this early in the morning just to secure a favored table on Belle Isle. They were going to work or to school. And they had no patience with anyone or anything that threatened tardiness or immobility.

Michael happened to be looking out the window absently when the car began to move again. It was then he saw what had been the bone of contention: A bare, life-size, inflated rubber doll was lying on the sidewalk. Evidently, the doll's escort had finally become convinced that the driver's threat to idle was not idle. Throughout the car, passengers nudged each other and chuckled as they pointed at the abandoned figure.

Michael was one of the few who did not nudge. His concern was whether he had committed a serious sin in gazing at this unclothed female effigy. The answer might well be in the affirmative; if so, he certainly was not going to throw temptation in the path of his buddies.

Meanwhile, the car recommenced its jouncing journey.

The atmosphere on board eased somewhat. One, most of the riders thought the doll was genuinely funny; two, the buffoons responsible for this caper were members of the U.S. Navy—though that branch of the service would at this moment be loath to claim them.

Anatomically correct or not, this doll, garishly painted and curvaceous, would be attractive only to a sex-starved adolescent. Which might have described the seminarians.

Regardless, the majority of passengers found the doll and the sailors highly entertaining.

By this time, the pranksters had reached mid-car, where they proceeded to give the conductor a hard time. They would have been ushered off the car had they not been servicemen. These were, theoretically, the guys who had won the war. Never mind that the war had been over for some two years. And never mind that these two "gobs" had stormed no beach more threatening than Coney Island. In this case, tolerance of bizarre behavior was the order of the day.

The sailors were in classic uniform: bucket hat, pea jacket, and bell-bottoms. The car swayed and jounced from side to side, and so did the sailors, never quite losing their balance, but never managing to stay totally steady. The duo allemanded down the aisle until they reached the horseshoe back of the car. There they stood, almost directly in front of the seminarians, who now had a good view of their backs.

The sailors might have found the students worthy of some sarcastic remarks were it not for the presence of a fresh, attractive young woman seated across from the seminarians.

The threesome naturally had been aware of her from the moment she boarded and took her seat. She was about their own age. Her features were well defined. A red beret topped wavy brunette hair. Her cloth coat was too warm for this car. But she was not about to remove it. That would have been bold on her part. Ladies frequently accepted discomfort rather than appear brazen by, say, removing an article of clothing in a public place.

She had seated herself as a proper young lady should, smoothing her coat beneath her as she lowered herself to the bench. Demurely, she had glanced at the three young men across from her. No more than a glance. She was left with her fantasies and they with theirs. The difference: They felt guilty and she did not.

Now, the situation was changed dramatically. All because of the two distractions in sailor suits.

Usually when a man is accused of undressing a woman with his eyes, the charge is the result of an educated guess. There was nothing ambiguous about the sailors' ogling. At first they confined themselves to nudges and sotto voce comments. But with no response from the subject of their gibes, their comments grew increasingly louder—and lewder.

No one said them nay, although each time the streetcar stopped, their ribaldries could be clearly heard by those nearby.

The conductor called out the next stop. "Michigan Avenue. All out for Michigan Avenue."

As the car ground to a halt and some passengers left and others boarded, one sailor could be heard saying, ". . . I'll bet I could get her to strip. Then we could see."

"What?" The other smirked.

"Whether she's got little tits. But solid."

They made no effort to lower their voices. Rather, they guffawed uncontrolledly.

The young woman was blushing furiously. Many nearby passengers were embarrassed—some for her, some for themselves, and some for both.

The three young men buried themselves more deeply in their books, though none of them was studying any longer. No one seemed impelled to interfere or intercede, although two or three passengers did approach the conductor to ask if he was going to "do something." But he was an older man, not at all up to taking on either of these two.

As the car started up again, the sailors ostensibly innocently bumped up against the young woman's legs, then snickered. The young woman seemed to shrink from the contact. As the two rocked back and forth, rubbing against her, Mike leaned across Bob Koesler and spoke to Manny. The streetcar noise drowned out his words to anyone save his two companions. "What," Mike was nearly shouting, "are the odds?"

"What odds?" Manny returned.

"Of these two guys being on this car doing what they're doing?" From his vantage Mike could see the sailors in profile.

Manny's eyes followed Mike's gaze. The taller of the two gobs was rhythmically rubbing his leg against the young woman's leg. She tried to tuck her leg farther under the seat, but could not escape him.

As the sailor turned to smirk at his buddy, in a flash Manny was able to see the face full on. Manny groaned. He knew where this was heading. Surely someone would intervene in the young woman's behalf. But not he. Please God, not he!

He'd had only one honest-to-goodness fight in his life. It had unnerved him much more than it had overcome his vanquished opponent. As a result of that one fight, Manny had learned something that he had hitherto not known about himself: that he had a terrible temper. What's more, he knew too that if ever he fought again, he might lose all control and go for the kill.

Ever since, Manny had lived largely on the reputation of that fight. Knocking opponents here and there on the football field was one thing; football was a violent game. But Manny played by the rules, even if he did occasionally draw blood. Probably, had he been a prizefighter, he would have done all he could to beat his opponent, while sticking scrupulously to the Marquis of Queensberry. But he would have, and could have, controlled the killer instinct.

On top of that, Manny had listened to the seminary rector warn his students that fighting could be a cause for expulsion.

All this ran through Manny's mind when he saw the sailor

full face. The young man was known to Manny only as Switch. Undoubtedly, Manny thought, the way his luck seemed to be running today, the bulkier sailor was Blade.

The last time Manny, Switch, and Blade had met, Blade was saved from death only because Mike and Switch had pulled Manny off him. Now they met again.

Manny looked down the aisle. Instantly, men became preoccupied with whatever they could pretend to be interested in. Some seemed disappointed and increasingly disgusted at the disgrace these young men were bringing to their uniforms. Still, no one was going to challenge the sailors.

Now, there was no doubt in Manny's mind that he had to get involved. He couldn't dump this on either Bob or Mike. Blade was too lethal for them. Indeed, he might be just as punishing for Manny to tackle.

The car stopped to take on passengers. The newcomers quickly became aware of a tense atmosphere. Riders aware of what had transpired were waiting for "the other guy" to do something. The car started up again.

Manny spoke loudly enough to be heard by everyone in the rear of the car. "Fella, it'd be a smart idea to get off at the next stop."

Blade and Switch turned with a "who—me?" expression to confront the idiot who had an evident suicide wish. Manny met Blade's stare without flinching.

"I got a better idea," Blade spat. "You get off. Even better, I throw you off."

The nearby standees backed away as far as possible, leaving the field to Manny and the sailors.

Clearly, Blade had no memory of their previous meeting. But Switch did. He lost a shade of his braggadocio as he mouthed just loudly enough for Blade to hear. "Don't you remember this crud? In the school yard? They were playing with a ball . . . remember? He kicked the shit out of you."

Blade shot an angry glance at his buddy, as if to say, Yeah, and after I kick the shit out of him now, I'm gonna do the same to you.

But he did remember. And remembering, he was momentarily overcome by severe qualms. The beating had taken place long ago. But it was the worst beating he'd ever suffered. He'd been bruised and sore for weeks after.

However, he'd learned a thing or two since then. And—his eyes slitted, his lips tightened in an ugly sneer, and his confidence returned—he was in the Navy now!

Manny was seated. Blade didn't have to seize the high ground; fate had delivered it to him. Manny had expected to absorb the first blow. He hadn't counted on its being so devastating. It was an arcing punch that caught him on the left side of the chin. The punch had all the power and impetus of having been delivered downward, carrying Blade's weight behind it. In the split second Manny had to think, he realized that Blade had come close to breaking his jaw. One more punch like that and he'd be sipping food through a straw.

Manny hunched his face turtlelike between his shoulders, compressed his body downward, and barreled up into Blade. He would have taken him to the floor but for the circle of onlookers; instead of going down, Blade was buttressed by the wall of standees.

Manny had removed his coat earlier. Thus, Blade's blows fell on thinly protected skin and muscle. Blade, on the other hand, still wore his heavy pea jacket. Manny's only open target was his opponent's back, but his punches had little punishing effect.

It was a combination boxing and wrestling match—a street fight. By sheer power of will, Manny worked himself to a standing position. His blows now could reach Blade's face.

Blade wanted desperately to destroy his opponent. But Manny drew on inner resources he hadn't been aware of. In a flash, Blade went down as Manny rained hammerlike blows, right and left, on the punching bag that was Blade's face.

It was over. Once again Mike, assisted this time by Bob, pulled Manny off Blade and literally saved the beaten man's life.

The fight lasted only seconds. Even so, Switch managed to get into it, punching Manny several times when his back was exposed. Bob Koesler moved to pull Switch away. But then, something unusual happened. The young woman who was the unwilling cause of all this, snatched off her sensible shoe and swung it with all her might, smashing Switch on the head. He crumpled to the floor.

Cheers rang out. In the few minutes they rode this car, the sailors had caused the passengers to move from an indulgent "boys will be boys" attitude to one of disgust and anger.

The two sailors were dragged from the streetcar. Several passengers volunteered to wait for the police to arrive. Military justice would follow police action and would be harsh.

The hero once again: Manny Tocco.

21 THE FIGHT WAS still within him as his buddies held Manny Tocco fast. Maybe, Bob Koesler guessed, it was like a powerful horse that had just won the Derby. The horse was not going to stop on a dime. Nor would Manny be as composed as he had been before Blade's onslaught.

Little by little, Manny unwound. He became aware of his newfound popularity as, one by one, his fellow riders congratulated him. He had seen what had to be done and he'd done it.

The young woman who'd been sitting across from them now slid onto the bench between Mike and Manny. "Thanks." From the tone of her voice she meant it.

Manny focused on her gradually as if coming out of a fog. "You're welcome," he said, not too clearly. His speech seemed to have some sort of impediment. He winced as he touched his jaw. Blade's first blow had done major damage. Manny was grateful nothing was broken.

She touched his jaw tenderly. It didn't hurt as much when she did it. "You guys go to school? College?" She included all three of the young men; she'd observed them studying.

"Yeah," Bob replied. He answered only to save Manny from having to talk, which was obviously painful. "We're at Sacred Heart Seminary."

Her eyes widened. "You're seminarians? You're going to be priests?"

"So we hope," Bob said.

She slumped in the seat ever so slightly. Then she

shrugged. "Nothing bad intended," she addressed Manny, "but if you change your mind, you could always go into prizefighting."

Manny's answering chuckle was broken off by a flash of pain. "You didn't do so badly yourself," he finally managed. "I saw you swing your shoe. Thanks. He was bothering me."

"What are you going to do now?" she asked. "I mean, you aren't exactly in shape for school."

Manny assessed his clothing. Nothing was torn, just soiled and mussed. "I think," he said slowly, "I'll go home and start over."

"You mean after all this, you're going to go to school anyway?"

Manny nodded. "As long as I don't run into those two again this morning, I should be okay."

"May I come along?"

He was incredulous. "Come along? With me? What for?"

"Well, I'm in college too. Marygrove. I'm a journalism major. I have a few contacts at the *Free Press*. If it's okay with you, I'd like to write this up and see if they'll run it."

His every instinct was "No!" If the story got published, the rector would surely read it. Manny was well aware of the boss's edict on fighting. Although this might be a special case, still it *was* a fight. On top of which, he had creamed a serviceman.

But . . . this had been a trauma for her as well. What the heck; the paper probably wouldn't publish it anyway. He nodded his okay.

She was overjoyed. She was certain this was a good human interest story—a chance for her to get into print. Go for it!

Manny and his grateful new friend left the streetcar to the applause of their fellow passengers. One enthusiastic fan began a chorus of "What shall we do with the drunken sailor, Earl-eye in the morning?" Enough passengers were familiar with the chantey to join in, making it a sort of accolade for the victors.

* * *

During the streetcar ride to Manny's home, he gave the fledgling journalist enough information for several stories. Words poured out of him. This was undoubtedly an after-effect, an escape valve for the adrenaline-based killer instinct that had remained even after Manny had been pried off Blade's pulpy face—and still had to be tamped down.

At this point, a bit breathless, the young woman left her deliverer to go in search of a typewriter.

Manny kept his explanation at home to a minimum. With a change of clothes, he returned to the seminary, where he had been reported absent from all the morning classes except for English. However, he had enough mnemonics at hand to please the teacher. He would gladly take the responsibility for tardiness rather than answer for the public brawl that had caused it. Mike and Bob had told no one about the fracas except Stan Benson, who by now was an adjunct member of the small clique.

All went swimmingly until the next morning.

The journalism student got her story. It was, as they say, buried on the front page. She had had a camera with her—Lois Lane was always prepared for any contingency—and there, swollen jaw and all, was Manny, just below the fold.

"Here's a future priest who thinks chivalry is not dead, just ailing." She thought her lead was pretty grabby. So did the city editor. Thus its appearance in a prized spot in one of the country's major newspapers. It didn't hurt her stock in a future at the Freep. And she'd been awarded what many aspiring journalists long for but never attain: Under the headline KNIGHT IN ROMAN COLLAR was her own byline.

The rector followed his usual routine: rise and shine, offer Mass, breakfast with the *Free Press*. Immediately, a blip in the routine occurred: Emanuel Tocco was summoned to the rector's office-suite. Manny didn't have to wait long, though to him the wait seemed sublime torture. He had seen the morning paper and he knew what was coming.

Another student emerged from the inner office. It was obvious that his appearance before the rector had not been a happy one; he resembled an early Christian just granted a temporary reprieve from the lions. As the victim passed, he nodded to Manny, gestured toward the door of the rector's office as if to say, "It's all yours."

Manny rose, summoned his resources, and entered the Colosseum.

The first thing to hit his eye was the morning *Free Press*, page one prominently displayed, on the rector's desk. Without formal greeting, the rector pointed to the news photo. "What is the meaning of this?" The statement was challenging but, oddly, the tone was more reproachful than reprimanding—almost conciliatory. That puzzled Manny.

"Well, Monsignor . . . uh, I think it was pretty much the way it says in the paper."

The Monsignor made no comment, just looked at him. Manny found the silence somewhat unnerving. "I think," he said, in an attempt at explanation, "that the girl kind of played down her own role."

"You mean the entire incident was her fault?"

"No, sir. I didn't mean that, Monsignor. She was a completely innocent bystander. Then those two started getting fresh, acting up, horsing around . . . uh, making improper advances." Manny was having trouble trying to come up with a term that might get his point across. He was uncertain how conversant the Monsignor was with the relevant parlance. "She didn't do anything to provoke them," he concluded firmly. At least he could get that point across.

"And then *you* entered the picture."

"I had to, Monsignor. What they were doing to her was wrong. And it was getting worse."

"She makes mention in this article that this was not your first encounter with these two men."

Manny shook his head. "My bad luck, Monsignor. When I was in grade school, they tried to bully me and . . . another boy." He thought it better not to drag Mike into this. "I couldn't believe the odds of our paths crossing again."

"What did you mean that the young woman played down her own role in this thing?"

"She whacked one of them with her shoe."

"With her shoe!"

Manny nodded. "Darn near knocked him out."

"With her *shoe?*"

"It was a pretty solid shoe. And . . . well, she must be a lot stronger than she looks."

"Mr. Tocco, have you given any thought to what you've done?"

"I've been over it again and again, Monsignor. I'm sorry, really sorry"—and indeed he sounded it—"that it happened. But I don't know how I could have done anything differently."

"Did you think they were going to rape her? In a crowded streetcar?"

"No, sir, I guess not. But what they were doing to her was already bad enough. They were . . ." Manny tried to choose his words carefully. "They were rubbing up against her. They weren't subtle. They were embarrassing her. She didn't deserve that kind of treatment. No woman does. And . . . well, I waited till I was certain no one else in the car was going to step in."

Silence. The rector studied the newspaper. Manny studied his shoes.

"Mr. Tocco," the rector said finally, "what if this incident were to have occurred some eight years in the future, when you were an ordained priest?" Manny looked startled, then thoughtful.

"Picture yourself on that streetcar when some sort of immoral conduct was going on. And there you are in your clerical garb. Would we find you wrestling on the floor? Or would we see you using peaceful means in coming to the aid of a victim?"

Manny did not respond immediately. He did not point out that his initial action was merely verbal, albeit threatening. He *had* invited Blade to leave the car.

He didn't mention that because, looking back, he was all too aware that his "invitation" had, in effect, been a challenge to duke it out.

Even less would he try to vindicate himself by pointing out that Blade had delivered the first punch. After all, he himself had thrown down the gauntlet by telling the bum to leave. From that moment on, Manny had known that Blade would throw the first punch.

As for the rector's scenario of a clerically dressed priest rolling around the floor of a streetcar, the point was well taken: Manny could not envision Bing Crosby's Father O'Malley wrestling with someone as a means of persuasion or to prevail or make a point.

Unexpectedly, the rector's attitude seemed to change. The change was so abrupt, it took Manny completely by surprise. In a sheer second the Monsignor moved from sternness to downright affability, with—was he imagining it?—undertones of amusement. "You don't offer much in your own defense, Mr. Tocco."

Manny shrugged. "I did it. I wish now I hadn't given that girl an interview. I truly didn't think it would get published . . . though she seemed pretty confident. But the fact is, I did it. And you're right, Monsignor: an ordained priest probably wouldn't have done what I did. So I'm guilty as charged."

Manny stood, shoulders drooping, before the rector's oversize desk, awaiting his sentence.

However, instead of passing judgment, the rector smiled. "I like your willingness to accept responsibility. That speaks well of you. Of course, I cannot condone your handling of the situation. But I can understand the courage it took for you to get involved.

"Had you been wearing clericals, you might have handled the situation differently. And be assured our formation program will eventually smooth out your rough edges.

"Besides, this publicity"—he gestured toward the newspaper—"is not all bad for the seminary and its students. The public can and will, by and large, understand that you are only in your first year in college. You have a natural immaturity that will disappear in time. But your willingness to step forward in a difficult situation is commendable . . . and should be nurtured."

The rector's affability disappeared as quickly as it had emerged. "However," he said, "we were speaking of formation. And as part of that formation, punishment must be meted out. I am, of course, waiving expulsion. Though that is the penalty for fighting, there are extenuating circumstances.

"So, Mr. Tocco, you will be jugged every Saturday afternoon for the coming two months." There was a pause, then: "That will be all, Mr. Tocco."

Manny was bewildered by the entire incident. From the appearance and conduct of Switch and Blade to the penance imposed by the rector. As he left the office, he encountered Koesler, Mike, and Stan.

"Did he throw you out?" Mike, of the three, was most concerned, since he had been witness to both battles—and a short-term combatant in the earlier one.

Manny shook his head.

"Did he give you any penalty?" Koesler asked.

"I'm jugged Saturdays for two months."

Mike was relieved. "That's just a slap, when you consider he could have expelled you."

"Come on," Stanley urged, "if we don't get to class, we're all going to be jugged."

Mike couldn't tear himself away. "Don't feel so bad. All you have to do is spend Saturday afternoons in study hall. You can do that standing on your head."

"You guys go on," Manny said, without looking at any of them. "I've got some thinking to do."

"You're not worried about the jug, are you?"

"No. No. It's not that. I just gotta think."

Wordlessly, the three left, each, in a sign of support, patting Manny's shoulder as they passed by.

Slowly Manny made his way to the impressive Gothic

chapel. All was quiet save for echo-like sounds. He was the sole occupant.

He made his way to St. Joseph's side altar and shrine. It was the Italian in him, he thought. Catholics of Italian descent seemed to have a special devotion to the husband of Mary. For Italians, March 29, the Feast of St. Joseph, was as important as March 17, St. Patrick's Day, is to the Irish—without the parade.

Getting down to the least common denominator, what had he learned from these two pivotal incidents?

He had a temper. An explosive temper. The temper now under his microscope was only a distant kissing cousin to the juice that flowed through him during contact sports. To react violently when provoked during football or hockey or the like was, he thought, natural. It resulted in no more than some penalty in yardage or playing time.

But being attacked by someone who was bent on seriously injuring him or another innocent party evidently brought out the beast in Manny.

Look, he admonished himself, you've been in a serious fight only twice in your life—both times with the same jerk.

But both times he had turned into someone he didn't recognize—sort of a Dr. Jekyll and Mr. Hyde. What would have happened had somebody not been there to pull him off? And each time, as he cooled down, Manny had realized he *could* kill.

How's that for your black suit and roman collar, Father O'Malley?

Manny had to program what he was discovering about himself into a future that was as yet unclear. Was the rector correct in projecting that the training he had yet to complete would smooth out his rough edges? Or was this tendency of his to go beyond the limit an uncontrollable element of his nature?

Now that the question was raised, would the mere fact that he wore clericals block him from a fight to the finish? Manny definitely didn't think so. It didn't seem to matter whether the provocation involved only himself. His first fight had started in self-defense, until he'd realized that Blade would not be satisfied by a Mexican standoff.

His second fight had had nothing to do with self-defense. Blade—and Switch as well—were harassing an innocent party. Once again, Manny had gotten involved. Once again, he had become so ferocious he might well have killed had others not restrained him.

And while he was at it, there had been a third—almost—encounter: The Vike. Once again, it was not self-defense: The Vike was harassing Rose. Once again, Manny had put his body on the line.

And if Jorgenson had responded to the challenge and he and the Vike had gotten into it, what then? Could he picture a Viking who would cry uncle?

Yes, he could. Strip the braggadocio from a pampered bully like Jorgenson and you have a coward.

Could he imagine *himself* giving up? Pleading for mercy? Not by a long shot!

If the rector was correct in supposing that the next eight years of seminary training would curb his violent inclination, then how to explain some of the priests he had encountered?

There were priests who had been heartless, cruel, insensitive, ruthless, rude, and the like.

Not that many, and not that often. But the ones who were sometimes brutal as priests must have exhibited signs of that disposition when they were seminarians. Did they hang in, keeping those tendencies under wraps until they were ordained? Were they ever homicidal? Did any priests ever kill? If they did, the secret was well kept.

As far as Manny could gauge his present state of self-knowledge, temper was his Achilles' heel. In all honesty, it could cost him his vocation.

22 CHRISTMAS 1947 HAD been, to borrow William S. Gilbert's term, modified rapture. At least for one postulant IHM candidate.

Alice McMann, now known as Sister Mary Benedict, was the possessor of good news and bad news. The good news was that the past holy season of Christmas had been the most profoundly religiously moving feast she had ever known.

The bad news was that it was the most lonesome period she had ever experienced.

When the Community was not in chapel, when the ethereal plainchant did not lift one from this earth, when the humdrum routine wore into one like a Chinese torture, even Christmas was a lonely celebration.

Loneliness multiplied because she knew she was under surveillance.

Sister Mary Bridget, the Mistress of Postulants, had had words with Sister Mary Jane, the Assistant Mistress of Postulants. The words concerned Sister Marie Agnes, formerly known as Rose Smith.

The subject: Particular Friendship.

The Postulant Mistress and her assistant had been around a long time. They knew what to look for in applicants to the religious life. They looked for stability, progress, humility, and, perhaps most, obedience.

They recognized that Sister Benedict was dependent. She was that to her core. It was her personality. But that, in itself,

205

was not a reason to discourage her from seeking the religious life.

As far as the Postulant Mistress was concerned, the problem was intensified by Benedict's attachment to Sister Marie Agnes. It was impossible to overlook the distinct possibility of a Particular Friendship. And that, very definitely would be grounds to dismiss the former Alice McMann from the convent.

Sister Mary Jane and Sister Mary Bridget pondered the situation, discussed it, and reached a decision.

Marie Agnes was summoned to the office after evening prayer. The other postulants looked knowingly at one another: It had to be about Benedict. All were aware of the tie that bound the two.

Was it a Particular or an Ordinary Friendship? The postulants were advised not to entertain these thoughts. This was for their superiors to handle and determine.

Sister Marie Agnes entered the office. Sister Mary Bridget was seated on a somewhat less than comfortable straight-back chair. Sister Mary Jane stood beside the Mistress's chair. Marie Agnes knelt with no support for her arms, which hung at her side.

"Sister Marie Agnes," Sister Bridget began, "you have permission to speak."

Rose nodded.

"I'll be blunt," Sister Bridget continued. "We have talked on this matter before. We continue to be concerned about your relationship with Sister Mary Benedict. We have observed the two of you and we are troubled."

Silence. Sister Mary Jane couldn't help noticing—and not for the first time—what a beautiful nun Marie Agnes made. Her beauty was not only external; her entire personality was most attractive. All in all, a beautiful young woman whose beauty was enhanced by the habit.

No poster ads could even hint at the special gift that such a gorgeous candidate of both inner and outer beauty could bring to the convent.

Religious life was not designed as a haven for women

who can't "get a man." It was for those who would settle for nothing but the perfection of Jesus Christ.

If convents were for castoffs, more likely Alice McMann would be there.

"I am truly sorry, Sister," Rose said. "We have tried to conform to the rule. Religiously."

The two elderly nuns wordlessly overlooked the pun. Indeed, Rose regretted it as soon as the word left her lips.

"We don't doubt the attempt," said Sister Bridget. "We wonder if there is any change as a result of the effort."

"We pray there is. Actually, Sister, there is little time in our schedule for any communication whatever. We never even sit together in most of our activities," Sister Marie Agnes said.

An ironic smile briefly crossed Sister Bridget's face. "For most activities," she said, "prayer, study, the Divine Liturgy, meals, and the like—alphabetical order is the rule. That is done for no other reason than to organize our routines."

"There are quite a few letters," Marie Agnes observed, "between our surnames, S and M, or our given names, R and A. Although not between A and B, our names in religion.

"My point is," she said, "that for two people who were the closest of friends in the world, we are learning to live apart."

"What you observe," Sister Mary Jane said, "about the separation your very names have caused, is valid. The only opportunity you two have to communicate freely is during recreation after dinner—at which time you are free to be near and converse with anyone you wish."

"Yes," Sister Bridget said, "and at such times, the two of you are invariably together."

Marie Agnes felt a blush beginning. She tried, but did not succeed in suppressing it. She was momentarily offended that anyone should take pains to spy on her. This was not, she thought, Nazi Germany. But she said nothing.

"The point is," Sister Bridget said forcefully, "no matter how much effort you have invested in controlling the situation, nothing much seems to have changed."

"But we continue to strive," Rose protested. "And she . . . uh, Mary Benedict is making progress."

Sister Bridget's eyebrows went up, as she and Sister Mary Jane exchanged significant glances, but her face quickly returned to its usual noncommittal expression. "I think that will be enough for now," she said. "You may return to your cell. Nothing about this to anyone, particularly during recreation period."

Effortlessly, Marie Agnes rose from her kneeling position. Both nuns couldn't help but note the ease with which the postulant effected the demanding movement.

Sister Mary Bridget reflected on her own osteoporosis. Long ago she had stopped blaming her weight loss on her meager diet and penitential exercise. She was fragile and growing more so . . . all due to the one thing she could not control: her advancing age.

After all, she was in her mid-eighties. It was remarkable that so many of the Sisters lived to such ripe old ages.

She was grateful for her mental alertness. That, along with her years of fruitful experience, made her especially qualified for the pivotal position she held in the Community.

Sister Mary Jane remembered clearly a time when she too could have sprung to her feet from her knees unassisted. And not all that long ago. Then, little by little, joints began to stiffen. Eventually, she'd had to surrender her driver's license because she was unable to turn her head sufficiently to see the blind spots on either side of the car. No one had demanded—or even suggested—that she stop driving. She had done so voluntarily, out of concern for others with whom she shared the road.

The doctors called her debility "degenerative." She could expect the condition to worsen. She only hoped that she could survive as well as her superior, Sister Bridget.

Both women watched as, with steady step, Rose left the room. Youth, they thought, and sighed softly.

Sister Mary Bridget sat impassively for a few moments. "I think it is time to speak to Sister Mary Benedict."

Sister Mary Jane nodded. "Yes, she is the Achilles' heel

in this twosome. Sister Agnes, I think, is finding this adjustment period difficult. But I also think she could cope very well if only Sister Benedict were stronger. I have noted that there is an invariable routine during recreation: Sister Benedict always waits before taking a seat to determine where Sister Agnes will be. Then she follows Agnes like a bird dog.

"And did you notice Sister Agnes's slip of the tongue? Agnes said that 'she'—referring to Benedict—is making progress."

"Yes," Sister Bridget said. "We simply haven't the time in postulancy to play games. It's time to take action."

"Shall I send for her?"

Sister Bridget nodded slowly and a bit sadly.

Sister Mary Benedict walked resolutely down the hall, wondering why she had been summoned to the Mistress's office—although in her inner heart she knew it had to do with Rose. That they might have to part was too painful to consider. The only thing worse than her being forced to leave the convent was the possibility that Rose would be forced out also. That simply would not have been fair. Whatever difficulty that presently existed was her own fault, not Rose's.

But maybe it wasn't that bad. Alice searched her conscience to uncover anything untoward. Something that in the outside world would have been meaningless, but in the convent would be grist for the public Chapter of Faults.

That must be it! That glitch tonight during the Chapter of Faults. The whole thing was so silly. It just sprang from ignorance. She could explain it all so easily.

Benedict had reached the door of the Mistress's office. She knocked and was bidden to enter.

It was like a tableau. Sister Mary Bridget sat statuelike in that uncomfortable chair. The arthritic Mary Jane stood by her superior's side. Their expressions did not change as Mary Benedict entered the room.

This was by no means a rare appearance for Sister Mary

Benedict before the Mistress and her assistant. By this time, Benedict had broken pretty much all the listed rules as well as some that had never been promulgated because no one had conceived of anyone's doing such things. Indeed, Sister Mary Bridget was constantly aware of Benedict's presence in the convent due to the regularity of broken rules.

So there they were again: Bridget sitting, Mary Jane standing, and Benedict kneeling.

"If," Benedict began, without waiting for permission to speak, "this is about what happened during Chapter of Faults this evening, I can explain."

Bridget almost smiled. She liked the girl. Benedict was a breath of fresh air—so spontaneous, so open, so irrepressible, so full of fun, so free of guile. But the girl's many likable characteristics did not necessarily recommend her for the religious life.

The incident at Chapter that Benedict thought was the problem involved the marble staircase—the one everyone was forbidden to use.

It seemed that Sister Rose—another postulant—was bringing in a shipment of dairy products for the communal kitchen. The basket containing the eggs was particularly heavy, and Sister Mary Rose was not a robust young woman. So, to catch her breath and renew her strength, she set the basket down on the sacred steps.

No sooner had she done so than she realized the enormity of her action. She had used the sacred steps! She looked around, but no bolt of lightning flashed. No thunder cracked. She was still alive and well. But, of course, in order to live with herself, she had to submit it—top of the list—at the Chapter. In doing so, she used unfortunate phraseology. "I laid my eggs on the steps."

Throughout the assembled community could be heard a ladylike titter. But it was Sister Benedict who sold the farm: She laughed aloud, openly, without shame. But only for a moment. Only till she realized that she was the only Sister who had reacted with lack of control.

Then, what to do about it? Guilt laid its heavy hand on

her. Should she confess this unnun behavior? Why confess something everyone could testify had happened? And if she did confess, how to do so? As you all know, I just made an idiot of myself publicly and at poor little Sister Rose's expense . . .

Or would the better way be to just let it sit where it was? At the end, that's what she had decided to do.

It must have been the wrong decision. Which was why she had been summoned to the inquisitor's office. The older Sisters had not laughed aloud—not because they didn't find it humorous, but because they had practiced self-control until it oozed from every pore.

Now, as Benedict recounted what had happened at the Chapter, the risibility of the event returned. Once again, Sister Bridget and Sister Jane called upon their ample supply of that self-control.

"No, Sister," Bridget addressed Benedict. "This has nothing to do with Sister Rose, or her eggs, or the Chapter of Faults. As a matter of fact, there isn't any rule about keeping a self-controlled silence during the Chapter."

"But, Sister, the Rule *is* part of the reason why you have been called in tonight."

Here it comes—whatever it is.

"There seems to be some enmity between you and the Rule," Sister Bridget said.

Benedict's brow furrowed.

"We think it has nothing to do with you personally," Sister Bridget went on. "It's just that with some candidates it seems that we can't think of enough things to tell you not to do."

Benedict thought that that was rather jocular. But she was done laughing aloud for the evening. And, as things transpired, it was well she controlled herself.

Sister Bridget nodded to Sister Mary Jane, indicating that the assistant should take over.

"Sister Mary Benedict," Mary Jane said, choosing her words carefully, "we have been watching you closely—as we have all the postulants. For everyone's benefit, the earlier we can make a decision about the candidates' future in the Order, the better it will be—the better it is for everyone."

Here it comes. O Lord, please let it not be Rose. Whatever has to happen tonight, it doesn't matter what they do to me. Just don't let it happen to Rose. I will take whatever they have to dish out to me. But not Rose. She will make such a good nun. Benedict squeezed her eyes shut and lowered her head.

"Sometimes," Sister Mary Jane continued, "it works to everyone's benefit to delay the process of moving into the novitiate and taking the vows. Once you move into that state, it is so much more difficult to turn back. The paperwork itself is taxing and troubling. Your difficulty with the Rule— particularly with regard to your relationship with Sister Marie Agnes—seems to tell us that it would be better on all sides for you to take some time off."

Benedict's blood pressure bounced at the mention of Rose. "This business with Sister Marie Agnes," she said, "there has never been anything remotely physical—"

Sister Mary Jane smiled. "We tend to agree that there is no reason for us to conclude there is any sort of Particular Friendship. But circumstances concerning the two of you, added to your regular problem with the Rule, prompt us to grant you a year's leave of absence."

Benedict paled.

"You know much better now what is expected of you. With this knowledge and awareness you will be much more able to understand the commitment required."

"Nothing will happen to Sister Marie Agnes? I mean, she can continue her life here?"

"Yes. For the time being we will see how she functions. At the moment, we feel we want her to continue. We believe she wants this too."

Some color returned to Benedict's face. Slowly an ambivalence took over. She was grateful to God for having accepted her bargaining prayer. She did not want to leave. Yet she couldn't really tell whether she was going to miss Rose more than she would miss religious life. Realistically, she admitted to herself, she knew she would more miss her friend.

And a leave of absence did not preclude the possibility of her returning after a year. She knew, however, that a year's absence would just about kill her closeness with Rose. If Benedict were to return, she would be a postulant once again, while Rose would be a novice. The gap between them would be wider and deeper—and their youthful closeness would be a thing of the past.

During the next couple of weeks, Alice spent every available moment in chapel, praying her way through this crisis.

Neither Sister Bridget nor Sister Jane pressed Alice for a decision. They knew the path Alice was taking and they could not think of anything better than prayer.

Soon, Alice was able to see the situation with clarity. She did not belong in the convent. She was sure of that now.

Rose had taken to religious life like a warrior to battle. But if Alice remained in the convent much longer, it would be a disgrace both for her and for her family when she eventually did leave. It was better all around that she go now.

Telltale wisps of hair peeked from out her wimple. Letting her hair grow out was a sure sign—which her sister postulants did not overlook—that Sister Mary Benedict was headed back to "the world."

Her decision was not reached overnight, but once arrived at was firm.

It was distressful to her buddy, Rose, who hated to lose her friend. But once Alice had left, Sister Marie Agnes was able to singlemindedly pursue her calling.

Suddenly, at afternoon prayer there was one postulant fewer. No one was surprised.

23

THEY MET AT the Smith home.

Rose of course could not attend. She was tucked away in the Monroe motherhouse. The meeting, called by Bob Koesler, comprised Alice, Mike, Manny, and Stan.

Stan traveled some distance to attend these periodic get-togethers. He did so more out of gratitude than anything else. If it weren't for Bob Koesler and Bob's friends—all of whom had adopted this solitary creature—Stan would have had no one to join him on his totem pole.

Alice was given the floor. She had some tears that needed to be shed. The four young men had understanding and sympathy that needed to be expressed.

Mike, perhaps more than the others, empathized with Alice. She had been a bosom buddy of his twin. Alice had spent so much time with Rose at the Smith home that it seemed from time to time that she too was his sister.

Alice gave a blow-by-blow account of her misplaced attempt at a religious vocation. The accounting was painful. There were embarrassing moments as she explained how ill-fitted she had been in Monroe. Silence followed her narration.

"What are you going to do now, Al?" Mike asked finally.

She sighed. "Try to get into college. Be a freshman instead of a postulant. Take a business course, I guess. Get out of my home as quickly as possible. The atmosphere there is kind of depressing. My folks had my future all solved. They had me filed away in a cabinet; they wouldn't ever have to worry about me again."

All four young men knew what she was talking about. Not in any practical way; after all, she had left and they were still in. But they had known of seminarians who had stayed in, even to the point of being ordained, rather than wound their families.

Of the four, Stanley Benson best understood. But he said nothing.

"Maybe I can help," Mike said. "My dad is on the archdiocesan Board of Commissioners. He's got a lot to do with how the money is collected and how it's spent." He smiled. "That's an oversimplification. But he does carry a lot of weight. I'm sure he could get you into any local Catholic college."

"But would he?" Alice was skeptical. "I feel like a kind of leper . . . like a failure."

"You're not! And we don't feel that way about you!" Manny said forcefully.

The others nodded agreement.

Alice was hesitant in believing anybody would go to bat for her. But Mike's confidence was absolute. "I think of you as another sister—even if you're not my twin—and Dad considers you as another daughter."

"Do you need time to settle on a major?" Koesler asked. "Do you know what you want to be?"

"No. I only know what I *don't* want: I don't want to be a nun. And I *don't* want to teach school."

"So much for the negatives." Bob chuckled. "How about the positives? What do you want to do?"

"I want to be a secretary."

"That's all!" Bob sounded incredulous.

That's all! Stan Benson thought. *That's all!* Like being a secretary was the lousiest job in the world! He himself would have given everything to be buried in an office, making things easier for his boss. Getting things right. Dotting i's and crossing t's. Writing speeches, not delivering them. *That's all!*

Yes, Stan mused, *that's all.*

Of course, he swallowed all he wanted to say. He wouldn't rock the boat for anything.

"Come on," Manny said. "If that's what she wants . . . good. She's had a religious vocation planned and imposed without her consent. Actually, when you come right down to it, without her even being involved. Just because her best friend seemed to have that vocation locked in. Well," he concluded, "I think it's time to support Alice's preference."

"You're right," Koesler admitted. "I didn't mean to put secretaries down," he said to Alice.

"Alice, I'm glad you spoke up," Mike said. "I was thinking of asking Dad to get you in at Marygrove—"

"Please, no," Alice broke in. "Not Marygrove. Not the IHMs. Not just yet."

"Right," Mike agreed. "How about St. Mary's Business School for Catholic girls? It's in downtown Detroit . . . right next to Old St. Mary's church."

"Sounds perfect!" Alice, for the first time, saw some light at the end of the tunnel.

"Just one more thing," Bob Koesler said. "The six of us banded together geographically—with the exception of Stan, who taught us that geography isn't that important. And, more so, because we all wanted—or thought we wanted—a religious vocation. I think that what's just happened here today maybe teaches us that friendship is more important than anything."

Spontaneously, they all joined hands.

"We're not the Three Musketeers," Koesler said, "in number or in purpose. But we *have* become friends. Good friends. Whatever happens to us in the future"—he spoke it as a prayer—"may we all be confident in our friendship. Okay?"

"Okay!" they fairly shouted, and then laughed the laugh of comradeship.

On everyone's mind was the pledge: All for one. And one for all.

The coming days would test that pledge.

24

THE DAYS PASSED slowly, as usually happens when one is young and eager to become an adult. Time was doing strange things to these six young people.

It was 1951, early in that marvelous decade of the fifties. Some later termed it the last age of innocence for the United States.

Sister Marie Agnes, IHM, had taken her final vows. Actually, the path had been smoothed by the absence of Alice McMann. Not that the two weren't still the best of friends. But without Alice depending on her, Marie Agnes could concentrate on her own formation. The Mistress was pleased. Everyone had taken it for granted that Mary Benedict—Alice—would not return from her leave of absence. Meanwhile, Marie Agnes was on her way to a spectacular career as a nun.

Her twin, as well as Manny Tocco and Stanley Benson, entered St. John's Provincial Seminary in Plymouth, Michigan, for the final four years of theology.

Bob Koesler was in his second year of the theologate. The scholastic year began with a bishop clipping a few strands of crown hair. The ceremony, called tonsure (a hair cut), symbolically made him a cleric, a clergyman.

Future ceremonies would promote the candidates to the minor orders of porter (gatekeeper), lector (reader), exorcist (one who has power over the devil), acolyte (altar server); and the major orders of subdeacon (who functions as such at solemn Masses and incurs the promise of celibacy and the monastic prayer of the breviary), deacon (who functions as such in a solemn Mass and may preach and baptize), and, finally, priest.

For these seminarians, things were getting serious.

Bob Koesler, for the first time, was aware that the priesthood was a definite possibility. Before these final steps loomed, he had doubted he was worthy of the calling he'd desired from the memories of his earliest days. The prospect awed him, and gave him sobering considerations.

Time for the final decision neared.

Mike Smith had no troubling doubts. He had just entered the major seminary and already he was living up to the promise he had shown at Sacred Heart. Time dragged for Mike. He was eager to get through these "preliminaries" and get on with saving the world. He felt he could learn all he needed to be an exemplary priest in far less than the appointed four years. He filled the empty moments by tutoring Manny Tocco, who did not particularly need the help. But it did sharpen Manny's grasp of ancient and now all-but-buried heresies. The doubts he harbored about the final steps of his vocation were deep. He kept them in his heart and told no one. He still had four years before a final decision. In the meantime, he wondered. Time was closing in on Manny.

Then there was Stanley Benson. For him, time was running ahead of itself. His seminary career had been passingly successful based on his academic record and evidence of his spiritual life. His teachers and guides saw little to recommend and even less to criticize. Stanley had been the very personification of mediocrity. That had not been easy. He was far brighter than anyone—except for Bob Koesler, who remained Stan's confidant—could have guessed.

Now Stan was in the major seminary. His mother was overjoyed. Even his father felt a deepening pride in his son. At one time, Stan's parents, especially his father, had feared he would amount to nothing much. They recalled mention of a secretarial future. Thank God and Father Ed Simpson that Stan had recognized his sublime vocation and was following the road. Please, his mother prayed, give me at least four years so I can share his triumph.

Stan wished time would stop dead in its tracks. He knew it would not.

Time was deceiving Alice McMann.

She had completed her business course at St. Mary's and gone on to take a bachelor's degree in Liberal Arts. She was now Alice McMann, B.A. Prospects would have been bleak for a prestigious position as secretary had it not been for two developments. One, she had specialized in the legal field. Two, she had the backing and endorsement of Henry Smith, father of Mike and Rose. She put together this package and took it to the legal firm of Schoenherr, Brady, and Rostovitch, one of Michigan's most prestigious law firms. She was interviewed by Johnny Piccolo, an up-and-coming young member of the firm.

The interview went well. Piccolo was a bit puzzled over Alice's seeming lack of ambition. But that, he thought, was all to the good: He wouldn't have to worry about her leaving him and trying to work her way up to being secretary to the head of the firm.

Technically, Alice was a dream come true. This was a day when, if there was a typographical error on a Last Will and Testament, no erasures were allowed; the typist had to start from scratch. Alice knew about the demands of this profession; the better the firm the less tolerance of imperfection. She was up to that and any other demand the firm—or John Piccolo, her boss, might make.

And there were some demands that would be made later on.

Time seemed to be on her side. She was only twenty-one. Her whole adult life was ahead of her.

Her social life was blossoming as well. The firm's other secretaries knew it long before Alice was aware of it. John Piccolo was putting the full court press on Alice. It seemed she was the last to realize what was going on.

It started with working after hours. Then late-night dinners. Then weekends aboard a friend's yacht on the Detroit

River, Lake St. Clair, or Lake Huron. Few would believe this relationship remained platonic. But it did. Perhaps not in the strictest sense . . . but there was no intimate sexual contact.

Alice began to wonder whether John might be homosexual. But a couple of his former girlfriends assured her that was not the case. They also implied that there were things that were worse than being homosexual. Either these friends were not convincing, or Alice was blinded by the respect John showed her.

In any case, he proposed, and Alice accepted.

Before even her parents, Alice told Rose—Sister Marie Agnes—who was pleased that Alice was so happy. But Rose had reservations—reservations she did not share with Alice.

Of course Rose could not attend the wedding. But she asked for—and received—all the details.

Italians tend toward Catholicism. So it was no surprise that Piccolo was Catholic. The wedding and nuptial Mass was celebrated at Old Saint Mary's downtown. Bob Koesler organized the liturgy insofar as arranging for himself, Mike, Manny, and Stan to serve the Mass. Since the theologate students were permitted to wear cassock, surplice, and clerical collar, it looked for all the world as if four priests were playing the part of altar boys.

The wedding brunch was held at Roma Café near Farmers' Market. There were toasts, an open bar, an Italian buffet, and plenty of Chianti.

The couple spent the night at a downtown hotel, and in the morning they were off to Acapulco. Then they virtually dropped out of sight.

When Alice quit her job, John Piccolo lost the best secretary in the firm.

Early May 1954. Only one month before the Class of '55 would receive the first of the major orders: the subdiaconate. In June, the Reverend Mr. Robert Koesler would become Father Robert Koesler. And Smith, Tocco, and Benson would become Reverend Misters.

Koesler was on cloud nine. Smith was in seventh heaven. Benson was resigned. And Tocco was uncertain.

Just as it was markedly easier for Alice to quit the convent while still a postulant without having taken vows, similarly it was far easier to leave the seminary before the subdiaconate and its commitment to celibacy. This was Manny's last chance. The subdiaconate was a commitment, not an empty ceremony.

Ordinarily, a candidate for Holy Orders who was doubtful at this stage would have a most serious talk with his spiritual director. However, peculiar circumstances led Manny to consult with his small but tight clique. He revealed and explained his uncertainty.

Koesler and Smith were shocked. Benson was envious. Backing away from the priesthood at this stage might devastate Manny's parents. Whereas, were Benson to follow suit, his parents would be rendered somewhere between psychotic and comatose.

In the end, Manny's advisers would agree that such doubts called for a request for a leave of absence. Manny concurred. He asked for the leave. The faculty thought it a wise move. The leave was granted. If Manny were to return after such a late decision, his would be a most rare case. Meanwhile, his parents would hang in, hoping against hope that he would go back and go on.

Back in "the world," Manny learned that there was no significant demand in business or industry for a theology major. But he applied to and interviewed with as many as possible. His parents provided some monetary help. But they did not encourage, nor did Manny want domestic welfare.

He was twenty-four and had never been on an actual date. He was attractive to the biologically eager females. But he didn't know that. He tried several dates with the young journalism major. Now a staff writer at the *Detroit Free Press,* she set up an interview with the paper's city editor. It didn't hurt that this editor happened to be Catholic.

Manny had an extensive background in English. Even Latin took a backseat to English in the seminary. It also didn't hurt that the city editor had just dealt with a tryout reporter who turned in abysmal copy. To the degree that on one occasion, the editor snarled, "Boy, you have misspelled Cincinnati so badly it can't be fixed!"

Manny was aware of and good at correct English. Finally, it didn't hurt that he'd been recommended by a competent reporter. He was hired.

With a job of which he could be proud, things began to look up.

Feeling a little carefree, he phoned Alice Piccolo. He brought her up to speed. He talked to her quite a while and he wondered that she didn't invite him over for dinner. He was about to hang up when the invitation was extended. More curious than offended, he accepted.

He arrived at 8 P.M. She opened the door. He was jolted. Her left cheek was bruised and her left eye was on its way to being swollen shut.

He stood in the doorway holding a bottle of wine. At sight of her injuries the normal amenities had stalled. He became aware that he was staring. Pulling himself together, he thrust the bottle at her.

She thanked him awkwardly. She seemed to find speech difficult. Perhaps there was more damage to her cheek than was obvious.

"Alice, what happened—" Manny was interrupted by a presence at her shoulder. It was John Piccolo, drink in hand.

"Well," Piccolo said, "if it isn't the Knight'n Shining Armor!"

Manny had met his host fleetingly at the McMann-Piccolo nuptials. He hadn't seen him since. Now he measured the man. A bit larger than Manny, Piccolo looked as if he worked out regularly. He was well proportioned. But, thought Manny, based on Piccolo's slurred speech, he sure didn't need that drink. Uncertain how to respond to his host's ambiguous welcome, Manny said nothing.

Piccolo addressed his wife. "Arnsha gonna invite your Sirlanslot in?"

Manny began to feel extremely awkward. He had expected to find adoring newlyweds, sharing a love that was exclusive and blossoming. He was finding its antithesis.

Johnny grabbed the bottle from Alice's hands. "Jus' what we need," he gurgled, "more booze." He shoved his wife toward the kitchen. "Go on! Get supp'r onna table. Show your ers'while boyfriend you're good for somethin'."

Alice stumbled from the shove and almost fell. But, wordlessly, she made it to the kitchen and quickly became absorbed in what she was doing.

"C'mon in." Johnny led the way into a living room that screamed of conspicuous consumption. He walked easily, in a controlled manner. Obviously, he hadn't had enough alcohol to affect his gait, but if his speech was any indication, he was getting there.

Manny stepped onto the carpet and sank into the deep pile. It would be years—if ever—before he would be able to afford such luxury. He hoped that when he reached that level of income he would have the good taste and common sense to be less pretentious.

Johnny dropped heavily onto the white-on-white couch and waved toward a nearby companion chair. Manny sat down, facing him.

"Alice told me about the time you saved her from the proverbial 'fate worse'n death' in the movie house. I guess I oughtta thank you." He chuckled without mirth. "It helped our honeymoon that she was a virgin. And, believe me, our honeymoon needed all the help it could get."

Whether or not this line of chatter was embarrassing Manny, Johnny's tasteless remarks were having that effect.

"Then," Johnny continued, "there was the other time, when you saved the virginal ears of that reporter on the streetcar. Alice didn't have to lecture me on that. I 'member reading about it. The newspaper account didn't say whether you got a roll in the hay for that one. You just go around getting girls ready for real men with your extravagant foreplay, dontcha, now?"

Manny, drawing on all the self-discipline he'd learned in the seminary, restrained himself before remarking, "You forgot the Viking."

A strange look crept over Johnny's face. He had not expected any sort of measured response. He had been trying to goad his guest into some sort of outburst, or at least into losing his self-control. Seemingly, he was not succeeding. "Viking? What Viking?"

"You ought to hire a more dependable clipping service."

"Clipping service?"

"You know: The guys who snip gossipy items and send them to you for your edification. The people you've got now couldn't find an elephant with a nosebleed in a snowbank."

"What?" Piccolo looked sullen. This was not going the way he'd planned.

Alice appeared in the doorway. "Dinner's ready." It was said without much confidence.

Piccolo bounded up from the couch. There was no indication of wooziness of any sort. Dudgeon seemed to have neutralized the effect of the alcohol.

He strode into the dining room, brushing by Alice, who shrank back, looked appealingly at Manny, then scurried after her husband. Obviously she had experienced this sort of treatment before.

After some hesitation, Manny followed. Arriving at table, he concluded that Alice had made an excellent presentation. That brief glance was all he saw of the dinner.

Johnny picked up a platter filled with delicious-looking meatloaf. Without a word, he flung it at Alice, who ducked in a practiced manner. The platter hit the wall, hurling the sliced pièce de résistance in every direction. The wall now resembled a modern expressionist exhibit.

Johnny kicked at Alice's buttocks, knocking her to the floor. "Stay where you are, you slut," he yelled, "and clean up this mess! You're not even capable of being a scullery maid!"

"Wait a minute, buddy . . ." Manny stepped forward.

Johnny, now completely out of control, turned and hurled the contents of his drink in Manny's face.

Before Manny could recover, Johnny was all over him. Manny went down with Johnny atop him. They scuffled, rolling from the table to the wall and back again, with dishes crashing down each time their bodies bumped against the table legs.

The combatants didn't speak, merely grunted as they invested every bit of strength they had in the battle. Johnny, larger and more powerful, was getting the upper hand. Manny could think only that he was rapidly losing this fight.

Alice was sobbing her heart out. Manny heard the sound. He knew then that he could not lose this fight. No telling how far Johnny might go or what he was capable of. The state he was in, he might even kill Manny and/or Alice.

Manny tried to free his arms, which Johnny held in a firm grip. Manny's reserve strength was nearing its limit. At this point, the winner would be the man with the greater desire.

Manny pulled free of Johnny and, dynamized with the same passion he'd felt in his previous fights, began pummeling, left and right fists, again and again. Now, naked aggression superseded mere self-defense. Manny was determined to ensure that his opponent would be in no shape to fight any further. If that involved Johnny's death—so be it. In his frenzy, Manny didn't recognize that Johnny was already dangerously injured.

Manny felt a tentative touch on his cheek. No more; just a soft touch. He stopped punching, pulled back, and surveyed the damage. It was considerable.

The dining room furniture was scratched and nicked; the chairs close to kindling. Alice's battered face was streaked with tears. The walls and carpet were splattered with food, blood, and sweat.

"Are you all right?" Manny gasped.

Alice nodded. "How about Johnny?"

Manny regarded his adversary. Piccolo was breathing. That was a relief. He might well not have been. "I think he won't be conscious before we get out of here. Even if he does come to, believe me, he won't have any fight left."

" 'We'?" Alice repeated, confused. " 'We get out of here'? What? . . ."

Manny noticed for the first time that some of the shed blood was his own. He also noted that in previous fights, he'd had to be forceably dragged off the loser. This time it had taken only a gentle touch from Alice to stop him.

"Manny, you've got to leave. John will be furious."

"I think I kicked the fury out of him."

"He's got guns—"

"Where?"

"Under lock and key . . . somewhere, I don't know."

Manny considered this. A gun could change the complexion of the situation. "Get your things together. Quick!"

"I can't leave. I'm his wife."

"We'll see about that. If I let you stay here now, he'd probably kill you. He'd probably kill me too. I think leaving is a better alternative. Take only what you need. C'mon," he said insistently. "I'll help you."

Alice hesitated. But Manny was right: Both of them had to be gone before John came to. "Okay. I'll do it."

While Alice collected the essentials, Manny had time to think, if briefly. What had he done? Did he have to solve everything with his fists? What kind of monster had he become?

Wait a minute: This was classic self-defense. He had fought for his life—literally.

Over the long haul, he was making enemies. Tough guys who could think they had reason to maybe kill him. He was going to have to do something about that.

But first, take care of Alice.

After stowing Alice's luggage in the trunk, Manny gently helped her into the front seat, then went around and slid behind the wheel. Before starting the car, he turned to look at her. "Shouldn't we get you to a hospital? That eye doesn't look so good."

"It'll be okay. It's happened before. It'll go down given

a little time. When it's safe to travel around, I'll see my doctor."

"This has happened before?"

"Uh-huh." She was embarrassed. "It's my fault."

"*Your* fault! You mean what he did to your meal and to you was *your* fault?"

"I just don't measure up. So he kicks me around a bit. But he always forgives me."

Manny shook his head. "Do you have a family doctor?"

"Yes. Dr. Laura Gaynes."

"When Johnny kicks you around, he leaves scars and bruises?"

"Most of the time."

"Your doctor sees the bruises?"

She nodded wordlessly.

"What does she say about them?"

"They're always superficial. I heal quickly."

"That's it? The doctor patches you up and sends you back for more?"

Alice tried to smile, but one side of her face hurt too much. "No. She's been after me from the beginning to leave him. She's disgusted with me."

"You get it from every side, don't you?"

"It's my fault."

"We've got to do something about that attitude of yours. But first, we've got to take you someplace safe."

"Where?"

"That's what I've been working on. I think . . . yeah . . . let's go home."

Neither 'Fredo nor Maria Tocco had gone to bed. They were watching the small-screen television that was, for them, a brand-new entertainment package.

Manny let himself in and held the door for Alice. He called to his parents. They could tell from his tone that this was not an ordinary visit. All they needed was one look at Manny and Alice, and they knew something was wrong.

Alice was one of "the six." They had attended her wedding. Of course she was welcome in their house.

Manny explained what had happened. He was going to have to deal with Johnny Piccolo. But for now, until they could enlist the help of Alice's parents, she needed a safe place to stay. The Tocco guest room would be reclaimed from the den.

Fortunately, Manny had found a sympathetic hearing. Maria fixed them something to eat, although neither he nor Alice had much of an appetite.

The next day the process that would lead to a divorce was begun.

Johnny waged a furious battle to retrieve and reclaim his favorite punching bag. But in the face of threatened testimony from her doctor, the neighbors, and several employees in the law firm, he eventually realized he didn't stand a chance.

Alice asked for and got nothing from Johnny. She wanted only to be free and have time to recuperate. Manny, in their final meeting, told Johnny that if he wanted to think of Manny as a Knight in Shining Armor, or as Sir Lancelot, no matter. But if Johnny ever touched Alice again—if he even so much as looked at her cross-eyed . . . well, a smart lawyer like him would have meticulously planned for a lavish funeral.

In time, Alice was granted the uncontested divorce. Meanwhile, Manny had informed Bob, Stan, and Mike. Alice herself told Sister Marie Agnes, who was heartbroken for her.

But life continued.

Bob Koesler was ordained and began his first assignment at an east-side Detroit parish. Mike and Stan were made deacons and began their final year at St. John's. Bob was inwardly convinced that the seminary had seen the last of Manny Tocco. Manny and Alice were spending so much time together that they had become an "item" to those who knew them well.

And, indeed, they did fall in love, and thought of marrying. But there was the matter of a previous marriage and the necessity for a decree of nullity.

Church law regarding marriage was taught in the seminary's final year. Manny was not there for the study. He was aware, however, that an annulment was not easy to obtain. The services of a priest were required to get a couple through this legal maze.

Neither Manny nor Alice wanted to ask Father Bob (as they chose to address him) for help. Which was no reflection on his competence. It was just that they were all too close—something like a doctor's reluctance to operate on a family member.

Manny had heard Stan speak of Father Ed Simpson. Something about how he'd gotten Stan into the seminary. They asked for an appointment. Reluctantly, Father Simpson agreed to see them. Stan was close to ordination now and Simpson, prematurely, was planning his new life in a desirable parish. If Tocco had not been close to Stan, Father Simpson would have refused to even see him. And that on sound grounds, since neither Alice nor Manny was a member of Guadalupe parish. After all, there was always the possibility that Tocco might do something to upset Benson's—and thus Father Simpson's—applecart.

But after hearing Alice's case, Simpson knew that her getting an annulment was another definition of Fat Chance.

Alice and Johnny were Catholic; neither had been previously married, neither had denied the other the right to have children, neither had held a gun on the other to force marriage. Wifebeating might belong in the confessional or the counseling office, but was not an impediment that would make a marriage null and void from its very inception.

Going down the short list of conditions that might favor a declaration of nullity, Father Simpson found theirs an open and shut case. A little too open and shut for the two young people. A more sensitive and caring priest would have let them down more gently. Simpson was not such a priest.

Manny was not the type to brood over a decision. He did

not think Jesus would be so tight in making rules and regulations for people whose only crime was that they truly loved each other.

Alice and Manny considered it, discussed it, argued over it, prayed over it, and finally reached a decision. They were married by a judge, the ceremony witnessed by two surprised but delighted secretaries who had been passing the judge's chambers at the time.

In the eyes of civil law, Alice and Manny were married. In the eyes of the Church, they were excommunicated. And as such they were no longer welcome in the homes of the Toccos, the Smiths, the McManns, the Koeslers, and even the Bensons.

Of the clique, only Mike Smith joined in the shunning. The others, for their own peculiar reasons, could not break off their long friendship. Still, the unconditional acceptance no longer existed.

25 Years accumulated.

Fathers Smith and Benson joined Father Koesler in the priesthood. Shortly after Stan Benson's ordination, Father Ed Simpson took up his vigil, waiting for the phone call that would at long last free him from Guadalupe and send him off to one of those plush, elegant parishes so prized by climbing clerics. It didn't have to be a suburban church. Those were more apt to be gingerbread buildings built to serve beginning families as well as the growing exodus of "white flight" from Detroit city.

Father Ed had done his part: He had delivered one medium-rare young man to ordination from about the least likely vocation producer in the archdiocese. Granted, it was a one-way contract; the diocese had promised no reward. But you'd think you could expect a modicum of recognition.

Nothing.

Father Ed was doomed to work this miserable parish until he dropped. He watched as, one by one, his elderly parishioners retired from mostly blue-collar jobs. During this era, retirement was not a consideration for priests. No one—or very few—wanted to be put on the shelf.

On the other hand, Father Mike Smith was carving out a splendid career for himself. After a brief parochial stint, he was shipped off to Rome, the fertile soil that grew bishops. He was sent back to Detroit to the chancery and an expected eventual monsignorship.

Father Stan Benson was disappointed in his early assignments. He was sent to parishes in the moneyed suburbs, first

231

to Grosse Pointe, then to Birmingham. It was easy—too easy—to be noticed. Whenever something happened to these parishioners—and it frequently did—calls came from reporters in search of sidebars . . . human interest angles that could flesh out a story.

The last thing Stan wanted was to be quoted in the news. It would thwart his secret goal of mediocrity. He wanted no one even to consider his background and discover a reason he should never have been ordained. His parents—especially his mother—were so proud of their son the priest. Stan was evermore determined to do nothing that would draw attention to himself.

Father Benson was making mediocrity a profession. And he was getting very good at it.

He was almost the personification of an Irish Bull: being so good at not being good at anything.

There were few internal conflicts within the Church of that day. Catholics were confronted with a brick staircase. The steps were rules and regulations. If one kept the rules and climbed the stairs one got into heaven, although there was always the possibility, even the likelihood, of a bad time in purgatory. In any case, it was a simple system that could get complicated only by people.

Take the situation in which Manny and Alice found themselves, for example. They had broken one of the biggies: entering an invalid marriage. This put them in the state of mortal sin. There was no escape from this state other than having the marriage convalidated or living apart.

The other biggie, the one that forced adult Catholics into frequent, fruitless confession, was "artificial" birth control.

Pope Pius XII had blessed the rhythm method of family planning. It offered some relief. Before rhythm, Catholics had a choice of intercourse open to life (i.e., unimpeded by any manner of contraception) or abstinence. However, the rhythm method was somewhat less than sure-fire; for those with irregular periods, it was more familiarly known as Vatican Roulette.

All heaven and hell was about to explode.

In 1958 Pope Pius XII died. The Cardinals assembled in the Sistine Chapel were initially deadlocked in finding a successor to Pius. The best they could come up with was an interim papacy. They elected Cardinal Angelo Giuseppe Roncalli, who became Pope John XXIII. Overweight, elderly, with an unconventional sense of humor, John was supposed to entertain for a little while. After which the Cardinals would get serious about a successor to Pius.

As his first public (official) act, John, in view of the fact that he weighed many more serious pounds than his predecessor, increased the salary of those bearers who carried him in the *sedia gestatoria* in and out of St. Peter's Basilica.

Then, in 1959, John called for a reform of Church law and the convening of an Ecumenical Council, which became the Second Vatican Council. He did not live long enough to see either the desired reform or the Second Council implemented. He had initiated the Council, but it was left to his successor, Pope Paul VI, to finish it. John would have had to wait until 1983 to see revised Church law published. And it was anyone's guess what he would have thought of it.

Detroit, as an example of dioceses throughout the world, could not help but be affected by Vatican II. Many priests, not to mention lay people, paid scant attention to what was going on in Rome. So a bunch of bishops were meeting; what's that got to do with the parish debt and yet another collection on the horizon?

Then, suddenly, these disinterested Catholics were hit by a vernacular liturgy. The Latin Tridentine Mass, with which everyone had grown up, was offered in English. And the priest, who had whispered much of the time, with his back to the congregation, turned around and looked at the Faithful.

26

BETWEEN 1965 (THE conclusion of Vatican II) and 2002 (the present) this humongous Roman Catholic Church changed to the extent that it would never be the same. No one person or no collection of people would be able to shut the windows that John XXIII had opened to *aggiornamento*—the letting in of fresh air. To try to close the windows against the winds of change would be to try to put the toothpaste back in the tube.

The Nicene Creed, a product of the Nicene Ecumenical Council in A.D. 325, is still recited at Mass. Most Catholics say it by rote, pleased that they no longer need a prayer book. Some theologians would deny its every assertion. Most of the dissent springs from the spirit of Vatican II.

Medical advances challenge a divided post-Conciliar Church.

- Cloning: Is it a reproductive phenomenon or a departure from the missionary position?
- Harvesting organs: Questioning the transplanting of organs (heart, kidney, liver, etc.) from a dead to a needy person.
- Stem cell research involving the destruction of human embryos: Leading to enhancement of life, or committing murder?
- Sexual ethics:
  Does personal conscience take precedence over abstract rules?

234

Are artificial contraception and sterilization always
  wrong?

Or should a couple themselves decide whether they
  should be open to reproduction?

If that decision is "not now," does it matter how preg-
  nancy is avoided?

Is the evil of masturbation the result of a misreading of
  the Old Testament story of Onan?

Or is autoeroticism intrinsically wrong?

Is anything intrinsically wrong?

Is homosexuality against the Natural Law? Or is there
  a genetic cause for that state?

• *In vitro* fertilization: Is it morally acceptable when
  only husband and wife are involved?

Is it morally wrong when it involves a third donor or a
  surrogate mother?

• Or, perhaps the most difficult and pressing question
  of all: The morality of abortion.

Is it always immoral?

What if the life or the health of the mother is threatened?

Roughly half a century ago and more, many of these and
related questions were not even asked, let alone answered.
But the documents of the Council and its spirit demanded
that the Church catch up with the real world and the knowledge explosion.

Over these most recent years it has, indeed, been interesting to be a concerned Catholic.

On the one hand, a number of Catholics, from Cardinals
to segments of the laity, have fought valiantly to preserve a
Church that has survived extraordinary persecution, the Reformation, scandal, and assault. They consider Vatican II to
be at worst an unmitigated disaster and at best a rank-and-
file seduction from Mother Church to the evils of the modern age.

On the other hand, a number of Catholics, from Cardinals
to segments of the laity, have fought valiantly to achieve

what they perceive as an "openness" to the Holy Spirit and to have confidence in the Spirit's direction—wherever that may lead.

Of course, these nearly forty years of internal turmoil had their effect on the young—now elderly—people we've been following. The questions posed by our age were addressed in different ways by Bob, Mike, Manny, Stan, Alice, and Rose. Though all now were in their early seventies, somehow most of them felt much younger. They had no idea what effect seventy years of life was supposed to have on humans; all they knew was that they just didn't feel like seventy.

And one of them would die of suspicious causes.

As we've seen, not all of the six achieved their primary goal in life. Yet all but one would be satisfied with what they had accomplished.

Father Robert Koesler became a simple parish priest. And so he would have remained had it not been for his accidental involvement in the serial murder of eight of the finest priests and nuns of the Archdiocese of Detroit. He happened by accident to come upon the second of these victims. Then, inexorably involved, he was helpful in assisting the police in the solution of those killings.

Evidently, the police knew a good source when they saw one. For Father Koesler continued to be a resource in succeeding murders rich in Catholic character.

When he wasn't helping solve crimes, he, as did most priests, tried to understand the Council and its impact on Catholic life.

At first, he vigorously dismissed the Council and its spirit. He grieved over the loss of the Latin Mass and argued that the Tridentine Mass of itself demonstrated the unity and universality of the Church. No matter where one traveled in the world, one had access to a Mass celebrated with identical vestments, the same gestures, the same rubrics, and most of all, the same language—Latin.

In time, Koesler's viewpoint evolved to the observation that Catholics could now drop in on a Roman Catholic Mass and *not* understand what was going on, in the same foreign language (Latin) in just about any country in the world.

Still, he continued to miss the beauty and pageantry of the Tridentine Mass in which he had been reared and with which he had a lifelong familiarity.

On the other hand, he accepted and became comfortable with the many humanizing aspects of the Vatican Council.

He was, in a word, eclectic, choosing the best of both worlds.

If any of the group of six had been undisputed leader, it would have been Robert Koesler. He was only one year older than the other five, but it was noteworthy the influence one year could carry in the context of the seminary and religious life. The reality of their relationship worked out in the way many hoped the Pope would eventually relate to bishops and leaders of all faiths and sects throughout the world—as "first among equals."

With that in mind, Bob Koesler was in position to evaluate the others. The sheerest of accidents had brought them together these many years ago. They grew so close they might have been blood relatives.

Emanuel Tocco developed into a man of honor. Honor was a character value his father had instilled in him. If your word was not dependable, neither were you. If your word was rock-solid dependable, so were you.

Koesler admired that in Manny.

Koesler, Manny, and Mike Smith had attended the same parochial school. Because this school was humongous, they probably would not have met had it not been that all three were altar servers. And because they grew to admire the priests they served and were fascinated by the mystery of the liturgy, each thought he might one day become a priest.

The linchpin of this continued association was their attending a diocesan seminary. Almost all the others from that parish who dreamed of the priesthood would test their vocation in a religious order setting.

For all practical purposes, Manny Tocco considered himself a worthy applicant for this calling. He was hard-working, dependable, concerned for the welfare of others and destined to be a man's man. If these were not the seminary's requirements, they certainly fit the paradigm of fictional priests of popular novels and movies.

In a hazy way, Manny was aware that he would be entering a womanless world. He wasn't concerned about this; indeed, he barely gave it a thought. His interests fell into the masculine category—sports, pranks, studies. He had no sisters or even close female relatives, other than his mother. As for Rose and Alice, they were . . . well, just there. Rose was his buddy Mike's sister, Alice was her shadow—and that was that.

He even was separated from the girls in his own school. This sort of separation—boys from girls, men from women—could be made to seem natural in what was then the world of "Do Black Patent Leather Shoes Really Reflect Up?"

With this prelude, it was almost natural to consider life without the opposite sex as perfectly normal.

Manny's native intelligence was surely sufficient to get him through the academic demands of the seminary. In addition to this, there was Mike's tutoring. Academically, Manny was set.

Of course, such a high aspiration as the priesthood would expose any deficiency that might be underlying. Manny identified his weakness early on: his temper. He worked on taming it.

Everyone has a temper. In the average person, usually this emotional drive calls for some sort of action. But tempers come in all degrees: Some people have a hair-trigger temper; others have such patience and self-control they rarely if ever lose their temper. The majority are somewhere in between.

With Manny, his mother was the model for restraint. From time to time she would become angry. But the anger was always justified and always controlled. Manny wished he could be more like his mother. He wanted to emulate her moderated response to provocation.

After much prayer and thought, his honest conclusion was that he took after his father rather than his mother. 'Fredo Tocco was quick to express anger, quick to get it out of his system, and quick to forgive. He had an infectious sense of humor. He could be counted on to handle most troublesome situations in a measured manner.

Manny walked in his father's footsteps, and a few steps further. He led a sheltered existence in the parochial school, then in the seminary. A temper was a part of everyone's makeup. Controlling it was part of every student's goal.

To be honest with himself, as Manny constantly fought to be, he did improve over the years. There were pushes and there were shoves. But by and large he marched closely to his father's example.

There were exceptions. Those were what Manny feared in his response to naked aggression. He could count on the fingers of one hand the number of times he had gone over the edge, or nearly so.

That idiot, Blade, for instance. Twice Manny had been presented with an unavoidable altercation with Blade. And twice had come close to leaving his adversary more dead than alive.

The first time, Mike—and even Switch—had intervened and pulled Manny off.

The same thing had occurred the second fight with Blade. Manny might have understood and forgiven himself had he feared that Blade might kill him. But Manny honestly didn't reflect on thoughts of his own possible death. The problem was that he had been totally irrational; he hadn't thought, just reacted.

Would he have backed off of his own volition after realizing that he had knocked out his opponent? Difficult to say. He, de facto, hadn't let up, even after Blade was unconscious. Had the fight been carried to extremes, he, Manny, could have been charged with manslaughter, no small matter.

As for that Piccolo jerk, again Manny had not provoked the fight. It was Piccolo all the way. Once again, Manny had responded in self-defense. And then he went further. If he hadn't been stopped, would he have pulled back?

Try as he might—and he tried and he prayed—he could not come up with a clearcut conclusion.

Funny, thinking of it, the first fight with Blade was stopped only because two other boys pulled him off. In the second go-round with Blade, again others had intervened to stay Manny's hand; otherwise he might well have killed Blade.

And in the fracas with Piccolo, a mere touch by Alice, and Manny had quit.

Then there was the Viking. In that instance, Manny had never come closer to a serious battle without actually engaging in one. That it hadn't developed into a knockdown, drag-out battle . . . well, that was probably a tribute to the Vike. For a change, a potential fight was averted by the would-be aggressor.

Emanuel Tocco didn't abandon the priesthood capriciously. For one, the timing did not speak of impulse. He left the seminary at the eleventh hour as it were. He'd entered in the ninth grade—the earliest possible point of entry. And he'd stayed through high school, college, and three years of the theologate. He had invested eleven years, stopping only one short of the required dozen.

Nor was it a single issue that caused his leaving. His temper had at times been close to and nearly homicidal . . . no mean consideration. However, he left for a wider spectrum of reasons.

A retreat master had nailed these reasons many years prior to Manny's final decision. It was an oft-told anecdote and one that Manny never forgot.

It seems, according to the story, that a bishop visited a Trappist monastery at a time when the monks never spoke. An exception to that rule was when a bishop initiated conversation. One such bishop, thinking himself an amateur psychologist, engaged one of the monks in conversation, thus interrupting the monk from field work.

"Brother," said the bishop, "you seem to me to be very depressed."

"Yes," the Brother admitted, "that's right, Bishop, I am."

"Let me see," the bishop pondered, "I'll bet it's this silence. You can speak to me, but you must not say a word to the people you live and work and pray with . . . that it?"

The monk thought for some moments. "No, it's not that."

"Hmmm." The bishop thought some more. "It must be your diet. It's meager at best, and there's no meat, ever."

"I don't think that's really it, Bishop."

"Hmmm. Is it the cubicle they give you for a bedroom? Straw mattress, lumpy, narrow . . . is that it?"

"No, Bishop, that's not it."

"Well, this *is* a hard case. Could it be your routine? Up in the middle of the night for prayer, then work and pray all day, then retire at an ungodly early hour. Is that what's getting to you?"

The monk seemed lost in thought. Finally, he said, "No . . . I'm sorry, Bishop, but it's not that either."

"Then I give up, Brother. What do you suppose is the problem?"

"I think, Bishop, it's the whole damn thing."

And that's what seemed to Manny to be his reason, or reasons, for leaving the seminary: the whole damn thing.

At that point two events occurred that would radically change the entire direction of his life. He got a job at the *Free Press,* Detroit's morning newspaper, and he married Alice McMann, albeit without benefit of clergy.

They tried for Catholic validity, but the effort proved fruitless. The couple continued to attend Mass, though they never received Communion or confessed sacramentally. This arrangement didn't much bother Manny. It was a matter of much moment to Alice, though she never let on. If questioned, she, like Manny, would have said that they'd given it their best shot, and there seemed nothing else they could do.

Having reached this conclusion, Manny did not let their sacramentless life bother him.

It bothered Alice.

In time, they had one daughter, who was baptized by Father Koesler. There would be those who criticized receiving a child of an invalid marriage into the Church. Koesler dismissed such criticism as, at best, pharisaical scandal. He knew this child would be raised Catholic, and a good Catholic at that.

Manny started as a copyboy at the *Free Press*. Under the tutelage of City Editor Nelson Kane, he climbed steadily, distinguishing himself as a no-nonsense reporter who got the story first, but first got it right. He discovered he had a flair for making an otherwise dull story seem interesting.

In short of due time, he caught the eye of several politicians and business executives.

It didn't hurt that he had built a solid reputation as a straight shooter. Even the crooks, in and out of political life, had to admit that Manny Tocco was an honest and honorable man.

After long, serious thought, and after discussing the matter with Alice, Manny left the *Free Press* to become press secretary/speechwriter for a top Michigan executive who had his eye on the State House.

There followed an admirable career that found Manny at home in the highest political and business circles. Though Manny was convinced that in the priesthood he had lost a noble vehicle for his life calling, still he was satisfied that he had done his best in his new profession. He was advised, respected, and, above all, trusted.

In a very few years, Alice McMann had packed in a lot of experience, starting as a teenager in a parochial school and then in the convent. As for her sexual awakening, it was frightening at worst and awkward at best.

She'd had her dream of sexuality, always as romance, tenderness, and fulfillment. That had been seriously damaged by the adolescent, clumsy, and crude advances of a fourteen-year-old boy. As a result, one of the things Alice had come to associate with sex was being groped by a pimply teenager in a darkened movie house.

As it worked out, the panting youth never even got close to what his crowd referred to as "first base." Manny Tocco's quick intervention had scotched that. It had taken no more than a threatening admonition from the redoubtable Manny to cool off the perspiring groper.

It wasn't much in the annals of knight errantry. Manny's open-ended warning was enough to quiet the situation. Alice was not only grateful, she was flattered. She couldn't bring herself to thank Manny, although she did try to subtly express her gratitude. But she was never sure that Manny had caught the drift.

Besides, she was committed to the convent and a life remote from groping males, or, for that matter, any type of male. And Manny was headed for the seminary and the priesthood.

Alice did not quite grasp what the priesthood demanded. But then neither did she understand what religious life entailed. A more than casual study suggested that nuns did all the work and priests got all the glory. But that was how things were if one chose to enter and proceed. So, romantic thoughts unspoken, Alice remained secretly in Manny's debt.

Then there was that brief interlude in the convent. Alice had learned in short order that she could never join Rose's friendship with the demands of religious life. Alice concluded that she could be closer to her best friend as a layperson than were she to remain in consecrated life.

Then came the generous support and help from Rose's father, followed by Alice's hiring on at the law firm.

Rose was kept informed of each step along the way. Her information as to the events of Alice's day-to-day life was far more detailed than it would have been had Alice remained in the convent.

Rose was disturbed by John Piccolo's interest in Alice.

Rose knew that Al had an undeservedly poor self-image. Rose noted how Alice had given herself over to John, almost as a slave to an owner. Rose suspected this relationship would degenerate as time went on, particularly if it led to marriage.

But Rose strongly believed that she could serve more constructively if she stayed on the fringe ready to help in any way she could in picking up the pieces. Besides, the communication between the two friends, while much freer now that Alice was unconstrained by convent rules, still was in no way what it had been before they had entered the convent.

Alice married John Piccolo. As a bride she was the centerpiece of the wedding day. She was immensely happy. She would need the memories of this happiness to give her strength to survive what was coming.

Alice tried to keep a stiff upper lip and hide from family and friends what she was suffering at the hands—and fists— of her husband.

Infrequently the couple would dine out, usually with John's coworkers. John used such occasions as a showcase of his mastery over his wife. These displays were humiliating to Alice, and embarrassing to everyone but John.

The couple never entertained at home. Had they done so, the fact that theirs was a sadomasochistic relationship would have been obvious beyond doubt. And John wanted that doubt to take precedence over any certain knowledge. He knew that the firm had no place in its higher echelons for an overt sadist. And John very definitely wanted to climb.

His approach left room for dalliances with lower-level stenos. Far from attempting to shield these sexually gratifying games from his wife, he boasted of them to her in nauseating detail.

The word divorce seemed not to be in Alice's lexicon. As a young girl, she had not always told the truth. On occasion, she had even lied to Rose—not often and not seriously. Sometimes she guiltily thought of what might have happened had Manny not intervened in the Stratford Theater.

That was it with Alice: guilt and punishment. She was supposed to love, honor, and obey—words that popularized the wedding ceremony but didn't even exist in the Catholic ritual.

So there it was: Lies and adolescent desire—she had sinned, done something wrong. She *must* have done something wrong. She must be *doing* something wrong to be slammed around as she was.

Then came Manny's phone call and finally her invitation to him to dine chez Piccolo.

It would have been outrageous for such an invitation to originate with Alice—something like inviting a friend to witness one's torture. But it would have been inconceivable that the invitation issue from John Piccolo. And yet, though Manny had no way of knowing, that's exactly whence it came. He had indicated to his wife, in no uncertain terms, that she should invite her friend—"this paragon of virtue"—to dinner ". . . so we can see what he's really made of."

John's behavior that evening was beyond insane. Alice had never completely gotten over the memory of it. Occasionally, even now, when the Toccos dined out or had guests in, Alice would find herself stammering from the memory of those events.

She remembered how strong and fit John had been. She had had the bruises to prove it. She also remembered her fear that he would humiliate Manny.

As it happened, her fear for Manny turned into a fear *of* him. A fear that he would kill John. She had never witnessed such an uncontrolled fury, even with John at his worst.

Yet at her first hesitant touch, Manny had stopped immediately and called up an unlikely self-control.

The divorce followed and, mostly because, in the end, it was uncontested, it was not overly bloody. Next came the attempt at an annulment. Compared with the civil action, the Church's procedures were like a bloodbath. Neither Alice nor Manny ever fathomed why the Church should demand in minute detail such intimate marital facts. In any case, the divorce was granted, the annulment denied.

Manny rationalized promptly and set his conscience at ease. Alice was not as successful. She never got over the fact that they were not validly married in the Church's eyes. It was a continuing source of embarrassment to her.

Nevertheless Manny and Alice kept up with Church affairs, reading some of the more thoughtful books and periodicals.

They had become actively involved for the first time only recently when their grandchild, Louise, was denied the opportunity of making her First Holy Communion.

27

MANNY AND ALICE named their daughter Rose, after Alice's best friend. Little Rose would have no siblings, although they were desired. The doctor blamed Manny's low sperm count.

Like most only children, Rose was cherished. She returned this affection. She loved her parents dearly, but bottom line, she was "Daddy's girl."

Manny and Alice attended Mass faithfully on Sundays and Holy Days of Obligation. But they never attempted to take Communion.

Rose was born in 1965 at approximately the conclusion of the Council. It was a much more love-centered time in the Church. So Manny and Alice didn't feel overly compelled to explain to their young daughter about her parents being condemned to eternal hell-fire because a priest hadn't witnessed their marriage.

Because the role was so natural to him, Manny was Rose's, as well as Alice's, white knight.

In time, Rose grew up, fell in love with, and married Ralph Rigby. Shortly thereafter—nothing bashful about Ralph's sperm—Rose became pregnant.

But something was wrong. The symptoms seemed to come out of the blue. First came the weight loss. Ralph had always been slim. But there was no obvious reason why he should be losing so much weight. Then there was bone pain, and a pins-and-needles sensation in the arms and legs. Blood tests revealed low levels of protein, calcium, and sodium.

All this had a disastrous effect on Rose. She was pregnant

with her first child, and her husband, in desperate need of care, seemed unable to get an accurate diagnosis. Doctors tried everything, to no avail.

Manny and Alice tried to help. They insisted that Rose and Ralph move in with them. After weak and unconvincing demurrals, the move was made.

Despite heroic efforts from all concerned, Ralph continued to deteriorate. He died during Rose's seventh month. The wake and the funeral were heart-wrenching.

Manny would have it no other way than that Rose stay on. Two months later, Louise was born. The happiness she brought to the Toccos and to Rose almost alleviated the sorrow of losing Ralph.

Then it began. The first sign occurred at the start of Louise's second year. The three adults took the baby with them to an all-you-can-eat restaurant. Somebody gave Louise a cookie. Although part of it got crunched in her hair and all over her face, still she managed to down most of it. She was the life of the party.

It was not long after that—after some bread and more cookies—that the symptoms kicked in. As they developed and increased, finally a specialist correctly diagnosed her condition as celiac disease, an inherited illness. Actually, Ralph's illness and death had been signposts leading to the identity of Louise's illness. Ralph's celiac disease had been passed on to his daughter. She had an allergic intolerance to gluten, a protein. In short, bread—among a few other foods—made her ill . . . very ill. And Rose, crushed by the death of her young husband, now faced a life-threatening disease in her daughter.

The family's friends gave of themselves unstintingly. But when night came—no matter who had been there through the day—the friends would leave.

Manny would tuck in Louise; then, just as he had in her childhood, he tucked in Rose. Then he and Alice would seek comfort in each other's arms.

As close families do, the Toccos took special care of Louise. The most important consideration in this case was diet. Even small amounts of gluten caused a reaction. All gluten had to be avoided. That abstinence included commercial soups, sauces, ice cream, hot dogs, as well as wheat and rye.

Rose, as did her family and friends, grew accustomed to recognizing and avoiding gluten in all its forms. Being aware became second nature.

By the time Louise was seven, the family had begun preparation for her long-awaited First Holy Communion. Of course there was the obvious consideration with regard to bread. But that had been handled for years with care and substitutes; surely it would be no problem now.

In the Catholic Mass, the priest consecrates bread and wine, just as Jesus did at the Last Supper. Catholic belief is that in this consecration the bread and wine become the living presence of Jesus Christ. Thus, bread and wine are central to Communion.

As Louise's First Holy Communion approached, this was of no grave concern to the Tocco family. It was no problem; they would find a substitute for the bread. They always had. For everyone in any way connected with Louise, this was to be a joyful banner occasion.

Manny and Alice called at the rectory to arrange for an accommodation. No point in dragging Rose along; she was no stronger than a piece of wet tissue paper.

28 FATHER ALAN STATNER had been a seminary classmate of Manny. Earlier he had tried to work out a solution to the Toccos' strained relation with the Church, but without success. Manny had seen Rose burned years previously in the Tribunal's Marriage Court. He wasn't about to go through that again, even with reassurance that processes had improved. Nor would he accept the "Pastoral Solution" wherein estranged Catholics could return to the Sacraments without going through a formal trial. It was against Manny's nature to take an easy way out.

Besides, Father Statner would not offer a Pastoral Solution. He had allowed Vatican II to wash over him and leave him gasping for fresh air that did not originate with Pope John's *aggiornamento*.

At the outset, Alice explained Louise's condition. The atmosphere was pleasant. There was no tension or sense of impending doom. Father Statner was familiar with the problem of gluten in celiac disease and its relationship to Communion.

"You see," Statner said, after Alice had made her point that a substitute for a wafer of bread with gluten would have to be used, "this question has been addressed by a document from the Vatican."

The Toccos found that mildly interesting.

"No substitute," Statner stated, "may be made."

"What!" Manny's fabled temper flared.

In response, Statner's back stiffened. "This isn't something I made up, Manny. It's the official stand on this question. After all, we are simply doing as Jesus instructed. 'Do what I have done,' He said when He gave His apostles the first ever Communion. And what He did was to change the substance of bread and wine into the Body and Blood, Soul and Divinity of Himself. And the bread He used undoubtedly contained gluten."

Manny's knuckles were white as he clutched the arms of his chair. "Tell me, Father," he said from between clenched teeth, "did any of Christ's apostles have celiac disease?"

"That's casuistry of the worse order!" Statner said. "But wait," he continued, "before we get carried away, there's a solution to this problem—"

"If you're going to suggest that we put a nongluten wafer aside in the ciborium with the other wafers, forget it. We've been down that road: the slightest crumb will set off a reaction in Louise."

"As it turns out," Statner said, "I wasn't going to suggest that. Let me call your attention to our belief that Communion now can be received under either or both species of bread and/or wine.

"The children will receive their First Holy Communion under both bread and wine. However, lots of Catholics receive only the bread. Most of them simply don't want to receive from a common cup."

"I think I know where you're going with this," Manny said. "You're going to tell us that Louise should receive only the wine, and skip the bread."

"Exactly."

Alice could almost accept the compromise. But she knew her husband well. She knew he would not. "I don't think we can tell Louise to do this, Father," she said.

"Every time Louise would attend Mass, she would be the only one to pass up the bread and receive only the wine. *The only one,*" Alice emphasized. "She already is set apart from 'normal' people in the care she must use in choosing her food.

"Now, to make a spectacle of her illness . . . no, we can't expose her to that."

There was a long moment of silence.

"I think we can all see," Manny said finally, "that neither of us is going to change our position—"

"Manny," Statner interrupted, "this is not *my* opinion. It is the official word on the matter from our Holy, Catholic Church. Ours is not to quibble or disagreee. Ours is to follow our faith."

"Well"—Manny helped Alice to her feet—"in this position, our Church is being silly at the expense of a little girl who has been hurt by nature and now is going to be hurt again by our Church."

By the time they left the rectory, Alice was afraid her husband's temper might be approaching the boiling point. She turned to Manny. "What'll we do? What *can* we do?"

"What we should have done in the first place." Manny's jaw was set uncompromisingly.

Father Statner dabbed at his eyes. He was not going to cry. Men don't cry. But he felt very low.

These people—his friends—probably could find a priest who, one way or another, would fulfill their wish and find a way to give Communion to their precious granddaughter under the form of bread that did not contain wheat.

It wasn't that Statner dismissed Vatican II out of hand. He went along with Conciliar changes to the letter. And that was the problem: Where many other priests had gone on to what they called the "spirit" of the Council, Father Statner continued to stick to the Letter of the Law.

The Council didn't ratify things like artificial birth control or back the idea of women priests, among many other practices that defied Church law. The New Age priests did that, pushed forward by a newly arrived laity.

Father Statner wanted to help anyone who needed help. But not by flouting Church law. How many times had he watched in sorrow as people like the Toccos walked away from him in distress. He found it particularly painful, as he knew his people would go on a priest-search. More than likely they would find someone who would satisfy their requests.

A growing number of the new, younger priests wanted to retreat to the pre-Conciliar era that Father Statner had experienced early in his own priesthood. He would not join them. He was in the middle. And he would stay there. But it was not comfortable.

29

THE NEIGHBORHOOD LOOKED as if it might implode. Most of the buildings appeared to be leaning on other buildings. It resembled a house of cards: Pull one out and all would come tumbling down.

This section of the city did not even have a nickname like so many other areas of Detroit: Greektown, Poletown, Black Bottom, Indian Village, Rosedale, Corktown, and so on.

Its only claim to fame had been the once-proud Olympia, the huge building that showcased celebrity boxing matches, the Pistons basketball team, and the Detroit Red Wings hockey team.

Once also, there'd been a parish here: Our Lady of Guadalupe, known simply as "Guadaloop." The church building itself still functioned as a place of worship: Truth in the Gospel of Jesus Christ. The rectory, oddly, was still a rectory, in that there was a priest in residence.

Father Ed Simpson had been the previous resident priest, the last pastor Guadalupe would have. It was common knowledge among "the boys" that old Ed had coveted a parish "worthy of his pastoral ministry." Everyone but Ed knew that was not going to happen.

No one else knew to what extremes he had gone in an attempt to win the chancery's favor. There were times that Father Simpson felt like Dr. Frankenstein—except that Ed's "monster" was a pussycat who'd become expert at straddling fences.

Whatever—Stan Benson had been picked, plucked, stuffed, and delivered. A real live priest from Guadalupe.

Few could fault Father Simpson on that. He had created what no one had thought possible: not just producing a priest out of Guadalupe, but a priest out of someone who didn't want to be a priest.

Father Simpson might have lived out his days in an alcoholic fog had it not occurred to the disciples of change that, while priests just go on and on, real people retire. The subsequent trickle of priestly retirees opened the door to a groundswell of discontented and/or ill priests.

They retired in droves. And one of them was Father Simpson. Unfortunately, he lived just long enough to acquire a Florida tan before joining that Great Offertory Procession in the Sky.

The rectory at Guadalupe survived, though it had ceased to function as anything official. It wasn't even vandalized; why not, no one seemed to know.

When it came time for Father Stan Benson to retire, he leaped at the opportunity. He returned to Guadalupe, moving his few possessions into the rectory that held so many memories. His father had died many years before. His mother, now in her nineties, but quite coherent, still gloried in her son's priesthood. He visited her regularly. She lived in an excellent nursing home, which provided the best care money could buy. Stanley had scrimped and saved, and now used those savings to ensure that his mother would want for nothing.

When Manny called for an appointment, Stanley was delighted. It was an occasion to celebrate, especially since Manny was a longtime friend and former classmate.

The Toccos parked in front of the rectory. It was early evening, but it had been overcast for several days, with intermittent showers.

"It looks," Alice said, "like the setting for one of those English murder movies. I'm actually afraid to get out of the car."

Manny smiled. "No need to be afraid, gal. I'll take care of you."

Of course you will, she thought. There had been no further temper explosions since the time her present husband had almost killed her former husband. But if there were provocation . . .

Actually, she felt very secure leaning against him.

Manny pressed the doorbell. He almost expected the chimes to sound the *Dies Irae* or some other spooky theme. But the sound was an innocuous buzz.

The door was opened promptly by an ebullient Stan Benson. "Come in. Come in. It's so good to have you here."

Alice reflected that he was among those of the six who had not been judgmental at the news of their marriage. Thinking back on it now, she couldn't remember that Stan had expressed himself at all regarding the marriage. But without committing himself in any fashion, he had seemed supportive.

As they were ushered into the living room, the Toccos were surprised to note that the interior of this ancient rectory was well kept up. Stan noticed their wonderment and was pleased. "We've put a lot of work into this place." He made it sound as if a crew had descended on the building and cleaned and maintained it. Actually, he had done it virtually by himself.

In response to Stan's offer, the couple requested white wine.

They settled themselves into old, but again well-maintained, chairs. The Toccos could hear kitchen sounds as well as smell the aroma of food cooking. Stan did not seem to advert to it. They wondered whether he had a cook . . . or perhaps a live-in housekeeper? Somehow both of them considered it highly unlikely that, given his druthers, Stanley would be living with anyone.

The three chatted about the past. They went back a long way, since junior high. Stan had entered the group only because Koesler had, in effect, sponsored him. But once he'd joined, the others had accepted him in the spirit of Christian charity if not genuine camaraderie.

A quiet bell sounded from the kitchen. Stan excused himself. A few minutes later, he returned to announce that dinner was served. He had been chef, cook, and bottle-washer.

The pièce de résistance was a delicious-looking beef stew that had simmered to perfection through the day. In response to Stan's invitation, Manny offered a prayer, after which they proceeded to pass the serving dishes. The conversation continued in the same vein as before, reminiscences of the good old days. Manny, Alice, Stan, and the others. How alive they'd all been. How healthy. How filled with anticipation of life to come.

By the time dessert and coffee were served, they had moved on to the present. Alice cleared her throat, a sign the serious side of this evening had arrived. So, thought Stan, still no such thing as a free lunch.

Alice launched into the sad tale of their daughter and their granddaughter. All had been going so well until their son-in-law had fallen to this strange disease. The effect his premature death had had on his pregnant wife. Then the arrival of little Louise. Followed by her reaction to gluten, the clue that provided the diagnosis for Ralph's disease . . . a disease he had passed on to his then unborn baby girl.

It had all proved too much for Rose. It was like a Greek tragedy: Just when they thought they had a handle on this string of disasters, something new would pop up.

During Alice's narration of these events, Manny experienced acute discomfort. He shrank from hanging his family linen out for others to see. Further, even before he and Alice had had the opportunity to plead their case, Manny was ashamed that he had to beg a favor. Particularly since, to Manny, this was no actual favor, but rather a claim to what was Louise's right.

Stan listened intently as Alice described the celiac disease that father had passed on to daughter. Stan had read something of the illness. Though it had principally to do with wheat, Stan had never made the connection with the bread used in Communion. Not until now.

The granddaughter of Manny and Alice had celiac disease and was expected to receive her First Holy Communion. A contradiction in terms. A classic dilemma. Rome had spoken. But all Rome had said was that wheat bread was the one and only bread that could be used for valid Communion. Something like a traffic sign that reads: DETOUR and adds, FIND ALTERNATE ROUTE. Not very helpful.

Alice plowed ahead with her plea, but Stan was no longer listening. In his mind's eye he could see what surely would happen should he do anything that would satisfy the Toccos.

PRIEST GIVES GIRL HER DAILY BREAD; ROME BURNS.

And the like.

Alice finished with an account of their meeting with Statner. The conclusion: Communion under the species of wine alone—valid, and skirts the issue of bread and gluten. But still too daring for Stan. One word to the media and he would get the publicity he had, for all these long years, managed to avoid.

In his heart, Stan could not have disagreed more with Statner's solution. Of course the little girl had every right to Communion in the same manner as the other children. If that meant a separate place on the altar for a nonwheat wafer, so be it. If anything, Stan would have had the entire Communion class receive nonwheat wafers. There would be no problem in finding an acceptable substitute for wheat, as Louise and her family had been doing for most of her young life.

Solving this sacramental issue in the fashion acceptable to the Toccos was what Stan's conscience dictated. But it was not what he would or could advise Manny and Alice.

He told the couple that he did not agree with Father Statner. At this, their hearts soared—only to be dashed to the ground once more. For Father Benson stated that the fact that Louise was unable to consume wheat bread was a sign from God that Holy Communion was not to be a part of her life. God undoubtedly would make up for the loss in some way.

If they wanted still another opinion they could shop around. But he knew they were unlikely to find a more liberal opinion than his or Statner's. Rome had been too crystal-clear on this matter.

And, thought Stan, take that, you media hounds! I'm not going to hand you my head on a platter. I've been hiding my light under a bushel for too long to let the sun shine in now.

Unconscious of having mixed his metaphors, Stan felt relieved that he had reasoned himself off the hook. But he was despondent over what he had done to these friends of his. These now *former* friends, he feared.

Manny stood abruptly, tipping over his chair, which fell to the floor. He was furious. Alice was apprehensive. She had seen her husband this angry when he had nearly killed her former husband. She touched his arm tentatively, tenderly. Manny slowly unstiffened. That meant at least he wasn't going to hit—and therefore annihilate—Stan.

Instead, Manny turned and strode from the room, Alice following at his heels. They retrieved their coats and Manny held the door for his wife, as they wordlessly let themselves out.

Leaving the neighborhood, he drove too fast. Alice touched his arm. He exhaled deeply, and slowed down.

"Is the world going mad?" Manny asked of no one. "I haven't heard theology like that since the forties!"

Now convinced that her husband wasn't going to make Gratiot a speedway, or return to maul Stan, Alice quietly sobbed. "What can we do?" she asked finally, dabbing at her eyes.

After some moments, Manny responded. "I'm not sure."

"Do we go see Bob Koesler? He might have some workable way out."

"No. I don't think so. I'm beginning to think this thing is a hot potato. I'm pretty sure Bob would help us. But I don't want to put any pressure on him. Besides, I'm tired of shopping around."

"Then what?"

"I've been thinking lately about the Episcopal Church."

"Leave the Catholic Church! How could we do that? You were almost a priest. I was almost a nun," she added after a moment.

" 'Almost' doesn't count."

Silence.

"There's an Episcopal church not far from us. We could look into it. The way I feel now, honey, it's the Episcopalians or nothing."

Nothing. Both quietly contemplated an existence without organized religion.

Could they break a lifelong habit?

Father Stan Benson finished the dishes. He surveyed the kitchen. It had been fun getting things straightened around. New windows and doors so tightly fitted that they were almost burglarproof. A stove fan that worked for a change. He moved into the living room. The interior painted, and the furniture reupholstered. Yes, it had been fun.

Why didn't they just leave him alone?

Most people thought of Stan—if they thought of him at all—as a relic of the thirteenth century. And they treated him like a relic. They venerated him, but considered him a statue on the mantelpiece.

Once in a while, someone from the past, friendly, would consult him. As Manny and Alice had just done.

Could he have helped them? But of course. Granted, he didn't have a parish now. But there were any number of tired pastors out there who would happily have let him "use" their parish to offer a First Communion Mass. Except that he had to protect his mother's reputation as well as his own. She at one time had been considered by Catholics as a whore—and he a bastard. His mother truly believed she had been released from infamy. Stan held the controls that kept her reputation safe. Under no circumstances would he allow the truth to be revealed.

Meanwhile, occasionally someone had to be hurt—usually by Church laws and Vatican directives.

Tonight was a case in point. He'd had to uphold one of the sillier rules that came from Rome. He just couldn't chance having his background revealed.

Why couldn't Manny see through this whole thing? He was smart enough. He shouldn't have let good old Stan Benson escape without challenging him. Maybe it was the *Father Knows Best* syndrome. Even for a savvy guy like Manny.

There was a point at the end of this evening when Stan had feared that Manny was going to hit him.

Manny should have done it. It would have saved Stan from the self-imposed hairshirt. God knows he needed to do penance.

30

THE STORY, PROBABLY apocryphal, is told of an electrician who, years ago, was called to a convent to repair some defective wall plugs. He had been toying with the idea of converting to Catholicism. He just needed some sign to push him over the edge.

He arrived at the convent during the nuns' late afternoon period of meditation. So all the while he worked the nuns sat silently around the spacious community room, deep in contemplation.

That very evening the man called at a rectory and told the priest he wanted to become a Catholic. The priest asked why, and the electrician replied, "Any religion that can put twenty-three women together in a room for an hour of silence has got to have something going for it."

At the time Rose Smith became Sister Marie Agnes there were rules upon rules upon rules. Those familiar with convent life of that era would not wonder at all that silence played a major role in daily routine.

Unlike Alice McMann—who briefly had been Sister Mary Benedict—Marie Agnes found comfort and deep meaning in silence. There even were stages of silence, culminating in the nighttime Grand Silence.

Virtually no one had an inkling that the Vatican Council was just over the horizon. But of the few religious Orders that were able to anticipate the new *aggiornamento,* the Sisters, Servants of the Immaculate Heart of Mary, were in the van.

It is almost impossible now to list chronologically the

changes in minds and lifestyles that took place. Among the
early transformations were the return to maiden names;
replacing the head-to-toe traditional garb with modified
habits; visiting family homes, albeit with permission and the
accompaniment of another Sister. A short time later, contemporary dress replaced the modified habits, with, perhaps,
a small cross pinned to the lapel. And Sisters could go where
they wished without permission and without any escort.

Sisters chose from a myriad of ministries, such as nursing, catechetics, the practice of law, and serving in parishes
that didn't even have schools, to mention just a few. Nuns
sought to go where the spirit called. Modern formation
sometimes ended in foreign countries. Communities might
be formed anywhere. For the very first time nuns could
choose their residences and their assignments.

A popular movement, Church-World-Kingdom, began in
Detroit. It featured discussions by small groups, in which
there was little differentiation between the laity, nuns, and
priests. Church-World-Kingdom would spread throughout
the country.

Perhaps because the IHMs were basically a teaching
order, there was more early transformation. These nuns studied the Conciliar documents before the ink was dry. Liturgi-
cal changes particularly were far-reaching and radical.

Long ago, Sister Marie Agnes had returned to her maiden
name. She became Sister Rose Smith. She was joined in this
by a high percentage of other Sisters, some fresh and new,
and some who claimed they had well earned their multiple
facial wrinkles. Men and women who had been students of
the teaching nuns no longer recognized their beloved and
memorable teachers by name. Sister Rose Smith hadn't
taught them; Sister Marie Agnes had.

And when there was an obituary for Sister Jane Doe, the
funeral of Sister Doe was nowhere nearly as well attended as
it might or should have been. The absent hadn't realized that
the Sister Consolata they had known was the middle identity
between the once and future Jane Doe.

As for Sister Rose Smith, she was simply at the right

place at the right time. She rose through the ranks inexorably. She taught at many schools and made many friends and few enemies.

In the end, she directed the once vast IHM Order. Sadly, she now presided over a disintegrating group. Attrition of the late fifties and the sixties had reduced Order membership from as many as seventeen hundred religious to a bare remnant of something like six hundred.

In those halcyon days, Rose would have been addressed as Reverend Mother. Today, she was Sister Rose, or simply Rosie.

In high school she was a very active member of the clique of six. That ended when she entered college and the convent. She parted company with the group and "the world." And, despite the occasional twinge of loneliness, she loved her vocational life.

She was saddened by the hemorrhage of professed nuns, including many in final vows. Moreover, she grew frustrated in all attempts to recapture the golden years.

But there were pluses. And one of the many pluses of renewal was the freedom to associate freely with friends and acquaintances of every stripe. From time to time what was left of her special clique would assemble. Of the six, four were still in religious life: Rose herself, Bob Koesler, Stan Benson, and Rose's twin, Mike.

Alice and Rose had remained the best of friends, sharing all they realistically could.

Sister Rose continued to admire Bob Koesler, and to be amused by his accidental role as Catholic resource to the Detroit Police Department's homicide division.

She could not bring herself to feel friendship for Stan Benson. Rose simply could not stand a fence-straddler. And Stan had proven so motivated to mediocrity that he could have been inducted into a Phi Wishy-Washy fraternity.

Sister Rose preferred those who took a stand one way or the other. Even if it was impossible to agree with all such people, at least one knew where they stood.

She didn't understand what motivated Father Benson. Whatever it was, she didn't care for it or him.

A perfect example of someone with whom she disagreed radically, yet not only liked, but loved, was her twin, the dynamic and controversial monsignor.

Even in the seminary, Michael Smith had stood out. He won oratorical contests. He was appointed head prefect in college, a role that put him in charge—so to speak—of discipline, of which plenty was needed. Occasionally, he directed the Schola Cantorum—the choir. While not the quintessential athlete, still he was proficient at all major sports. He was on the good side of nearly all the professors. Last, and by no means least, he was a far better than average student.

Michael's broad field of accomplishments attracted the influential eyes not only of the seminary's rector but also of the majority of faculty members.

He was sent to study in Rome, and on his return was assigned to the Chancery. In time, he was made a monsignor. Everyone assumed that one day he would be consecrated a bishop. Initially, he would be an auxiliary bishop, helping out (literally) the Ordinary. Eventually, he would have his own diocese. Then possibly he would graduate to running a major archdiocese—Los Angeles, Boston, perhaps even Chicago or New York. Maybe he would become a Cardinal and elect a new Pope. That would in all probability be the limit. But not a cheap achievement by any standard.

Even in the sixties Mike had outdistanced his five special friends. But he didn't abandon them. He got together regularly with Koesler and Benson. He palled around with them and vacationed with them. By this time, Sister Mary Benedict had returned to being Alice McMann. As a seminarian, Mike had served at Alice's wedding to John Piccolo. He would have been involved in Alice's nullity case, had he not been excused due to their friendship.

However, when Alice married Manny in a civil ceremony, the future Monsignor Smith dropped them.

The Second Vatican Council took Monsignor Smith, and almost everyone else, by surprise. Mike understood the portent of Pope John's Council; he just could not guess how far it would go, nor how deeply it would affect him.

Just prior to the conclave that elected Pope John XXIII, Cardinal Edward Mooney died. He was succeeded by Archbishop Mark Boyle, whose reputation placed him at the far right of center. But at the four sessions of the Council, Mark Boyle went to school. He even played a major role in a radical change in the Church's understanding of marriage.

Michael Smith was caught up in his bishop's enthusiasm over the Council. After all, the Conciliar documents spelled out the Church's position in the modern world. But Smith went further than Boyle. Michael was captured by the arguments of activists. He knew not where the spirit would lead, but he was willing to follow.

Perhaps it was a mistake—certainly in conservative eyes—that Michael was appointed to a commission studying the reasons why so many were leaving the priesthood. This commission quickly concluded that so many priests did not, after five, ten, or twenty years, simply discover, "Hey, there's women!"

The Church had changed. Those who took the Council seriously and followed its directives perceived that the Church had, indeed, changed. It was no longer the cut-and-dried institution that claimed to have all the answers in neat, discrete piles.

Many of those priests who were swept up in new questioning of Church precepts also began to question their own commitment to the celibate life.

And so, for various reasons, many left the priesthood. Most did not leave the Church. Mother Church had supported them in the infancy of their priesthood. It was time, they thought, for them to help Mother through Her change of life.

Michael Smith was one who questioned, searched, and sought answers. When the answers he received did not agree with his educated concept of what Christ's Church was meant to stand for, he left the priesthood behind.

Were he to marry, in order to remain in good standing with the Church he would need laicization—permission granted by the Pope to return to the lay state. He would still remain a priest; nothing could change that. But, with laicization, the needed permission to function as a priest would henceforth be withheld.

Paul VI was a vacillating pontiff. How else could one describe a Pope who appoints a commission to study the Church's position on birth control and then rejects his own commission's conclusion? In the matter of laicization, there were times when the Papal policy granted the decrees and times when it did not. As well acquainted as Mike was with Rome and bishops and chanceries and those who had the Pope's ear, Michael would have known when to apply.

But he did not apply. Nor did he attempt to marry. He took seriously the promise he had given to live an unmarried life.

Michael spoke, lectured, and taught extensively. Frequently his path crossed that of Manny and Alice Tocco. Convocations, symposia and the like, such as Church-World-Kingdom, and Call to Action, frequently featured photos and a brief biography of Michael, and occasionally of Manny and Alice.

When the three met, they were cordial. But not as they had been in their youth.

As for his twin, Rose agreed with Michael on many churchly essentials. The two more frequently disagreed on how to right wrongs, or on how far to go. They were particularly popular when they appeared on the same program. The fact that they were twins who could disagree yet remain close drew a crowd.

Michael got along well with Bob Koesler. Koesler was always open to Michael's insights, whether he agreed or not. They remained friends.

Not so Michael and Stan Benson. Michael regarded Benson as a man who had no convictions or willingness to take a stand. He looked on Stan as one who seemed to have no opinions.

Michael didn't hold this total negativity against Stan. But since Stan appeared to have no opinions on any of the major controversies, Michael could not grasp why Stan did not at least agree on any of the subjects. Or why, if he felt no sense of agreement, he would not defend his lack of conviction.

To Stan it was all so simple. But he understood why he appeared as having a tabula rasa mind that was not used for any creative purpose. Outsiders simply thought he was dull . . . unimaginative.

Stan was in hiding. Joining in any adventure such as Michael's would be to throw open the door to questioning and subsequent exposure. For Stan that was unthinkable. He preferred to seem a dunce rather than to become vulnerable to having his secret exposed.

Michael had only disgust for people such as Stan. Here was a priest of some forty years who had lived through some of the most exciting times of the age-old Church of Rome. He had imaginative, involved friends. And yet, with all of this, he was still a blank wall.

He should have known. He should have participated. That he did not was a disservice to the Church.

Stan Benson should be gotten rid of.

Gotten rid of? Michael shuddered. What was he thinking!

But one thing Michael Smith had learned over the years: Nothing conceivable to man is impossible.

31

"I WONDERED . . . WOULD you give the eulogy?"

"Sure, Stan," Father Koesler responded without hesitation.

Most priests consider it an honor to be asked to give the eulogy of a priest's relative—or of a fellow priest. In the laity's parlance, the practice might be termed a professional courtesy. To priests, it is another manifestation of bonding. At this most solemn moment, the celebration of the end of mortal life, priests tend to gather and offer prayer and moral support.

"Lily . . ." Koesler said. ". . . that was your mother's name, wasn't it?"

"Yes."

"And how old was she?"

"Ninety-four. She would have been ninety-five next month."

Koesler had never felt at ease with the small talk exchange that usually followed a death notice. Obviously, Stan's mother had lived an uncommonly long life. It was no surprise to Stan's few friends that his priesthood was his mother's pride. She had basked in the sublime vocation of her son the priest.

"Well," Koesler said, "you made her proud of you. You know that, don't you?"

"I know." No one knew what Stan had paid for that pride. It had cost him his life. He had paid a profound price for his mother's happiness. But, he felt, the price was worth it.

The Bensons were a reclusive family. Koesler had known

them as well as or better than anyone else. He was inquiring into Stan's memories of his mother to get more personal detail for the eulogy. It was like pulling impacted teeth.

This was Monday. The funeral would be Wednesday morning, with a wake Tuesday evening.

As it turned out, the wake was peculiar in that hardly anyone attended. That was extremely odd for a prayer service and viewing of a priest's mother. But very few were in any way close to either Stan or his mother.

Manny and Alice, Sister Rose and Michael Smith attended. But they spent most of their time in conversation with each other. The Toccos and Michael had long since buried the hatchet, although not very deep.

A more representative crowd showed up for the funeral itself. A couple of auxiliary bishops attended, some priests concelebrated. A few of Stan's former parishioners were there. Lily had outlived most of her contemporaries.

Stan Benson was the picture of self-control. Inside he was screaming. Now his mother knew. Now she knew what her joy had cost him. Could she be happy knowing this? He loved her. He always had. He didn't regret the sacrifice he had been forced to make.

It's unfair, Momma. I shouldn't have to stand over your casket. I can't cry. No one will let me. I don't mind your wanting me to be a priest. I would have done anything for you. I proved that by sacrificing my life. Don't blame yourself, Momma. You wanted what you thought would be best for me. Rest now, Momma. You've had a long and mostly happy life. I will probably follow you shortly. I pray you will be there to welcome me home.

The funeral service continued toward its conclusion. Stan had presided over so many similar liturgies, he scarcely paid any attention to the routine that washed over him. He did hear Father Koesler's eulogy. For what little he had to work with, Bob did a fine job. He just had not known her very well. Perhaps not even Lily's husband, Stan's father, had known Lily Benson as well as did her son.

The final requiem was sung. The congregation left to go

about their business. A few journeyed to the cemetery. Koesler was the only priest besides Stan at the graveside. The ceremony was characteristically brief. Finally, only Benson and Koesler remained.

"Thank you, Bob," Benson said, turning to his most dependable friend. "The eulogy was beautiful."

"I wish I had known her better. There was probably lots more to touch upon."

"The 'lots more' would've had to come from me. And I didn't have the gumption to say it. But there is one more thing you could do."

"Anything."

"I need to talk to you."

"Of course."

"Tonight?"

"Sure. Where?"

"St. John's. Our old alma mater."

"Eight o'clock okay?"

"I'll meet you at the foyer."

They shook hands and parted.

32

THEY MET PROMPTLY at eight.

There was a wedding going on in the chapel. But the room they chose to use was empty and available. In the distance, they could dimly hear the sounds of a wedding and the organ.

"I have been keeping a secret for a long, long time," Stan said. "Since I was an altar boy at Our Lady of Guadalupe parish."

"Man, that is a while!" A thought occurred to Koesler. "Did you want to make this a Confession?"

"No," Stan replied. "That won't be necessary." He paused several moments. "This is very difficult," he said finally.

Koesler nodded sympathetically, understandingly, supportively.

Another long pause.

"Maybe," Koesler suggested, "if we walk around? Like we used to do?"

"Maybe."

They left the building and began walking together through the various gardens and shrines.

"Are you sure you want to do this?" Koesler asked.

"I'm sorry. I don't want to waste your time."

"You're not wasting my time, Stan. It's just that I've never seen you like this before."

"Okay. Here goes." Stan seemed to take a deep breath. "It begins with my parents."

"Yes?"

"They weren't married in the Church."

"Well, they must have had their marriage convalidated; they went to Communion regularly."

"They did . . . and they didn't."

Stan recounted his days as just about the only faithful altar boy Guadalupe parish had. His father had been married before and couldn't qualify for a nullity. His parents had gotten married eventually, but only civil law recognized the marriage. Stan's mother had been carefully taught by the Church that her marital state was leading her into everlasting hellfire.

Koesler understood. He'd seen this sort of case many times. He knew about the torture of the threat of hell. In his later years as a priest he had tried to alleviate that threat and restore couples to confidence in God's love.

Stan continued. Because of his fidelity as a Mass server, his mother thought that he wanted to be a priest. Actually, he just loved the Mass. He didn't want to "do" Mass. He didn't want to be a priest. But his mother never knew that. All she saw was his fidelity. Like too many people who assume something is so just because they want it to be, Stan's mother added two and two and got five. After all, how could a boy be faithful to Mass and not want to be a priest?

Whatever, her convoluted thinking only added to her torture. Not only was she responsible for her own damnation, but she had led her husband down the same path. If their marriage was invalid, it couldn't be invalid for only one partner. And now, the final blow that intensified her torture: Her nonmarriage had made a bastard of her son. And that bastardy would block his entry to the seminary and his vocation as a priest.

Enter Father Ed Simpson.

There was something wrong at this point in Stan's narration. Koesler could not put his finger on it. He would have to wait till Stan completed his story. "You mean Ed Simpson, pastor of Guadalupe?"

"The very one." Stan had never figured out why Father Simpson was so determined that he become a priest. But the old man certainly seemed determined that Stan do just that.

Simpson effectively built a dilemma around the boy. Simpson was going to completely save Mrs. Benson's soul—as well as Mr. Benson's. But Simpson was also going to shepherd little Stan into the seminary.

Lily would be ecstatic. But to complete her happiness, Stan would have to become a priest. It's what she wanted more than anything in the world. She had been convinced from the start that Stan wanted to be a priest. She wanted that too. With her marriage fixed, no obstacle stood before her son. But should Stan fail, his mother's bliss would be shattered.

As a final touch, Simpson gathered the necessary documents, forging at least Lily's marriage record. With that taken care of, the marriage repaired and all, nothing stood in Stanley's path to the seminary and the priesthood. Should he back away, Mother would be crushed—which was the last thing in the world Stan wanted.

"How," Koesler interrupted, "did Simpson convalidate the marriage? I haven't heard a single word that sounds like Tribunal."

"That's almost the weirdest part," Stan said. "Did you ever hear of a 'Missionaries' Privilege'?"

"I must confess I've heard of the Missionary position."

Ignoring the levity, Benson proceeded to explain Simpson's claim to have received Pontifical permission to let owners of harems select one member as his true and only wife and thus conform to Christian monogamy.

"Half of that is believable," Koesler said. "I have heard of the custom in mission territories to downsize to one wife. But that Simpson had one of those alleged permissions left over, and that he would spend it on your mother . . . well, I find that just ridiculous."

"That's what it seemed like even to me at the time."

"Then why didn't you tell your mother it was a hoax?"

"God forgive me . . ." Benson bowed his head. ". . . but Simpson had made my mother happy and at peace for the first time in many long years."

Koesler nodded. "Of course. As long as she believed Simpson's malarkey, she would be happy and at peace."

"Happy and at peace," Benson repeated. "I dedicated my life to that—keeping her happy and at peace. I could never let her know the truth. And so, of course, I had to get into the seminary, and the priesthood.

"But I had to keep all this a secret. Her welfare—her happiness—depended on no one's knowing our secret. The truth would've destroyed her.

"So I've gone through my life keeping what is now termed a low profile. That meant I had to divorce myself from any and every decision or action that might be the least bit controversial.

"A good example: When Manny and Alice wanted me to solve their granddaughter's problem with a Communion wafer having no gluten, I knew what they requested was correct. I also knew that if I didn't follow the Church guidelines, I almost certainly would attract a spotlight. Some reporter, some bitter conservative or Church official, might start digging around, talking to my mother, finding out about Simpson's crackpot privilege. That could destroy the fiction I'd created. Actually, the fiction I'd built on Simpson's fiction."

"I would never have guessed," Koesler said in wonderment. "What a story!"

They walked on in silence. Koesler found the tale difficult to sort out. "So," he said finally, "you said this isn't a confession. Besides, I can't think of any sin you might have committed. So . . . why? Why tell me now? Because your mother is gone?"

Stan shook his head. "Because I don't know what my status is. I knew there was some kind of impediment to Orders if a guy was illegitimate. I was illegitimate in the eyes of the Church. If you want to discount Simpson's make-believe convalidation, I'm still illegitimate. So, what's my standing in the Church? I honestly don't know."

"I know the Canon Law prof skipped over the Order impediments for our class," Koesler said. "Yours too?"

Stan nodded.

"I think," Koesler said, "he passed over them because there were two thousand four hundred and fourteen laws to study and he could be pretty sure that if any of us had an impediment, the system—records and so forth—would have flushed them out.

"But you had a vested interest in the answer to your situation. How come you didn't look it up on your own?"

"Because I'm weak!" Stan's reply was almost shouted.

"Keep it down," Koesler cautioned. "Somebody else might be out here." After a moment, he asked, "What do you mean you're 'weak'?"

Stan sighed. "Did you ever come across somebody who had the symptoms of, say, cancer, but didn't go to a doctor for a checkup because he was afraid of what the examination might disclose?"

Koesler knew any number of people—including himself—who would fit that bill. "Sure."

"That's how I am about this. I was afraid to dig into it for fear I would find something really wrong. I can't tell you how many times I've opened the *Codex Iuris Canonici* and came close to looking up everything in there about impediments to Holy Orders . . . especially regarding illegitimates. But . . . my life was in delicate balance. Momma was happy. I couldn't chance upsetting that cart."

Koesler shook his head. "I wish you had told me what we were going to discuss this evening; I would've looked it up. But I do know enough about it to address your question."

Stan stood still and shut his eyes tight. "Go ahead."

"Okay. First of all, there were certain impediments to Orders in 1917 when the earlier Code was promulgated. The idea was to avoid—well, shocking the Faithful. The hierarchy of about a hundred years ago feared the Faithful would be distracted in their worship if the priest was 'deformed.' Maybe he had a hunchback, or a clubfoot, or a shriveled arm, or a cleft palate, or a stammer . . . or maybe there was merely a general awareness that the priest was illegitimate."

Stan winced. Now he really expected the worst.

"But," Koesler continued, "there wasn't any specified penalty to illegitimacy. Illegitimates were termed 'irregular.' They could be dispensed by a bishop. It was as simple as that." Now Koesler knew what had distracted him a few minutes before. It was Stan's statement that his illegitimacy had blocked his possible ordination.

"Then what about my illegitimate cousin in Ohio?" Stan's voice was challenging; he wanted to be permanently rid of his doubts. "He was told in no uncertain terms that he couldn't go to the seminary because his father had been divorced and his parents hadn't been able to marry in the Church. So he couldn't be a priest . . . and that was the only thing he wanted."

Koesler shrugged. It had gotten too dark for Stan to see the gesture.

"Lots of people made up their minds that illegitimates were banned from the priesthood," Koesler said. "If you believed this hard enough, it came true. Your cousin got bad advice—undoubtedly from some priest . . . maybe some priest who even believed it himself. But in any case, when the guy was told by a priest that his illegitimacy barred him from the priesthood, well, of course he believed it. And so it became a fact.

"And you believed the same thing. And it became a fact for you too—at least until Father Simpson made you believe that he could 'fix' it." Koesler shook his head again. "Stan, illegitimacy isn't even mentioned in connection with Orders in the new 1983 Code."

"Then . . ." So heavily had Stan perspired that his clothes were clinging to him. ". . . nothing terrible happened? I mean, I ruined my life, but nothing else bad happened?" He felt a wave of relief wash over him—much like the patient who feared having a fatal illness only to find his condition benign. He felt like going out to celebrate. He felt like baying at the moon. He felt like leaping off the ground.

Gradually, Stan sensed that Bob Koesler was not sharing in this elation, this relief, this ebullience. Doubts began to creep into his troubled conscience. "Bob, what's wrong? You just gave me terrific news. You couldn't have made me happier. Can't you share in my happiness?"

Try as he might, for Stan's sake, Koesler could not. He stood silent.

"What is it, Bob? Tell me!"

Koesler sighed. "I suppose I must . . ." He hesitated. "But . . . well, once your awareness settles . . . uh . . . you'd probably figure it out for yourself. Or somebody would bring it up in casual conversation. So we should try now to figure some way out of it—"

"For the love of God, Bob," Stan's voice was rising again, "what are you talking about?"

Koesler steered Stan to a nearby bench, and the two sat down.

"Stan," Koesler began, "you feared there would be dire consequences to your becoming a priest because you were— or are—illegitimate. There aren't any such consequences. And for that I rejoice with you. But—"

"But what!?"

"Okay. You've heard of a shotgun wedding?"

"Of course. It doesn't have to be a real gun. Just something that forces . . ." Stan's voice trailed off. "Just something that forces . . ." He saw clearly where this was heading. He didn't want to go there.

"One of the questions," Koesler said, "that we probe when we are preparing a couple for marriage is whether each of them is entering this life together willingly, under absolutely no force or coercion, or fear. Not infrequently, when someone challenges the validity of a marriage, the contention is that he or she got married to please parents. Or because someone or something was threatening them.

"Now if that's really the case, the marriage can be declared null and void. In other words, from the very beginning of the couple's life together, there was no marriage . . . all because of force and fear."

Stan's head drooped until it was almost touching his chest.

Koesler wondered whether he should have brought this

up. He tried to convince himself it was better that Stan learn it from a friend than from anyone else. Worse still if Stan had come to this realization himself. And he likely would have; Stan was the type who, if he could dismiss a worrisome concern, would find another one as a replacement.

"What does this mean?" Stan murmured. "I gave my mother a happy life she wouldn't otherwise have had. I gave Father Simpson whatever—whatever the hell—he was looking for. But at what cost? At . . . what . . . cost?"

They sat in silence for what seemed a very long time.

"You didn't have a chance, Stan," Koesler said finally, trying to console his friend. "Whichever way you turned, you were boxed in. Your mother was the innocent in all this. She received a bogus miracle from Simpson. You alone could destroy it. And you wouldn't do that. You *couldn't* do that. Not many feeling human beings could destroy their own mother."

Koesler knew he was talking in circles now. Always returning to Lily Benson and the love between mother and son. Mother was able to assist son in what she thought was his undying desire to be a priest. Son could not turn down her gift and lead the sort of life he really wanted. A perfect dilemma.

"At what cost? At what cost?" Stan kept repeating the question like a mantra.

"Don't do this to yourself," Koesler said. "It wasn't your fault."

"It's not a matter of whose fault it is. I am not a priest. I never was a priest. I was forced into a false ordination."

"Don't go on like this!" Koesler admonished. "Maybe we can work out something. There is a law—*Ecclesia supplet*—that the Church supplies what is needed. The Church can take care of canonical glitches when there's been a blunder committed. Like when a canonical detail has been forgotten or overlooked and the bride is about to walk down the aisle. The Church can supply the proper jurisidiction or permission—or whatever is missing. Maybe we can work out something like that."

So concerned was Koesler about his friend's emotional health that he was grasping at straws.

"It's one thing," Benson said softly, "to build on a mistake. It's something else to work with nothing.

"The hundreds, thousands, of Masses!" He spoke as if to himself. "The hundreds of thousands of absolutions I've given! The marriages I've witnessed! Can the Church supply validity for all these?"

He turned to look at his friend, although it was too dark to see Koesler's face. "Bob, it's not that I forgot something on the way to the altar. It's more like Joe Blow stepped into a Confessional and began giving absolution. I am not a priest. I never was. I've never wanted to be a priest. And I never was."

Moonlight shone into Benson's eyes. They were moist with tears and somehow childlike. "I've wasted my life and brought nothing good into anyone else's life."

"That's not true, Stan. God would never let it be true."

"We're not talking about God, Bob. We're talking about law."

Silence.

"There's a rollaway bed in my apartment, Stan. Why don't you stay with me for a while? Until we straighten this all out?"

Benson shook his head. "I've got some thinking to do. Don't worry about me, Bob. I'll be all right."

"Stan . . ."

"Please, Bob: It'll be okay. I've just got to be by myself. I'll be in touch.

"And, Bob: Don't feel bad that you were the one to open my eyes. If you hadn't done it, I'd have done it myself in time. And it was so much better to have you around when I found out. Besides, I asked you for a rundown on my status. I'm grateful. Honest."

"Stan . . ."

Benson chuckled. "I'm a big boy. I'll be okay. Go home. I'll be in touch."

Most reluctantly, Koesler departed, but not before he

placed his hand on Benson's shoulder and gave what he hoped was a reassuring squeeze.

Father Koesler was engaged in one of his favorite forms of relaxation. Eyes closed, stretched out in a recliner, he was enjoying the glorious voice of Jonathan Swift. Koesler had filled the CD player with Swift's recordings, from operatic selections to songs of the tenor's birthplace, Scotland. Scenes of the breathtakingly beautiful Scottish highlands filled his mind's eye, as Swift's rendition of "Loch Lomond" wafted throughout Koesler's living quarters.

The priest smiled, recalling his own visit to Loch Lomond many autumns ago. He almost chuckled aloud, recalling how he had sat below in the cabin, while a boatload of tourists faced the loch breeze above on the deck. Finding himself alone, Koesler had broken into his own rendition of "Loch Lomond." He had sung at the top of his lungs, confident that the grating rattle of the boat's engine would provide cover for his frivolous action.

Frivolous action. Had Stan Benson ever enjoyed anything frivolous? Koesler wondered. He tried to think back over what he knew of Stan's life. He couldn't recall Stan ever doing anything frivolous or being anything but serious and sober. Now that he thought of it, he realized that Stan had always seemed to have the weight of the world on his shoulders. Koesler had never before adverted to this. He was reasonably sure that none of the others in the circle of six had ever adverted to it either; all of them had been too busy making their own way through life.

The CD player had switched to "Songs of Italy," an early recording, made before Swift's light baritone had evolved into a liquid tenor.

Italy. Once more, scenes of yore crowded into Koesler's mind. His trip to Rome when Cardinal Boyle had received the red hat. Rome, the mountaintop of Catholicism . . . whence had been handed down the 2,414 laws that had ruled so many lives . . . and ruined not a few. Like that of Stan Benson.

Stan. Koesler brought his recliner up to sitting position. His brow knitted. Three days had passed since his meeting with Stan at St. John's Center. Koesler had been expecting a call from Benson, and if truth be known, as the day wore on he had become increasingly anxious. Funny, under ordinary circumstances, Koesler would think nothing of it if he and Stan didn't meet or even speak for months. But now, given the fraught nature of their recent conversation, Koesler felt that contact was overdue.

Koesler resolved that if he did not hear from Stan by this afternoon . . .

As if on cue, the phone rang. Startled, Koesler almost leaped out of his chair in his haste to answer it.

"Father Koesler? This is Mrs. Schultz."

Koesler's gorge rose. He had to fight back nausea. He knew Mrs. Schultz, although he had met her only a few times. She was Stan's occasional housekeeper. That she should be calling now . . .

"I hate to be the one to tell you," she said. "It's Father Benson."

"How bad is it?"

"He has expired."

"Oh, God!" Koesler pulled himself together. "Can you tell me—uh, how did it happen?"

"I can't tell you much of anything, Father. I found him this morning. The police came. And I don't know what all . . ." Her voice betrayed her anxiety.

"I'll be right over."

"Before you come, Father, you should know: The police found Father's Last Will, and you're the executive."

"Executor," Koesler corrected. "He never mentioned that. But I'm not surprised. Is . . . is Father's body still at home?"

"They took him downtown . . . to the morgue."

Good, thought Koesler. He and Dr. Moellmann, the County Medical Examiner, were friends. Dr. Moellmann would have, literally, the last word on the cause of death.

* * *

Father Koesler arrived at Our Lady of Guadalupe to find the neighbors, such as they were, gathered in front of the rectory. Whatever had happened, they figured it must be important. After all, a couple of marked Detroit police cars, as well as a couple of unmarked ones, were parked at the curb. And—the real drawing card—a television van had just pulled up. Maybe Father Benson's neighbors would find themselves on TV tonight! They would have to settle for considerably less than fifteen minutes of fame.

Koesler had placed a call and left a message for Dr. Moellmann, who was busy even then with Father's Benson's autopsy.

In the meantime, the priest found the will. Koesler marveled at how little Stan Benson had possessed. Obviously he had wanted little from life. And life had given him little. Everything was to go to Maryknoll, a missionary order. The Order would never survive solely on Stan's bequest.

As executor, Koesler felt he should be doing something; he wasn't quite sure what. He rummaged perfunctorily through a chest of drawers. He was brought up short when he came across a hairshirt, an item worn as a means of self-inflicted penance. The priest quickly decided to dispose of it. Stan would not want it known that he had a medieval monastic bent.

An officer approached Koesler. There were some routine questions. A confused housekeeper had been of little help. The officer had reassured her that these questions were not of supreme importance. He would ask around. Koesler knew the answers to most of the questions. For the rest, he suggested the officer contact the Chancery. They were likely to know all the minutiae.

Stan had left no specific request for a liturgy. Koesler elected himself principal concelebrant. He hoped that some of the Detroit priests would attend. Koesler, the Chancery, and the funeral home would take care of lingering details.

The phone rang. Mrs. Schutz answered it, then handed the receiver to Koesler.

"Father Koesler . . ." It was the familiar, Teutonic-accented voice of Dr. Willie Moellmann. "I'm sorry I couldn't get back to you sooner. I was waiting for the lab report."

Good old Dr. Moellmann: He placed his own phone calls. It was never, "Just a moment please for the doctor."

"That's okay, Doctor. I'm grateful you returned my call. Do you have anything on Father's death?"

"Yes. Death was due to asphyxiation. The cause was carbon monoxide poisoning. From all appearances, most likely accidental."

Koesler breathed a sigh of relief. He hadn't wanted to think—! "You're sure?"

Dr. Moellmann chuckled. "When am I *not* sure? It wasn't difficult. From what I'm told, the rectory is an old house with a gas furnace, and a large fan and vent in the kitchen. It was recently renovated; the doors and windows were replaced. Also new insulation was added. All in all, an accident waiting to happen."

"How so?"

"Obviously, no fresh air could enter without cracking open a window or door. The fan was running, creating a backflow down the chimney, instead of exhausting from the chimney. The furnace goes on under negative pressure. Carbon monoxide replaces oxygen. The victim suffocates."

Koesler automatically almost asked again, "You're sure?" but stopped himself. Dr. Moellmann had already committed himself on that, and did not suffer foolish questions gladly.

Koesler would rephrase the question. "There's nothing else involved?"

"I just got the lab report. The carbon monoxide binds to the blood and the blood turns a dark cherry color. It was an easy test. There was no sign of struggle—or anything of that nature that would suggest homicide. There was no indication of suicide like a note. So, it will be termed an accident." It was obvious that Dr. Moellmann's statement was a conclusive one. Sort of, thought Koesler, like *Roma locuta est; causa finita est*—Rome has spoken, the matter is closed.

"Thank you, Doctor. Maybe we can do lunch sometime."

"*Ja*. Call me." And he hung up.

One thing more, thought Koesler: We have to have a gathering of the group.

33

IT WAS 6 P.M. The five remaining principals were assembled in the cafeteria of St. John's Center.

"We haven't been together as a group in a long, long time," Koesler said.

"And now," Sister Rose Smith said, "it is funerals that bring us together. First Mrs. Benson, and then our friend Stan."

"He never really belonged to this group." Michael Smith had a perceptible chip on his shoulder. "Bob dragged him in and the rest of us adopted him like a stray dog."

"Come on, Mike," his twin said. "Lighten up. We just buried the poor guy. If anything, we ought to be examining our conscience and see what we did to cause his death."

"Rose is right," Alice said. "And, in a way, so is Mike. We weren't exactly gracious to Stan. He was always odd man out. Maybe if we had been kinder, more welcoming, this wouldn't have happened."

"What did we have to do with it? It's been declared an accident. That means nobody is responsible," Manny said. "After all, it's not as if he committed suicide . . ." He turned to Bob Koesler. ". . . did he?"

Koesler had been mulling over the medical examiner's conclusion: accidental death. But Koesler couldn't rid himself of the bee buzzing around in his brain. What if . . . what if . . . what if Stanley, so upset and depressed over the news Koesler had given him, had indeed decided that life was no longer worth living? Just because Stanley hadn't left any note didn't necessarily mean that he hadn't taken his own

life. Maybe in committing suicide—if that was the case—
Stan had thought of that old legal term, *res ipsa loquitur*—
the thing speaks for itself.

Did "the thing" speak for itself? Was it so evident that
Stan felt his whole life had been a waste, a lie, a farce; was
that enough to cause him to turn on the exhaust fan, set the
thermostat, and calmly lie down to go to sleep for the last
time?

And if so, how would anyone ever know? Maybe Stan
had intended for his death to be ambiguous, believing that
his old friend and classmate, his fellow priest, Bob Koesler,
would get the message and understand?

Oddly, Father Koesler, upright man that he was, had not
till now even thought to consider the possibility that someone
else—who?—could have set up the circumstances leading to
Stan Benson's death. But now that the horrid possibility occurred, all he could think of was: Who would do that? And
why? The old rule in mysterious deaths was: Who profits?
But nobody would profit from Father Stanley Benson's death.
What little he had—a pittance—would go to Maryknoll.
And it was all Father Koesler could do to keep from laughing at the very image of any Maryknoller creeping into
Guadalupe's ancient rectory to commit murder. No way!

He was brought back to reality as Manny repeated his
question, this time somewhat insistently. "He didn't commit
suicide, did he, Bob?"

"If nobody is responsible," Mike interjected, "then what
are we all doing here this evening?" He looked at Bob.
"Maybe we're here," he said, answering his own question,
"so that Bob—amateur detective that he is—can pace back
and forth like Sherlock Holmes and tell us which of us
'dun it.' "

"For heaven's sake, Mike," Rose said, "will you stop
being such a jerk!"

Michael shot an irate glance at his sister but said nothing.

"In a way, all of you have a piece of the truth as I understand it," Koesler said. "I think Stanley Benson has something to teach us—all of us. I think we owe it to him—and

to ourselves—to learn something from his life . . . and from his death."

Mike laughed. "He's going to become St. Stanley?"

The others were growing short of patience with Mike. When no one responded to his jibe, Mike looked around the circle. One corner of his mouth pulled down in irritation. But he seemed to be getting the message.

Manny picked up Mike's baton. "What, exactly, do you mean, Bob? What can we possibly learn from Stan's life . . . or his death? That he was too cruel to be a priest?" They all knew that Manny was alluding to Stan's sloughing off Manny's granddaughter's problem. "Or," he continued, "that we should provide ventilation when we are dealing with carbon monoxide?"

Manny recalled Stan's bragging that he'd had the rectory repaired and the windows and doors replaced. So the ME's finding was that the cause of death was asphyxiation due to carbon monoxide fumes. The large kitchen exhaust fan was left running, eventually pulling inside the living quarters the poisonous fumes from the chimney. It appeared that Stan had forgotten to turn off the fan, had gone to bed, fallen asleep, and never awakened.

Now Manny too began to have second thoughts. Was it possible—? No! He dismissed immediately the idea that anyone had killed Stan. But suicide? Was that more likely? Manny shook his head. If truth be known, he didn't think enough of Stan to consider that Stan had the grit to commit suicide.

Manny straightened up. "Sorry," he said, in apology for his seemingly shallow or mean comments. "But"—he looked at Koesler—"why *are* we here now?"

This wasn't going as Koesler had planned. He'd better get things on track and keep them there. "I think it's important for us to understand Stan. And I confess I myself didn't understand him until about a week ago—the night after we buried his mother.

"At his invitation, I met with Stan here at St. John's. He told me pretty much everything about his life."

He had their complete attention. They had not expected a biography of someone they'd thought they knew pretty thoroughly.

Koesler took them through Stan's experience with the Mass, and his fidelity as a server. Mike and Manny could understand; they'd had similar experiences. Except that in their case, the fascination with the Mass and with the priesthood that produced it had led them toward the seminary. They were startled to learn that while Stan had shared their attachment to the Mass, the priesthood had never held the slightest attraction for him.

"Then why," Alice asked, "did he go to the seminary?"

Koesler explained the linchpin role that Father Simpson had played. The phony annulment, the fake convalidation, the alleged leftover annulment from missionary days, locking everyone concerned into unbreachable secrecy.

"You mean to tell us that the Bensons and Stan fell for that!" Manny couldn't believe it. "That's incredible!"

"Not if you're a tortured soul convinced you're going to hell," said Koesler. "Along comes a trusted priest, their pastor, and tells Mrs. Benson that she doesn't have to go. No matter how fanciful this scenario seems to us now, she wanted so badly for it to happen that she would have believed anything . . . and she did believe everything Father Simpson told her."

"And Stan?" Rose asked. "He didn't have to have a fairy tale to clutch."

"He didn't have to swallow the myth. The motivation Simpson used on Stan was his mother's happiness. She had always believed that Stan wanted desperately to be a priest. He hadn't set her straight because it didn't matter: He was an ecclesial bastard and was led to believe that his condition was an irreversible impediment to Orders—that it made it impossible for him to ever become a priest.

"Then," Koesler continued, "Father Simpson waves his magic wand, and Mrs. Benson is back in the Church's good graces. So, of course, she assumes there is no longer any impediment to Stan's becoming a priest; now he can pursue what both of them wanted so desperately—the priesthood."

"What kind of a monster would manipulate a family like that!" Rose stormed. "What kind of monster would manipulate *anyone* like that?"

"Good question," Koesler replied. "Who's to know? There must have been some reason other than sheer whimsy on Simpson's part. Maybe it was for selfish purposes—or maybe he actually thought he was doing good. But, as I said, who's to know?"

The silence was almost pregnant as each searched his or her brain for a possible answer. Finally, an oddly sympathetic Michael spoke. "I think," he said, "all you have to do is look at the parish."

"The parish? What's the parish got to do with it?" Manny asked.

"Guadaloop!" Mike said in a don't-you-understand tone. "It had gone to seed. Simpson was miserable. It was no secret that producing seminarians was the mark of a properly pastored parish. So if Simpson could produce a seminarian—even better, a priest—the Chancery might move him to a much more prestigious place. Actually," he said, almost as a side thought, "*any* other place would've been more prestigious than Guadaloop.

"Believe me," he said, "in the time I worked in the Chancery, I saw lots of guys like Simpson . . . although, now that I think of it, none of them were as mean-spirited and manipulative as that guy—at least, not that I know of."

"Okay," Koesler said. "Stan gave me the skeleton of what got him into the seminary and kept him there—and in the priesthood." He looked around at the others. "We've put flesh on Stan's ordeal." The others nodded.

"The next thing on Stan's agenda was to get lost in the crowd, as it were, and to stay lost. He was deathly afraid that someone might stumble on the secret he was keeping so diligently. So he deliberately led a life of colorless mediocrity."

"I've got to confess," Manny said, "I did wonder about

that. I always thought Stan knew more—much more—than he showed."

"In fact," Koesler said, "he specifically mentioned you, Manny, and your granddaughter. I can tell you now, he agreed with you totally. But he was afraid that if he solved your problem, if he went along with you—which he could have done, and which he wanted to do—he would have smashed to smithereens clear Church law. The spotlight would be on him, and he feared what might be revealed. It tore him up to refuse you."

Manny, and even Mike, were moved by this simple revelation.

"And I gave him such a hard time," Manny said.

"We all did at one time or another, in one way or another," Alice said.

"Long before Pope John called for a reform of Church law," said Koesler, "Stan believed that Canon Law was just an effective way of keeping people in line. If he had become what he wanted to be—a good secretary—he wouldn't ever have thought about Canon Law. Now he had to enforce it in its most literal and exact demands.

"The final blow was his status. He insisted that I tell him what his situation really was. I told him, of course, that his illegitimacy was an impediment that could be dealt with . . . that it was no great problem."

"How come he didn't know that himself?" Rose asked.

"He explained it that night," Koesler said. "He was like someone who feared he had cancer and was too frightened to go to a doctor and find out for sure. Too frightened that the doctor would confirm his worst fears.

"I can't tell you how relieved Stan was when I told him that the impediment didn't really make that much difference."

"And then you told him, didn't you?" Mike said. It was an accusation rather than a question.

"Told him what?" Alice asked.

"He just didn't have an out, did he . . . they just didn't leave him an out," Mike said.

"That's right," Koesler replied. "He owed his priesthood to the very force that surrounded and engulfed him."

"He wasn't really a priest!" Manny's tone was almost awed.

"That is, indeed, the bottom line," Koesler said.

"When I think," Rose said, "of the things we suffered—or thought we were suffering in our lives—!"

"They don't seem much in comparison," Alice said.

"Now," Koesler said, "you know what the cause of Stan's death was . . ."

"Officially, it's listed as an accident," Mike said.

"That's right. Not wanting to throw my police weight around"—Koesler bowed to Mike—"I talked to the medical examiner. He found nothing to indicate anything other than accidental death. There was no suicide note. No sign of a struggle or anything you'd be likely to find in a case of homicide. Which leaves only accidental death."

"After what we've heard," Manny said, "I'd say it probably was suicide. But if so—and I never thought I'd say this—it was justifiable suicide."

"I guess I was the last person to talk with him—before he let his life slip away," Koesler said. "He was like a trapped and hopeless animal. He couldn't have been responsible for what he did. I have to agree with Manny: justifiable suicide."

"After all," Mike added, "the Church nowadays considers that an apparent suicide was just that: apparent. The presumption is that the guy was not in full command of his faculties. I agree with Bob and Mike: justifiable suicide."

"And I agree," Alice said.

"And I too," Rose said. "But something's missing."

"I can't imagine what . . . ," Alice said.

"I'm surprised"—a smile played at Rose's lips—"with good Catholics like us, I'm surprised we haven't come up with 'who dun it.' "

"You mean who's responsible?" Manny said. "My nominee has to be Simpson. He screwed everyone: Mr. and Mrs. Benson, and, of course, Stan. Just to get—if Mike is correct—a chance at a better parish."

"I think," Rose said, "maybe we all share a bit of the blame."

Judging from the looks the others gave her, it was not a consensus.

But Koesler would not be bulldozed. He took a piece of paper from his pocket and unfolded it. "Indulge me as I read," he said. "This is a column by Sally Jenkins of the *Washington Post*. It ran August 4, 2001. It impressed me so much that I've kept it. I think it speaks to our present situation.

"Anybody remember a pro football player named Korey Stringer?"

"He played for the Minnesota Vikings, didn't he?" Manny said.

"Yeah," Mike said. "He died . . . heatstroke, wasn't it?"

"Yeah," Manny echoed. "It was August and the heat index was something like a hundred and ten degrees. And the team was working out in full pads and everything."

"What a memory!" Rose said.

"Football!" Alice's lip curled.

"Okay," Koesler said. "That's the background all right. Now I'd like to read you excerpts from the column, which I'll paraphrase, and comment on as we go along.

"Minnesota's coach contended that Stringer's death was 'unexplainable' and said that no one in the organization should feel guilt over it. But the cause of death was quite specific: heatstroke. If you accept the coach's word 'unexplainable' you let the whole organization off the hook. 'The inference is that because it was unexplainable, it was not preventable.' But experts were unanimous that it was preventable. One expert called it 'inexcusable.' 'No pro football player,' he said, 'should die of heatstroke . . . if the most basic attention is paid and precautions are taken.'

" 'Unexplainable. Inexcusable. Stand those two words side by side and you see why [the coach] clings so hard to his. If Stringer's death was explainable, it was preventable. And if it was preventable it was inexcusable.'

"Then the writer asks what was so important about two-a-day practices in such crushing heat? Nothing, say physiologists everywhere."

Koesler put aside the paper for a moment. "It just goes to enforce the image of the macho pro player," he said. "Nothing stops the athlete. Not heat, not snow, not most injuries. 'Suck it up,' coaches say.

"There were lots of things the coaches could have done to avoid this useless and meaningless death. In weather too hot for football, they could have practiced without pads and merely walked through play patterns. They could have practiced early in the morning or late in the afternoon when the temperature was less hazardous and more conducive to survival. They could have seen to it that the players were taking enough liquids. And so on.

"The point this columnist makes is that Korey Stringer's death was preventable, therefore inexcusable.

"Something like that could be said about Stan Benson. He could have confessed to his mother that he didn't want to be a priest, that he wouldn't be happy as a priest. His mother would have been hurt—maybe even devastated. But if she loved her son—and she did—she would have recovered.

"Father Simpson could have made the best of Guadalupe. Or he could have found a less hurtful way of trying to move up or be transferred . . . if that was, indeed, his motive—and that we'll never really know; we can only guess.

"In any case, we ourselves could have been more sensitive in picking up signs. They were there—if more subtly.

"The solution to Stringer's life-threatening episode is clearly more evident. But in either case, death was preventable."

Koesler picked up the paper again. "Finally," he said, "we turn to Rose's question: 'Who dun it?'

"There's enough blame to go around in both examples of Stringer and Stan. But the point the columnist makes is worth thinking about. After puncturing the mystique of football and its insistence on the players pushing themselves beyond ordinary human endurance, the writer addresses the question:

" 'Stringer's death was all too explainable: He was killed by an old idea. He was the victim of an archaic concept of toughness.'

"And," Koesler said, "I'd like to suggest that Stan Benson was killed by old law. Forget the coaches, the physical therapists, the heart, the pads, the dehydration, and all the rest. 'Stringer was killed by an old idea. He was the victim of an archaic concept of toughness.'

"Forget us and Lily Benson and Father Simpson.

"In 1959, Pope John XXIII called for an Ecumenical Council and for the reform of Church law. He got his Council. But the Catholic world had to wait twenty-four years for the new code. The preceding code was promulgated in 1917. That was the code we studied in seminary. That was the one Pope John said needed revising. It was old law—but more than that, it was *deficient* law.

"Now, take deficient law and misinterpet or misapply it, and you come up with the cross Stanley Benson carried almost all his life. Hide behind deficient law to avoid recognition that it is unjust law, and you apply bad law to almost every problem.

"Illegitimacy *was* an impediment—though dispensable—to Orders. But to show how unimportant it proved to be, it's not even mentioned in the new code.

"Stan was killed by old law. He was a victim of an archaic concept of law that was badly out of date.

"So this becomes not 'who dun it?' but '*what* done it?'

"Stan believed one thing and dispensed another. And he felt there was no escape in either case."

Koesler knew that he was preaching to the converted. But from their facial expressions he perceived that he had given them a fresh concept to think on.

"When we began this evening, I mentioned that we might learn something from Stan's life and his death. If we can help those who touch our lives—so that they never have to become victims of force or fear, so that they need never doubt God's mercy and forgiveness, then I think we will have learned some valuable lessons from Stan Benson."

Silence. Then Rose spoke. "Amen."

The others nodded affirmation.

"How about we use this place for what it was intended," Manny said, "and get something to eat and some coffee . . . and have some more talk."

The group, now all smiles, stood and headed for the vending machines. Koesler held back. "Go ahead. I'll be with you in a minute."

He thought of all that had gone on over the years and—in an intensive way—the past few days.

He thought of a remark one of the gang had made tonight: "St. Stanley."

Why not?